The Seed

The Seed

❧

Tempe Brown

32-BROW

Library of Congress Number:		00-192269
ISBN #:	Hardcover	0-7388-3940-X
	Softcover	0-7388-3941-8

This book was printed in the United States of America.

To order additional copies of this book, contact:
Xlibris Corporation
1-888-7-XLIBRIS
www.Xlibris.com
Orders@Xlibris.com

Contents

ENDORSEMENTS

(In Alphabetical Order)

IN WRITING *THE SEED*, Tempe Brown has uniquely presented a powerful picture of the Conquering Christ. In this day of intense spiritual warfare, a book such as this gives us comfort in knowing that people of faith have a great Champion who will never be defeated. The message of *The Seed* has been woven throughout scripture from Genesis to Revelation. Once the reader begins this book they will not want to put it down until finished.

Paul D. Cantelon
Retired Pastor of Christ Church of Washington
Washington, D.C.

* * *

The Seed, by Tempe Brown, is an extremely valuable tool for evangelism. Within just a few moments, you are completely engrossed in this exciting Gospel journey. Taken primarily from Scripture, *The Seed* gives you a clear and accurate picture of Christ our "Rescuer", and His plight on this earth. Just as accurate is Brown's portrayal of Satan and his demons of Jealousy, Murder, Pride, Greed, and Deception. Tempe Brown has written a novel that is certain to change the lives of many.

Dr. N. Benjamin Crandall, President
Zion Bible Institute
Barrington, Rhode Island

* * *

Tempe Brown's dramatic and intriguing novel, *The Seed* is a fresh and exciting view of the Gospel. The story is as old and reliable as the Bible itself (with plenty of solid scripture to back it up) yet it carries us to a dimension few have visited. We are taken inside the realm of the Spirit and see the mighty battle taking place for our very souls. The Great Plan of God is in place and the Holy Warrior Jesus has come to wage all-out war against the enemy of God and man. His mission: to set the captives free from Satan's kingdom of darkness and bring them into the kingdom of God. This book is a must for those who long to win their friends and families to Christ. It is a mighty evangelistic tool in the hands of the Church in these last days: a sharp sickle to harvest a multitude of souls. You won't be able to put it down. Get ready for an exciting, action-packed adventure!

Stephen Hill, Evangelist
Brownsville Revival
Pensacola, Florida

* * *

Tempe Brown has served with me as assistant pastor and has provided invaluable service to the body of Christ. She is a godly woman of impeccable character; one who loves and upholds the Word of God. Although her ministry is broader than to the local church, she continues to serve as an elder at Christ Church. I'm honored to endorse Ms. Brown's first novel, The Seed. Utilizing her keen wit, combined with extensive research, she has produced a riveting Biblically based novel. It caused me to love Jesus more!

Jesse Owens, Senior Pastor
Christ Church of Washington
Washington, DC.

* * *

One of my favorite hymns is entitled "I Love To Tell the Story". In this magnificent hymn, there is a line in the chorus that says, "T'will be my theme in glory, to tell the old, old story, of Jesus and His love." There is no better story to be told, and yet I am thankful for those who endeavor to tell the "old, old story" in brand new ways.

Tempe Brown has replaced the non-fiction of scripture into an action-packed novel. All of the drama the Gospel presents is interwoven into a fictional story that will captivate the hearts of the pre-Christian and the Christian as well.

For those who want to hear the "old, old story" again, or those who need a story that will eternally change their lives, I invite you to read *The Seed.*

Dr. Dwight "Ike" Reighard
Pastor, NorthStar Church
Atlanta, Georgia

* * *

The author herself has experienced the miracle of being delivered from the darkness of this world and her novel challenges all Believers to conquer over their fears of the principalities of evil. What a vivid insight to the Light of Jesus Christ and the victory He has already given us. Thank you Tempe for delivering this spiritual insight at such a vital time.

Rev. Ruth Schofield, Founding President
Embassy of the Prince of Peace
Washington, DC

* * *

The Seed reads like a novel, but it is certainly not fiction. This retelling of God's plan for his human creation is told in a C.S. Lewis style and with the drama that is a page-turner. Anyone who wants to understand the battle of good against evil–this is a winner. Especially put this book in the hands of new believers, and especially non-believers.

Ms. Brown takes the reader into the inner chambers of Satan's kingdom that makes you feel you have a ringside seat at his demonic strategy sessions. But she then takes you from there to the divine strategies of God as every challenge of the evil one is thwarted, and ultimately defeated.

The story of Jesus is told unlike anything I've read before. Ms. Brown does justice to the accuracy of the Scriptures, while telling the greatest story ever told with fresh, exciting new imagery.

I hope you realize by now how much I like this book. You will too!

Don Wilkerson
Executive Director
Teen Challenge International

ACKNOWLEDGMENTS

FIRST I WANT TO thank my Lord and Savior Jesus Christ for His love, mercy and salvation. Thank You for coming as the Holy Warrior Who came to set us free. I am eternally grateful that You came into my life and the lives of my children twenty-three years ago. I thank the Father for such a Great Plan and for the Holy Spirit who continues to carry it out to this day.

Next I thank my mom, Jeanne Field, for her constant support and prayers. I thank my children and their spouses: April and Jim Summer, Melinda and Ray Duvall, and Tommy and Michelle Brown. Thank you and my grandchildren for cheering me on with this book and believing in me. I thank my brothers and their wives, Don and Jackie and Jim and Jean Cockrell for the priceless encouragement and prayers. I thank my friend Elaine Fetter for the endless hours of listening to me chatter about the book. Thanks for being my bud.

Thanks to John and Vivien Weller for taking me under their wings and teaching me so well when I was a young Christian, and for all the encouragement they have given me for this book. Thanks to Rev. Paul and Lucille Cantelon, my former pastor, who encouraged me from the beginning and even preached out of the book before it was finished! And to my good friend Sharie Cantelon for her love and prayers over the years. A profound thanks to my dear pastors Jesse and Kay Owens who have worked diligently to help me to get this book into the right hands and for encouragement regarding my writing skills.

I thank my dear friend Kay Beard for her invaluable insight and courage to tell me like it is and for those last minute suggestions and changes. An enormous thanks to my friend and fellow writer Christine Lamson White for the endless hours of editing and guidance. To my friends Rod and Melissa Hemphill for their priceless friendship and support. Melissa spent hours checking for errors and the hard part, checking the endnotes.

Thanks to Jay and Shirley Lecher who believed in this project so much they made the dream come true. Thank you, Jay, for your legal counsel, your untiring assistance with the editing and formatting, and incredible wisdom and advice; and thank you, dear Shirley for giving up precious time with your husband and for storming heaven on my behalf. I thank my friend Josephine Darner, a lovely poetess, who believed in this book and helped make it happen. Sincere thanks to Diane Givens for her suggestions and for the courage to point out some areas of sensitivity in the manuscript.

My profound thanks to Dr. N. Benjamin Crandall, President of Zion Bible Institute in Barrington, Rhode Island. What a privilege to have you endorse this work. I am grateful to Rev. Tom Grazioso for the inspiration for the second chapter and for the permission to run with it! An immense thanks to writer/editor Kristy Johnson in New York for the incredible book review, wonderful editing and priceless suggestions. My sincere thanks to Rev. Edward Nelson, M. Div., Evangelist and Hebrew scholar. Thank you for the significant suggestions you made. God sent you just in time.

Sincere thanks to Rev. Steve Hill, the mighty evangelist so used of God in the Brownsville Revival in Pensacola, Florida. Thank you, Steve, for your endorsement. What a blessing you are! My thanks to Dr. Dwight "Ike" Reighard, Pastor of NorthStar Church in Kennesaw, Georgia, for your endorsement and for being such a blessing to my family. I thank my friend Rev. Ruth Schofield, Executive Director of the Embassy of the Prince of Peace in Washington, DC. Thank you, Ruth, for the countless hours of prayer on my behalf. To Rev. Don Wilkerson, Executive Director of Teen Challenge International. Thanks, dear brother for believing in this book and your valuable help.

My profound thanks to Bob and Lyda Mosier. Bob's professional skills and encouragement helped me tremendously early on. Thank you, Paula North, for putting my book in the hands of Dr. Ron Mansdoerfer, who gave me some great suggestions, and for the use of your beautiful ocean side home where I could write in peace. Thanks, Dorothy (DJ) Jackson, for your encouragement and for your eagle eye, catching those last minute errors. Thanks to Elaine Holbrook who read my manuscript early on. Your encouragement spurred me on. Thanks to the Nankievel family for the use of your cabin in the Black Hills of South Dakota and for letting me write uninterrupted. Thanks, Stuart and Robin Barth for your encouragement from the beginning. You empowered me. Thank you Kurt and Laurel Gentemen, pastors of Vine Life Christian Fellowship in Athens, Georgia, for the prayers and support from your dear flock. Thanks to Rev. Retha Garten, Pastor of Northern Florida Christian Center for her prayers and encouragement. And thanks always to Lilya Patterson who prays for me every single day. David and Audrey Fleming, thanks for years of friendship and prayer in my behalf.

There were many who helped me along the way, but unfortunately I cannot thank you all by name. While traveling and speaking, I was a guest in many homes, and you allowed me to slip away and write for hours uninterrupted. My profound thanks for that. Thanks for the prayers and support of my North Carolina, Georgia, Indiana, Kentucky and Colorado pals–you *all* know who you are. And last, but most certainly not least, thanks to my precious church family at Christ Church in Washington, D.C. for cheering me on over the years. You have all prayed so diligently for this book. It finally came into being.

PREFACE

THIS BOOK CAME ABOUT over a period of more than ten years. The inspiration for it was hidden in my heart for five years and when I began putting down my thoughts it came easily. However, since I am not a theologian and have taken on such an extraordinary subject, the gospels, I have approached it with much trepidation. And since I am not a scholar but an evangelist, I felt I needed to have several learned men and women read the manuscript carefully to make certain it is biblically sound. With the help and suggestions of these men and women, I feel that this book is indeed solid. I have already found, through those who have read the manuscript, that *The Seed* has brought the Word to life in a new and refreshing way, and as my friend Alice Boseman said, "It makes me want to run to my Bible." No greater compliment could be paid this work.

Secondly, I am well aware that it is risky writing a novel about the gospels and calling it fiction. When fictional characters are introduced and when one puts words in the mouths of the characters, the book is considered fiction. However, those who have read it have said that the treatment of the scriptures has been handled with great care and respect and that the truth comes through with power. I have taken liberties with the chronology of events. But then so did gospel writers. Much of the book is speculation. But so are many commentaries on the lives of Jesus and His disciples and the multitude of subjects in the Bible. Keep in mind that it is a novel based on truth. Regarding certain characters in the Bible that are mentioned, but we know little about them, I have marked in the endnotes that literary license is used.

Third, I have purposely not quoted verbatim any translations except the King James Version. I have paraphrased the scriptures for flow and simplicity. If a phrase or two matches word for word one of the various translations, it was unintentional. I did not go through the manuscript with the countless translations that are out there to make sure that I did not use the exact same wording. If some phrases match, it is sheer coincidence.

As you read this book, I pray you will be blessed and that you will gain much spiritual insight. I invite you to use this book as an evangelical tool, plus, I encourage you to look up the scriptures that are marked in the endnotes which in itself can be a series of Bible studies, especially for young people. God bless you as you read *The Seed.*

Tempe Brown

Dedication

I dedicate this book to my first pastor, Reverend Lyman B. Richardson, now with the Lord, and his dear wife Louise, who laid such a strong and loving foundation in my life.

CHAPTER ONE

The Great Plan

IN THE MIDST OF the glorious praise around the throne, something happened that would change the course of heaven.

The celestial atmosphere was filled with the music of rapturous anthems. Songs of praise rose like incense to the very heights of heaven, and then hung like a glittering veil around the Throne of God. The great seraphim flew high above, their bodies pulsating like live, glowing amber coals. In humility they covered their faces with their wings and cried out "Holy, Holy, Holy art Thou, O God!"

The train of His garment was pure, dazzling light and filled heaven with His glory[1]. The light of God drew their gaze to Him, for the light was the glory of His goodness. Utter joy exuded from within the light and came forth from Him in powerful rays like streaks of lightning, stirring the hearts of the angels, and setting off again another strain of glorious praise. His love came down upon them like a mighty waterfall, bringing them to new heights of adoration. Unable to stand, their knees bowed and many fell on their faces in worship.

The praise that came from the myriad of angels roared and thundered so powerfully that it shook the very portals of heaven. But amidst the lively worship, God distinguished a sound that disturbed Him. The angels' anthems continued to peal and then swell into a crescendo of adoration. Suddenly, like a Great Conductor, He signaled for the praise to cease. In perfect obedience, the angels instantly fell silent. Out of the millions of worshiping tongues of angels, one voice continued to sing. The most powerful and magnificent angel of all, Lucifer, had not been gazing upon the glorious countenance of God at all, but saw his reflection in the glassy sea and was fascinated by his own beauty, and failed to heed the signal. His voice rang out, sounding like a loud, brassy gong and a clanging cymbal.[2] God distinguished it above all the multitude of voices.

Never had anything but perfect peace been felt in the atmosphere of heaven. Now the sea of glass surrounding the Throne of God began to churn.[3] The troubled waters were merely a preview of what was at hand.

The defiant solo ended and one third of the angels surrounding him applauded. God knew they were deceived. They failed to recognize the brassy tones of loveless worship, for they were deafened by the folly of their wayward hearts. When the applause ended, Lucifer turned his haughty face toward God, his eyes glistening with pride.

At that moment, the arrogant angel gave the signal and an insurrection broke out, bringing about a massive upheaval in heaven. The entire universe was aghast. The galaxies would have careened out of their orbits had the Father not held out his hand and steadied them.

Lucifer changed from a magnificent angel into a hideous dragon before their very eyes. The great archangel Michael and his angels fought against the dragon in a great battle. The dragon violently thrashed his tail as the mutinous angels that followed him in his apostasy were violently expelled out of heaven to a place of gloom and darkness. None were spared.[4]

They were now fixed in their evil condition with no possibility of redemption. The faithful remaining angels who had resisted Lucifer's lies were also fixed. Fixed in holiness, for they loved God more than themselves. Yet they were bewildered by the catastrophic events. The unthinkable had happened. Their perfect heavenly home, the place where joy and complete harmony abounded, had been defiled.

The Triune Godhead, three different and distinct entities, yet remaining perfectly One,[5] was grieved beyond measure by this turn of events, yet He was not taken by surprise. God knew that when you create a self, you risk self-centeredness. But He determined the risk was worth it. In His perfect love, God did not create a mass of meaningless robots programmed to worship Him. Worship must come from the heart.

God was so full of love–so full of life–that He let it explode out of Himself and made life live all around Him. Life had to be celebrated! He made Heaven profuse with life and surrounded Himself with beings of life and poured out His love on them and gave them the capability and the capacity to give love back to Him. The individual will God gave His angels was a great gift. Lucifer used his gift, the prerogative of choice, to turn his love inward. It was a cataclysmic decision.

The heart of Lucifer was the birthplace of evil.[6]

The environment in heaven took an extraordinary turn. A battle plan was laid to deal with this new thing called evil. It was a foreign element to the heavenly beings, for it had never before existed. Only the wisdom of God could combat such a perilous manifestation as this.

The Godhead began to move in ways the angels had never before seen. The Word had stepped down to obey the will of the Father, and the Holy Spirit moved aside to carry out the Great Plan. The Word was nowhere in sight. The angels had never been apart from Him before. In obedience to the Father, He had gone to a remote place and had not returned. It was the talk of heaven.

Multitudes of God's mightiest angels were chosen and trained for war. Before they could bear the name of Heavenly Host, they must fulfill one last requirement. The command seemed strange.

There was something they must see.

The angels were taken in small companies to a secluded place where they had never been before. It was called the Theatre of War. Had the first campaign already begun? Bands of angels stood waiting their turn to go. As those who returned from the mysterious place silently marched past them, the expressions on their faces caused the others to tremble in awe.

One of the angels said breathlessly, "Look at their faces."

"I know! Wh-what did they see?"

The countenance of each angel had changed completely. Their eyes glowed in awestruck wonder. What they had seen intensified their humble devotion to the Almighty and they were empowered as never before.

A massive angel stepped toward the edge of the winged throng and spoke gently. "Do not fear. It is part of God's Great Plan and we shall all be a part of it."

"What is this Great Plan?"

"We know only what we need to know for now. He will reveal more to us when the time is right. Come. It is time for us to go."

The glorious spirits followed the lead angel to the place where few had been in heaven; a place that had been set aside, for what they did not know, but soon they would.

Their journey took them to a place that seemed far removed from anything that they had ever known. Up ahead they could see what seemed to be a large curtain suspended in space. All around them was an aura of stillness. Almost like a heartbeat had stopped. They moved toward the curtain. It was like a veil–very heavy–deep blue and purple in color,[7] the same hue as the atmosphere around it, making the edges seem to disappear. It was made of material they had never seen before. They were told it would be transported to the place of the Great Plan, but they did not yet know what it was.

The lead angel approached the curtain timidly. "This is as far as I go," he whispered breathlessly. "I'll wait here. You go in."

The others looked at him with searching eyes. He pulled the edge back slowly and stood aside. They stepped behind the curtain, walking slowly and peering over one another's shoulder. In the distance, they saw what looked like a flat table-like surface. A dim light was shining down on something there, but they could not make out what it was.

They moved closer, holding each other's trembling hands and clinging to one another.

Then they saw it.
"Oh my God!" they gasped, and turned their eyes away.
"My God, my God!"
They fell on their faces and cried out in anguish. "Father!"
There, lying on an altar
in a crimson pool of blood,
was a perfect, spotless,
unblemished,
snow-white
Lamb.[8]

And she brought forth her firstborn son, and wrapped him in swaddling clothes, and laid him in a manger; because there was no room for them in the inn.

Luke 2:7

The prophecy from Eden had begun. The woman's Seed was here to crush Satan's head. This Child did not come from Adam's seed, for his seed contained the fallen nature. It was the Seed of God, and a virgin birth was necessary to fulfill His perfect plan. No man touched this birth.

CHAPTER TWO

The Invasion

GOD'S HEAVENLY HOST WAS on a high-level secret mission that cold, starry night; the night that would split the calendar right down the middle. The shining winged creatures poked through Earth's atmosphere and did a fly-by over the City of David, the chosen beachhead where PHASE ONE of a major counter-offensive would be launched. Its ultimate objective: the takeover of Planet Earth.

The placid little village of Bethlehem was the target site for the most ingeniously camouflaged tactical action in the history of warfare. The plan was carefully drafted by God Himself, aided by His Heavenly Host who came to assist in the overthrow of hostile rebel forces who were holding hostage the inhabitants of the chosen planet.

In a nearby pasture, bearded shepherds pulled their cloaks around them and gazed into the glittering cosmos. To the human eye, the skies looked bright and clear. All seemed peaceful. But the shining winged creatures saw the atmospheric layer with different eyes. They saw another realm. Earth's atmosphere, once melodic and jubilant, when the morning stars sang together and the angels shouted for joy[9] was now boiling with demonic activity.

The enemy lines, an impenetrable defense shield masterminded by Satan, whose air power had ruled the skies unchallenged for over four thousand years, had been infiltrated. Satan had been the undisputed prince of the power of the air[10] –until now.

Legions of demons on patrol moved slowly across the skies, their red eyes scanning the horizon. As they came nearer, the angels disappeared into thin air. The ominous patrol circled the area, and continued their surveillance. As soon as the enemy's minions were out of sight, one of the glorious celestial spirits, an archangel named Gabriel, veered right, plummeted straight down and stopped silently in mid-air over a stable-cave. Spreading his powerful wings in a vaulted arc, he slowly lowered himself through the ceiling of the humble grotto. His golden eyes saw the culmination of a Plan that had been laid before the foundation of the world.[11]

Upon seeing the tiny God-man, he rejoiced in his heart and began worshiping. It worked! He was here! Glory to God!

PHASE ONE of the Great Plan was complete. The Rescuer had come! And in the most unexpected form–a Baby! God wove a part of Himself into a young virgin's womb and birthed Himself right behind enemy lines.

God spoke a Word and the Holy Spirit placed the Word inside a young maiden and a heavenly Child was conceived. And now–now, miracle of the ages, He was born!

The Word had become flesh.[12]

The most ancient prophecy of all had begun. God Himself spoke it in Eden to His great enemy Satan immediately after the fall of man.

"The Woman's Seed will crush your head."[13]

The Woman's Seed. A strange declaration, for women do not have seed. It was the Seed of God, and a virgin birth was necessary to fulfill His perfect plan. This Child did not come from Adam's seed, for his seed contained the fallen nature. No man touched this birth.

David of old had written of this event:

"I will declare the decree: the Lord hath said unto me, Thou are my Son; this day have I begotten thee."[14]

The prophecy was fulfilled that Isaiah had spoken centuries before:

"Therefore the Lord himself will give you a sign; Behold a virgin shall conceive, and bear a Son, and shall call His name Immanuel," which being interpreted is God with us.[15]

Immanuel. God with us. God had come to dwell among His people.

God had waited until the fullness of time[16] to send His Holy Warrior, the One Who would soon set the captives free from the Satan's hold. Since the fall of man the enemy of God had the world enslaved, in misery, in sickness, in poverty, out of hope and out of their minds. For centuries it was his turf. Evil was his expertise: hopeless, helpless creatures were under the cruel reign of the devil and his hideous hierarchy.

Gabriel could hardly contain himself for the joy at what he had seen. He shot straight up, gave the signal and joined the radiant formation. The glory of God blazed all around them as the heavenly spirits fanned out and began rejoicing. All of heaven joined in the chorus; even the stars seemed to enter the celebration. The angels shouted with all their might, "Glory to God in the highest!" Their praises exploded in the heavenlies, cascaded to the earth in a shower of dazzling light, and rolled like great waves through the valleys, up the hillsides and across the seas. The whole earth was filled with His glory![17] The resounding adulation burst forth throughout the universe and then fell again and sank into the earth and her foliage. The trees and the hills clapped their hands[18] and the waters roared with rapturous joy.

The sky was as light as day, yet it was only the third watch. The shepherds were terrified at first, crying out, "What does this all mean?" but the peace and joy that inhabited the glorious praises of the angels sank into their innermost beings and brought forth praises out of their mouths, almost involuntarily.

The angels continued their exaltations, "Glory to God in the highest, and on earth peace, and God's good will toward mankind!"[19]

Those words were not just a proclamation of peace,

they were a Declaration of War.

Man's Rescuer had arrived! The One Who would free them from Satan's power. No one had ever attempted it before. No one had ever challenged Satan. Not Abraham. Not Moses. Not Samson, David or

Daniel. No one had come for the express purpose of destroying the works of the devil.[20]

Several of God's select angels left the glorious chorus line and surrounded the stable-cave. Some slipped in to see the tiny Lamb of God. Their golden eyes glowed in wonder as they beheld the heavenly God-Child. They sighed at the sight of their Holy Master encased in this wee Form. The angels laughed as they watched His tiny fingers fan out, then close again in a tight little fist. He rubbed his nose then pulled his legs up in a bunch, kicked again and waved His arms.

The Babe's crying disturbed one of the angels. "Is He all right?"

Gabriel, the angel in charge of the Child's safety, smiled and spoke tenderly, "He senses the atmosphere of the world's sin that surrounds Him and it disturbs His sleep." Mary reached down and picked up her Newborn. Gabriel continued, "He has never carried the weight of the sin environment before. The earth is permeated with it. All its inhabitants that He has come to rescue were conceived in sin,[21] born into its environment and born with a sin nature. It all feels very normal and natural to them. But this tiny baby Boy, our Lord, has never experienced it."

The angel gasped, "No wonder He cries."

They watched His young mother bend low and kiss her Infant's soft, velvety brow. She never dreamed that one day a cruel crown of thorns would be crushed down upon it.

Gabriel sighed, "She must be weary from the long trip from Nazareth."

The other angel nodded sympathetically.

"Come, we must be going."

The mighty angelic spirits spread their glorious wings, floated straight up and away. Several massive guardian angels remained, surrounding the humble sanctum. They would keep contestant watch-care over the tiny Seed.

Indeed, Mary was weary from the difficult trip and lack of sleep, but the birth of her miraculous Son brought such joy she hardly noticed. She pondered the last few hours as she gazed upon her Newborn's face. Strange visitors from faraway lands had come to visit. They were noble men, stately in manner, yet they had humbly fallen to their knees in their fine robes and worshiped Him and gave Him gifts of great worth.[22] She wondered, *How did they know He was here?*

The shepherds in the field had come as well: the field of *Migdal Eder*,[23] the same field where Jacob tended his flocks,[24] that lies between Jerusalem and Bethlehem. The very name, *Migdal Eder*, meaning "watch-tower of the flock", prophesied of Jesus, for this was the field where the priesthood raised sheep for sacrifice in the Temple.

These shepherds left their flocks to see the real sacrificial Lamb of God.

Joseph, her husband, seemed overwhelmed at the responsibility he faced, knowing he must protect, teach and rear Him. He wondered how on earth could he train up and be foster-father to a Son born of the heavenly Father? Yet a great peace rested upon Joseph, knowing that he was not alone in this enormous endeavor. He had been called, chosen; thus he would be enabled from Above.

The Baby fell asleep in His mother's arms. Joseph watched his young wife as she studied her sleeping Infant's face. She was dazed and awestruck that her arms were cradling a human, yet alien Being from another realm. He was so small, so fragile and so vulnerable. Each time she looked into His eyes, she felt a sense of Eternity.

"Try to get some sleep," Joseph whispered. She nodded and laid her little Son in the crude bed of hay. There was a lovely cradle Joseph had made with great care back in his carpenter shop. Now it pained him to see the long awaited One lying in, of all things, an animal's trough.

That sleepy little manger scene was not all it seemed. They didn't know that little Babe lying in the manger was a Holy Warhead sent from Heaven launched upon the earth to wage war against sin, disease and death.

And when that little Baby cried
it sent shock waves
into the very epicenter
of Satan's domain.[25]

Strange how each time a type of Jesus appears on the scene

Babies die.

Moses was a type of Jesus as Deliverer.
When Moses was born,
Babies died.

Passover was a type of Jesus as the Sacrificial Lamb.
When the first Passover took place,
Babies died.

When Jesus was born,
Babies died.

Babies are dying again.
Do you think Jesus is at hand?

CHAPTER THREE

The Search For The Seed

HEROD'S COURT HAD BEEN a pit of intrigue, violence, and murder. For decades, Satan and his minions happily wreaked havoc by launching schemes of suspicion and paranoia among the royal family, servants and friends. Between a string of ten wives and a scheming brood of sons, the mad monarch had been driven to kill one of his wives, her grandfather, her mother, two brothers-in-law, and three of his sons, plus numerous subjects. The emperor Augustus, at one time his confidante and friend, acknowledged woefully, "It is better to be Herod's pig than his son."

The night was wearing on and Herod's head was throbbing. Hours before, a large entourage accompanying a delegation of rich eastern kings with strange dialects, had stirred up all of Jerusalem with their impressive arrival, carrying with them much wealth. Their importance was such as to gain immediate audience with Herod. Their report was incredible. They claimed to have followed a star that was to be the birth announcement of Israel's King. The Messiah. If their story were true, this rival King, Who was rumored to have been born, would indeed summon the allegiance of all Israel. He could even invoke a major uprising. The thought of it struck terror in Herod's heart.

He sank onto his tapestry-covered couch in a slump, his belly, like his ego, piled upon itself like a serpent layers when it reclines.[26] At one time he boasted a strong, vibrant physic, but he had let himself go. Sumptuous living and poor health was taking its toll. He was jittery and irritable. A Ruler? A King? The Messiah? Why hadn't his court magicians told him about this? He had to stoop to call upon those absurd priests and scribes to confirm the Magi's report. The words the priest had read from the Scriptures still resounded in his ears like a gong resonating throughout his mad being:

"For out of Bethlehem shall come a Ruler that shall lead my people Israel."[27]

After his meeting with the exotic dignitaries, attempting to trick them into leading him to the Christ Child, he told them, "Go to Bethlehem and search carefully for Him. And when you find Him, come back and tell me where He is so that I too may go and worship Him." But his little scheme failed. When they found the Child, they were filled with great joy, and they opened their treasure chests and gave Him gifts of gold, frankincense, and myrrh. When it was time to depart, they left another way because God had warned them not to return to Herod.

"Where are those foreign fools that went to seek Him?" Herod bellowed, his eyes wild with suspicion. "I told them to report back here to me when they found Him!" Looking out the palace window, where he usually admired all the great architectural fetes he had created, he seethed with rage, realizing the wise men had mocked him and were probably long gone by now.

Jealousy, the prominent ruling demon that controlled Herod, began to stir violently within him. The sinister spirit knew he must get word to his master, Satan, the message of the Magi. He summoned the demon captain to personally relay the message of utmost importance.

The Seed was here.

* * *

Satan's eyes were wild as the demon captain reported the wise men's strange story. He slowly rose from his throne of darkness like a volcano ready to erupt, his hideous face contorted with hatred. "Are you certain?" he hissed. "Are you absolutely certain that is what they said?"

The demon captain knew the importance of the message. "Y-yes, Sire, that is what they said." The hair on his wings stood on end. He feared his master more than anything, and dared not move, knowing this kind of news could greatly invoke his wrath.

Satan stared at the trembling captain, his icy eyes glittering with almost frenzied excitement. The dreaded prophecy had finally been fulfilled. It had to happen sooner or later.

The Seed.

Every single day Satan had relived the awful oath that God had made to him that fateful day in Eden–the words that kept him constantly looking over his shoulder–the words he knew so well:

"I will put enmity between you . . . and the Seed of the woman, and He will crush your head."[28]

For centuries the devil watched, constantly scrutinizing; always looking for the Seed. The enemy of God stepped down from his throne and began to slowly pace. His steps were deliberate as if he was tracking some invisible footprints; his movements corresponding with the events he was retracing in his evil mind–the times he thought he had eliminated the Seed.

I thought surely that Abel must be the Seed. After all, he was the woman's seed and had found favor with God, so I moved upon his brother Cain, to slay him.[29] *Not a difficult task, but I had a feeling it was too easy. I always wondered–what if it wasn't him?*

He knew God meant what He said, *"The woman's Seed will crush your head."*

Not if I get Him first, he had vowed silently.

The demon captain dared not speak. He watched the foreboding figure silently move across the floor like a lion stalking his prey.

The evil one's thoughts continued. *Pharaoh did my bidding by slaughtering all the male Hebrew children, but Moses slipped through my fingers.*[30] He stopped and stared at a javelin fastened on the wall. He had provoked Saul to kill David, but he too had escaped.[31]

Who was it? Joseph?[32] Daniel?[33] He could never be sure, so he attempted to kill them all. But now he was sure. They have seen His star. Now he had Him at last.

The Seed.

Those very words brought a shudder of hatred through Satan's being; a being that had once been called Lucifer,[34] the most beautiful angel God had ever created, and the most notable. He had been the highest-ranked archangel in all of heaven, exquisitely formed with golden pipes designed within his body, covered with every precious stone: sardius, topaz, diamonds, beryl, onyx, jasper, sapphires, emeralds and carbuncle. Beautiful music had flowed from them each time he spread his wings. He was the worship leader of heaven; whose glorious wings had covered the throne of God, just as the cherubim spread forth their wings over the Ark of the Covenant. His name meant "light-bearer" and his bejeweled body had reflected the Divine Light and splendor of God in all its glory. But iniquity was found in him. His heart was lifted up.[35] Now there was no light in him to bear at all, but rather gross darkness, which he now carried and spread throughout the world.

Because of his magnificence and grandeur, he had set his heart to be as God. No longer satisfied to reflect the glory of God, he saw himself as having glory within himself, and that he, more than God, should receive honor and authority over all of heaven. He even said himself, "I will ascend to heaven and rule the angels. I will take the loftiest throne and preside over the councils of Heaven. I will rise to the highest heavens and be like the Most High."[36] The once anointed angel of worship, who had walked with God on His holy mountain, profaned himself and his office, and was cast out of heaven, along with the mutinous fallen angels that had followed him in his rebellion.[37] Like a fiery meteor shower of fallen stars, they plunged through the layered levels of the heavens, transmuted from glorious heavenly spirit beings into hideous devils.

Satan's pride had brought him down. No longer the radiant archangel, he was now a hairless, dragon-like beast, stripped of his glory, with nothing to cover his nakedness. The gorgeous wings that had once lifted Satan to the glorious heights of heaven were now black and leathery, shaped like the wings of an enormous bat. The light that had shown in his eyes was now red and yellow, glowing wildly like a rabid dog. The gleaming, bejeweled pipes that had graced Lucifer's magnificent form, and had blown forth rapturously anointed heavenly music, were now shriveled up like dried prunes, and covered with layers of horned, scaly incrustations that occasionally emitted a rather disgusting, gassy belch. A hideous mimicry was all that remained. Once bathed in the warm light of God's love and Presence, he now emanated light that was harsh, terrifying, and chilling. Able to change forms at will, he transforms from the snake that he is, to an angel of light.[38]

Now faced with the fact that he had been stripped of his divine power and no longer possessed magnificence and authority, he was enraged, and resolved to get even with God at all costs. Hatred exuded out of his dark heart. Hatred for God and all that He stands for. Hatred for His truth, the Word of God, and hatred for God's earth-children. Seeing that they were the very essence of His pleasure, Satan saw a way to inflict pain upon his old Enemy. He would use His beloved children to carry out his vendetta.

They were the only creatures God had made in whom He had breathed His own Spirit,[39] opening them up to the unseen world of the spirit realm, introducing spiritual communion. He could fellowship with them Spirit to Spirit, whisper exquisite secrets, and walk with them hand in hand in the cool, misty veil of the withdrawing sun that filtered through their garden wonderland.[40] He had made a heaven on earth for them. In six days He spoke it into being. Just for them. And at the end of each day, He proclaimed, "It is good," declaring that it was consistent with Himself, and that all that He had created was good; making it clear to the ages to come that He did not create evil. A good tree cannot bear bad fruit.[41]

God created it all and then gave it all away; a magnificent, sumptuous, lavishly dressed garden, filled with an abundance of luscious trees bearing fruit of every size, shape, color, texture and taste imaginable. Everything in the garden was theirs, all delighting to the senses. They had need of nothing–intimacy and companionship with God, His goodness, His generosity and His glory were lavishly poured out upon them. They were Man and Woman, perfect creations of God, the Lord and Lady of the planet with dominion over it all.[42]

Their home was a lush garden where earth and heaven were one. Heaving contests of the world were yet unknown. The only fracas was the flowers. Riots of roses, a tumult of tulips and a blast of bluebonnets. Antelopes and angels were their playmates. They were cradled in contentment and lullabied by a Spirit-breeze. They slept in blissful peace under a canopy of palms on a fragrant bed of mint. Little did they know a stalker's steely eyes were watching their every move. There was a serpent out there with a score to settle.

The Adversary's plan was simple. First he would throw suspicion on the trustworthiness of God, and would make them question His character and goodness. Then he would offer a distorted image of life. Still seething with the disappointment that he could not attain the throne of God in heaven, he would usurp the throne of God in their hearts. Furious that God had made man in His own image, he was determined to make man into a mockery of that image. He had exalted himself above God, so would he incite them to exalt themselves. By making them rebel against God and His authority, he would detach them from Him.

Everything was created with the spoken Word. *"Let there be–"* The sun, the moon, the firmament and the living things made in just six days.[43] Satan resolved to eradicate it all with the spoken word in just six seconds.

The stalker watched their every move until the time was right. And then the serpent struck. He spoke to the Woman. "Has God said you may eat of every tree except *that* one?"

The bait was set. A hint of uncertainty. It was clearly implied: There's a hidden treasure in *that* tree and God is keeping it from you. The seed of suspicion was planted: God is denying you something? Maybe you can't trust God. Perhaps He's holding out on you.

A faint trace of doubt brushed across her face. The Woman had the authority to trample on the serpent,[44] but instead she chose to dialogue with him. She answered hesitantly, "We must not eat of it or touch it, or we shall surely die."

The enemy of God, knowing the Woman's confidence had been disturbed, boldly took the next step and threw mistrust on God's very Word. "You shall not surely die." He accused God of being like himself: a liar and a deceiver. God alone was God–a simple truth–yet the one truth Satan could not and would not accept. Now he would pass along the greatest lie of all time to the woman. You'll be God.

"God knows that if you eat of *that* tree, you'll be like Him." The serpent leaned closer to the Woman. "Just think," he hissed, "You'll be as God!"

God was the God of life. Satan offered fruit that contained seeds of death.

The Man, too, was intrigued by the new idea that there might be another element that God had not yet shown him; a realm that would let him explore his world outside of God. It felt strange to think such thoughts. He had never entertained any ideas independent of God before. The serpent had awakened in him too a vague mistrust–and the beguilement of prohibition. Temptation was something he had never experienced. It was foreign to him, yet exhilarating. *That* tree. They had freely eaten of every tree, but *that* one.

They had passed that tree daily and thought nothing of it, until the serpent focused their eyes on it as being something more than they had been told. It began a process that would begin the greatest cataclysm since the rebellion of heaven. Suddenly their thoughts began to move outside of the simplicity of obedience. A simple command–you may have everything in the garden except that. God had to put something there for them to be reminded that He alone was God and that one could not breach His authority and Word.

Were not the mysteries of God enough wisdom for them to explore? Did they not commune with Him personally–face to face? Would He not allow them to experience new joys evermore? Must they run to the forbidden to find pleasure? Sensual wisdom was desired above the wisdom of God. A turn was made. Suddenly they were self-confident and not God-confident. They wanted to be their own god, and in the imperfection of their own wisdom, they felt they no longer needed God's wisdom. A fatal mistake.

A curious fascination gripped Adam as he watched his beloved reach for the captivating morsel. She took the fruit and drew it to her lips. A strange uneasiness came over him. His heart began to pound. New feelings of uncertainty burst within him. Never had he experienced anything but perfect peace. Evil was foreign to him, and he had nothing with which to relate these emotions of turmoil. But it was too enchanting to resist.

Their eyes fixed on the object of the temptation made the warning of God, *"If you eat of it, ye shall surely die,"*–forgotten.

She bit slowly into the rare pulpy morsel, then handed it to Adam. Her expression said it all. Ecstasy! He followed her into this exotic adventure and he too ate of the fruit.[45]

Immediately the glory that had clothed them like a luminous veil–vanished. Adam watched in horror as the light in his wife's beautiful, lucid eyes–went out. The lovely countenance that he so loved to gaze upon changed before his very eyes. The juice of the forbidden fruit still wet on her lips, her innocent smile turned into a haunted grimace. A great shudder of fear rushed through Adam's being. What had he done?

God's words rang in their ears. *"You shall surely die."*

They did not die. Their Spirit did.

The serpent threw back his head and laughed horribly, and then burst out viciously,

"Got–cha!"

Doubt, fear and the sin nature were firmly planted in Adam's fallen nature and had been passed down throughout the centuries to all the generations.[46]

Satan smiled at the thought of it. Quite a memorial to his craftiness, if he did say so himself. But now, he had to deal with the Seed. He wanted to end the agonizing pursuit once and for all–he had to get this Enemy and destroy Him and he must not fail this time.

The serpent had deceived the woman, which led to the downfall of all mankind. Little did he know that through the woman's Seed, Redemption would come for all mankind.

The evil one continued to pace and laugh out loud intermittently. The demon captain knew not to interrupt his master's thoughts. He stood silently, watching him move back and forth across the chamber floor.

Breaking the silence and causing the nervous captain to jump, Satan jerked around and roared, "These three star gazers say the Seed is here? Where?!"

The captain shrugged nervously, "Uh, He m-must be somewhere in Bethlehem, Sire."

Satan got in his face. "I know that, you idiot. But where in Bethlehem?" His eyes were wild. "Don't you see? I must get Him–and I won't take any chances of missing Him this time, do you hear?"

"Y-yes, Sire!"

The devil turned and moved toward his throne. He yelled over his shoulder, "Get Murder in here!" He sat down and sneered viciously, "I've got a juicy little job for him to do."

"Yes, Sire!" The captain moved quickly toward the door. He was glad to be leaving.

Satan settled back on his throne and adjusted his wings. *That star may have appeared at the Seed's birth. It could have taken two years for those eastern imbeciles to make their journey.* He smiled an utterly evil smile. Herod had killed three of his own sons. It would be easy to get him to kill the sons of Bethlehem. The bitter bile of hatred surged through his being.

I've got to get Him this time.

I must get the Seed.

I must get Him . . . before He gets me.

* * *

An angel shot through the ebony midnight sky like a golden arrow. He could see a hideous black swarm of demons led by Murder at work in and around the palace. Herod was at that moment calling his royal guard together. Jealousy, the large demon with thin, grape-like skin, green and transparent, had completely taken possession of Herod's body. Red, hate-filled eyes leered through the sunken sockets of the maddened king.

Murder arrived and Jealousy welcomed him. They had worked together many times. Murder moved slowly toward Herod. Jealousy nodded and moved aside. Murder drooled as he sank his razor-sharp talons into Herod's skull. The order was given.

* * *

Gabriel slipped silently into the stable-cave and bent over the Child's bed and gazed worshipfully at the sleeping Babe. Gently touching Joseph's forehead, he spoke to him. "Arise quickly, Joseph, and take the young Child and His mother and flee into Egypt. Stay there until I bring word to you. Herod seeks the Child to destroy Him." The heavenly messenger was gone as quickly as he had come.

Joseph's eyes fluttered open. He sat up with a jolt and looked around. His heart was pounding. Was it a dream? Or was there really–something here? An angel? The message of the dream was real enough. He quickly and quietly gathered up his little family and stole away into the cover of night to Egypt.[47]

* * *

Before the break of dawn, the tiny sleeping village was awakened with the horrible sounds of bone-chilling screams. The hair stood up on the necks of those nearby. They bolted upright in their beds and cocked their heads to one side listening intently. Another gut-wrenching scream, then another, followed by the mournful wails of women.

An old man and his wife in near panic peered cautiously out their window and saw swords gleaming in the red light of dawn.

Swords drawn? For war?

No. To impale the innocents.

To murder the meekest.

To stop the Seed.
Children.
The first martyrs
for the Messiah.[48]

And he came and dwelt in a city called Nazareth: that it might be fulfilled which was spoken by the prophets, He shall be called a Nazarene.

Matthew 2:23

The angels, still covert, saw many demonic entities moving about within the sacred walls, seeking anyone whom they may use, harass or torment. The glorious guardians' assignment was to guard the young Messiah and to allow Him peace on His first visit to the Temple.

CHAPTER FOUR

The Country Boy

JOSEPH'S LITTLE FAMILY REMAINED in Egypt until the death of Herod. A glorious angel of the Lord appeared in a dream to him and told him, "Get up and take the Child and his mother back to the land of Israel. Those who were seeking to kill the Child are dead." Joseph was beginning to get used to these strange messages from On High, and without hesitation, he returned to Israel with Jesus and His mother. When they approached Palestine, they stopped to rest for the night and in another dream, he was cautioned to go to Galilee. They could finally go back to their hometown of Nazareth.[49]

To the onlooker, they seemed like any other normal Nazarene family; a young mother caring lovingly for her household; the husband, an honest businessman working diligently as a carpenter, and a precocious little Lad Who had playmates and a little dog that slept at the foot of His bed. Little did their neighbors know that God's very own little Son lived in their midst, being raised as a country Boy in their small Galilean village. Nor did they know that multitudes of angels protecting the young Child were all about. His identity must remain concealed.

Another prophecy was being fulfilled. The great prophet Isaiah spoke of a *Netzer*, a Branch that would spring forth: *"And there shall come forth a rod out of the stem of Jesse, and a Branch shall grow out of his roots."*[50] Nazareth: town of the Branch.

His childhood was humble but normal. He loved His mother's cooking and enjoyed walks in the cool of the evening after supper with His parents, greeting and talking with their neighbors. And, as with all children, there came a time when that precious, innocent childhood viewpoint of life was ruptured like a fragile membrane with the sordid ways of the world. The purity of childhood perception was overpowered by the stench of sin. It struck Him like a stinging slap the first time He heard His neighbors cursing and telling tawdry jokes. His heart broke when He observed the ways of men, their fallen natures exploiting one another for selfish gain.

He felt deeply about the poor beggars in the streets of Nazareth, the outcasts and the sick, and often took His own bread from the table to feed them or a weary passerby, and prayed silently for them in His bed.

Mary was proud of her Son. He was intelligent, considerate, meek and gracious. She watched Him interact with the other boys in the village and strange thoughts and emotions rose within her heart. Sometimes she felt He was hers, yet He was not hers. He belonged–to them. She knew He was different and always would be.

One spring morning, Joseph announced to his family they would be going to Jerusalem to the Passover Feast. An excitement stirred within young Jesus. At last, He would see the Temple, which He had focused upon in His small boy's heart. He dreamt about it for days. Finally the time came to load the supplies. He helped Joseph load the cart full of goods and hook it to their little donkey.

The trek across the sun-baked terrain was slow, but filled with anticipation of joining the throngs in sharing in the Great Feast. Their hearts raced with excitement the moment a jumble of domes, towers and minarets emerged out of the pulsating sandy horizon. Their gait changed from plodding to skipping and dancing as the weary little band of Galileans crossed the last stretch of their long journey toward the golden city cradled in Israel's history. A hearty song of praise burst forth from their dry, smiling lips as they merged into a growing stream of chanting pilgrims coming to the Feast.

Young Jesus ran ahead of His kinsmen, His determination spiraling with every step. His eyes brightened as He took it all in. "Look! There it is!"

Two enormous angels surged ahead with Him, encircling Him with their mighty wings. The specially chosen guardian angels were invisible to Him.

Smoke rose majestically from the midst of the glittering city, announcing the faithful ritual of the daily sacrifices. As He beheld the Temple with His penetrating gaze something seemed to awaken in Jesus.

"Son! You must stay close now!"

The unlikely little Tourist held Joseph's rough, carpenter's hand tightly as they entered the gates. High above the entrance of the city, bright banners of crimson, blue and purple fluttered and snapped against the cloudless azure sky, extending a grand and stately welcome.

An explosion of color, sights, sounds and aromas burst upon their senses. The bustling city was teeming with people. Never had Jesus seen such a wall of humanity. He was completely enthralled with the people and their activities.

Enterprising street vendors and wealthy merchants engaged vigorously in commerce along the labyrinth of narrow streets lined with bazaars, crowded shops and markets. Some sold imported oil, honey and smelted ore from Phoenician refineries of Sardinia and Spain. Young and old women carefully arranged various sized baskets of vivid flowers: scarlet chalcedonicum lilies, royal purple bell-shaped rose of Sharon, brilliant yellow narcissus and plump fruits and fresh vegetables along the narrow avenues.

Musicians played flutes, pipes and lyres on street corners, hoping a penny or two would be tossed their way. Noisy beggars clamored for coins from kind passersby. White-robed priests and Levites looked away as they walked past them. Some of the more humble and devout priests stopped and spoke to them, offering quiet prayers. Sellers of purple draped strips of various shades of dyed fabric across their shoulders advertising their wares. Tradesmen working in iron, brass and copper hammered and clanged like an orchestra without a conductor.

Jesus watched the throngs of people walking the serpentine streets of the city. Some of their faces were locked in a stupor of hopelessness; bearded old men shading their eyes from the sun, reeking with the pungent odor of wine; busy people working hard at the game of survival. *They're like sheep without a shepherd,*[51] *He* thought sadly.

Various types of demons rode on the shoulders of many of the people, controlling their thoughts and keeping them in bondage. Had they seen young Jesus, they would have shrieked in terror and dispatched a message to Satan. The archangels remained invisible to the demons and kept Jesus covered so that no evil spirit could know His presence.

The old Jewish sages were aware of the presence of demons among them. Many believed that evil spirits were so profuse that they were constantly brushing up against them in the marketplace and streets, and that the wearing down of their tunics and sandals was the direct result of rubbing up against them. The demons enjoyed such prominent notoriety.

Indeed their influence *was* plentiful and ever present. Some of the religious leaders were their favorite prey. The demons had access to those whose lives were open to them through intense pride, prejudice, and self-righteousness. They controlled many of their thoughts and thus, their actions. Those devoted spiritual leaders who were sincerely and humbly seeking God and remained true to the spirit of the *Torah*, obeying it's commands and living it out in simple faith, were a threat to the demons. They left them alone, going after easier prey.

Jesus and His group followed along behind the hundreds of pilgrims who had come to worship at the great and holy place. The grand Temple proper was constructed of gleaming white stones, each one twenty-five cubits in length and eight cutis in height. Crowning the Temple was a massive white dome crested with gold. They began the long incline up Mount Moriah toward the Temple. Animals in pens, and pigeons and doves kept in rickety wooden cages, protested for their freedom as they walked past.

Several bleating lambs were herded past them. Lambs born to die for man's sin–man's sin that could only be cleansed by the shedding of innocent blood. Jesus looked at them and a deep stirring began within His soul.

Finally, they stopped at the foot of the wide steps. Jesus' eyes followed the steep rising of the pinnacle of the Temple. They moved up the steps. He took a deep breath as they entered the massive gate and walked across the outer court.

Porticos covered with roofs of cedar and supported on gleaming, exquisite marble pillars soared twenty-five cubits high above the paved mosaic floors. Within these colonnades were benches for those who wished to sit and meditate or pray.

As they entered the wide Court of the Gentiles, His young cheeks flushed when He saw the market of sacrificial animals for sale and the tables of the noisy moneychangers in the courts of the Temple. The holy angels protecting Him gasped in horror at the sight.

They moved further toward the fourteen steps that led up to a terrace, which was enclosed by the walls of the Temple buildings. Strict inscriptions on the walls reading, *"NO GENTILE NOR LEVITICALLY UNCLEAN PERSON MAY PROCEED WITHOUT COMING UNDER THE PENALTY OF DEATH"*[52] frowned down at them. Another flight of steps led them up to more splendid gates. They entered the largest and most ornamental gate called Beautiful into the Court of the Women where two separate galleries were set aside for the women. In this spacious court, several Levites rehearsed the music that would be conducted throughout the festive ceremonies of the Feast. Mary stayed behind with the other women and smiled as she watched Jesus and Joseph climb the twelve steps to the Sanctuary.

Manifold impressions stirred the young Lad as He encountered a multitude of glances. Some of the Pharisees and Sadducees were warm and friendly; others were proudly robed and austere. Many scribes had kind, pleasant smiles; others were smug and elastic. The solemn Temple officers nodded to the religious leaders as they moved quietly through the wide halls. They spoke in whispers and low tones as though telling each other secrets. Their leather sandals snapped against their heels in syncopated rhythms echoing against the Temple walls with each footstep.

The angels, still covert, saw many demonic entities moving about within the sacred walls, seeking anyone whom they may use, harass or torment. The glorious guardians' assignment was to guard the young Messiah and to allow Him peace on His first visit to the Temple.

Jesus felt strangely tense, yet there seemed to be a delicate embrace that made Him uniquely aware of a familiar Holy Presence. The overwhelming impression that *This is My Father's House* swelled within Him.

He gently but purposefully pulled His hand out of Joseph's. A strong shaft of sunlight suddenly appeared through a high window and kissed Jesus' face. An irresistible magnetic power imparted a deep unspoken love to Him, which could only be accepted by awed silence. Impulses of His Mission and Being began to stir deep inside. His Divine Personage increased to some measure and, for a moment, He was reunited with His remote past.

The three-fold blast of the silver trumpets from the Temple Mount echoed through all of Jerusalem and beyond that the Passover had begun. The Feast was an indescribably intimate experience for the young Lamb of God. Does He yet know that He is the Passover Feast? Silent wonderment and unspoken questions could no longer wait. He must seek audience with the Doctors.

Following the Feast, Mary and Joseph rejoined their friends and began the long trip back to Nazareth. Assuming that their self-reliant Boy was with the caravan, they went a day's journey and upon coming to a resting-place and gathering for the evening meal they first missed His presence. Hoping to find Him among their kinsmen and acquaintances, they began to question them frantically if they had seen Jesus. Not finding Him, Joseph and Mary returned to Jerusalem and made a frenzied search in the marketplace, bazaars and, finally, the Temple.

The distraught parents moved silently from place to place with pleading eyes peering into chamber after chamber in the now-empty hallowed halls and finally approached the Hall of Instruction. They heard voices that sounded like men asking and answering questions in quiet, awed tones. Timidly, they looked around the corner through the wide door and there was Jesus sitting in the midst of the most distinguished Doctors of the Law.[53]

"Son!" Mary ran to Him, tears of relief flooding her eyes. "Son, how could You do this to us? Your father and I have been worried sick! We've searched everywhere for You!"

Jesus looked at them puzzled. "Why did you have to look for Me? You should have known I would be in My Father's House and about His Business."

Joseph's eyes widened in amazement. He knew He was not speaking of carpentry.

The Doctors of the Law shook their heads in bewilderment. The questions and answers that had come from this Child had completely astounded them. His wisdom and understanding was overwhelming to them. His questions burned in their minds. He had asked things for which they had no answers. Who was this Boy and how did He know all that He knew?

They spoke to Mary and Joseph. "Quite a young Man you have here. As His father you have taught Him well."

Joseph smiled as he thought, *Yes, His Father has taught Him well indeed.* The angels smiled and nodded. "Please excuse us now, we must be leaving."

Jesus looked at the Doctors. There was so much He wanted to talk about. So much He longed to tell them. They were the teachers of the Law and yet there were so many things they did not understand. How He longed to be about His Father's Business! He wanted to stay there and yet it was not time for his mission to begin. He must remain in His parent's home and be obedient to them until the time came. He returned to Nazareth and humbly and gladly submitted to their authority. Mary never mentioned the incident again, but quietly hid it in her heart.

* * *

Jesus grew in wisdom and understanding and in stature, and in favor with God and man.[54] As Joseph's Charge, He was to learn his trade as a carpenter. His tall, erect frame grew muscular from cutting trees and hauling wood to the shop.

He loved to roam the hills that surrounded the basin in which Nazareth was cradled. He joyfully watched the birds dart about, tending their nests. He splashed happily in the clear, cold brooks that wound lazily along the countryside. His eyes watched in wonder the tiny insects and the timid animals. From the lofty view of His highland home He could see the fertile hills and valleys below. Gleaming, prosperous cities dotted the panorama, the greatest of which was Sepphoris, and snow-capped Mt. Hermon stood proudly in the distance.

As He grew, He gathered tremendous insight watching the sheep grazing peacefully near the shepherd; walking through the lilies of the field, and watching the hen gathering her brood under her wings; the sowing of the fields and the reaping of the harvests.[55]

From time to time, as He gazed upon the rising of the red morning sun, memories would echo through the prisms of His mind of creating the universe: the sun, moon and stars–with a word.[56] When He walked the shore of the sea, He remembered like a faint dream commanding the waves, *"You may go thus far, and no more."*[57] Retained in His inner history were distant images of His heavenly home, yet He felt strangely comfortable with Earth and its downtrodden inhabitants. He was one of them, and one with them. He was God entered into man's skin to experience every facet of humanness that they experienced, but uncannily, without sin.[58]

Jesus was the eldest of several children,[59] the first-born Son of Mary.[60] Truly the Big Brother. From the little irritations of family life and the pressures of being a teenager, to the drawing temptations of a single young Man, He lived a life of perfect poise. God in an earth-suit. The Divine Alien Who disguised Himself as a Nazarene country Boy. Robed in flesh, He went about the strange business of fulfilling the requirements that needed to qualify Him as man's Substitute.[61]

PHASE II of His Mission was
to enter the arena of association.
For the time being,
this was
His Father's Business.

I indeed baptize you with water unto repentance: but He that cometh after me is mightier than I, whose shoes I am not worthy to bear: He shall baptize you with the Holy Ghost, and with fire.

Matthew 3:11

Jesus looked up. His eyes locked onto the eyes of the demon captain, sending chills up his scaly spine. The demon gasped and violently jerked away, his eyes sharply stinging. It was a mere taste of the power that would soon break forth upon their evil kingdom.

CHAPTER FIVE

The Lion And The Lamb

IT WAS THE FIFTEENTH year of the reign of Tiberius Caesar. The harsh Roman Emperor was a drastic contrast to Augustus, whose thirty-seven year reign had been generally moderate and had allowed the Jews to live peaceably. Tiberius was merciless in his treatment of the Roman Jews and his hostility towards Judaism reached Palestine with untold hardships to the people. The first Procurator that he appointed over Judea removed four high priests from their office before finding one who was sufficiently submissive and compliant to Roman rule. His name was Caiaphas.

It seemed that the crushing exaction of heavy taxes and the complete disregard for the needs and interests of the Jews had reached its extreme limit, when it only worsened at the appointment of Pontius Pilate. Under his governorship, violence, persecution and malicious murders without even the formality of a trial were not uncommon.[62] Pilate was without respect of the religion of the Jews and set himself in complete defiance to Judaism in Jerusalem, in Galilee and even Samaria, so much so that the Emperor himself was forced to intervene on occasion.

This was the condition of Israel when word got out that a strange, rugged hermit clad in ascetic attire of camel hair had come out of the desert and was preaching and baptizing at the river Jordan. Word spread like wildfire. A prophet was in their midst. The four-hundred-year silence had been broken, bringing hope to the tiny nation straining under the burgeoning weight of Roman bondage.

From every niche of Israel they came; from Jerusalem, all of Judea and all the around the Jordan Valley people went out to hear him preach. Every level of rank and class made their way to the lower Jordan where it narrowed into a beautiful, lush inlet near the place where the waters parted for Joshua on Israel's entrance into Canaan.

The glorious rays of truth of the ancient prophets, that the long-foretold Deliverer was near, burned in John the Immerser's heart. His message, like refracted light, blazed through the land and struck the very souls of men that a better kingdom was at hand, bringing them to readiness and repentance. But he was not that Light. Darkness covered the earth; even gross darkness lay oppressively upon the people. But nearby the promised Light was already casting a golden edge on the horizon.[63]

John's anointing had come from before his miraculous birth, a birth not unlike that of Isaac, the promised child of Abraham and Sarah. He was a gift from Above to aged parents; to a mother who was barren, and he was filled with the Holy Spirit and angel-called from the womb.[64] It was no wonder that the power of his preaching brought such multitudes.

John's booming voice as one crying in the wilderness could be heard for miles by the hundreds of travelers tramping through the high grass to join the multitudes waiting their turn to confess their sins and enter the water and be baptized.

The banks were thick with people. Large trees leaned over the river as if they were studying its depths. The area was fertile with flowering shrubs and tall, reed-like papyrus plants. John stood waist deep in the middle of the muddy river. His fingers and the soles of his feet were wrinkled like prunes from having been in the water for so long. His followers stood in line hanging onto every word. One by one they came:

the lowly and the lost, those who were weary of the delusions of sin, and those who were under the heavy burdens of the laws of their hypocritical spiritual leaders. Even the tax collectors came to be baptized.

John's fearless preaching had even reached the ears of Herod, alarming him greatly. Concerned about his growing popularity, he felt John's strong influence over the masses could lead to an uprising. According to the reports, the people seemed ready to do anything John might propose. Herod sent Roman soldiers to keep an eye on him, but they, too, fell under deep conviction and asked what they should do. Bold as a lion, John minced no words instructing them to stop accusing people wrongfully and to end their heavy-handed cruelty. He aroused the feeling of expectancy in the multitudes as he cried out with a loud voice, "Repent! For the kingdom of heaven is at hand!"

* * *

A small patrol of demons was perched on the limbs of a dead sycamore tree high above the scene. Like a row of rumpled vultures, their scrawny necks jerked back and forth and their knotty heads bobbed up and down as they listened intently.

Squinting yellow eyes watched John intently. "What does he mean the kingdom of heaven is near?" the captain of the patrol growled suspiciously. His voice sounded like somebody shoveling gravel. The large, gargoyle-like demon grunted, "Each day the crowds grow larger."

"So what?" squawked a lesser-ranked, shaggy imp perched just below him, scratching behind his ear like a dog. "What can he do? He has no power. He's just another loud-mouthed prophet."

"Yeah!" chimed in another underling. "We've killed all the prophets so far.[65] What's to stop us from eliminating this loudmouthed boor?" They punched each other and shook with gleeful laughter.

"We're already working on that," the captain smirked. The scales on his lead-colored wings opened and closed as he breathed. "Our master has big plans for the Baptizer." He lowered his voice and glared at John. A sly grin crossed his bat-like face. "A very special birthday party is being arranged."[66]

The demons squealed with delight. "Ooh, a birthday party! Can we go? Huh? Can we?"

Just then the crowd below began to buzz with breathless excitement. Several Pharisees and Sadducees in their immaculate, long, flowing robes had come to spy on John. They pushed their way to the front. The crowd respectfully moved aside and made way for them.

The demon captain smiled, "Our puppets have arrived."

The cool, damp air was pierced by John's thundering voice. "You brood of snakes!" His penetrating voice sent birds scattering in every direction. The multitude's eyes widened that he dared to address the religious leaders in such a sharp manner.

The demons on the lower branches flapped their stubby wings furiously up to the branch alongside the captain. "Is he t-talking to us?" they screeched, their teeth clattering like hailstones on a tile roof.

"No, you fools!" snapped the captain. "Shut up and listen!"

John's lion-like roar sent a chill across the necks of the hushed crowd. The stiff religious leaders lined the bank of the dusky river like pallbearers at a gravesite, and carefully drew their robes up around them fearing they might get soiled. Their cold eyes studied the young preacher, watching him with a mixture of resentment and awe.

For weeks, John had called out loudly for those in highest authority, the High Priest, Caiaphas and President of the Sanhedrin, Annas, and all religious leaders, to repent and to turn wholly to God. He pleaded for them to help turn the hearts of the people back to God and to the good news of the kingdom. But they refused and turned deaf ears to his cries. Some came to hear John preach and even to offer themselves to be baptized because it was the popular thing to do, but John recognized their hypocrisy and made it clear that he was not impressed.

John's voice swelled, as did the veins in his neck. "Who warned you to flee from the wrath of God that is coming? Bring forth the fruit of repentance by changing your lives. And don't say you're exempt because you're descendants of Abraham! God can raise up children of Abraham from these stones!"

They glared at him in disbelief. No one had ever talked to them that way before. The crowd was speechless.

"Already the ax is lying at the root! Every tree that does not bear good fruit is cut down and thrown into the fire!"

They were incensed at his remarks. "If you are not the Messiah or Elijah, what authority have you to baptize these people?" The spokesman's words hung in the air like a foul odor.

"I indeed baptize you with water unto repentance. But He Who is greater and mightier than I . . ." His words grew softer, "Whose sandals I am not worthy to carry or even untie." John's voice rose again into a great crescendo, his shaggy mane shook as he cried, "He shall baptize you with the Holy Spirit and with fire!"

The demons' eyes were wild. "Wh-what?" They fluttered their hairy wings frantically.

"He is ready to separate the chaff from the wheat with His winnowing fork, storing the grain in His barn but burning the chaff with never-ending fire!"

They grimaced at his words and frowned at him with disgust. They dared not speak against the powerful prophet for fear of an uprising among his followers.

Just then John's voice rang out like a bell reverberating through the air, as a robed Figure stepped out from among the crowd.

The captain shifted his position for a better view. He lowered his head and squinted his yellow eyes, not believing what he was seeing. "No. No, it can't be," he wheezed.

"Behold the Lamb of God!"[67] John cried.

The crowd gasped. The demons grew dizzy with fear and the captain felt queasy as his eyes beheld

The Seed.

Jesus looked up. His eyes locked onto the eyes of the demon captain, sending chills up his scaly spine. The demon gasped and violently jerked away, his eyes sharply stinging. It was a mere taste of the power that would soon break forth upon their evil kingdom.

John stood in awe as he beheld the One for Whom he had been preparing the way. Here was the long-awaited Messiah, the One Who would aright all the wrongs; the One he had been waiting for and dreaming of all his life. John was amazed at His humble appearance, which did not seem to befit the One he had been announcing, Who would bring the wicked to fiery judgment.

The morning light formed a luminous sheen on Jesus' hair as He stepped into the cool water. The Son of Man had come to be baptized. The lump in John's throat grew with every step Jesus took toward him. "It–it is I who need to be baptized of You!"

Jesus smiled, "It's alright, John. It's the right thing to do."

The two historic figures, of whom the prophets had spoken long ago, the forerunner and the One Who was to come,[68] stood waist-deep in the shaded Jordan.

All of heaven stood still.

His ministry was to begin.

John trembled as he attended Jesus, watching Him slowly descend into the swirling water. He did not know the significance of the moment, never dreaming that a little drama was being performed that would resound throughout the ages, and would be repeated myriad of times in the coming centuries; a drama depicting the death, burial and resurrection of the Savior of the world.

The water gurgled in Jesus' ears and then a serene quiet enveloped Him as the water closed over His face. He knew that death scene would one day become a reality.

Upon coming up out of the water, Jesus saw the wonder on John's rugged face. John clung to his Lord, the One for Whom he had been born to be His forerunner, to announce His coming.[69] He realized at that moment that he must withdraw from the forefront. He would decrease, while his Lord's ministry must increase.[70]

Just then a clap of thunder was heard. A flourish of little gasps moved through the crowd like a wave. The heavens opened and the Spirit of God descending in the form of a dove lighted upon Him, nuzzling His wet cheek. Glorious rays of light fell upon the scene. The wonderful, familiar Voice of His Father spoke tenderly His public endorsement:

"This is My Son Whom I love; with Him I am well pleased."[71]

The dove remaining on His shoulder suddenly transformed into an invisible mantel, publicly anointing Him as Messiah. Jesus felt power enter His Being.

Awareness of His Mission became clearly defined. Compassion for the lost sheep of Israel had been there all along, but now–now they were captives that must be rescued. He saw the bondage of the downtrodden. And the poor–they must hear the good news! His heart broke for the brokenhearted. He wanted to cry out at that very moment, "You are accepted! This is the year!"[72]

But not yet. There was a matter He had to attend to.

He looked up at the gaping, shivering demons clinging to the tree. They took off in terror when His holy eyes blazed a white-hot Light into theirs.

He had an appointment.

An encounter.

The Seed was here
and He was ready to meet
His archenemy
face to face.

For we wrestle not against flesh and blood, but against principalities, against powers, against the rulers of the darkness of this world, against spiritual wickedness in high places.

Ephesians 6:12

Evil loomed in the air of the War Room like a gray mist draping the atmosphere. They were in a planning session. Since Satan was neither omnipresent nor omnipotent, he used the one means he had to spread his evil throughout the nations. Strategy.

CHAPTER SIX

The War Room

A BLACK ROBE COILED about the clawed feet of the figure sitting silent on the grotesquely ornate chair at the head of a massive conference table, around which sat thirteen of Satan's choice demon princes. The master spirits and principalities were the rulers of darkness in high places.[73] Each one reigned over entire nations, regions, great cities and small hamlets throughout the earth, commanding vast armies of wickedness in the spirit realm. Some of their territorial generals even named themselves after the nations they ruled.

Evil loomed in the air of the War Room like a gray mist draping the atmosphere. They were in a planning session. Since Satan was neither omnipresent nor omnipotent, he used the one means he had to spread his evil throughout the nations. Strategy.

One wall was covered with maps of nations. Fiery darts had pierced each strategic area where they concentrated their efforts. At the center of the charts and graphs was the tiny area that would one day be known as the nation of Israel. More darts were leveled at that one site than any other on the face of the planet.

The multilevel hierarchy fiendishly fed on one another in common evil interaction. They thrived on their ability to complicate, agitate and subjugate the loathsome human element that cohabited the haggard planet. Their twisted, calculating devices brought untold levels of misery and horror. Each devious scheme was structured for a prospective course of action. No evil idea was denied. Each wild whimsy and beguiling fantasy would eventually be introduced into human society. They prided themselves in the subtlety of their insidious incursions into the fluid logic of mankind. Each new perversion was carefully infused into man's imaginations, resulting in agreeable acceptance and application.

A dim light played on the jelly-like surface of one of the more prominent princes named Seduction, the ruler over all seducing and unclean spirits.[74] His voice was hoarse and sensuous as he whispered a sinister scenario to those around the conference table.

"Eeyyyoeeee!" Squeals of delight cut through the room. His corrupt comrades like his idea.

Next to him sat an enormous barbed demon named Fear, a powerful prince who commanded an army of spirits of fear,[75] who enjoyed throwing their weight around, intimidating and paralyzing the lesser ranked demons, and bringing terror, dread and panic to the weak, mortal souls of Earth. Under his command were sub-princes that did his bidding through subtle enticings. Their names were Discouragement, and the twin entities, Doubt and Unbelief.

Next to him was an immense grisly prince named Murder[76] and his comrade, Hatred. Together they had conducted every kind of carnage, killing and butchery imaginable.

Seated by them was a pasty-faced demon called Infirmity. Legions of spirits of infirmity[77] were under his command, bringing untold sickness, disease and misery upon mankind.

To his left was a perverse spirit called Debauchery, a wild-eyed, loud-mouthed demon who worked closely with Seduction. Between the two of them, countless indecent, unbridled, lustful perversions were unleashed upon the earth to find their places in those who were open and willing.[78]

Rebellion,[79] seated next to him, paved the way for the latter, and was given much power and rank. Rebellion's partner was a ghastly demon called Witchcraft,[80] not present at this conference. He was on a mission in various regions yet uncivilized by man. Under his command was an intimidating spirit by the name of Manipulation, sometimes characterized by the name Jezebel. For centuries she had been combing the nation of Israel for a particular victim, and had found one. She was unable to attend the conference. She was busy working on Herodias,[81] Herod's new wife.

Bitterness and Jealousy[82] were next. Their favorite ploy was to offend. And their playing field was unlimited: families, friends, neighbors, social acquaintances, government and religious leaders with their own countrymen. Within virtually every relationship, they could find a way to plant their ruinous trap, often bringing Murder onto the scene. Throughout their heinous history, these demons influenced countless civil wars to erupt quite effortlessly over a single offense.

Next to them was Death, a shadowy, ominous entity who sat quietly, seldom speaking a word. He, Murder and Infirmity worked together, but Death often moved closely behind Fear, his stinger ready to strike,[83] seeking the right moment to clutch a panicked heart. Rebellion and Debauchery called upon him regularly to put the finishing touches on their tasks as well.

Next to Death sat Strife, a nervous, fidgety demon who loved to cause trouble, especially in the earthling's households and among the religious leaders. He, too, worked closely with Hatred.[84]

To his left was Pride, the largest, most imposing and highest ranked demon prince among them. He was Satan's alter ego. It was he who rose up in Lucifer and incited him to seek to be exalted above God.[85]

Pride sat at Satan's right hand; and to his left was one of Satan's favorites, and next highest ranked demon of the thirteen, named Deception,[86] a monstrous evil prince who enjoyed a place of great honor among the dark powers. He and his protege, Spiritual Blindness,[87] took great pleasure in their work. They controlled an army of religious spirits, large, brooding demons that worked in and about the places of worship.

Since God had created his creatures to worship,[88] the demons implemented a plan to merely get them focused on some object other than God. It had worked for centuries. Anything would do. A golden calf,[89] a statue, a pillar. Empty, inanimate objects that man in his folly were deceived into holding up as gods.[90] Deception and Spiritual Blindness consorted together to draw the weak-minded worshipers into fashioning every sort of hand-hewn idol, giving them names and rank, setting them up as patrons of fertility, agriculture, sex, war, anything the demon prince and his underlings could heave into their minds. Some worshiped animals, trees, rivers, the moon, stars and the sun, each one constituting a separate deity and form of worship.[91] They even turned their faces to the east and worshipped the sun in the very porticos of the Temple.[92] The faithful sun seemed to blush in anger at the very thought of anyone worshiping it.

The participants indulged in every evil perversion they could muster. Hoards of demons inhabited each idol, and thoroughly enjoyed the homage paid them. Once the people gave themselves over to these abominations, the demons were given the right to take possession of the deluded idolaters, and could move them to engage in the most horrific acts know to man. Even to the point of offering up their children to be mutilated, even burned to death in the fires of their pagan gods.[93]

Satan received great pleasure in seeing God's creatures ignoring their Maker, and instead, paying homage to himself through idolatry. The deceived earthlings had become a distorted image of all God had created them to be. They worshiped Satan and he loved it.

The demons gleefully exchanged pitiless plots around the table, belching out all sorts of maniacal modes of baseness. Their evil network was successful and far-reaching.

Satan usually enjoyed their bantering, but he seemed nervous, agitated. He stood abruptly, causing a hush to fall over the assembly. Evil embodied him. Sweeping away from his chair, he began to pace. Their yellow eyes watched him move restlessly across the War Room floor; his long, black tail slithered behind him like a water moccasin.

Suddenly, he turned and spoke. "I accept your reports and ideas, and, of course, your new schemes will be implemented as soon as possible". The thirteen smiled and nodded to each other. "However, I must tell you that Pride and Deception have brought me greater satisfaction than all of you put together!"

The smiles faded, their eyes narrowed and their heads sank down into their shoulders like a line of toads. Jealousy's sickly green skin turned even greener. Pride sniffed, drew a huge breath and coldly looked down his nose at the others. Deception leaned forward and grinned.

"It brings me great pleasure to see God's ridiculous creatures indulging in idolatry, but nothing pleases me more than to pull the strings of our little puppets, the priests and Pharisees."

As he moved closer, the demon committee could see the rancor rising up in his hideous face. A low hiss rose out of his throat. He fixed his beady eyes on Deception. A grisly smile played about Satan's grotesque mouth. Deception returned the smile with a knowing nod. "Nothing gives me greater satisfaction than to see . . ." His voice changed to a singsong mocking tone; the corners of his liver-like lips turned down and his head wagged back and forth as he punctuated each word. "Than to see the–word–of–God entrusted into the hands of those fools." Taking a deep breath, his barrel shaped torso swelled, his evil heart exuding hatred. "I enjoy seeing how they use it to put the people in deeper bondage, rather than to set them free from my hold."[94]

The thirteen began to enjoy their master's excitement and sat up listening intently.

"How very unsuspecting they are. Pride has given us an inroad to their hearts." He laughed out horribly. "Little do they know that pride is the very thing God resists the most![95] Yet they wallow in it. And you, Deception, have beguiled them to believe they are serving God wholeheartedly when I am ruling their hearts. What a wonderful game! Nothing wounds the heart of God more than to see His own Word used to tighten them in my stranglehold."

Deception pushed back from the table and rose slowly, turning to his master.

Satan looked at him and smiled wickedly. "Well done, Deception. It is a plan that shall continue forever."

Deception bowed deeply. "Thank you, Sire. It is my pleasure to join you in the honor of exacting revenge." The light from a nearby torch played on his two faces, causing them to appear and disappear like a subliminal hologram. Taking advantage of the moment, he spoke again. "Master, we are implementing a new campaign to recruit even more into the Pharisaical order."

The strong man's ears went up. "How so?"

"They draw them in by offering the young ones a challenge, exclaiming, 'Take the yoke of the Law upon you, and learn of it! It shall be life to you!' And they're only too eager to oblige."

"Life!" Satan loved it. "Life! Yes, yes, I like it!"

Deception continued, "Some will be sincere, but that is the chance we will have to take. My religious spirits are working feverishly to rob them of their devotion and turn their fervor into focusing on their silly traditions, which eventually neutralizes and makes ineffective the Word of God."[96]

Satan nodded gleefully. He was elated. "Yes! Go on, go on!"

"Their traditions become the focal point in their teachings and their worship. Then when they recruit others into their order, they merely pass along their religious drivel."

"What a marvelous plan!"

"We shall coerce them to travel great distances to win a single convert." His four fangs gleamed as he smiled. "And when he becomes one, we shall make him twice the sons of hell as they themselves are."[97]

Satan picked up the thought. "And they will return to their towns and spread the bondage there! It shall become even more widespread." Deception closed his eyes and slowly nodded with a smile.

Satan was excited and began drooling. "And make them add more laws–and more and more!" His voice was high and shrill. "Yes! Make them slaves to the letter of the law! Thinking it is life, it shall be their death!"[98] The fiendish fallen angels howled and cackled with delight.

"Keep them on this course," the devil continued. "I like nothing more than to see God's dismal little creatures trying to reconcile to Him by their good works!"[99] The wickedness of his demented mind began to blaze out of his eyes. "Nothing! Nothing can ever bring that about! I have them! They are mine! And they are lost forever! I've outsmarted God! I've killed the Seed!"

The vile beasts cheered wildly as their insane master, intoxicated with evil, bragged and boasted of his stratagems.

Waves of laughter rang through the massive chamber doors where two large demon bodyguards stood sentry. They smirked at one another. "Must be going well in there."

Just then, the grotesque guards were startled by a frenzied commotion at the end of the corridor, raising the coarse, gray hackles on their thick necks. They gnashed their teeth and growled vehemently at the swiftly approaching demon captain and his excited subordinates, as they raced each other to be first to tell the ghastly news.

"The Seed! The Seed!" they screeched like banshees, their wings slapping each other in the face.

"Quiet, you insolent little creeps!" one of the bodyguards bellowed in a gale-force voice. "The master is in conference!"

The demon captain sharply signaled the others to be silent. They back-peddled and cowered. Panting laboriously, the captain turned to the bodyguards who had situated themselves in a heap in front of the chamber doors.

"We must see the master!"

"Impossible! I told you he's . . ."

"The Seed is alive!"

"What?!" the guards gasped, their eyes wide with horror.

"The Seed is alive! We've seen Him!

"We–uh–we–

botched Bethlehem."[100]

And He was there in the wilderness forty days, tempted of Satan; and was with the wild beasts; and the angels ministered unto Him.

Mark 1:13

The nights were the worst. Forty terrifying, sleepless nights animals encircled Him in the dead of night. He could feel the hot breath of hungry lions just as Daniel had in the lion's den.

CHAPTER SEVEN

The Wilderness

JESUS' THROAT WAS DRY and ached from swallowing the hot dust in the burning wilderness air. His parched lips were pursed as He pressed on deeper into the wilderness, driven by the new Power coursing through His Being. With the anointing of the Holy Spirit, the power and dynamics were there to carry out His mission and to work miracles. The Holy Spirit was within Him without measure.[101] He was now able to communicate fully with His Father and He had power over the enemy. Now the power and passion to save the world must be put to the test.

He had been fasting for forty days and nights, alone with the reality of the staggering destiny that lay before Him. He must set firmly in His mind and heart the purpose for which he was sent: to fulfill His Father's predetermined Plan.

The atmosphere was heavy with demonic oppression. Unlike the First Adam, who was tempted in the midst of Paradise, where he had provision of the lush garden, the warm companionship of his mate, of God,[102] and friendly animals all about, the Second Adam[103] was forty days in a desolate, dangerous place, without warmth, shelter or food. Forty days He was away from the companionship of family and friends. His only companions were the wild beasts.[104] He was in the wilderness–the dry places–the abode of demons.[105]

The nights were the worst. Forty terrifying, sleepless nights animals encircled Him in the dead of night. He could feel the hot breath of hungry lions just as Daniel had in the lion's den.[106] Each torturous night He could hear the low guttural snarls of jackals and the eerie howls of hyenas ricocheting against the barren canyon walls. The terror of night was just one of many temptations the enemy had designed for Him.

Although the final confrontation would be between Jesus and Satan, for forty days and nights the savagery of hell was unleashed against Him. The fiery darts of His adversary the devil[107] assailed Him without ceasing. As each day went by, His enemy attempted to wear Him down with hideous thoughts. Every demon in hell had their turn at Him. Doubt and Unbelief worked Him over attempting to get Him to question His mission.

"If God really loved You, He wouldn't put You through this, would He?" Satan's favorite ploy: to lob thoughts of suspicion and distrust against the Father–to plant offenses in the minds of men to make them feel God-betrayed.

"How could God do this to You? Look at You! Out here all alone. He doesn't care about You! Why would God let you go through this?" This was a temptation that would resound throughout the ages. But Jesus would not be worn down by the empty lies of the devil and his hoards.

The demons became almost frenzied in their desire to outdo one another. To make the Seed fall would mean a great reward for them forever. Their contests to tempt and torture Him and to erode His resolve were uttermost in their evil minds. They sought to build a stronghold in His mind by pelting Him with one corrupt thought after another, but He disallowed any evil imaginations to remain in His mind. He cast them down as fast as they hit Him. Unlike His adversary, He would not entertain thoughts that exalted themselves higher than the knowledge of God.[108]

On the fortieth day, Jesus was feeling the full impact of His hunger. The hot breath of the desert wind lashed His hair around His face like tiny whips. Looking up, His sun-tortured eyes saw the silhouette of a large, foreboding figure standing with his back to the sun. An old trick. Make your enemy look towards the sun and blind him. The old enemy of God slowly walked toward Jesus, his leathery, snake-like skin gleaming in the bright sunlight. Their eyes locked for a moment. The Light in Jesus' eyes was brighter than the morning sun, blinding Satan. Quickly he turned away, his eyes burning. The old sun-in-the-eyes trick had backfired. And–so much for staring Him down.

A strange, moaning wind moved through the canyon below. Little swirls of dust danced about their feet as they walked slowly toward each other. Two sets of footprints were left with each step in the blistering sand. One of scaly, clawed feet that had downtrodden humanity for centuries; feet that paced up and down, to and fro upon the earth, seeking whom he may devour.[109] The other, footprints of sandals. God's feet in a leather thong. Every footprint He left was on ground that was cursed.[110] The dry, desolate, cracked wilderness floor was a grim reminder indeed of the reason He was here. To bring life from death.[111] To bring hope from despair.[112] Beauty from ashes.[113]

They were not alone. The atmosphere was electric with spirit beings. Satan's evil hoards were still nearby, watching intently. They were nervous and agitated and kept swooping up, and diving back down like a swarm of bats. Satan had instructed the menacing horde to fly about Jesus' head like attacking hornets to distract Him, but they could not get near. Even in His weakened human condition, the brightness of His countenance drove them aside and the twisted inky cloud surged back and forth as they screeched in pain. They were distressed that they had not been able to bring Him down. Now it was up to their master to finish the task.

The angels were there too, watching every move, held back by the command of the Lord of Hosts. Dazzling like the hem of God's garment, they encircled the arena of the Great Test. Oh, how they longed to rush to His aid! But they could not. He had to go through it. The whole universe was watching. The destiny of all creation was at stake.

Satan eyed Him carefully and was surprised to see his enemy halting slightly. Jesus stopped abruptly. He had a rock in His sandal. The evil entity smirked as he approached Jesus and thought to himself, *Well, well, the Son of God with a rock in His shoe. So this is the dreaded Seed. He doesn't look like that much of a threat to me.* "Maybe He's going to crush my head with that little stone in His sandal," he cackled to his minions. Suddenly his laughter stopped as he remembered David's victory over Goliath with a single stone,[114] and hunched over defensively, eyeing Him intently. The old lion began to circle Him, walking round and round.

Jesus would not be intimidated by Satan's tactics. He sat down on the ground and calmly shook the stone out of His sandal. He then stood up and dusted off His robe.

After the initial shock of the abhorrent news that the Seed was alive, Satan had been devising his strategies. The devil had forty days to prepare. He saw as the days and nights went by that the usual enticements were not working. Though his plan was simple, he was confident he could bring Him down. It had worked with the first man.

Why wouldn't it work now? he thought.

The lust of the flesh.

The lust of the eyes.

The pride of life.[115]

Works every time.

But not this time.

Out of his vast arsenal of temptations, he chose three final ones. Circling his mortal enemy like a hungry lion, his wicked mind concluded, *If I can get Him to take just one of the three, I've got Him.*

Just one act of–selfishness.

The first test: the physical realm.

The tempter stopped and picked up two large stones the size and shape of loaves of bread. The early, yellow morning sun cast a buttery, golden hue on them, giving them the appearance of fresh-baked bread.

Jesus experienced the full range of the human experience. He salivated and His parched lips tingled. He was hungry.

Sadistically, Satan began his enticement. "If You are the Son of God, command these stones to become bread."

With that pronounced "*if*", not only was the shrewd enemy attempting to get to Jesus' hunger, he was also trying to get to His ego. Jesus didn't fall for it. He didn't have to prove He was the Son of God. He knew He was. He smiled as He remembered the words of His Father: "This is My beloved Son in Whom I am well pleased." He knew His Father would give Him manna[116] if He asked for it. Satan wanted Him to cheapen His miraculous power by reducing it to tawdry pagan magic to be used for His own self-interests. Jesus knew a better way. His Father's way.

Without batting an eye, Jesus, The Bread of Life,[117] answered him, "It is written, man does not live on bread alone, but on every word that comes from the mouth of God."

The devil raised one eyebrow, sneered and dropped the stones. *Ah! So He's going to use Scripture against me!* Strangely enough, Satan knew the Word of God forward and backward. He knew how to twist it, distort it, pervert it and turn the double-edged sword[118] so that it could slit your throat. *Alright,* he thought, as he removed his long, black cape. *You're going to quote Scripture–I'll play Your little game.*

The cape fell to the ground. Massive leathery, bat-like wings unfolded and spread wide. Grabbing Jesus' arm, they were airborne in an instant at dizzying heights. The thought crossed the devil's murderous mind to drop Him, but he knew the angels would catch Him, and perhaps an all-out war would transpire. He knew he was outnumbered two to one. Maybe he could get Him to jump.

Jesus could see the Holy City below. The streets were a beehive of activity. People were so busy with their bartering and selling, they didn't notice the Figure that was being lowered onto the highest point, the very pinnacle of the Temple.

The second test: The spiritual realm.

Jesus' robe flapped in the wind like a banner. Again the devil assailed Him. "If You are the Son of God, cast Yourself down–" A smirk crossed his crafty face as he thought, *Two can play this game of quoting Scripture.* "For it is written, God will give the angels orders to catch You!"[119]

He was offering a shortcut that translated: "Imagine the shouts of acclamation when they see their long-awaited Messiah descending dramatically into their midst! Why, the very heads of Israel will be convinced of Who You are and pave the way for Your ministry."

Had He succumbed to this temptation, Jesus would have raised Himself up to the rulership of the world through the spectacular, and in doing so, force men to pay homage to Him and do His will. But Jesus would not compel obedience, but would reveal the love of the Father and allow mankind to make the deliberate choice to make Him Lord of their hearts. Unlike the dialogue with Eve, which was on the serpent's terms, Jesus spoke to His enemy on *His* terms, the authority of the Word.

In calm majesty He replied, "It is written again, 'You shall not tempt the Lord your God!'"

The devil clenched his teeth and took Him up to an extremely high mountain and showed Him all the glittering riches of the kingdoms of the earth and the treasure and wealth of them all.

The third temptation: the political realm.

More desperate now, Satan's voice changed from a mocking tone to a frantic falsetto. The wind howled in their ears. Foam began to form around the corners of his hideous mouth. Stretching his long, wiry arm out and sweeping it from left to right, he cried, "All these things will I give to You if You will fall down and worship me!"

What an empty trade that would have been! The sin-soaked world with all its deceitful lies for selfish satisfaction rather than the Great Plan of Salvation. Yet many throughout the centuries to come would make that choice and would succumb to that very temptation–the devil over God–the pleasures of the world over the ecstasy of heaven–the carnal over the spiritual–the second-hand indulgences over the first and greatest joy of all. And all wrapped up in one simple moment of choice.

Choice. What a powerful gift God had given–and how recklessly it could be used. A simple turn of the key–to hear the tumbler of a moment's notion for self-indulgence. Click. And then it is done. Instead of unlocking the door of excitement and pleasure, it locks the one in–in to the shocking, horrible surprise of imprisonment and bondage, locking ones own hands and feet in the stocks of sin–and once the bolt is locked, no amount of twisting and turning can free them.

Looking beyond the luxury and prestige of the world, He saw the tarnished, tainted, condition of it all. He was not here to inherit third-hand the earth–from Adam–to Satan–to Him–but to rule and reign as King of Kings and Lord of Lords. He would not be subordinate to Satan, but would overthrow his kingdom. He was here to rescue the world from Satan's power. To join forces with him now would be dividing His own kingdom.[120]

Jesus looked at the glittering cities displayed before Him. Satan and his minions ruled them. There were powerful princes over each of the cities. The devil offered them to Jesus–to turn the ruling Princes over to Him and let Him become their Commander. But first He would have to bow down and worship Satan, the most blasphemous proposition of all.

He was not interested in becoming the commander of demon Princes; He was here to destroy the works of the devil and to crush his head!

As hungry, physically exhausted and humanly weak as He was, His Spirit and resolve were stronger than ever–for the Spirit within Him was far greater than he who was in the world.[121]

He was asking Jesus to turn His back on all that He had been sent to do–to join forces with the enemy–to become as the First Adam. And all hope for redemption, restoration of creation, and His Father's Great Plan would be lost.

Worse, Satan would win his evil heart's desire.

God would have worshipped the devil.

Jesus realized at that moment more than ever how completely insane Satan was to attempt to "offer" the earth to the One Who spoke it into being. For by Him and for Him were all things made that were made.[122]

A holy wrath rose up inside of Jesus that this mocker of God would dare to suggest that He join him and his dissidents against His Father; that he would dare throw in His face the very words that he had used to deceive one third of the angels, causing the greatest cataclysm of all time–in the very courts of heaven. Once again Satan was demanding worship. And he ordered it from a member of the Godhead!

He was soliciting Jesus to revolt against His Father and the Holy Spirit!

A powerful rebuke rose up from the innermost depths of Jesus. It did not come from His aching, parched throat, but from the annals of history that began before time was set into motion–a rebuke that split the rocks and shook the foundations of hell.

The Lion of Judah[123] roared, "Depart from Me, Satan! For it is written: Worship the Lord your God, and serve him only!"

The devil threw back his ugly head and screamed an eerie wail that bounced off the shadowy cliffs.

It was over. The Truth triumphed over the Liar. The devil was violently ejected into the searing desert air with all his dejected demons listlessly trailing after him, and in a faltering, raging voice he cried, "I'll be back!"

God released the angels to come to minister to Jesus.[124] At once the glorious guardians completely surrounded Him. They gave Him food and drink and bathed Him in the glory and light of the Father's love. Theirs is to constantly stand in the Presence of God, and the strength, power and fire of His holiness radiated from them and were infused into Jesus. They broke into worship and thundering praise that

The Second Adam did not fall.

And that PHASE III of the Great Plan
had been accomplished.

* * *

"It is written! It is written! How I despise these words!" Satan exploded in a tirade of cursing, his fangs showing fiercely. The frightened demon attendants cowered, not daring to make a move while their maniacal master raged violently, unleashing his fury like a blazing firestorm. The Seed had outmaneuvered the old Deceiver with the one weapon he could not override. The truth. It completely debilitated him, leaving him powerless.

The towering, arrogant demon prince, Pride, was not willing to accept defeat so easily. "Sire, defeat is not yet!"

Satan jerked around and stared at him. "What are you saying?"

"There are other ways to get around this impudent intruder." Pride smirked, "He is nothing more than an irritating little anthropoid. A mere human born of a woman, therefore He is not impervious to our devices." A hush fell on the room. Satan's tantrum began to subside. His cold steely eyes fixed on his alter ego, absorbing his confidence and composure.

"Our arsenal is not yet exhausted, Sire," Pride announced.

Satan's eyes narrowed. "You saw how He uses the Word of God. He is no fool. He knows I cannot penetrate the force field of truth. Furthermore, I find no breach in His character upon which to encroach."

Pride protested, "You say He is no fool. Indeed He must be the grandest of fools to attempt to pervade our empire, which, by the way, was legally handed you by that silly simpleton Adam."

"But," Satan reminded him, "Adam made the mistake of venturing outside of the protection of God's Word, naturally making him an easy mark. But this–this nettle in my craw is a veritable walking, breathing enclave of truth." The words left his mouth like overflowing bile.

"Yes, my lord, but those whom He shall attempt to convince are not."

"What do you mean?"

"Think for a moment, Sire. If you were He, who would you first approach to obtain their allegiance and aid?"

"The religious leaders, of course! But I gave Him opportunity to dazzle them by descending into their midst from the pinnacle–"

Pride waved his answer off. "Obviously He intends to win their confidence another way."

"How?"

Pride chuckled haughtily, "With the same instrument He used against you, the truth!"

Satan groaned, "We're back to where we started, like a dog chasing its tail."

"No, Sire! For the truth must be believed to be effective. You yourself said it at our last conference. Those mindless pawns, the religious leaders, are so deadlocked in their rituals and the letter of the law that they have no room for the truth of it!"

"Then they won't believe Him!" Standing on the dais of his massive throne, he threw back his hideous head and laughed, snorting loudly. The attendants, relieved that his tirade was over, quickly ran to prepare drinks.

Satan stretched his wings and waved his arms excitedly. "Yes! Yes! Drinks!" he shouted gleefully. "Perhaps we should celebrate tonight!"

Pride smiled confidently, congratulating himself for saving the day.

A spidery little demon approached the throne with a tray holding two jeweled goblets filled with wormwood.[125] Satan lifted one of them from the tray and smiled, "Our friend Deception will be delighted to hear that his assignment will be heightened."

Pride frowned, "Deception?"

"Yes! He shall intensify their brain-locked bias and blind them with such darkness they won't be able to recognize their measly Messiah if He stands before them!"

Pride took the other goblet and chose his words carefully. "Um, as usual, I have had your best interest at heart, Sire. I'm certain you will think of some way to reward me as well."

Satan sneered, "Serving me is reward enough. However, I do have something in mind for you. You shall work with Deception. He will fill their minds and you shall fill their hearts." He took a long drink from his goblet and wiped his mouth with the back of his bony, clawed hand. "That should completely close their spirits to receiving the truth!" The demon attendant refilled his goblet.

Pride grinned a fiendish grin. "But *we* are the truth, Sire."

Satan almost choked on his drink. "What's that?"

"Does God's word not say that their Messiah will be despised and rejected?"[126]

Satan eyed him suspiciously. "Yes, so?"

Pride's chest swelled, "Well then! That must mean that we ourselves are the truth!" He raised his goblet high and shouted arrogantly, "For *we* shall bring it about!"

Satan sat back down with a jolt and stared blankly at the floor. Suddenly he was no longer sure

who was the pawn and
who were the players.

And he came to Nazareth, where he had been brought up: and, as his custom was, he went into the synagogue on the sabbath day, and stood up for to read.

Luke 4:16

Blinded by familiarity, they could only see one of their hometown boys who did not yet have a steady job.

CHAPTER EIGHT

The Announcement

THE DISTANT HILLS WERE bathed in the soft, yellow light of morning, a perfect day for His announcement. Jesus walked the short distance along the narrow streets of Nazareth toward the synagogue. A gentle breeze rustled the trees and a chorus of birds chirped their joyful little praises.

Memories of Jesus' childhood came tumbling into His mind–the marketplace now closed and empty for the Sabbath–the simply constructed houses strewn across the gentle hills–the well where women would gather about in humming clusters passing on the latest gossip. He had often accompanied His mother there and watched her draw water countless times from that deep well and expertly heave the large clay water pot upon her head. Her strong back carried her gracefully up the long, steep hill toward home. Her tiny bird-like features gave one the notion that she was weak, but she was strong as a lioness in body and spirit. Jesus smiled as He thought of how she had cleaned the house thoroughly with His homecoming in mind.

On His way to the synagogue, many of His old friends and neighbors greeted Him. Jesus remembered His childhood neighbors with benevolence. The tight bond to children among the Jewish people was strong.

Some of the young men He had grown up with were now married and had started their own families. One of them caught up to Jesus and introduced his young wife and baby daughter to Him. The cowlick on the young man's thick black hair was as unruly as ever; his wide, boyish grin was now slightly pinched, yet cordial. Jesus greeted them warmly. He touched the little girl's soft, pink cheek and blessed her silently. The young man chatted as though in a breathless hurry.

"So, Jesus, are You married yet?"

Jesus smiled, "I–uh, have a Bride in mind."[127]

"Wonderful! When is the big day?"

"Not for a while. I still have to prepare a place–"[128]

"You're going to settle down here in Nazareth, I hope."

"Nooo, I don't think so."

"Well, be sure to send us an invitation. We'll want to come."

Jesus looked at him tenderly. "You most definitely will receive an invitation and I truly hope you will accept it and be there."

The little family waved and walked on ahead. Jesus nodded and greeted other familiar faces. An elderly gentleman called out to Him. Good morning, Jesus! You're looking well. And where is Your dear mother?"

"She'll be along," Jesus smiled. "She's coming with my brothers, James and Jude." The old man gave a satisfied nod and moved on.

Jesus rounded a corner and entered the courtyard of the stately synagogue. He stopped and looked at the richly decorated facade that proudly faced Jerusalem. Several of the old sages from His early days were standing in a little knot near the gate, loudly complaining of the rising, widespread influence of the hated Gentiles. Upon seeing Jesus, they quickly dropped their wildly waving arms and abruptly ended their conversation. They looked at Him cautiously and nodded.

Strange rumors had been circling about Jesus. They heard He had spoken to a Samaritan woman of ill repute, and even drank water from her pitcher! It was also reported that the entire village of Sychar had turned to Him. They heard He had even slept in that horrible place and spent several days with those godless half-breeds![129] Word also had it that He had healed the son of one of Herod's officers.[130] A Roman! And another Gentile!

Other tales had been brought to their ears of stunning miracles done at His hand. They didn't quite know what to make of it. He had been such a quiet boy Who seemed to have a fervor for God. His worship had always been so different from theirs. Some thought He might one day enter the ministry, but He had never applied Himself to become a scribe or Pharisee. They took note that as a young Man Jesus had never entered into the broiling discussions of politics, and had never, to their knowledge, gossiped or spoken ill of anyone. They found Him odd, yet intriguing in His serene, almost regal manner. Never had He shown any sign of grandiosity. And now it seemed He was gaining fame throughout the entire Galilee doing unusual feats of healing. Surely He would perform something even more spectacular for them. After all, He was their very own townsman!

They watched Him closely. Jesus smiled and stepped through the entrance into the dimly lit synagogue. The old, familiar meeting house had not changed. The lamps were flickering, throwing dancing shadows on the thick plaster-covered walls. That same damp, musty odor was still there.

The synagogue ruler approached Him, smiling. "Jesus, we heard You were in town. We would like for You to read the Scripture and perhaps expound upon it following the morning prayers."

"Yes, thank you, it is time for Me to accept."

The ruler motioned to Him to sit forward in a place of honor with the elders and officials. The elders cupped their mouths and whispered among themselves as He sat down. They leaned forward and peered past one another at Him.

Jesus saw His mother, sisters and brothers enter and take their seats. Mary and the girls moved to the women's area. His family took their place in the back of the room. It was the first time Jesus had sat up this close.

Waiting for the service to begin, Jesus slowly scanned the beautifully adorned lintels over the wide doorway, and gazed at the engravings of vine leaves and clusters of grapes. If only His countrymen would accept Him as the Vine and they the branches.[131] What life they would know! They would bear the fruit of love and kindness[132] instead of bias and intolerance. His gaze moved across the engraved moldings and cornices, and down the double columns. The somber atmosphere, once joyous with revival brought by devout Pharisees who reminded their hearers of the grace and kindness of God, had now become lifeless and dull through the legalism that had crept in, so unlike the Breath of Life that sat among them.

Finally the service began and the prayers were offered. The bearded old minister held up his arms and began to pray. How often Jesus had worshiped there. The well-known, well-remembered words of the rote blessings and prayers were the same.

This was the place of His early religious instruction. It was here that He began to see the deviations from the truth and the extreme bondage that was being put upon the people. Instead of revealing the love and mercy of the Father, they heaped pride and prejudice into their lectures, and mixed impurities into the Law like stirring poison into one's wine.

Several prayers were offered and finally the last prayer: "Blessed art Thou Jehovah God. Thou art Holy and Thy name is Holy. Thou art the God who preparest Salvation, and hast chosen us from among all nations and tongues; and hast brought us Thy commandments and Thy Law. Reveal Thy Deliverer to us, O Lord, that we might see Thy Great Salvation."[133]

The prayer they just prayed was answered. Their Deliverer was seated among them.

The prayers ended, the minister brought out the scroll of the prophet Isaiah from its case. He removed the linen cloth, unwound the large scroll and handed it to Jesus as He rose to take His place on the platform.

They were completely blinded as to His true identity. Whatever bonding they had to Him was condescending and obligatory, relative only to His having been one of their townsmen. Before them stood not One Who was in such a dubious and nostalgic attachment, but was the Messiah

Himself, the greatest Bond of all. Blinded by familiarity, they could only see one of their hometown boys who did not yet have a steady job.

He stood straight as a tower. His smooth forehead, void of frown or worry lines, sloped into dark, straight brows. His cheekbones were high and regally sculptured, His chin strong and purposeful. The *Maaphoreth* draped over his head and descended gracefully over the back of his neck and shoulders, a garment that was considered imperative for anyone who would publicly read or *Targum* the Scriptures. His inner garment, the *Kittuna,* was without seam, woven from the top throughout, and fastened with a long girdle. It descended to His feet, which were shod with leather sandals. Over this He wore a square outer garment, the *Tallith*, with the customary *Tsitsith*, fringes of four long white, intricately knotted threads that represented the *Torah.*[134]

He chose a passage and scanned the familiar words penned by Isaiah by the breath of His Father, and with clear, peaceful eyes, began to read without a flaw:

"The Spirit of the Lord is upon Me–" He looked up and smiled.

Here it comes. The Holy Warrior Who was sent to rescue them from Satan's power

was announcing His arrival.

"–Because he has anointed Me to heal the brokenhearted–" He pronounced the words with a deep longing in His spirit.

"–To preach deliverance to the captives." How different those words sounded in His mouth.

"–And recovering of sight to the blind–"

They nodded to each other with side-glances of approval at how beautifully He read. One of the aged elders gave a sideways yawn and squinted up at Jesus as though he could barely stay awake.

Jesus continued with unruffled peace.

"–To set at liberty them that are oppressed and downtrodden."

He handed the scroll back to the minister and sat down. The eyes of everyone there were fastened on Him. They all wondered at the gracious manner in which He read, but in their carnal realism, mistook power and anointing as a mere extraordinary ability to read well. They waited in awkward silence. Is that it? He's finished with His sermon?

He didn't expound, teach or lecture. Little nervous coughs and whispers wafted across the room.

Finally, He spoke. "Today this Scripture is fulfilled in your presence."

They looked at each other stunned.

"I am the One of Whom I just read."

What was he saying? They were aghast that He was claiming to be the very One of Whom the prophet of old had written. Even His brothers were disturbed and glared at Him in disbelief.[135] His mother's heart began to race.

One of the elders spoke, "Isn't this Joseph the carpenter's Son? Isn't His mother's name Mary? And His brothers, James, Joseph, Simon and Jude[136]–and His sisters–don't they live here among us?" James and Joseph looked at each other and sank down in their seats. Mary sat up straight and smiled at Jesus through worried eyes.

His townsmen could not bear His intense, penetrating gaze. They did not know that behind that gaze was the Rock of Ages, the Great I Am, the wondrous love of the Lamb of God Who would one day, without reserve, lay down His life for them.

He saw the hatred mounting in their hearts. "I suppose you will now quote the proverb, 'Physician, heal yourself'; or prove Yourself by doing here in Your own home town what we heard You did in Capernaum. How true it is that a prophet is without honor or acceptance in His own home town or country."

They looked at each other, incredulous that He had not viewed their having allowed Him to take part in their service as an honor; and that He had the gall to call Himself a prophet and to mention those so-called miracles to the loathsome Gentiles.

Knowing their thoughts, He continued, "Many widows were in Israel during that three-and-a-half-year drought that so ravaged the land, but Elijah was sent to but one, a Gentile widow in Sarepta in Sidon.[137] And there were many lepers in Israel in Elisha's time, but only one was cleansed, a Gentile by the name of Naaman of Syria."[138]

Outraged that He dared to compare Himself to the great prophets Elijah and Elisha, they jumped to their feet and took hold of Him, forced Him out the door and into the street. The service, instead of ending with a blessing and benediction to which all would, in one accord, say "Amen" was ended abruptly with cursings and insults which they all hurled at Him in one voice of hatred and contempt. Their amen turned into an abomination.

In silent sadness He allowed Himself to be pushed and shoved to the edge of the cliff that bordered their town, all the while He was praying within, "Father, this is not the kind of death we discussed together in the courts of heaven." Seeing they might throw Him off, He suddenly turned around and gave a look of commanding power and majesty. They stopped in their tracks. He parted the red sea of bloodthirsty eyes, and silently walked through them all. Even His boyhood friend and the elderly gentleman glared at Him with disgust.

He had come to His own and His own received Him not.[139]

Jesus knew in the centuries to come that many believers would experience the same. They would believe on Him and would be despised and rejected by their own families, friends and countrymen, some even unto death.

The day had come for which they had waited and watched for centuries; the day they had mentioned in their daily prayers of looking for the Blessed Hope of Israel; the day they had told their children about for generations; the day all heaven had looked to. Their Messiah had come, and through the dimension of men's minds, they dismissed Him. And in doing so, they dismissed themselves.

Instead of throwing themselves at His feet, they tried to throw Him off a cliff.[140]

Strangely, those same men loved the Word of God. They loved to dissect it, scrutinize it, analyze it and debate it, but when the Word stood up and confronted their prejudices and unbelief, they wanted to cast Him down to His death.

Spiritual Blindness had indeed left his mark.

Jesus' brothers quickly led their mother back to their house.

She alone knew the words He had spoken were true.

And she knew
the hourglass
had turned.

And Jesus, walking by the sea of Galilee, saw two brethren, Simon called Peter, and Andrew his brother, casting a net into the sea: for they were fishers. And he saith unto them, Follow Me, and I will make you fishers of men.

Matthew 4:18,19

The captain swooped down and ordered the demons within him to interrupt the service. His voice was frantic. "We can't have them hearing truth!"

CHAPTER NINE

The Call

THE NOON SUN GLITTERED on the Sea of Galilee like diamonds scattered on a blue silk cloth. The aroma of roasted fish filled the air. Simon, a fiery, foolhardy fisherman and his more amiable brother, Andrew, were enjoying the catch of the day, along with their neighbors and fishing partners, James and John. James was strong and silent with a serious outlook on life, yet he often surprised his friends with a quick, dry sense of humor. His brow remained in a constant furrow, etching a deep crease between his penetrating eyes.

"Did you hear what He said today?" Simon asked, taking an enormous bite. John looked up. His thin, bearded face was weatherworn from the sun and many encounters with the capricious Galilean Lake winds.

He carefully pulled a tiny bone out of his mouth. "Which time?" he said, raising his sun-bleached eyebrows, "He said so many extraordinary things."

James reached across the table for a third helping of fish, stabbing it with his knife and landing it expertly in the middle of his plate.

Simon smacked, "About the kigum of Go' being at han' an–"[141]

"Simon! Don't talk with your mouth full!" his dark-eyed, round little wife interrupted, shoving a napkin in his beefy hand. He pushed back from the table and let out a staggering belch, beating his chest with his open palm like a mother burping her baby.

"All I know is, His teachings make more sense than all that legalistic quibbling we get sometimes."

"Simon!" his wife scolded with a giggle. "You shouldn't speak about the holy men that way."

Simon smiled and said, "Aw, I've got nothing against them personally. Its just that a man can't live with all those rules and regulations. It's impossible!"

The four men finished their meal and went out and sat on the edge of the harp-shaped lake they so dearly loved and from which they made their living. A gentle breeze caressed their rugged faces.

"You know what John the Baptizer said of Him?" Andrew began. His long, thick lashes shaded his soft brown eyes. "He said that this Man is the Messiah."[142] There was a long silence.

"Do you believe him?" Simon asked finally, his hands clasped around his knees.

Andrew turned and looked straight into his brother's eyes. "Yes, I do."

Simon quickly looked down.

John spoke up. "I do too, Andrew."

"Me too," piped in James.

Simon picked up a white stone and skipped it across the lake. For once he had nothing to say.

That night Simon tossed and tumbled in his bed for an hour. He wasn't the type to lose sleep over anything, but he couldn't get the young Preacher's words out of his mind. And those eyes. They seemed to plumb the very depths of his soul. *Why is He affecting me this way?* he wondered as he sat up, scratching his thick, curly hair. Simon was a man given to causes and had been involved in a few, but this . . .

The next Sabbath, he got up early, washed and put on his best robe.

"Where are you going?" his wife asked as she prepared a tray for her sick mother.

"Uh, to the synagogue," he answered, half embarrassed. She knew he had not been in six months.

His wife didn't seem surprised. "You're going to hear the Nazarene, aren't you?" she smiled. Simon nodded, waved and disappeared out the door.

The Temple at Capernaum was more crowded than he had ever seen it, and he lived but a stone's throw away from its steps. He spotted his brother Andrew who had saved him a seat. "How did you know I'd be here?" he whispered as he sat down on the cool, white marble bench.

"I just knew," Andrew grinned.

The crowd was engaged in lively conversation. The women sat in the upper level. Some held small children on their laps. Others fanned themselves with one hand and cupped the other over their mouths as they whispered little bits of town gossip. The men crowded together on the lower level. Some of the younger ones sat on the floor.

Jesus stood up to teach. A hush fell over the crowd. His voice was golden. Every word He spoke was a love song straight from His Father's Heart into theirs. His Word was as one Who possessed authority, not like some of the scribes with their pious platitudes and clever little anecdotes. Their ears had never heard such wisdom. Every eye was on Him. The young lads sitting on the floor leaned forward, cupped their tanned chins in their hands and listened closely. Even the Temple priests were thrilled to hear such wisdom.

* * *

A small patrol led by the demon captain circled over the gleaming white marble temple. Looking below, they spotted a poor wretch whom they had held captive for decades, and in whom several demons abode. The captain swooped down and ordered the demons within him to interrupt the service. His voice was frantic. "We can't have them hearing truth!"

The demons stirred violently inside the man and goaded him to enter the temple.

Jesus moved slowly about the room so He could make eye contact with each person there, including the women who dared to peek over the balcony.

Suddenly, a commotion broke out across the room. The man under the power of demons leaped into the center of the floor and rushed toward Jesus. Simon lunged forward. An unconscious desire to protect Him surged within him.

Andrew held him back. "Wait!" he whispered. "He'll handle it."

Simon sat back slowly, watching intently, his huge fists tightly clenched, just in case.

Immediately the wild-eyed, demonized man raised a deep and terrible cry from the depths of his throat. "What have You to do with us, Jesus of Nazareth–?" Everybody in the room was bug-eyed. "Have You come to destroy us?"

The answer to that was a definite "Yes!"

The voices were like a drone of angry hornets. "I know Who You are! The Holy One of God!"

Indeed they knew Who He was. They had just witnessed His victory over their leader in the wilderness just a few days before.

Jesus by a word of command rebuked him, immediately gagging him. "Be silent and come out of him!"

The unclean spirits, throwing the man into convulsions and screeching with a loud voice, came out of him, and took off like bats out of a cave.

The demon patrol looked on in horror as the unclean spirits shot past them, shaking and glaring furiously at the captain.

Simon and Andrew looked at one another wide-eyed, as did everyone present. They were all amazed, almost terrified. They did not yet recognize that the kingdom of God had come upon them and that war had broken out in their very midst; a war that would soon rage violently in the unseen world.

"Did you see that?" the man in front of them said, his voice high with excitement.

"What is this? Is this some kind of new teaching? With total authority He gives orders even to the unclean spirits and they obey Him!"

"What new doctrine is this?"

It was the doctrine of the rule of God. To be free!

The disturbance was over and the crowd began to disperse. Immediately rumors began to fly, and would soon spread like wildfire throughout all the regions surrounding Galilee.

Jesus came over to Simon and Andrew. "I'd like to visit your home today," He smiled. His teeth were as bright as the whitecaps on the Sea of Galilee.

They were flabbergasted. "S-sure!" Simon stuttered. "I don't know if my wife will have a meal prepared. Her mother has been very sick."

"I know," Jesus smiled warmly.

Simon's wife nearly fainted with surprise and embarrassment that such an honored Guest would come when she had made no preparations. Her arms folded tightly as she gave a "How could you!" look at Simon.

He shrugged sheepishly as he introduced her to Jesus. "This is the Teacher from Nazareth I've been telling you about."

Jesus immediately put her at ease with a warmth that melted her icy stare that was aimed at her grinning husband. She smiled apologetically at Jesus. "Please forgive me, Sir. I have nothing prepared. My mother has been so ill."

"May I see her?" Jesus asked tenderly, His eyes already studying the frail figure lying on the bed beneath a window in the corner.

Clay pots of flowers lined the windowsill, lovingly placed there by her daughter in an effort to cheer her. Pink, purple and red anemone lilies spilled over the edges of the pots, jostling one another for sunlight. A gentle breeze from the lake brought relief to the warm room.

Jesus' face grew serious as He approached her bed.

Simon followed. "Can You help her?" he whispered. "She's been like this for days." A yellow kitten stretched and squeaked out a sleepy meow at the foot of her bed.

Jesus looked at her aging face etched with wrinkles that told stories of hardships and laughter. Beneath the flush of the fever He saw an outline of a demon coiled about her head, fire burning in its beady eyes. Its impish grin faded quickly when it saw Jesus approaching.

It hissed, "Oh no! The Seed!"

Jesus' eyes locked onto the evil spirit and rebuked it sternly. "Fever, leave!"

At once the wild-eyed demon jerked back in horror and fled past the lilies and out the window.

The woman opened her eyes. The first thing she saw was the smiling face of Jesus. What a face to wake up to! He took her by the hand and helped her up. She began fumbling with her hair. "Oh, my, I must look a sight!"

Jesus grinned at her. "You look beautiful."

She smiled a grateful smile, washed, dressed and headed straight for the kitchen.

The setting sun cast an orange and lavender hue on the little lakeside cottage. A passerby saw Simon's mother-in-law through the open window, looking quite healthy and busy serving her family and Jesus. Quickly he spread the word that Jesus was doing miracles at Simon's house and within minutes, a large crowd developed. Nearly everyone in the village showed up, both those who where sick, and those who brought someone with an ailment.

Jesus went to the door and looked at the gathering crowd. Without hesitation He went out to them, touching them and healing them one by one. Many who were demon-inflicted were set free with a word, sending dozens of demons screeching in terror, "You're the Son of God! You're the Son of God!"

Jesus wasn't about to be announced by these evil entities and ordered them to shut their mouths, refusing to let them speak. They knew too much. They knew He was the Messiah and they were rendered powerless at His command.[143]

Simon watched in amazement as He operated in authority and power. This same quiet Man Who had reclined at his table just a few hours before was now straightening bent limbs, opening deaf ears, cleansing diseased bodies and liberating tormented lives from demonic spirits. Who was this Man? Was He indeed–the Messiah?

Again that night Simon laid awake, his mind replaying the scene that had taken place just outside his door. Incredible miracles. People he grew up with healed of maladies they had had all their lives. He knew these people. He watched them in their daily struggles to survive, their abilities to work impossible because of deformities, deafness, crippled legs, chronic diseases and tormented minds. Some, known as the "village idiots," those poor, pitiful creatures who went through life slobbering, grinning blankly and mouthing gibberish, were suddenly released from the horrible bondages that had robbed them of their lives. And with just a word! Jesus just clamped His eyes on them and commanded the tormenting spirits to leave.

"And they did!" Simon said out loud, causing his wife to stir–and even startled himself. He patted her arm gently and whispered, "Go back to sleep."

He turned over and put his arm behind his head and stared at the ceiling. Moonbeams dancing on the lake reflected shimmering ribbons of light on the walls. But Simon was seeing something else. He was seeing spines straightening, eyes opening and lives restored.

"How can these things be unless God does it through Him?" he wondered, his eyes glistening with tears. "He has to be–the–Messiah."

* * *

A few days later, Simon and Andrew were scrubbing their nets after a hard night of fishing and had caught nothing. Looking up they saw Jesus walking over to them.

"Hello and Shalom! How's the fishing?"

The two burly brothers looked at each other and sighed, "Not so hot."

Jesus climbed into Simon's boat and asked him to shove out a little from the shore.

"Huh?" Simon squinted into the sun. Jesus nodded toward the fast approaching crowd.

He pushed out quickly just in time to keep from getting trampled. "Man! Don't they ever leave You alone?"

Jesus smiled. "They're the reason I'm here."

The crowd began to beg Jesus to teach. Using the boat as a pulpit, He began to teach them many things. Little waves gently rocked the boat as His words, riding on the natural acoustics of the water's edge, rang out.

Astounded that he was once again in the company of Jesus, Simon quietly watched the faces of His hearers. He knew something strangely wonderful was happening in their midst, but he was afraid to let himself believe that the Messiah Himself had eaten at his table just a few nights before, and was now preaching from his boat! It seemed that Jesus had intentionally sought him out to befriend him. *Why would He ask to come to my house the other day? And now He chooses my boat to sit in. Why me?* Simon asked himself silently. *I have no status, no wealth, no pedigree. Why would He want to get to know me?*

Little did Simon know that his question would be humbly asked throughout the centuries: "Why me, Lord? Why did You choose to befriend me? Out of all the millions of people on Earth, why do I have the privilege of knowing You? Why do I have the honor to call You Friend?"

When Jesus finished teaching, He turned to Simon, "Push out into the deep and let your nets down for a catch."

Simon dropped his head and looked up at Jesus past his bushy eyebrows and said condescendingly, "Uh, Master, the fish are not schooling. We fished hard all night and caught nothing." Jesus' smiling eyes seemed to look right through him. Simon sighed, "But if You say so, I'll give it another try."

Halfheartedly he lowered one net into the water, wishing he didn't have to witness the embarrassment of the good Teacher when the net came up empty.

Suddenly, a familiar tug grabbed Simon's attention as the net strained to hold the enormous catch. His eyes wide in amazement, he let out a hearty shout to his partners to come help him. The boats nearly sank with the abundant catch.

Simon, when he realized what was happening, looked at Jesus' smiling face and fell to his knees. "Master, please leave. I'm a sinful man and I can't deal with Your–Your holiness. Please, just leave me to myself."

Jesus leaned forward and looked straight into his eyes. "Don't be afraid, Simon. From now on you'll be fishing for the souls of men and women."

Simon and Andrew beached their boats, followed by their fishing partners James and John, Zebedee's sons. As though some invisible force moved in their hearts, they dropped everything, nets and all, and followed Him up the beach, speechless.[144] Jesus had done a sounding inside the big fisherman's heart, deeper than the Sea of Galilee.

That night, Simon slept like a baby, snoring loudly, never dreaming in a million years that one day his very shadow would produce the kinds of healings he had witnessed a few nights before,[145]

and that great cathedrals
would one day
bear his name.

For this cause shall a man leave his father and mother, and shall be joined unto his wife, and they two shall be one flesh. This is a great mystery: but I speak concerning Christ and the church.

Ephesians 5:31,32

The wedding ceremony itself had brought wondrous longings to His heart to hastily begin His ministry of betrothing those who would say yes to His proposal of love.

CHAPTER TEN

Wedding Invitations

THE LARGE ROOM WAS beautifully adorned with bright oil lamps and candlesticks. Garlands of white myrtle blossoms draped over the doorways and lampstands. The guests listened carefully as the bridal blessing was spoken. Then the bridal toast was made and the happy couple drank from the cup while the guests looked on wistfully.

Jesus and His first disciples[146] were invited to the wedding, along with Jesus' devout mother, Mary. His Presence at the wedding at Cana of Galilee was a time of joy. He had just left the tenseness of the wilderness and the painful confrontation at Nazareth, and was now enjoying the carefree gaiety of a wedding.

He had recently called four fishermen as His first disciples, along with Philip of Bethsaida and Nathanel of Cana. He joyously entered into deep friendship with them. The gladness at the wedding in Cana added to the festive cheer in the hearts of the devoted men and their Master. Although His disciples did not yet understand Who He really was, or what He was all about, they would learn in time, just as the young couple for whom the wedding was celebrated, would learn about each other. There would be good times and hard times, but the commitment of their love for one another would see them through.

The feast was in progress. The lively music caused many of the guests to tap their feet and sway to the beat. They reclined at tables on tapestry-draped couches cushioned with soft pillows and many were seated in chairs that lined the walls of the spacious room. The tiles on the floor were strewn with flower petals. The festive mood was high with laughter ringing out throughout the house.

Jesus' mother overheard a servant tell another that they were running out of wine, a situation that would bring intense embarrassment to the bridegroom and his family. She leaned over and whispered to Jesus, "They're almost out of wine."

Jesus sat up straight, looked deeply into His mother's eyes and said respectfully, "Woman, why are you telling Me this? It is not yet My time."

The difficult and painful moment had come when Jesus was no longer her natural Son. Her earthly relationship in the context that she had always known was over. When she spoke as His mother to supply a miracle for the wedding, she was inadvertently crossing the invisible line into His Father's Business.

"Woman, what have I to do with you?" was a quiet, tender reminder that she could not dictate His ministry. His hesitation was not a reluctance to provide wine for the wedding, but to do so upon His mother's request.

He now was leaving His father and mother and would cleave to His Bride. He was no longer subject to His earthly parents, but was a full-grown Man and was fully entered into His Mission.

Mary understood immediately, but trusted completely His wisdom and compassion. She said to the distraught servants, "Do whatever He tells you to do."

Jesus beckoned to the servants and whispered to them to draw water into their largest waterpots. They looked at Him, completely bewildered, but obeyed without question, and filled them to the brim.

"Now draw out a pitcherful and take it to the host."

When the governor of the feast tasted the contents, he motioned to the bridegroom to bend his ear toward him. "This wine is the best I've ever tasted! Usually they serve the best wine early in the feast, and after everyone had drunk their fill, bring out the lesser wine. But you've saved the best until last!"[147]

The bridegroom looked at him puzzled, shrugged his shoulders and returned his attention to his bride.

It was fitting that Jesus' first miracle was supplying wine for a wedding. His Presence among the precious masses of Planet Earth was an occasion to celebrate. He was the New Wine. His very Essence was to minister joy; to set people free, to wed their hearts to His own. He had not come to bring them another ascetic religion of bondage, but a relationship of a Husband to His wife,[148] a union of natural joy. Jesus' wedding gift of wine was His blessing upon marriage. He Himself would one day be wed–married to His Bride, the Church.[149]

The burly, leather-skinned fishers were the first of His Bride, a profound contrast to the soft-skinned, veiled bride of the hour. No longer would they catch fish but would trawl the deep sea of souls that would one day make up His Church, His Bride. She would be filled with the New Wine of His Spirit, and His joy would be complete when they would finally be joined together forever in His heavenly kingdom. He would remove her from her earthly home to the home of His Father.

The wedding He was attending brought it all to His mind. Gladness welled up in Him as He watched the young couple. One day Jesus would remove the veil of flesh from His Bride and would drink the wine of the New Covenant with her. The wedding ceremony itself had brought wondrous longings to His heart to hastily begin His ministry of betrothing those who would say yes to His proposal of love,[150] the Holy Spirit His ring on their finger.[151]

He was now wholly free to go about His Father's Business; to woo to life those dead in their sins and to become one with them, just as the marriage He had witnessed would bring oneness to the happy, garland-clad couple.

The excited servants could no longer keep quiet. They whispered to the bridegroom what had taken place. He and his bride peered with eyes of wonder through the rosy glow of the candlelight and past the crowd at Jesus. They timidly held up their glasses, nodded reverently at Him and smiled. The blush of the miracle wine matched the blush on the cheeks of the beautiful young bride. Jesus sat back, lifted His glass, smiled and returned the nod. A deep joy filled His heart.

Soon He would be sending out
wedding invitations of His own.

And Jesus passed forth from thence, he saw a man named Matthew, sitting at the receipt of custom: and he saith unto him, Follow me. And he arose, and followed him.

Matthew 9:9

He stamped papers, took the hard-earned money of his countryman and dared not allow himself to look up for fear someone would see the longing in his eyes.

CHAPTER ELEVEN

The Tax Collector

THE WARM AFTERNOON SUN played on the gleaming, fluttering sails of the little ships that had come to do commerce in Capernaum. Business was good. The day was so hot that Levi-Matthew moved his table outdoors in front of the customhouse. Grumbling locals and weary travelers stood in line to pay their taxes along with those paying duty on their imports and exports. Levi was a publican.

The tax-gatherers, known as publicans, were the most despised men in Israel. Even more than the cruel Romans who occupied their land. For though the Romans taxed them heavily, the publicans, who were native Israelites, willingly and greedily worked for them to collect. Then they added their own staggering amounts, skimmed it off the top, and lined their pockets with money from their own hardworking countrymen.

Levi-Matthew had developed skin sufficiently thick to handle the scowls and insults from anyone he encountered. The Pharisees taught that it would be impossible for the likes of him to be saved, for he and the scum like him aided and abetted the substitute kingship for that of Jehovah God, and considered them to be traitors, not of Israel only, but of God Himself. For such a man as Levi-Matthew, heaven was but a hopeless dream. His heart dared not hope for anything beyond this life except the fires of hell. Those Pharisees had indeed shut up the kingdom of heaven against them.[152]

It mattered little whether or not he was liked, or whether he sinned little or much. It made no difference. This was as close to heaven as he would get, so he might as well enjoy it. At least that had been his philosophy until recently.

Levi had another motive for moving his tax table outdoors besides the heat. He hoped the Nazarene Teacher might once again come and preach to the gathering crowds near the shore. He had heard Him teach a few weeks before, and His words had lodged in his heart, stirring up hope–a luxury he had not allowed himself since he was a boy.

So much was the impact of His teachings that he began to feel conviction concerning his sinful life and for his penchant to greed and lust. He had begun to lighten the load of taxes upon some of the people to the point of releasing a poor family from their debt, making them promise not to tell anyone.

Beads of perspiration formed on the faces of the men waiting in the long line to grudgingly pay their taxes. Little wisps of wind would occasionally cool Levi's ruddy face when the sun dipped behind the drifting clouds. "Next!" he yelled as he stamped the papers of a scowling businessman, who, upon paying his tax, promptly spat on the ground, his eyes never leaving Levi's.

Just then, Levi heard the excited shouts of a man near the end of the line. "Look! There He is! There's the Teacher!"

Jesus was walking along the shoreline, a crowd following, pleading for Him to stop and teach. Levi's heart began to race. He tried to see Him, but the sun was in his eyes. "Next!" he bellowed, trying to act as though he hadn't noticed the growing excitement. He stamped papers, took the hard-earned money of his countryman and dared not allow himself to look up for fear someone would see the longing in his eyes.

Was there really hope for him? Was God really the God of love and mercy the Nazarene had spoken of? The Teacher had talked about God as if He knew Him intimately. He had spoken as though there was no cavernous gap He could not bridge. Could a man like himself truly know God? Not according to some Pharisees. He was contemptible, without hope and deserved hell. Even his name, Levi, was a mockery, a name that spoke of priests and servants of God.

The line was growing shorter. He was glad, and hoped he could soon go home. Never had he felt so ashamed of his occupation. He wished he could hide the moneybox and close the customhouse for good. He longed to run and join the gathering crowd that was following Jesus. His heart pounded excitedly. *I long to hear His words*, he thought. *I hope He teaches today.*

"Next!" It was hard to concentrate on his business with his heart aching so within him and with the Teacher so nearby. Even his voice became gentler as he called, "Next," allowing the break between customers to give him a chance to look to see where Jesus was.

"There He is," he whispered to himself. He recognized four of His followers, the fishermen Simon-Barjona, his brother Andrew and James and John, the sons of Zebedee. Levi winced at the memory of the last time he had dealings with Simon. He had protested the taxing of the huge draught of fish he had caught a few weeks back. He claimed it had been a miracle catch and therefore should not be taxed. "Will you tax God?" was his heated argument. They had gotten into a wordy dispute and finally Levi let it go when he heard that the miracle was connected to the Nazarene Teacher.[153] Levi had heard that these four were now Jesus' disciples. He wondered why He would want those simple fishermen as His followers.

He stamped the papers of a glowering man before him, took his money and shoved it into the moneybox, slamming the lid. He hated what he was doing. He wanted to run. He wanted to run to Jesus. Without looking up, he hollered, "Next!" He wondered whom else the Teacher would call to be His disciple.

A man stepped up to the table. Levi looked up and saw Jesus smiling down at him. Levi gulped hard.

Jesus grinned
and quietly said,
"Next."[154]

* * *

Lively music could be heard up and down the narrow streets of Capernaum. Every publican in town had been invited to Levi's party, along with several of his closest friends, many of whom were considered to be of ill repute. Gaudily dressed women of no better reputation sat among them while others busily served the guests.

Jesus sat beside Levi-Matthew at the place of honor. Levi was ecstatic having his Master in his home and wanted all of his friends to meet Him. Upon the news that he had become Jesus' follower, the reactions of his family and friends ranged from a cool, "That's nice" to being ready to disown and disinherit him. Most showed up out of curiosity. Many simply came because Levi-Matthew threw great parties.

Jesus was glad to come to Matthew's party. He was delighted to meet his friends and family. His love and acceptance of the "riff-raff" of society was the hallmark of the all-encompassing friendship toward mankind. They were surprised at His genuine, easy grace and acceptance. No holy man had ever given them so much as a second look. Now, the holiest One of all was sitting with them and thoroughly enjoying their company.

No one had ever treated Levi-Matthew with such love and respect. Jesus had noticed him at his tax table for several days. When the Pharisees looked at him, they saw a loathsome tax collector. When Jesus looked at him, he saw a man.[155]

But a man the way God had created him to be.[156]

He already saw him . . . redeemed.

Just outside the door were the ever-present Pharisees, those of that legalistic sect, watching closely Jesus' behavior.

His disciples sat across from Him and to the right, near the door facing the window. Simon felt uncomfortable among these tax-gatherers and was still having a hard time accepting Matthew as one of the inner circle. He and the other disciples were unusually quiet, as they watched the interaction of the noisy crowd. The music was loud and high-spirited, forcing those who wished to converse to yell at the top of their lungs.

Simon leaned over, cupped his hand around his mouth and hollered at James, "If my wife knew I was here, she'd kill me!" James grinned and nodded knowingly.

The shrill flutes and laughter only added to the insult of the Pharisees as they stood outside and watched through the open door, Jesus laughing and talking with Levi and his seedy friends. It was bad enough that He had four backward, lowly, uncouth fishermen as His disciples; now He's added a publican!

Their laughter sparked even more controversy. Laughter in Israel was usually confined to banquets and weddings. But His Life was a banquet and His words were a wedding. Each word He spoke married Him to their hearts and celebration bubbled forth like sparkling wine.

Simon looked up and there in the doorway beckoning to him was a stone-faced Pharisee. He punched James and pointed toward the door with his thumb, "Come with me. Let's see what they want." They left the table and went to the door.

The Pharisees' arms were folded tightly in a defensive manner. They glared past them at Jesus as His uneasy disciples approached the door. "Uh, you wanted to see us?"

Simon couldn't see the dual demons, Pride and Deception, standing behind the Pharisees listening intently. They had been sniffing out sinful flesh, which was one of their favorite things to do. They were drawn to some of the Pharisees, for they could smell bitter anger a mile away.

They were looking for potential candidates to manipulate in order to destroy the Seed. To their disappointment, they found that many scribes and Pharisees were delighted and electrified at Jesus' wisdom and knowledge. Some were merely bewildered and upset at His presence. Others were enraged at his teachings and behavior. These especially interested the demons.

Mere disagreement with Jesus was not enough for them to work with. They sought those who were filled with hatred and vicious anger–those who had allowed their jealousy and rage to fester and grow–for such behavior indeed gave place to the devil.[157] Anger gave the evil spirits inroads into their lives, upon which they could easily build their strongholds.[158] Just as Cain, who did not heed the warning of God to deal with his anger and thereby opened himself up to the spirit of Murder,[159] some of the Pharisees were dangerously close to the same trap. The evil spirits were delighted.

The demons were also after the minds of the disciples, hoping to lodge in their hearts a seed of doubt concerning Jesus' obvious improprieties as a Rabbi. Rubbing elbows with publicans and sinners was profoundly and blatantly against their law. Unknowingly the Pharisees were doing their work for them. "Why does He eat with publicans and sinners?" they spat with hateful arrogance.

Pride and Deception screeched in horror and pulled back as Jesus walked up behind His freshmen disciples and answered for them, "Who needs a doctor? The healthy or the sick?" The Pharisees glared at Him in startled speechlessness. "You need to go learn what this Scripture means: 'I'm looking for mercy, not sacrifice.'"[160]

As far as they were concerned, showing mercy *was* a sacrifice.

Jesus looked deeply into their eyes and continued, "I am not here to minister to the strong, but to those who are weak." What loving words! Yet, in their determination to make clear their displeasure of His behavior, they missed the depth of Jesus' answer. His deep concern for them went unnoticed. They only glared at Him in stony silence.

Soon some of John the Baptizer's disciples, who had also been closely watching Jesus' conduct, came with questions, though theirs were not as the arguments of the Pharisees. The religionists had coerced their inquiry in an attempt to further discredit Jesus' testimony, though John's followers certainly had doubts of their own. Their master was in prison for publicly calling Herod an adulterer for having married Herodias, his brother Philip's wife.[161] It seemed to John's followers that this should be a time of fasting and prayer, not of feasting and revelry! It was a staggering contradiction to them. John was rotting in a hot, rat-infested dungeon, and the One Whom he declared as Messiah was partying with publicans!

Jesus' answer was, as always, suited to their understanding. John himself had gladly proclaimed himself as "the friend of the Bridegroom,"[162] so it was in this context that Jesus answered them. "Why should the Bridegroom's friends be downcast and mourn while He is with them? The time will come when I, the Bridegroom, will be violently taken from them. Then they will indeed fast."

They did not understand that He was speaking of His own impending crucifixion. It was inconceivable to them that the One Who John had proclaimed as Messiah would be taken away and killed! It was a strange context to place such a happy occasion as a wedding–the Bridegroom–with such grievous words that He would be violently taken from them.

Many of the Pharisees, who genuinely desired spiritual renewal and were truly seeking God's rule in their lives, had introduced more fasts to their already rigorous way of life, as had John with his followers,[163] in the intense pursuit of God's rule in every aspect of their lives. During these fasts they would plead for God's mercy and forgiveness. They had implemented these fasts to accelerate spiritual awareness in themselves and the people. The question had been asked, "Why do Your followers not do the same?"

In this context, Jesus continued, "Who would patch an old garment with new cloth? The patch will shrink and pull away from the old cloth, leaving an even bigger tear than before. And no one puts new wine into old wineskins. The old skins would burst from the pressure, spilling the wine and ruining the skins. New wine must be stored in new wineskins. Then the wine and the wineskins are preserved. But no man who has had the old wine wants the new, for he says the old is better."[164]

The rich heritage of Judaism that His Father had implemented, the old wine, was better than the multitudinous laws and rigors that had been executed. Not the new fasts and extended laws that the religious leaders had added to the people who were already burdened under their heavy load. More fasting was not the answer for true spiritual renewal.

Jesus was not here to introduce more religious rites, but to bring beauty and fulfillment to what His Father had already given them. The old wine, the Torah, would not be cast away, but would be fulfilled through His perfect life. In doing so, He would introduce New Life, a New Wine[165] that would be sweeter and richer than even the rich old wine of their past. As a Wise Instructor, He brought forth out of His treasure house of teachings the new and the old, the fresh as well as the familiar.[166]

Because their spirits were open to Jesus' wisdom, John's disciples were satisfied, for the time being. But the handful of Pharisees closed their spirits even more to the truth,

which flung
the gate
wide open
for Deception.

There was a man of the Pharisees, named Nicodemus, a ruler of the Jews: The same came to Jesus by night . . .

John 3:1,2

To come close to the young Teacher was to stand dangerously close to the precipice of one's inner emptiness, a vast chasm that the law had never been able to fill. An emptiness Jesus' words seemed to implore to satisfy.

CHAPTER TWELVE

The Summit Meeting

THE PHARISEES AND SADDUCEES, as always, were watching Jesus' every move as He taught in their streets and synagogues. Some of them felt He represented a threat to their religion. Jesus' disregard for the stringent rules of purity and His shocking fraternization with publicans and sinners was a stinging offense to them. Little did they know that He was, in truth, fulfilling every jot and tittle of the Law[167] before their very eyes. If only they would see it.

The Pharisees, in their immaculate long robes and wide-fringed shawls, listened intently with their arms folded. Some wore phylacteries, those small leather cases containing brief phrases of the Pentateuch, strapped onto their foreheads and left arm. Wearing them on their person was not only a constant reminder of the Law, but some believed it could engender the Word of God into their innermost being. A few even believed superstitiously that these tiny scrolls had power, like amulets, to ward off evil and drive away demons. A few had widened the fringe on their shawls and made broad their phylacteries to make them more conspicuous and show themselves to be more pious and eager than most to remain close to God's law.[168]

On the periphery of the crowd, a more-than-middle-aged man stood. He was a notable member of the Sanhedrin. He could barely sort out the words that so moved his heart. Words that, for the first time, were spoken in context of their true meaning; words that came from the Man from Nazareth.

As he listened to Him teach, questions flew about in his mind like frightened birds caught in a storm. To even allow himself to seek the answers was a profound move of conviction on the old Sanhedrist's heart. He had to overcome one stumbling-block after another to get to the place of even considering Jesus to be sent from God. Prejudice against an untrained Galilean was intense in his circles. To remotely acknowledge Jesus as God-sent was to compromise everything he believed.

But the miracles. How could they not be from God? And His words! No man had ever spoken like this Man. The authority in His teaching was not mere human charisma with which He was endowed. And the power He demonstrated when He performed miracles was more than real.

"Nicodemus, what do think of the words of this Teacher from Nazareth?" asked one of his fellow Pharisees. Nicodemus kept looking straight ahead, ignoring the question. There was no point in debating Jesus' teachings. Some of the lawyers had tried, only to be left dumbfounded and silenced. They couldn't touch this Man's wisdom.

Nicodemus didn't want to debate Him, but he had questions that had to be answered. But could he trust Him? In his heart of hearts he hoped He was all He seemed to be. It was the fear of man that grabbed Nicodemus by the throat at the very thought of approaching Jesus. Not that he was afraid of Him. No kinder, more caring Man had he encountered. No, he was afraid of his peers–and perhaps himself. To come close to the young Teacher was to stand dangerously close to the precipice of one's inner emptiness–a vast chasm that the Law had never been able to fill–an emptiness Jesus' words seemed to implore to satisfy. How he longed to talk to Him!

He could delay no longer. Perhaps if he waited until dark he could secretly draw near and have a private meeting with Him. Nicodemus had overheard one of Jesus' disciples discuss with another the place where they would spend the night. Tonight would be his perfect chance. The Sanhedrin was meeting at the Temple and he would send his servant to tell them he had important business to attend. Certainly that was no falsehood, for it might be the most important meeting of his life.

The crimson sun went to bed behind the hills, and under the welcome cover of darkness, Nicodemus made his way to the olive grove where he knew he would find Jesus. The flickering campfire helped him find his way through the thick brush. His heart pounded with a mingling of apprehension and excitement.

Jesus welcomed Nicodemus warmly. It was as if He was expecting him. The handful of disciples quietly moved away from them, allowing their Master privacy, although their curiosity leaned hard on them to eavesdrop.

The moonlight strained through the trees. An owl hooted softly in the background, seeming to ask the same question Nicodemus had in his heart.

Who–Who–Who–are You?

Jesus motioned to him to have a seat on a log beside the crackling fire. Nicodemus' eyes were full of unasked questions. Jesus sat near him and leaned forward, his expression affirming that he had His undivided attention.

The old Pharisee approached Jesus like an ambassador of one kingdom to another, coming together in a quiet, secret summit meeting of the minds. "There are some of us who believe that the things You do and say are from God. It is obvious that no one can perform such miracles unless God is with him." This was Nicodemus' first step of truth.

Jesus, as always, ignored the polite diplomacies and went straight for the spiritual jugular. "Unless you are born again, you will not see the kingdom of God."

His directness startled Nicodemus. And His statement! Everything he had lived for as a leader of Israel was based on the hope of one day seeing the kingdom of God! "How can a man be born when he is full grown and old? Can he enter a second time into his mother's womb and be twice born?"

Nicodemus asked questions. This was the difference between he and the others. This was the difference between life and death.

Jesus was glad for his questions. "Nicodemus, that which is born of flesh is just that–flesh. Flesh can never enter the kingdom of God. But that which is born of the Holy Spirit is Spirit–Life–the kind of Life that God has and originally intended man to have before the fall."

Nicodemus sat up straight and said skeptically, "How can these things be?"

He was not used to such Spirit-talk. The Spirit of God was in the *Torah,* and when understood and lived out in the context in which it was originally given, it brought peace and joy, for it was the perfect Law of Love. God's Spirit-blessing was upon all who lived it out in faith, which was accounted to them as righteousness.[169] Such sublime simplicity! Love God with all your heart, soul and mind, and love others as yourself. All the Law and the prophets hung on this simple truth,[170] which was a tremendous danger to Satan.

Deception had manipulated the minds of men in order to subvert the Law and complicate it with man's earthly wisdom. It had become nothing more than a rigorous book of rules, which left Nicodemus and many others empty of heart. It had become a taskmaster–without the Spirit of Life and Love–but death. Spiritual Blindness had turned their eyes inward to focus on their own attempts to please God with their traditions, rites and good works, a subtle deception that would carry on for centuries, another part of the captivity of the kingdom of the world. But Nicodemus could not yet see it.

You don't know you're captive when you're born into captivity.

Spirit-talk was no longer prevalent in their teachings, a fatal mistake when dealing with the things of God.

Jesus continued, "Why are you surprised that I tell you this? You're a respected teacher of Israel and you don't know these things? For days, I've been teaching truths to the crowds. You've been there–you've heard them. If I explain how to live here on earth, and you don't believe

Me, how are you going to believe Me when I tell you about heavenly things?"

Nicodemus leaned forward, "Please go on, Sir."

Jesus began to explain Spiritual birth. "After the fall, because of Adam and Eve's rebellion when they made the decision to live their way, they separated themselves from the Life of God, and from then on, all of mankind was born spiritually dead. Life apart from God is death."

Dead? Apart from God? Had he not lived his life for God? His words shocked him. "Then what must we do?"

"Trust and believe that the Father so loved the world that He sent His only begotten Son to redeem them."

There! He said it! He admitted that He was the Messiah! The Pharisee's heart was pounding. Jesus was telling Him plainly Who He was!

Jesus' words were vigorously direct, yet were spoken in love with the most sublime simplicity. "There are many *created* sons of God, Nicodemus, but there is only one Son Who is begotten of God.[171] And whoever believes in and adheres to *Him* will not perish but have Life eternal, in God's kingdom."

The old Pharisee was speechless.

Jesus continued, "And, when faith is placed in Him, like a gentle breeze, the Holy Spirit comes into him, fuses with his dead spirit, awakening him into New Life, so that in truth, he is born again from above. And this, Nicodemus, is the only entrance into the kingdom of God. Your flesh, nor the works of the flesh, can ever enter heaven, only your spirit imbibed with the Spirit of God."

Nicodemus began to tremble at the magnitude of these words. Because his heart was open and searching, the Holy Spirit breathed on him, whispering to his heart that it was indeed true. Jesus could see the revelation-light begin to glow in his eyes.

"I have come to open the eyes of the blind, deceived citizens of this world, to save them, not condemn them."[172]

Nicodemus' theology suddenly seemed impotent and empty as he listened to the depths of truth and wisdom that flowed like uncorked wine from the mouth of his gracious Host. Jesus' words, like a lovely melody, sweetly bathed his longing heart, while firm conviction pushed its way to the forefront, exposing the sin and sham of his life. The tenderness in Jesus' eyes melted the Sanhedrist's heart. Nicodemus now understood that he was looking at the very embodiment of the kingdom of God. And faith, like a lovely fountain, sprang up within him and opened his heart to believe that Jesus was the Way to eternal Life, the precious Gift given of God because of His great love for the world.

Tears rolled down his cheeks into his graying beard. He quietly reached into his robe and pulled out the phylacteries, and with trembling, liver-spotted hands, he handed them to Jesus. He no longer needed them. He now had the living Word of God in his heart.

The angels and that great cloud of witnesses[173] watched with euphoric joy as the old Sanhedrist, trembling on the brink of eternity, opened his spirit and his heart to receive the truth of the ages. Suddenly, the glorious light of God shot into his heart and blazed throughout his being and out of his eyes. Nicodemus was delivered out of the enemy's power of darkness and the kingdom of this world, and was immediately translated into the marvelous light of the kingdom of God.[174]

With utter joy in his heart, he left the physical company of His Savior, but took with Him His Spirit that would never leave him or forsake him. The questions he had were answered and the longings of his heart were filled. At this momentous summit meeting, a high-ranking ambassador of the world surrendered his heart to the opposing kingdom,

and quietly
and joyfully
defected.

Judge not, that ye be not judged. For with what judgment ye judge, ye shall be judged: and with what measure ye mete, it shall be measured to you again.

Matthew 7:1,2

He was teaching them to "kill" them with kindness. Even though it was a gracious manner of warfare, it was violent to the prince of darkness and his kingdom.

CHAPTER THIRTEEN

"Two Worlds Collide"

THE FIRST WORDS JESUS spoke when He began His ministry were, "Repent, for the kingdom of heaven is at hand."[175] This was bad news for the devil. Another kingdom was here and war was declared. Kingdom against kingdom. Light against darkness.

Two kingdoms. One programmed by God. One programmed by the devil.[176] Those two worlds collided each time Jesus opened His mouth to preach. His teachings, though alive, vibrant and exciting seemed–well, backwards from what his hearers had been taught. They seemed upside down. Wrong-side out. Foreign. Strange. Bordered on weird. But they were words of authority and of power. Words of life.

His teachings far extended the limited horizon that had been set for them, which kept them earth-bound and under man's burdensome control. He lifted their eyes higher and when He spoke their hearts took flight like eagles into new realms. When they entered His Presence to hear His words and looked upon His wonderful open face, their minds that had been obscured with questions began to focus clearly as truths of God were finally put into context for them.

His powerful voice rang out through the clean, sharp mountain air. Nature had spread her carpet of soft green grass and dancing wildflowers of shocking pink and pale lavender for His audience to recline upon. The sun embraced their weathered faces while He bathed them in the light of truth.

Many of the devout Pharisees who loved God with all their hearts believed. Because of their willingness to humble themselves and seek truth, the Holy Spirit worked in their hearts and gave them grace. God gives grace to the humble.[177]

Jesus did not speak as some of the more rigid Pharisees, whose starchy words polarized the people from God and pummeled them with religious plaster. His teachings fed their starving souls with words that were sprinkled with honey, spice and salt. His sermons, sayings and precepts were unequalled.

Jesus looked at the masses with compassion and love in His heart for them. They had been born blind in a dark world. But the Light had come,[178] opening the spiritually sightless eyes to the bright, sparkling treasure houses of kingdom truth. Many of the religious leaders had left out the most important message God had given in His Word. God loved them. He was on their side.

The Pharisees certainly knew of His compassion for they knew Him as *Adonai El Racham,* the Lord God of Compassion, and they prayed the words of David's great Psalm three times a day, *"The Lord is gracious and full of compassion; slow to anger, and of great mercy. The Lord is good to all, and His tender mercies are over all His works."*[179] But many did not teach or live this mercy and compassion. Somehow they became entangled in the letter of the law and missed or ignored the true spirit of it, which is love.

God, like a diamond, is multi-faceted. Some scribes and Pharisees had mostly pointed to only one facet of God. Judge. No one can stand in God's presence with the light striking that one facet without being destroyed by its fire. They became like the God they worshiped. Many of the religious leaders worshiped a God whom they saw only as Judge and Law Giver. Therefore, they became Judge and Law Giver.

God was so much more than that. And He sent His Son to reveal

His true Self. Jesus showed them the other facets of Father. Love. Mercy. Kindness. Gentleness. Longsuffering. Faithfulness. Goodness. Even joy![180] He told them of a love unlike any they had ever heard of. A love that loved them so profoundly that it was nearly unimaginable. A love that reached a part of them that they never knew existed. The truth of God's love searched their hearts and introduced them to those places inside them that were not yet explored. The excitement of His words fanned the feeble, sputtering fires of hope in their hearts. It caught on like wildfire in the wind and spread through their dry, parched hungering souls.

His teachings were so unlike anything they had ever heard; it staggered them and shook them to their very foundations. They had been taught, "Hate your enemies" Jesus taught "Love your enemies, even feed them and pray for them!" They had been taught, "An eye for an eye." Jesus taught "Turn the other cheek."

He taught them how things are measured where He came from. He said the amount of mercy, forgiveness, judgement and even money that is measured out will be measured back to them in kind.

"–With the measure you use, it will be measured to you. The same way you judge others, you will be judged. Don't condemn and you won't be condemned. Forgive and you will be forgiven. Give and it shall be given you. Do to others as you would have them do to you. Be merciful just as your Father is merciful. Love your neighbor as yourself. Don't seek worldly things, but seek first the kingdom of God. Everything you need will come to you. Seek first. Not second, third or fiftieth. Don't keep God standing in line behind all your worldly appetites."

He taught them sure-fire ways to tap into His kingdom's blessings: Be poor in spirit, be mournfully repentant, be meek, hunger and thirst after righteousness, be merciful, pure in heart, make peace, expect persecution and even rejoice in it. Eight "killer" concepts that would bring more blessings than they could contain.

All they had ever been taught was the Torah. God's Law, which was complete, based in love and was quite enough for man to handle. But they added hundreds more until it was impossible for anyone to keep them all, placing upon them the helpless feeling that they had no hope of making it into the kingdom of God.

Jesus came to remedy that. He had not come to abolish the Law, but to fulfill it for them. He would accomplish every jot and tittle, and all they had to do was believe and trust in Him and His perfection, and they would become one with Him. He told them, "I'll do the fulfilling, you do the faith. I'll do the work, you do the worship. You believe in Me, I'll birth you. Then just pass it on. Gift wrap your life and then give it away."

He even taught them how to pray. The only begotten Son said they, too, could call His Father *Abba*–Daddy. "Always remember to honor His name, for it is hallowed, sacred. Invite His kingdom rule to come and His will to be done in your lives and upon all the earth just as it is in heaven. Pray for your daily needs such as food and the Bread of life, and keep a clean slate, always asking forgiveness of debts and sins, and forgive those who have sinned against you. Ask Father to lead you out of the way of temptation and to deliver you from the evil one. And always remember to acknowledge that it is His kingdom and power that should be honored, and glory belongs to Him forever. Amen."

He spoke with such authority that man's hearts were gripped with truth. Those who had ears to hear received His words gladly, and in doing so, their spirits were awakened. Jesus saw the Sword of the Spirit reach into the heart and divide the soul from the spirit.[181] At last the longing spirit was free and could embrace truth unfettered. Free from the grasp of the mind, will and emotions, yet all were at his service, but now in a higher sense.

Each day more and more became a part of His Army and He armed them with weapons of warfare. Unconventional weapons that were not carnal, but weapons of His kingdom, mighty through God:[182]

Instead of meanness–mercy.
In place of hatred–humility.
Not grudges–grace.
Instead of prejudice–peace.
Not by force–by faith.
"Bless them that curse you.
Walk the extra mile."

Such weapons! He was teaching them to "kill" them with kindness.[183]

Even though it was a gracious manner of warfare, it was, nonetheless, violent to the prince of darkness and his kingdom.[184] It left Satan and his accursed army confused and debilitated. And every time believers put these weapons into practice, they grew stronger. The Sword of the Truth with one sharp blow set their spirits free. Free from the power of sin and free from the power of Satan. Darkness began to vanish. Demons had to flee! The devil was resisted[185] and the kingdom of God was advanced.[186]

Two worlds collided.
Jesus was on the attack and
a hostile takeover from heaven
was imminent.

Now when John had heard in the prison the works of Christ, he sent two of his disciples, and said unto Him, Art thou He that should come, or do we look for another?

Matthew 11:2-3

Go tell John you saw a kingdom being overthrown, all right, but not the political kingdoms of the world, but a spiritual kingdom of darkness. I'm here to destroy the kingdom of the devil.

CHAPTER FOURTEEN

"The Wrong Kingdom"

JESUS HAD COMPLETED HIS recruiting of the twelve men who were called to be His disciples: The four fishermen, Simon and Andrew and their business partners, James and his younger brother John, Matthew the publican and Philip, who brought his friend Nathanael (also known as Bartholomew) to Jesus. Thomas, a twin and a very intense, analytical young man, James, the Son of Alphaeus and the smallest in stature among the Twelve, Thaddaeus, also known as Judas, son of James, Simon, a Zealot, a sect of militiamen and extreme nationalists, and finally Judas Iscariot of Kerioth, a village in Judah, the only non-Galilean among them.

All twelve had come to Jesus with preconceived ideas. Their motives were patriotic. Thinking that the Messiah had come to set things right politically, they thought they were being groomed to be politicians, and would aid their new Ruler in setting up His kingdom. None had a clue they would be preachers.

Jesus had modeled ministry for His disciples, and was prepared to send them out. He had taught them, and gave them power and authority in His Name. Now it was time for them to go and proclaim the kingdom of heaven.

He sent them out to ignite the kingdom life in the hearts of men; to preach the good news of the kingdom and to heal the sick and even cast out demons, much to the chagrin of the demon captain whose unseen eyes watched their every move. He and his patrol listened intently. They had heard that the Seed was ready to attack in a much broader sense. He had given an incredibly dangerous weapon to them. He had given them His Name. "His Name is perilous!" The captain warned his diabolical horde. "Anyone who is given that Name can tread us underfoot![187] Even if we attack and swarm around them like hornets, they can destroy us all in that Name!"[188]

"What shall we do, then?"

"We'll send Strife and his minions ahead of them to cause confusion and dissension–the people will fight over who will let them stay in their homes. Strife opens the door to all of our evil work!"[189]

"Yes! And we can make people think they're heretics and reject them!"

"We'll keep them in want and make them wish they were in the comfort of their own beds!" They cackled with delight and slapped one another on their backs at their clever plots.

Jesus showed no interest in them and continued giving His disciples strict instructions concerning where to go, to whom to preach, even lodging and meals. "When you stay in friendly homes, bless it with the blessing of peace." Jesus wanted their home base in each village to be peaceful. He discerned the enemy's evil schemes and knew that the very adversary whom they were to defeat thrived in the midst of strife.

The demon captain got a knot in his scrawny throat.

Judas' eyes narrowed when Jesus instructed them not to carry money–not even an extra coat or pair of shoes–on their first journey of ministry. Jesus wanted them relying totally on His Father's provision. He wanted them to come to understand and trust His kingdom's economy and not to rely on the economy of the world.

The disciples' faces were solemn as He warned them, "I'm sending you out as sheep among wolves. Use wisdom, but remain calm and when in combat resist intimidation. Your message will not be accepted by everyone. In that house or that city, upon departing it, knock the dust off your feet as a notice to them that the judgment that will befall them will be worse than for Sodom and Gomorrah. They'll hate you because you minister in My Name." His expression was serious. "The student is not above his master, nor the servant above his lord." The coarse realism with which He spoke startled them. He continued, "Don't be afraid of those who can kill the body, they can't touch your soul."

Jesus could see the perplexed looks on their faces. *Kill the body? Are we facing that kind of danger?*

"Think about this for a minute. How much is a sparrow worth? Money-wise, practically nothing. Yet not one of those little birds falls to the ground without your Father's notice." Their faces relaxed a little. Jesus walked over to James and tousled his hair with His hand. "The very hairs on your head are all numbered. Not counted–numbered. This morning when you combed your hair and a few of them fell out," He chuckled, "Your Father said, 'Well, there goes number 1,462 and number 917.'" They all laughed. "So don't be fearful. If you are, you're operating in the wrong kingdom."

"You are of much greater value than a million flocks of birds. You who fearlessly confess Me before men, him will I confess before My Father in heaven. But whoever caves in to fear and intimidation and denies Me before men, him will I also deny before My Father in heaven. Don't think for a minute that I have come to make everything easy. We are at war. There are two kingdoms. My kingdom and the devil's kingdom. But My Word is a Sword."

The Word of the Lord was too much for the demons. They began to shriek, "Stop! Stop! We can't bear Your words!" The Sword of His Word sent them flying and screeching in every direction.

Jesus ignored them and continued, "There will be some lines of demarcation drawn, even in families. Some of your worst enemies can be those of your own family. If you are more devoted to your parents, or even your own children, for that matter, than to Me, you are not worthy of Me."

Judas frowned, still concerned that he had to leave the moneybag at home. This didn't sound like the kind of motivational speech he had expected. He wanted to know how they would be advertising His political Messiahship. He had dreams of power and prestige in His kingdom rule. This sounded like nothing but a hindrance to that dream. Jesus looked at him and continued, "If you're not willing and ready to lay down your life for Me you're not worthy of Me. Remain attached to this earth-life and you'll lose true life."

Judas looked away. Jesus walked over to Simon. "You're representing Me. If they receive you, they will receive Me and the One Who sent Me. Those who accept a messenger of God will receive the same reward as the prophet. The same with receiving a righteous man. Even giving a cup of cool water in your honor will be rewarded."

Finished with this discourse, Jesus turned and headed for other villages to preach and teach.[190]

* * *

John the Baptizer was still in the dark dungeon. He had boldly and publicly confronted Herod concerning Herodias, his brother Philip's wife whom he had married, saying, "It is not legal for you to have your brother's wife," plainly calling it adultery. Herodias seethed with hatred toward John and would have had him killed if Herod had not intervened. Herod feared John. But Herodias wouldn't leave it alone and vexed Herod until he gave in and had him arrested and put in chains.

Herod knew John was a just and holy man, and gave him some special treatment. Whenever he could, he would visit him and would listen to him, knowing he would straightforwardly address his sin, and he would leave his presence stinging with guilt. Yet he could not seem to stay away.[191]

Part of John's special treatment allowed his disciples to visit him from time to time, bringing him startling news of Jesus' activities. Jesus knew the reports had reached John's ears: the reports of His eating and drinking with sinners and of His teaching and healing the masses. This was not the kind of activity John expected from Messiah. Jesus was not surprised when John's disciples came with a message, a question asking, "Are You the right One, or should we be watching for another?"

Jesus knew that the bold preaching of John, declaring that the kingdom of God was at hand, implied the setting of all things right by the Anointed One, and the swift vindication of His power. That He would establish the Messianic kingdom on earth and perhaps John himself would be freed, as Messiah would consume all the kingdoms of the earth, including Herod's.

John's followers were expecting Messiah to be like King David, coming in battle array to fulfill the role of righteous judge and king of the nations. Or a deliverer like Moses who would work miracles and lead His people in a second exodus out of the bondage of Rome.

Surely He had seen His forerunner's plight. Did he not deserve to be set free from Herod's chains? Had he not done his work well? Had he not turned the hearts of the children toward their heavenly Father[192] and prepared the way for the Lord? Now would He not bring peace and freedom to His people? He should be at war! Their enemy had their leader hostage!

But the reports. He spent his time with sinners and quietly healing and teaching.

If John's disciples had held out any hopes of Jesus toppling Herod and liberating John, they were dashed by now. So, the messengers came with their painful question, "Are You the right One or should we look for another?"

Jesus knew this had to be a gut-wrenching question for John. Had he been mistaken? Had he missed it? God forbid.

Jesus quietly asked John's faithful followers to stand by and watch. He continued His work evangelizing the poor, opening blinded eyes, healing the lame, cleansing the lepers, opening deaf ears, even raising the dead.

At the end of the day, Jesus approached them. "Now, go and tell John what you have just seen and heard. The blind receive their sight, the lame walk, the lepers are cleansed, the deaf hear, the dead are raised up and the gospel is being preached to the poor. And blessed is he who is not offended in Me or the things I am doing."[193]

Their eyes were beginning to open and they began to understand what He was saying. Go tell John–yes, I am at war. I am at war with sickness, disease, blindness, ignorance, poverty, death, and all the works of Satan. I am here to set many hostages free. I am here indeed to overthrow a kingdom, but not the political kingdoms of the world, but a spiritual kingdom of darkness. I'm here to take back what is Mine.

I'm here to destroy the kingdom of the devil.

With that, John's disciples left in peace.

And the demon captain perched high above them
took off in horror
to report what he had heard.

For God, who commanded the light to shine out of darkness, hath shined in our hearts, to give the light of the knowledge of the glory of God in the face of Jesus Christ.

II Corinthians 4:6

"Did you say seeds of–Light?" Deception moved closer to the captain and loomed over him, his two faces mutating into various shapes and forms, leering at him. "And some seem to be weaker in illumination than others?"

CHAPTER FIFTEEN

Seeds Of Light

EVERY MOVE JESUS MADE the demon captain watched, from a safe distance, of course, taking notes of the places He went and the people He spent time with. He became quite nervous when he observed Him keeping company with some of Satan's choice slaves: tax collectors, prostitutes and sinners.[194] He wasn't just hanging out with them, He was changing them! Seven of the captain's own trainees had been cast out of the prostitute from Migdal![195] That was a real loss.

Greed, a notable demon, became quite upset when the Seed recruited Matthew the tax collector into His inner circle. The Light had entered Matthew's heart and Greed had to loose him, sending him screeching in pain. In fact, the Light was popping up everywhere. Satan's domain of darkness was dotted with tiny Lights from Judea, all the way to the Galilee.[196] The demon captain wrote in his report:

"He had a chance encounter with a woman at a well. She received the Light and blabbed it to the entire village. Now practically the whole region is lit up. Of all places, Samaria![197] He seems to speak to them by telling stories that they can easily relate to. When speaking to fishermen, He speaks of being fishers of men. When speaking to farmers, He speaks of sowing seed. The woman at the well, of water." The captain smiled an impish grin. "Of course He didn't speak to her about being a fisher of men. It seems she is already well-versed in that."

The captain's eyes squinted in the Light of Jesus' countenance and of those who followed Him. He could not take the brightness of His face. Wiping his eyes with the edge of his wing, he realized he would have to move farther away to continue his observations.

The crowds were growing daily, and so was the Light. The captain could not keep up with the losses. One thing he took note of, however, was that the tiny seeds of Light in the hearts of His followers varied in intensity. Some burned brightly and seemed to gain brilliance with each day. Especially if they were in His company and listened to His teachings. It was as if His words actually fed the Light within them![198]

But of even greater interest to the demon captain was how the little seeds of Light seemed to grow in size and in brilliance as His adherents prayed! He had to get a closer look. He knew his master would want a full report.

That night he followed the Magdalene to her meager room. He didn't have to wait long before she fell to her knees and began to pray. The captain could barely stomach the worship preceding her prayers. He knew he would not be able to remain for long. It was sapping his strength fast.

The Light within her heart seemed to stir like hot coals in a hearth. Then intensifying in radiance, it began to spread from her heart throughout her entire being. Suddenly, a shaft of Light appeared from above, engulfing the Magdalene like a ray of sunlight. It was the Glory of God! His very Presence was inhabiting her praises![199]

The captain grew dizzy with faintness and fear, and nearly choked at the sight of it. Wobbling in flight, he went out the window, his wings quivering with weakness. He had to get away from the Light. He headed straight for Satan's lair. He knew he would gain strength in the presence of his lord, though he feared him greatly.

Glad to have a few minutes to catch his breath, he waited outside the chamber doors. His master was in a meeting with Deception. The two grotesque bodyguards leered at him as he waited. He ignored them and went over in his mind the last words he had heard from the Seed. Finally the doors opened and Deception beckoned for him to enter. He didn't like Deception. He didn't trust him.

Satan's snakelike eyes glared at the captain as he stuttered and stammered through his report. "We've lost a tax collector, a p-prostitute, even the wife of Herod's household m-manager![200] Entire villages are turning to Him!" He braced himself for the explosion. He knew his master could be dangerous when provoked.

Deception stood in the background in the shadows, listening quietly. Only his sibilating breathing could be heard.

"Each time someone believes His w-words, a tiny seed of Light enters into their heart, Sire. It's most distressing!" Satan's eyes narrowed. "They s-seem to be at various levels of strength. I don't quite understand–"

"Enough!"

The captain's mouth clamped shut. Satan was clearly agitated. He motioned for Deception to approach his dark throne. The captain stepped aside, bowed low and yielded his place.

Deception moved slowly across the chamber floor with cat-like movements. He was in deep thought, his insidious mind already at work. He turned to the demon captain. "Did you say seeds of–Light?" Deception moved closer to the captain and loomed over him, his two faces mutating into various shapes and forms, leering at him. "And some seem to be weaker in illumination than others?"

"Y-yes, sir, or so it seems." The captain could hardly concentrate on the accuracy of his report with Deception right in his face.

Suddenly the large demon prince stood straight up, as though snapping to attention. He turned to his master. "I have it, Sire."

Satan leaned forward, his cold eyes wide with anticipation. He said slowly in a hissing voice, "What is it?"

"Seeds must have certain criteria in which to flourish, do they not?"

"Yes, yes, go on."

"Seeds must–take root, correct?"

"Take root? Yes, I suppose so."

"The entry of the Light seems to come from the Words of our enemy, the wretched Seed. Correct, Captain?

"Y-yes, Sir."

"Then we must see to it that the little seeds never take root."

"How so?" Satan's face was almost gleeful.

"The ones with very little Light are most likely weak in some way. Perhaps in understanding. Certainly we can snatch those seeds away.

"Others with a bit more illumination, but the brightness seems to ebb at times, must be vacillating. A sure sign of weakness. We must send trouble and persecution to keep them from taking root. They shall last no time at all."

"And the others!" Satan picked up the ball and ran with it. "We will plant our own little seeds. The root of all my evil!"[201]

"Ah, yes! The love of money!" Deception grinned, his fangs exposed in all their horror.

"Yes! The deceitfulness of riches!"[202] Satan fell back against his throne and laughed loudly. "I love it!"

"S-Sire, may I speak?" The captain took a deep breath, sending ripples through the scales on his wings. "There's more. I heard the Seed Himself say that He is here to take back what is His and to destroy your kingdom!"

"He said that?"

"Yes! He said that and more!"

Satan squinted and twitched. He was getting nervous. "Is that supposed to frighten me?" He looked at Deception for assistance.

"Yes, Captain, is that supposed to bring us to our knees?" They laughed.

"And Sire, speaking of knees, we also must do something about this–this praying. It seems to strengthen them considerably."[203]

"Of course we will, you idiot!" Deception snorted. "Do you think we cannot take care of such things? Perhaps you do not remember how Pride's choice general, the prince of Persia, fought against those miserable archangels Gabriel and Michael when Daniel prayed! Did we not hinder his prayers from being answered?"

The captain cringed and rolled his eyes. "Yes, Sir. For twenty-one days. And look what happened because of his prayers. Our hierarchy's position was weakened enough that even that stupid king Nebuchadnezzer came to his knees."[204]

Deception leered at him. "Would you teach me about strategy, Captain? Perhaps we should place you in authority over a nation!"

"We are well aware of the dangers of prayer, Captain. Just stick to your business and we'll handle the stratagems." Satan said condescendingly, smiling tautly at Deception.

Deception saw the look on Satan's face. He knew he was expecting him to head this one up too. "Sire! All my demons will be kept quite busy dealing with these–these seeds of Light. I cannot take on anything else. You do wish me to continue my efforts with the religious leaders, do you not?"

Satan dismissed the problem with a wave, "Of course. Continue concentrating on those assignments. We shall give this one to another."

Satan beckoned to the captain to come close. The nervous demon approached the throne. An order was given and he left. Within minutes, he returned with an excited little demon that was thrilled to be getting such an important assignment. His appearance was like a winged ferret with fangs.

His name was

Distraction.

And when Jesus was entered into Capernaum, there came unto Him a centurion, beseeching Him, and saying, Lord, my servant lieth at home sick of the palsy, grievously tormented. And Jesus saith unto him, I will come and heal him.

Matthew 8:5-7

He had listened as others talked at the bazaars and in the marketplace of how, with a word, demons left the bodies of those they had tormented for years. And he surmised one thing: it takes authority to do that.

CHAPTER SIXTEEN

The Sharp Soldier

UPON HIS RETURN TO Capernaum, a centurion who was well loved in the community approached Jesus. He had funded a couple of building projects for the village and had a good reputation from the townspeople. He was a high-ranking official in the military and his name had been on the list of Who's Who in the community for years.

Jesus could see the concern in his eyes as he came near beseeching Him, "Lord, my servant is terribly sick. It's the palsy and he is grievously tormented."

Jesus instantly replied, "I'll come right now and heal him."

The centurion took notice of His willingness to take the time to drop everything to go and minister to his servant, a person of no rank, no status, of no importance to anyone except himself. He began to see that Jesus held *all* human life as sacred.

He, a non-Jew, knew his house was considered to be "unclean" according to Levitical law. He said, in utmost reverence to Jesus, "Lord, I'm certainly not worthy that You should come under my roof."

Jesus ignored his statement and headed for his house.

"Speak the word only, Sir, and my servant will be healed." He had heard of the hundreds, perhaps thousands of people that Jesus had healed on those crowded mountainsides as the evening shadows grew long. He had listened as others talked at the bazaars and in the marketplace of how, with a word, demons left the bodies of those whom they had tormented for years. And he surmised one thing: it takes authority to do that.

The centurion understood authority. He had been in the military for decades and had served under some of the most gallant of leaders, and some of the toughest, most arrogant and cruel. He was in the service of Herod Antipas. He knew what authority could do to a man. It could be used or abused.

He saw this Man Jesus using authority for good. He heard of His willingness to heal the poor wretched folk that gathered around Him everywhere He went. Hour upon hour He would touch them, hold their faces in His compassionate hands, rejoice with the newly healed blind, run and dance with children who had never walked, and laugh with those who, for the first time, could hear. He knew he could heal his servant, and he knew He could do it long distance. With a word. Jesus' words. There was authority in them. When He spoke, things happened. The centurion understood authority.

He humbly continued, "I am a man under authority, having soldiers under me. I merely give an order to this man to go and he goes. And to another, come–and he comes. And to my servant, do this and that, and he does it."

When Jesus heard this He marveled. The One Who created the universe was impressed.[205] This man's faith caused the One Who flung the stars into the galaxies to do a double take.

"Wow! I've not seen faith like this in all of Israel, the very ones who should understand how God's authority works!" He turned and spoke to those who were gathering around hoping to see a miracle. "This man is one of the first of many Gentiles who will one day come from all over the world and will dine in My Father's kingdom alongside Abraham, Isaac and Jacob. And those who claim to be heirs of the kingdom–

those for whom the kingdom was prepared–will be out in the dark, crying and gnashing their teeth."[206]

Jesus turned back to the centurion, placed His hand on his shoulder, and squeezed it lovingly. He looked into his eyes and said, "Go, friend. What you believed for has already come to pass."

The centurion understood Jesus had authority over the powers of darkness and so did the demons that were watching and listening from the eaves of the roof above them.

"Oh no!" the demon captain gasped. "If His followers grasp this truth,

there will be no hope
for any of us!"[207]

And Jesus asked him, saying, What is thy name? And he said, Legion: because many devils were entered into him.

Luke 8:30

Jesus was thankful the Twelve could not see what He could see. A black, boiling swarm of demons like a million bats hovered over the craggy terrain. It was a hideous haven for evil spirits.

CHAPTER SEVENTEEN

Wildman Of The Tombs

IT HAD BEEN A long night. The disciples were worn out from battling the ferocious storm that they encountered crossing the Sea of Galilee. Their bodies ached; their clothes were drenched; their heads were throbbing and their sandals squished. But their hearts were in awe of the mighty miracle they had witnessed. Jesus, with a word, had calmed the violent storm.[208]

They looked forward to some much-needed rest, drying out their clothes and getting the water out of their ears. But upon reaching the shore, they were immediately met by an uneasy feeling. This was the place where the legendary Wildman of the Gadarene Tombs roamed. The disciples had heard shuddering stories about the Wildman. Over the years men had tried to bind him with chains and fetters. Some had even tried to tame him, but he snapped the fetters like dried needles and the chains like flimsy thread. Those who attempted to tame him ended up running for their lives, screaming in terror. He was stronger than ten oxen and moved about the tombs screaming and beating himself. Often he would cut himself horribly with sharp stones.

His shrieks would echo through the limestone caverns and caves, bounce off the steep cliffs and bluffs and across the lake's edge, sending eerie sounds like wild animals into the ears of the nearby villagers. Children often laid shivering in their beds at night, eyes wide and blankets pulled over their heads on those nights the Wildman was particularly boisterous.

The pale silver morning light lay over a gray film of hazy fog that only added to the weird, ghostlike scene. The hair stood up on the necks of the disciples. Goose bumps the size of pebbles popped up on their arms. Fear scraped along their spines like a thumbnail against a piece of slate as a bloodcurdling cry cut through the mist.

Jesus was thankful the Twelve could not see what He could see. A black, boiling swarm of demons like a million bats hovered over the craggy terrain. It was a hideous haven for evil spirits. Jesus was not interested in them, but only in those who suffered by them. The wails and moans of the Wildman cut to the depths of His heart. One of God's creatures was a helpless hostage to His archenemy, who had vandalized his very soul.

Suddenly, a massive figure appeared out of the dense fog. It was the Wildman of the Tombs! The disciples stood frozen in their tracks, their eyes bugging out. Their welcoming committee was a few thousand raging demons packed into one wild-eyed man.

From a distance the demoniac saw Jesus. He half ran, half stumbled toward Him, crying with a loud voice, "What have You to do with me, Jesus, Son of the most High God?" The swarm of demons in the region shrieked and fled in every direction when they saw Jesus. Simon's mouth hung open like a barn door. The Wildman writhed like a snake. "I implore You by God, do not torment meeeeee!"

Jesus' locked eyes with the tortured man and commanded, "Come out of him, you unclean spirit!" The man's eyes rolled back. He began to moan as though he would retch. Jesus demanded, "What is your name?"

A multitude of voices answered Him, "My name is Legion, for we are many!" The very presence of Jesus reduced the evil entities to cowering cowards, unable to continue their cruel mutilating of the man. They were failing and were in a panic. The demons pleaded with Jesus not to send them into the deep.

The fog began to burn off as the morning sun slowly rose, causing deep shadows to replace the hazy veil. Jesus looked up and to His left. A huge herd of swine was feeding on top of the high, grassy bluff. The devils begged Him to let them enter the bodies of the pigs. He pointed to them and yelled, "Go!" The demons ripped out of the body of the man, leaving him in a heap on the ground. They swept up the steep incline and swooped down upon the herd and entered into them.

The pigs' eyes were wild. They squealed and began to stampede, nearly running over one of the herdsmen, their hooves thundering like a thousand drums. They ran violently toward the precipice, the herdsmen screaming at the tops of their lungs, "Stop! Stop!" The herd lunged, as though purposely committing suicide, over the edge of the cliff. It was a horrible sight. Hogs flying, herdsmen screaming, disciples gawking, swine splashing, bubbles boiling, demons–drowning? And then–silence.

The herdsmen stood at the edge of the cliff, gaping down at the water, wide-eyed, watching the last bubbles disappear. They looked at Jesus in horror, turned and ran to report to a nearby city what had happened.

Jesus knelt next to the naked man, cupped his face in His strong hands and wiped away the foam from his parched mouth. "You're free," Jesus said softly.

The disciples quietly began to encircle him. James tore off one of his sleeves, dipped it in the gently lapping waves of the lake and tenderly washed the man's face. Philip took off his outer garment and put it on him.

Jesus looked into his eyes, now lucid and peaceful and filled with awe and wonder, and said, "You're going to be all right."

Tears streamed down the rugged, bearded face of the man, who just moments before was the legendary Wildman of the Tombs. He quietly worshiped Jesus with a heart of gratitude and thanksgiving. He would have followed Him anywhere, and pleaded with Him to let him stay with Him.

God and the angels filled the heavens with rejoicing at the sight of the setting free of the precious soul.[209]

Just then, a crowd started to zigzag their way down the steep bluff led by the herdsmen. "Where's the Wildman?" one of them questioned suspiciously. Jesus looked down at the teary-eyed man and smiled. The herdsman followed Jesus' gaze in disbelief, and saw the man who had terrorized their region for years, sitting quietly at the feet of Jesus, clothed, and in his right mind. Instead of bursting into praise that a possessed soul had been set free and that an insane maniac had been healed, they demanded Jesus to get out. They were paralyzed with fear and superstition, and were unwilling to allow such supernatural Power to remain in their midst. This was an atmosphere in which He could not have continued.

The people had just seen a great miracle. They had seen a man set free from demonic control, but they cared more for their herd of swine than their own people who would have greatly benefited from this great miracle and His presence among them. They were fearful. Superstitious. Set in their ways. Set in their traditions. Jesus merely got into the boat and sailed away. He sailed to a place where faith was–where they were open and longing for more of Him.

When Jesus again crossed over to the other side of the lake, a large crowd welcomed Him, for they were all expecting Him. And He sent the one who had been set free into the ministry. The once crazed man would go home and share his testimony, and would broadcast the mighty things God had done for him in the Decapolis, a ten-city federation where Jesus would later come.

The Wildman of the Tombs
would pave the way
for the Gospel.[210]

And behold, there cometh one of the rulers of the synagogue, Jairus by name; and when he saw him, he fell at his feet, and besought him greatly, saying, My little daughter lieth at the point of death: I pray thee, come and lay thy hands on her that she may be healed; and she shall live.

Mark 5:22-23

Jesus stopped in His tracks. "Who touched Me?" Peter was flabbergasted. "Who touched You? Master, we're in a crowd here. Half the crowd has touched You!" Many in the crowd had touched Jesus. But only one effectively.

CHAPTER EIGHTEEN

Miracle On the Way to a Miracle

JAIRUS KNELT BESIDE HIS dying daughter. The young synagogue ruler had been on his knees praying all night. All through the endless hours he had struggled with echoes of the voices of his colleagues who considered Jesus a threat, his wife's pleadings that he go to Jesus, and a spirit of fear that had been flitting about his head, tormenting him.

He had heard of the healings of the Centurion's servant and the court-official's son. Surely He could heal his little girl. But He was gone. He had been away for many days. "God," he cried. "If Jesus is truly from You–if He is truly your Son, let Him come and heal my child."

Just then, he heard the shouts outside his window. "Look! There he is! It's Jesus!" A crowd began to gather on the shores of the lake at Capernaum. They picked up the excited shouts. "He's coming! He's coming!"

Jairus was amazed. God had answered his prayers. Jesus was here!

He struggled to get to his feet. His knees were sore and his legs nearly locked as he tried to walk.

His wife ran in from outside and fell into his arms. "He's here!" she wept with joy. "Hurry! Go beseech Him to come!"

Jairus squeezed her hand. "Pray He will be willing!"

The disciples beached the boat and Jesus stepped on shore. The crowd greeted Him enthusiastically. "Jesus! Welcome home!"

Jairus could barely elbow his way through the crowd. "Please! Let me through! Please!" Finally he was face to face with Jesus. "Oh, thank God! Jesus, please! I beg of You. My little daughter lies at the point of death. I beg of You, come that she may be healed and live!"

Jesus didn't hesitate. He immediately turned to walk with him to his house. The crowd had grown greatly and nearly trampled one another to get a glimpse of Jesus. The disciples tried to control the crowd but it was almost impossible. They surrounded Him in an effort to keep Him from getting crushed.

Suddenly a small, pale hand reached through the throng in an attempt to touch Him. She was knocked sideways and nearly run over. "Please!" she cried. "Please. Wait!" She pushed through a mass of arms, legs, hips and elbows. "If I can but touch His clothes!"

She had been hemorrhaging for twelve years and had been badly treated with useless remedies by a string of physicians, leaving her worse off than she started out and all her money was gone. People had told her about Jesus and she believed with all her heart that He could heal her. "Please!" Her body was weak but her faith was strong. She gave one last heave, using the last of her strength. Her trembling fingers barely brushed the edge of the *Tsitsith*,[211] one of tassels on the hem of Jesus' tunic. Immediately she knew she had been healed.

Suddenly, Jesus stopped in His tracks. "Who touched Me?"

Peter was flabbergasted. "Who touched You? Master, we're in a crowd here. Half the throng has touched You!"

Many in the crowd had touched Jesus. But only one effectively.

Jairus couldn't believe He had stopped and was asking such a question. What difference did it make who touched Him? *My daughter is dying! Let's go!* he cried out in silence. Jesus turned around and began to scan the crowd. Jairus gently pulled at His arm. "Master, please, my daughter."

"Just a moment."

Jairus' dropped his arm. *We don't have a moment!*

The crowd began to move back revealing a small, trembling woman on her knees with tears streaming down her face, weeping half for joy and half in fear. She knew she was considered Levitically unclean[212] and could very well be stoned to death. Her lips quivered, "It was I, Master."

The crowd fell silent. Jesus looked at her with eyes of pity and slowly moved toward her.

Jairus' heart sank. *How could He do this? My daughter is dying and this woman can't wait? She isn't dying! Can't He minister to her later? Precious seconds are passing. Jesus, please!*

Jesus only did what He saw His Father doing.[213] He never moved out of urgency or pressure. At the moment, He was seeing His Father healing this dear woman.

Jesus reached down and took the shaking woman by her hand and lifted her up. She burst into tears and poured out the whole story.

Jairus was aghast at how calm Jesus seemed to be. *Doesn't He understand we have a crisis here? My daughter is dying! How can He be so blase and nonchalant at a time like this? Almost indifferent!*

Simon's eyes oscillated between the woman and Jairus. One face was filled with relief and joy and the other filled with anxiety and fear.

Jesus smiled warmly at the woman. "Daughter, your faith has made you whole."

Faith? What about my faith, Jesus? I've been praying all night. Don't You understand? This is life and death!

Death. That dark place of the eternal unknown. The unspeakable. The unthinkable. The inevitable. The subject was best avoided. But there were times it was unavoidable. It was thrust upon them each time someone close to them went to that undefined place. Even the most religious, the most pious among them feared death. No matter what their legends and ancient writings had taught, they were still uncertain of their eternal future and death-talk was left unspoken.

Peter could see the distressed look on Jairus' face. "Master . . ." he whispered.

Jesus smiled, "Go in peace and be whole from your plague."

She wept for joy and said, "Bless You! Bless You!" One of the women put her arm around her and led her away rejoicing.

Just then a man came up to Jairus and quickly spoke in his ear. "Sir, your little daughter has just died." The words ambushed him, hitting him like a spear in the gut.

"Dead? She's–dead?"

"Yes, Sir. No point in troubling the Master any further."

Jesus would not let death-talk move Him. It was an enemy He was ready to face down. The Rescuer had come to set the captives free. Free from every kind of bondage that Satan had placed upon them: sickness, disease, insanity, ignorance and demon possession–and the worst bondage of all–the fear of death. The very thought of it horrified them. The enemy kept them paralyzed with fear throughout their lifetime.[214] God saw this as the near-ultimate captivity, second only to His children' souls being seized and taken to an eternal, tormenting hell, that permanent captivity without chance of escape.

Jesus looked at Jairus. Fear screamed out of his eyes.

"She's dead," he said it breathlessly, as though someone had just kicked him in the stomach. All hope had drained out of him.

Jesus spoke hope right back into him. He knew the threat of his failing hope.[215] "Don't be afraid," He whispered. "Only believe."

His words staggered him. *Believe? There's still hope?*

"Let's go." Jesus took his arm. They walked a few yards and the crowd followed. Jesus stopped. "No," He said gently. "Please. Don't follow." He looked at Peter. "You, James and John. Come." The three quickly moved to His side. The other disciples stayed and quickly began sharing the exciting news with the crowd of the miraculous deliverance of the "Wildman of the Tombs" and how Jesus had calmed the storm. That would keep the crowd's interest for awhile.

As Jesus and the others entered the spacious courtyard of Jairus' home, they could see a large crowd of neighbors had already gathered, some wailing loudly, others bustling around making funeral arrangements.

"Boy, it didn't take them long, did it?" Peter muttered under his breath. The mournful sound of the flutes only added to the gloomy atmosphere that was pervading.

Mourners would lament and wail loudly during funerals and burials, not only for sorrow and the raw pain of losing a loved one, but for themselves as well, for fear struck their hearts each time death claimed one of their own.

"They must go," Jesus said quietly. He moved quickly into their midst and spoke firmly, "Take your mourning elsewhere. The child is not dead but asleep."

These people were professional mourners. They knew a dead body when they saw one. "You're mad!" they scoffed and laughed at the Giver of Life. They laughed themselves right out of witnessing a great miracle.

There were others laughing too. Hundreds of demons gloated and cackled that they had beat Jesus to the punch. They dared not come close, but Jesus could see them swarming all around the village, taunting Him among themselves.

"It's too late!"

"We beat You to her!"

"Shouldn't have taken so long to get here!"

They congratulated Death on a job well done and continued their mocking.

Jairus' wife ran to him and buried her face in his chest. "Our little girl! She's gone!"

The demons crowed and chortled all the more.

Jesus gently led them into the house along with Peter, James and John to the chamber where the young maiden lay. Her small face was chalky white, her hands folded upon her still breast.

Although death was a natural ending of life, it was a powerful blow to Jesus each time precious lives were cut short by the enemy. The devil had come to kill, steal and destroy.[216] He was a murderer from the beginning.[217] He had cut short the lives of many, including a lad in Nain,[218] and now this young maiden in Capernaum.

Jairus and his wife watched in dazed silence as Jesus took one of her hands.

This was unheard of. If a priest touched a dead body, he would be considered unclean and would have to separate himself for a time of cleansing, unable to perform his priestly duties; his anointing obviously rendered void.[219] Jesus, the great High Priest[220] not only was not "infected" by the unclean thing, but His anointing "infected" that which He touched with power and healing–first for the woman with the issue of blood and now . . .

Jesus spoke just two words:

"*Talitha, cumi!*"

"Maiden, arise!"

Suddenly, from the Source of all Life,[221] life sprang into her being. It rippled up from the springs of heaven and rushed through her still body. Her heart began to beat, blood began to flow in her veins, cells began to resume their vital little tasks. Her eyes fluttered open and she looked up into the Divine face of Jesus.

Her mother let out a little cry as she saw her child rise up from the dead. Jairus ran over and threw his arms around her. "My child! My daughter!" They held her close and wept with joy. Jairus then looked at Jesus through tears, and with a lump in his throat, whispered, "How can we thank You?"

Peter, James and John wiped the tears from their rugged faces. They had seen enough miracles in the last twenty-four hours to last them a lifetime!

"Keep this to yourselves," Jesus admonished the parents.

Peter, grinning, looked at them and thought, *Yeah, right. Like that's going to happen.*

Jesus flashed a glorious smile, "And give her something to eat."[222] Her parents' joyful sobs were thanks enough for Jesus.

The demons screeched when they saw Death cast out. The boiling swarm of evil spirits turned into a riotous display of confusion. A band of angels, golden and shining, swept through them, sending them shrieking and tumbling in every direction.

Jesus restored life back to the little maiden, giving her back to her loved ones, friends and neighbors, and giving them a little preview of His Resurrection Power and the power over that great enemy, Death.

He only did what He saw His Father doing.

And soon He would see His Father
removing Death's stinger.[223]

For Herod had laid hold on John, and bound him, and put him in prison for Herodias' sake, his brother Philip's wife.

Matthew 14:3

Her mother stroked her daughter's silky black hair and whispered in her ear her plan. Murder smiled and spoke to Salome to dance.

CHAPTER NINETEEN

Dance Of Death

THE GUESTS IN THEIR finest apparel stood and applauded as Herod made his grand entrance into the banquet hall, dressed in his finest robes. The beautiful and exotic Herodias was on his arm, dressed in exquisite silks and rare jewels. Her eyes were heavily lined in purple to match her long, flowing gown; her thin lips were painted dark violet and set in an amused smirk.

"Welcome! Welcome!" Herod bellowed. "Welcome friends and guests to my birthday celebration! Let the music begin!"

John the Baptist could hear music and laughter ringing through the darkness, echoing along the corridors and through the rock-hewn walls that held him prisoner. A drilling depression plagued his mind–not from loneliness or lack of comfort–he had wandered the wilds alone for years apart from the comforts of society. Nor was the gloom due to the impending consequences of being under the power of Herodias, who, like Jezebel, had incited her husband to do evil,[224] yet Jezebel did not succeed in her plot to murder the prophet Elijah. John, who had been heralded as the very spirit of Elijah,[225] wondered, would he escape Herodias' desire to eliminate him?

Elijah, who had stood up courageously to the prophets of Baal,[226] was terrified by the wicked queen Jezebel.[227] John was not afraid of Herod and his guards, nor did the Jezebel spirit intimidate him. He was not a reed shaken with the wind.[228]

No, these thoughts were not the cause of the awful foreboding in his soul. John feared neither man nor woman. King or queen. It was something else. Something he could not seem to shake.

He could feel evil lurking in that dark dungeon, like serpents slithering out of the walls. He was not alone. Depression, a hideous, menacing demon hissed in his ear for hours, ghastly thoughts of self-doubt and uncertainty. Was it all a dream? Had he made it all up? Had there been some terrible mistake on his part? *Was I right? Or was I in error and leading others into error? God forbid!*

The music and laughter seemed to mock John as he sat chained like an animal in the darkness of Herod's dungeon.

The monstrous demon continued his silent assaults. "There's no tangible success to your long, arduous mission, John. You preached on many occasions to Herod himself and with what results?[229] And your warnings all went unheeded by the religious leaders–if anything they have turned for the worse. And at the very height of your ministry, you turned your disciples over to this One who seems to have overlooked your plight. What if He is not the right one? He certainly doesn't seem to be the Messiah you were looking for. What if you were wrong? And now look at you. Your life is at its end and completely wasted."

Far from John's memory were the powerful effects he had on the populace. He had set their hearts on fire for God and had brought a keen awareness of the nearness of God's kingdom to their hopeless lives. He had preached with a power and an anointing that brought even publicans and Roman soldiers to their knees. But Depression's attacks had so shrouded his mind that he could barely think.

Some of the most powerful men in history had been under Depression's attack with fear of failure resulting in self-condemnation. He would cloud their minds with thoughts of deficiency and defeat. "Look at you," Depression whispered, "You've gotten nowhere. You must not have heard God right. Look at all the time you've wasted.

Who are you to take such responsibility? Someone else could have done it better. You're a failure. You might as well give up."

John shook his head as if trying to throw the vexing thoughts from him. "God help me," he whispered.

Only a reminder of truth could bring him back to reality. In answer to his prayer, suddenly John remembered the account of King David who had been under fierce attack from every side–even his own people were ready to stone him. *"But,"* John remembered, *"David encouraged himself in the Lord."*[230]

John cried out to God from the depths of his soul. "Father! Help me! I-I can't think–I can't even pray! Help me, Lord."

A shaft of invisible light from on high came into John's spirit. The Light of Truth. The words of the message that he had received from his Lord Jesus, the Holy Warrior of God, suddenly came to life:

"The lame walk, the deaf hear, the blind see, the gospel is preached and the dead are raised up." Bright revelation shot through his being and truth overpowered the lies of the devil.

"He's taking back what is His. You'll not win, Satan," John whispered. "Your days are numbered. Now get out of here!"

Depression jerked away, screeching with pain and flew out between the bars above John's head. John had resisted him. The demon had to flee.[231]

John's strength returned to him in an instant, and that dungeon became a prayer closet for John. He prayed for His Lord and His disciples. He was taking over Satan's domain! The truth had set John free. Although he was still captive physically, his spirit was unfettered. And with great joy he worshiped God and sang so loud that he drowned out the noise of the party, startling the guards.

The defeated demon fell in a heap outside the compound. The power and authority of John's rebuke had shaken him badly. The sounds of laughter and music caught his attention and he decided he might as well join the festivities. As he entered the banquet room he could see Lust coiling about Herod like an anaconda, aiming his eyes at young Salome, the teenage daughter of Herodias.

Murder was stroking Herodias' hair and whispering suggestions into her mind. Herodias despised the Baptizer because he had challenged Herod's right to marry her, his brother's wife. She wanted to be rid of him and it had become an obsession with her. John wasn't afraid of her. This had inflamed the Jezebel spirit that loved to intimidate and control.

Her daughter whispered to her, "See how he looks at me."

Herodias leaned over and kissed her cheek. "It's all right, Darling. We shall use his desires to get what we want.

Salome shrank back. "What do you mean?"

Her mother stroked her daughter's silky black hair and whispered in her ear her plan. Murder smiled and spoke to Salome to dance.

The musicians began playing an exotic melody that invoked the young girl to sway with the music. "Dance! Dance!" Herodias cried.

Herod and his guests joined in. "Yes! Dance for us!"

Excitement gleamed in her dark eyes as the music drew her out onto the glassy floor. The rhythms seemed to draw her out of herself. Her bare feet kicked and twirled, the bracelets on her ankles jingling with each step. Her undulating movements mesmerized Herod. She seemed to read his mind as she swayed before him. She knew he was drunk and she knew he wanted her, but her mother was near, so she was safe.

Lust and Perversion tightened their hold on him and began to whisper, "Give her anything she wants."

Salome seemed to enjoy tormenting him. She danced closer and closer to him–so close he could smell her perfume–and as the last notes crescendoed to a climax, she fell at his feet, her breast heaving for breath. The guests applauded wildly.

Herodias leaned forward and watched intently as her daughter slowly raised herself up to a sitting position. Salome glared at Herod, then threw back her head and laughed. He grabbed her ankle and slid her across the marble floor and leaned over to kiss her, but she turned her face away and pulled back.

"I'll give you anything," he whispered hoarsely, his breath heavy with wine.

"Really?" she asked coyly.

His head was spinning with wine. "Up to half my kingdom." He knew he said it too loud.

She stared at him a moment and smiled tauntingly. She glanced at her mother and then back at him.

"I want the Baptizer's head."

Her young voice rang out clearly. Every guest heard and gasped.

"On a silver platter."

A stunned silence fell over the room. Herod was horrified. He pulled back and stared at her. He knew his guests had heard his drunken vow to give her anything. They were watching him, waiting to see what he would do.

"Well?" she smiled teasingly, feeling the power of the moment. She knew she had him and she was enjoying it.

Herod was sorry he had made the oath, but to save face he reluctantly ordered it done. Salome got up, smiled haughtily, her ankle bracelets jingling, and walked back over to her mother who was smiling like the cat that ate the canary.

Lust and Murder cackled with delight as the guards left to carry out the order. "What a lovely birthday party this has turned out to be!"

John heard the footsteps above him. Somehow he knew they were the footsteps of the executioner and that they were coming for him. His time was up. He continued to worship His Lord.

The grate above him was removed and a guard lowered himself down. Unchaining John, he spoke quietly, "Come with me."[232]

As John's saintly head was laid upon the block, he whispered, "Oh God, Whose kingdom I have announced, I now humbly enter in."

Suddenly John opened his eyes and saw angels, thousands of them, running toward him and applauding. "Welcome! Welcome!"

Then a golden voice that sounded like a waterfall of love said joyously,

"Well done,
My good
and faithful servant.
Enter now into the
joy of your Lord.[233]
Welcome Home!"

And he saw them toiling in rowing; for the wind was contrary unto them: and about the fourth watch of the night he cometh unto them, walking upon the sea–

Mark 6:48

They put up the sail and followed the white, wavy, shimmering ribbon the moon lay before them on the water. The demon captain saw his chance and grabbed it. He shouted to his squad of demons, "This is it! Attack!"

CHAPTER TWENTY

Attack And Counterattack

THE AWFUL CRISIS HAD come to such a head, the demon captain reluctantly sent for Deception to witness it for himself. The two of them flew high above the twelve disciples and watched in horror as they healed the sick and cast out demons by the score, both a direct attack of the Seed upon Satan's domain. The kingdom of God was breaking forth in a violent manner, and those who heard the good news were pressing in as well.[234]

"On and on it goes," the demon captain groaned, watching the Twelve emulating the same tactics as the Seed. "First there's the wretched Seed, which is bad enough! Now He has multiplied Himself by twelve! They have power and authority to execute His loathsome attacks upon our domain and are furthering His influence at a greater rate than I can possibly report!"

Deception was incensed at the ghastly sight. "We must destroy the lot of them!"

"But how? They have dominion over us!"

"We must find them at a weak moment. They cannot continue like this forever. At some point they shall become vulnerable. Continue to watch them. At a safe distance, of course. Report directly to me when you see an opportunity."

"What if there is no time to send for you? Such an opportunity may require immediate action!"

"Take whatever steps necessary. They must be stopped! Keep me posted!" he yelled as he lifted his enormous form into the morning sky.

The news reached the Twelve that John the Baptist had been brutally murdered. They knew they must return to their Master, much to the relief of the demon captain. "At last they cease from their assaults!"

Jesus already knew of John's death. He knew that His faithful forerunner had completed his course and was now with his Father in heaven rejoicing with the angels over the souls whom the Twelve had set free and delivered. He knew that John now understood and there would be no more tears,[235] no more painful questions.

The Twelve hurried up the hill toward Him, their eyes showing traces of fear mixed with grief. "Lord! We heard the news!" Jesus' quiet demeanor and majestic peace stilled their hearts immediately. He motioned for them to come with Him. Heading down the gentle slope, He moved toward the place where they had moored their little ship.

Simon was glad to be back in his familiar, trusty little vessel. "Where are we headed?" he grunted as he helped shove off.

"To a secluded place. It's time to come away and rest now."

The breeze felt good on their faces. Their weeks of ministry had been successful but tiring. They were glad to be back in the presence of their Master and to once again hear the sweet sound of His melodious voice.

John's disciples and the multitudes that had heard of his death were in complete shock and turmoil. Their eyes, puffy from tears of grief, searched the hills surrounding the Sea of Galilee for Jesus, the One John had named as their true Master–the One to Whom they should look. But they were too late. They could see the familiar little sail billowing in the quiet wind. The lake glittered like broken glass in the brilliant noonday sun. Their hearts sank at the sight of the boat growing smaller by the minute in the blue distance.

"Come on!" someone cried. Before anyone could argue the length of the shore's perimeter, the crowd, like a herd of frightened sheep, began running to go around to the other side to meet Him.

People in the villages and cities dotting the rim of the lake saw the crowd coming and pointing at the forging boat. Many joined them as the running, panting crowd neared their towns. By the time Jesus and the Twelve put in to shore, an enormous mass of people was waiting for them. Many were sick and diseased, most just wanted to be near Him, but all had that haunted question in their eyes upon hearing the frightening news that yet another great prophet had been murdered. Jesus was moved to the depths of His being with compassion. Without hesitation, He began to minister to them, healing their sick and touching them with His blessed hands of kindness.

The disciples sat with the people and listened to Him for hours as He taught. Simon noticed the evening star had appeared and he became concerned about the people's need for nourishment. He, Andrew and Philip approached Jesus. "Lord, it's getting late. This place is pretty desolate. Shouldn't You send the people away to the surrounding towns to buy food?"

Jesus answered with a smile, "You feed them."

"Huh?'

"With what?" asked Simon.

Philip spoke up, "Do You want us to go to town and buy food for this crowd? That would cost a fortune!" Judas listened silently nearby, tightening his grip on the moneybag.

"Go ask the people how much food they have."

The three walked away shaking their heads. "Let's split up. You guys go survey that bunch over there, and I'll check with these over here."

"This may take awhile," Andrew groaned.

They approached the periphery of the crowd. "You got any food?"

"Nope."

"How about you, got any food?"

"No."

Just then a young lad approached Andrew. "I have a little bag lunch."

Andrew smiled, "Okay, son. We'll take it to Jesus." Andrew remembered Jesus' teaching on the mustard seed. A little is a lot in the kingdom of God.[236]

Simon and Philip gave up and turned to walk toward Jesus, shrugging their shoulders and holding their empty hands out as if to say, "See? We told You!"

Andrew moved in ahead of them, his huge hand on the small lad's shoulder, leading him toward Jesus. "Master, this young fellow here has a small bag lunch of five barley loaves and two sardines. But what good are they among such a multitude of people? I'll bet there are at least five thousand men here, not counting the women and children!"

"Bring it here to Me." He then directed the people to sit down on the green spring grass in ranks of hundreds and fifties. The Great Shepherd had them lie down in green pastures. The multitude obeyed, their longing eyes filled with anticipation, wondering what He might do. A hush fell over the crowd and the disciples watched in silence, their hearts fluttering with awed expectancy.

Jesus lifted up the scanty provision and looking up to heaven, He gave thanks for what seemed to be lack–as though it were enough–and asked the Father to bless it. He then broke the loaves into twelve fragments and likewise the fish and handed them to His dumbfounded disciples. "Now. Go feed them."

They looked at the tiny fragments in their huge, fishermen's hands, then looked at the massive company of people, some who were very large, very hungry men, and then looked back at Jesus.

"Go on," He grinned.

Simon timidly stepped toward the first bunch seated quietly on the grass. It was a total step of faith. Jesus watched His beloved friend cautiously step towards the crowd and was reminded of Moses stepping toward the Red Sea with nothing but a rod in his hand.

As he leaned down to hand the fragments to the first people, a young man and his wife, the morsel of bread and tiny piece of fish multiplied right in his hand. Simon's eyes nearly popped out as did the young couple's who received the miraculous meal, watching it compound right in his hands. Simon let out a little squeal of joy and hurried to the next and then the next.

"It's just like the widow's cruse of oil that never failed in Elijah's day!"[237] Matthew shouted. Little flourishes of gasps and laughter and squeals of joy rang throughout the throng. The disciples began to laugh and dance through the joyful crowd and soon began to toss the food into the outstretched hands. Tears of laughter and joy were streaming down their faces.

"Whoopee!" John yelled as he flung the Divine delicatessen.

Jesus slapped His knee and rejoiced with laughter at the merriment, knowing that laughter was indeed the medicine[238] these dear folks needed. He had turned their mourning into joy.[239]

After everyone had eaten and were filled, the disciples took up twelve baskets of leftovers. Simon laughed, "As always, Jesus' Divine supply is more than enough!"

John grinned, "Yeah, He made 180 gallons of wine at Cana for that wedding!"

James laughed, "That's right! And they had already drunk the place dry. There was enough left over to last that young couple's entire married life!"

Andrew joined in as he walked alongside them toward Jesus. "Yes, and remember the draught of fish after we had toiled all night and caught nothing?"

"It nearly sank the boat!" Simon said loudly.

"How many people do you think we fed?" Thomas shouted as he brought his basket of leftovers.

"More than five thousand!" Nathanael cried. I counted the ranks of men alone!"

Andrew grinned at Simon. "See. I told ya."

They brought the baskets to their smiling Master. "Well done!" He shouted, patting them soundly on their broad shoulders.

Suddenly one of the multitude stood and shouted, "Surely this is the Messiah that was prophesied!" Jesus saw the fervor stirring in the hearts and minds of the people and knew they wanted to force Him to be their king. They began to rise and move toward Him, shouting, "Jesus! Be our king! Be our king!"

Judas' eyes blazed with excitement, as did the other disciples. The time had finally come! He would be made king!

Jesus knew He was to be their King in a higher sense and must dismiss them before a riot ensued. He held up His hand in commanding majesty and the crowd stopped in its tracks and fell silent to hear His answer. "Go back to your homes, My children." They were stunned, as were the disciples.

"But–"

"Please," He smiled, "Go before it gets dark."

Quietly and solemnly they turned to go. Judas' eyes narrowed and a deep furrow formed between his eyebrows. His mind shrouded with questions, he watched in dismay as the people made their way toward their villages.

Jesus turned to the Twelve. "I need to have some time alone to pray. Go to the ship and head for home. I'll see you before long."

Simon started to protest, but John put his hand on his arm. "Let's go," he whispered.

As they shoved off, they looked back at the lone figure walking up the hill to be alone with His Father. The sting of disappointment of His refusal to allow them to make Him king brought questions to their minds. But for now they were just glad to be going home. The silver moon shone brightly upon the lake. The hills began to fade behind them in the darkness. They put up the sail and followed the white, wavy, shimmering ribbon the moon lay before them on the water.

The demon captain saw his chance and grabbed it. He shouted to his squad of demons, "This is it! Attack!"

The sudden wind didn't surprise the disciples. The Sea of Galilee was notorious for its sudden and violent storms, but there was not a cloud in the sky. They could see the stars trembling in the distance. There was only an invisible black cloud of demons led by the excited captain in an all-out effort to drown the hated followers of the Seed.

The wind grew stronger,[240] striking the white caps and turning them from waves to spray. Simon and Andrew realized that it was more than a good strong, helpful wind. It was going to be a fight. But they had fought the Galilee lake winds many times, and the other disciples trusted the four fishermen to know what to do.

Simon quickly lowered the sails and John passed out the oars. They were barely midway across the six-mile width of the lake. The little boat rolled and bounced back and forth. The waves swelled beneath them, then crashed over the side. Thaddaeus was turning green, as was Judas.

Jesus was deep in prayer when He sensed His Father telling Him to go to His men. He immediately got up and saw the little ship tossing about like a cork in the brilliant moonlit sea, and headed down the hill toward the shore.

Their arms were burning with pain from hours of rowing and getting nowhere. The spray of water was like a barrage of flying, stinging needles against their skin. Suddenly their eyes caught sight of something coming toward them. The bright moonlight was iridescent against the approaching Figure. The fisher-disciples had all heard from their youth the legends and myths of water-spirits sent from Baal to assault fishermen. There was no natural explanation for what they were seeing, and like the children of Israel who had wandered in the wilderness for forty years, they had not allowed the last miracle that had been done for them to sink in and acquaint them more deeply with the God of miracles.

They cried out in terror, "It's a spirit!" They were dangerously close to blasphemy, attributing Jesus' manifest Presence to that of satanic origin.[241] They didn't recognize Him because their minds were shrouded with fear, which put them back into the wrong kingdom. Fear was the devil's faith. They didn't expect the miraculous; they were unprepared for it. They thought it was the devil.

Jesus intended to pass them by, to bring deliverance from the assault of the enemy without making His Presence known, until they cried out in terror. He quickly replied, "It is I! Don't be afraid!" That was good news to them.

Simon, in the excitement of the moment, decided it would be safer to get to Jesus than to stay in the water logged boat. "Lord! If that's really You, let me come to You!"

Jesus could not have answered otherwise. "Come, then!"

Simon slung his leg over the side of the boat and began walking. He was walking on water, but more importantly, he was walking on the command of the Lord, "Come."

The demons saw this and shrieked in horror. "Make the waves louder!" screamed the captain. "Drown out that word!" The winds became even more fierce and the waves more boisterous, causing Simon to take his mind off the command to 'come' and his eyes off Jesus, so naturally, he sank. He screamed, "Lord! Help!"

Immediately Jesus reached out His hand and caught him and pulled him back up to the churning surface of the water. "What happened to your faith? Why did you doubt My word?"

Together they walked back to the boat. When they climbed in, the demons took off in terror, scattering in every direction, and the wind ceased immediately. Simon sat down with a thud, his head spinning from exhaustion and the incredible phenomenon he had just experienced.

The Twelve began to rejoice and worship Jesus. "You really are the Son of God!" They were beside themselves with wonder and amazement that this Man could even walk on water![242]

Jesus, like Peter, was walking on a command.
His Father told Him, "Go."
Jesus told Peter, "Come."
His word
is a sure foundation.[243]

He saith unto them, But whom say ye that I am? And Simon Peter answered and said, thou are the Christ, the Son of the living God.

Matthew 16:15,16

Jesus could see His mortal enemy lurking in the shadows, hurling evil imaginations into Peter's mind. It was like the temptation all over again. He jerked His arm away, gritted His teeth and shouted, "Get behind Me, Satan!"

CHAPTER TWENTY-ONE

A True Witness

AFTER SEVERAL JAUNTS BACK and forth across the Sea of Galilee, Jesus and the Twelve came to a place called Caesarea-Philipi, located at the foot of Mount Hermon. They built a small campfire and were grateful for a time of quiet reflection and prayer.

In the background they could hear the rushing water of one of the major sources of the Jordan. It gushed from the mouth of a cave at the base of a steep cliff, on its way to join its sister sources of the great river.

Although they were weary, they were excited about the things they had experienced in the last few days.

"Did you see Him heal that lame man?"

"Which one? Everyone He touched was made perfectly whole!"

"I still can't get over how the loaves and fishes kept multiplying right in our hands!"

Jesus smiled as he listened to their excited chatter. His eyes searched each face. It got quiet. His gaze stopped at Simon. "Who do men say that I am?"

One of them piped up, "Some say You are John the Baptist."

Another said, "Some say You are Elijah."

A third said, "I heard a man say You are Jeremiah, the great prophet." They snickered a little.

Three different witnesses. Three different opinions.

He looked at each of the twelve faces, His gaze more expectant now. "But who do you say that I am?"

There was a long silence. Only the song of the river and a chorus of frogs could be heard. As if he had just "gotten it," Simon leaped to his feet, and with a loud voice proclaimed, "You are the Christ! You are the Son of the Living God!" His voice echoed against the night. He even startled himself.

At last, Jesus had a true witness. He stood up and walked over to Simon. Putting His bronzed hand on his massive shoulder, He said, "You are blessed, Simon-Barjona. You did not come to that conclusion by yourself. My Father has revealed it to you."

The well-watered area was thick with wild grapevines, flowers and shrubs. It was like a tropical garden. Jesus knew the beautiful oasis was also a hotbed for demon activity. Centuries before, it had been set aside for the worship of the demon gods of Baal and Pan. And it was still a haven for the hideous entities. A fitting place for such an announcement. What better place to launch the very foundation of His church. Right in the middle of one of Satan's favorite haunts.

Jesus turned so His back wouldn't be to anyone. Looking at Simon He said, "Tonight I give you a new name. You are Peter, a little rock. And on that boulder-sized rock of the confession you just made, shall the foundation of My church be built." He seemed to look past them and raised His voice, "And the very gates of hell won't be able to stand up against it!"

Peter, still looking stunned, slowly sat back down on the large rock he had jumped up from. Suddenly that rock became more than just a seat. He stared at it, thinking about his new name.

The disciples could hardly contain themselves. He finally and frankly admitted it! He said plainly that He was indeed the Messiah. He confirmed it! Now surely He would unfold His great plan and would spread before them the blueprint, the grand design of His Messiahship. Surely now He would reveal His strategy to dethrone Herod Antipas and destroy the Roman rule.

Jesus continued, "I will give you the keys of the kingdom of heaven . . ."

They all leaned forward, their eyes shining with anticipation. Keys of the kingdom! This was more than they had even dreamed. He was giving them the very keys of the kingdom! A heady moment indeed!

". . . And whatsoever you bind or declare to be unlawful on earth must be what is already unlawful in heaven. And whatever you loose or declare lawful on earth must be what is already lawful in heaven."

Peter blinked in amazement and the others looked at one another in wonder and excitement. Such power! He was handing over to them unheard of authority. They would have a say in what was legal and illegal. They did not understand the spiritual implications of such a statement, as was the case on several other occasions when He spoke of the spiritual, they assumed the natural.

Keys of the kingdom! The very words exuded with influence and prestige. No more would they have to endure the heavy-handed despotism of the pagan Herod. No more public rejection and vicious attacks from their fellow countrymen. Kingdom rank would at last be theirs and the glorious Throne of David would be established. It was almost too much for them. Their hearts beat wildly at the thought of it.

Jesus walked around to the other side of the campfire. The glowing firelight flickered and danced against His face. The moment was right. Now was the time to tell them. "You must keep to yourselves what you have heard tonight–that I am the Christ . . ."

Their brows furrowed and their jaw muscles tightened. *Keep it to ourselves?* Their minds were racing, trying to understand such an admonishment. Remain covert? Surely He meant only until they reached Jerusalem where He will make His great proclamation, and all of heaven's angels will descend to crown Him on the portals of the Temple.

". . . For the Son of Man must go to Jerusalem . . ."

Yes! Yes! Their eyes were bulging with excitement.

". . . And suffer many things at the hands of the religious leaders and be killed . . ."

What? Killed? Messiah killed? Unthinkable! Peter's veins stood out on his neck and forehead.

". . . And be raised again on the third day."

They didn't hear that last part.

At the highest point of their faith and expectancy, their hopes and dreams were dealt a staggering blow. Scarcely could they take it in. One moment they were soaring in the heavenlies of ecstasy like great eagles, the next they were shot through the heart and came crashing down to the jagged crags of the reality of His words. In an instant they went from the sweetness of long-awaited victory to seeming defeat.

Peter could keep quiet no longer. Jumping off his rock again, he grabbed Jesus by the arm, pulled Him over to the side and began rebuking Him. "Not so, Lord! This shall never happen to You!"

Jesus could see His mortal enemy lurking in the shadows, hurling evil imaginations into Peter's mind. It was like the temptation all over again. He jerked His arm away, gritted His teeth and shouted, "Get behind Me, Satan! You offend Me because you esteem the things of man more than you do the things of God!'

The rebuke sent Satan hurling through space like a missile, sending him miles away from Jesus, in a straight line directly behind Him. Legions of demons went screeching in every direction in terror at the rebuke and at the sight of their master's violent ejection.

Peter was shocked. His mouth dropped open in disbelief. Had he heard Him right? *Did He just call me–Satan?* The disciples were stone silent. It was an awkward moment.

Once again the adversary was appealing to Jesus' human side, pulling at His flesh, attempting to draw Him away from His Father's way. Choosing man's way over God's way–the very core of the Lie. The Lie that caused the fall of man. It was Satan's favorite ploy.

For the disciples to be His true witnesses, the Lie had to be dealt with. Jesus knew His "witness," Peter, had the first part of the confession right. But the confession that Peter had just proclaimed had a second part. He knew if dear, loyal Peter could be deceived, His future Church could be too. Now was the time for the second part of the confession to be revealed–the very core of faith:

First confession.

Then crucifixion.

"If any man comes after Me with this confession–that I am the Messiah–on his lips, then he must deny himself, pick up his cross and die daily. Only then can he follow Me."

Peter, still dazed, went back to his rock and sat down. He leaned forward and listened intently to Jesus.

"If you plan on preserving your fleshly life, things that please and exalt self and man, you are lost. But if you lose your self-life for things that please God and for My sake, you will gain true life. I am endeavoring to have you become like Me–for you to shoulder your cross in life as I will shoulder the world."

Peter's confession that Jesus is the Christ was true. But when he opposed His word and His reason for being there, his testimony was no longer true. He was "savoring the things of man."

Just prior to their landing at Caesarea Philippi, Jesus had warned His disciples to "beware of the leaven of the Pharisees," the leaven of hypocrisy, of appearing to be what they are not. The devil had already deceived many of the religious leaders in the Lie. These scribes and Pharisees were well versed in "savoring the things of men." They were expert man-pleasers and certainly had no intention of dying to self. Self was the central figure of their doctrine, for they counted on their self-righteousness to get to heaven.

Jesus knew the confusion that had been brought to the world by such a doctrine. That they could "earn" their way into heaven. That by "being good" they could impress God to allow them heavenly entrance.[244]

They would even miss the Great Plan, the
mighty atoning work
He was about to do.

Jesus taketh Peter, James and John his brother, and bringeth them up into an high mountain apart; and was transfigured before them; and His face did shine as the sun, and His raiment was white as the light. And, behold, there appeared unto them Moses and Elias talking with Him.

Matthew 17:1-3

Just then, he looked up toward Mount Hermon again. This time he saw a bright cloud engulfing the entire peak of the summit. It was glorious! Even majestic! What was it?

CHAPTER TWENTY-TWO

Fire On The Mountain

"DID YOU SEE THAT?"

"Wh–what?"

"That light! There was a flash of light up there."

"Up where?" The sleepy shepherd sat up reluctantly and rubbed his eyes.

His partner jabbed his finger toward the mountain peak, poking the air with each word. "Up–there!"

"It was probably lightning. Maybe a storm is coming," his friend yawned, squinting toward the top of Mount Hermon.

"No lightning ever looked like that. It was different, like fire in the shape of a man–or men. Three of them! One was much brighter than the other two."

"You were dreaming. You're supposed to be on watch." The tired old man groaned as he turned over, hoping his partner would get the hint and stop jabbering so he could get some sleep.

He stopped talking all right, but his mind wouldn't let him rest. *What was it?* He stared toward the top of Mount Hermon and remembered his grandfather telling stories of the old days when they would light fires on the tops of the mountains around Jerusalem as a signal for those far away that a solemn feast was called. He could picture it in his mind and wondered at what he had seen.

It reminded him of other strange fires he had been told of on other mountains. A burning bush when God spoke to Moses.[245] Fire, smoke and lightning on Sinai.[246] Was it an omen? Or was he just imagining things?

The sun said goodnight to the earth and yielded to the moon, leaving a thin edge of white against the gathering darkness for the eyes of the world to behold. The brilliant masterpiece of God somehow stirred the middle-aged shepherd to deep introspection, an exercise he had not allowed for several weeks since he had left the company of the Nazarene Teacher.

His decision to disassociate with Him had not brought peace, but a gnawing apprehension, and life was more uncertain than ever. A part of him seemed to be missing. The return to "normality" was a let down. He had seen the miraculous and had tasted the phenomenal. He had been among the five thousand that were fed from a few loaves and fishes, had heard the sermons on the grassy slopes, and had seen the young man of Nain raised from the dead.[247] The natural was dull after the supernatural had touched him. And the Teacher's words! After hearing such words of life, the rhetoric of the mundane was uninteresting and uninspiring.

The night wore on and his eyes grew heavy. Finally his head slumped to his chest. It was a fitful sleep–the kind dreams weave in and out of. He dreamed he was walking along the craggy terrain toward Jerusalem. The hills surrounding the city were each crowned with glowing fires that seemed to beckon to him and those far away to come. Come to a feast.

A lamb bleated nearby. He awakened with a start, grabbing his staff in case of danger to his flock. It was only a hungry lamb looking to feed upon his mother's nourishment. He looked around and then settled back down.

His mind returned to his dream. *A feast? Call to a feast?* Was God speaking to him? He could not get the blaze of fire he had seen on the mountain, nor could he get the Nazarene out of his mind. He had followed Him for months. Hadn't he believed? Hadn't he been faithful? Or had he followed only to see Him give signs and to feed his belly?

Jesus' words haunted him. "I am the Bread of Life. I am the Manna, the Living Bread which came down from heaven–If any man eat of this Bread, he shall live forever."

What did it all mean? It sounded so mysterious and startling.

"–And the bread I give you is My flesh, which I will give for the life of the world–"

He sighed loudly. He wasn't the only one back in Capernaum that day who had asked how can this Man give us His–flesh to eat? It was a question he had expected Him to answer immediately, certain He would clarify Himself, but it only got worse.

"He that eats My flesh and drinks My blood, dwells in Me and I in him."

The shepherd had scarcely heard the last seven words of that last sentence. The cannibalistic tone brought such revulsion that he had not considered the rest. Only now could he find it in his heart to reconsider Jesus' words:

"–dwells in Me and I in him."

The shepherd ran his fingers through his thinning hair. *Could all this talk of eating His flesh and drinking His blood mean some sort of–inner communion? Was He calling me to allow my hungry soul to feed–on Him?*

He rested his arms on his knees and leaned forward, dropping his head and closing his eyes tightly. He was afraid. Afraid to believe. And afraid not to believe. He shook his head slowly and rubbed his eyes with the base of his palms. Leaning back against a large rock, he nestled his head between his staff and the rock and began to doze again.

Another dream. Sinai. Lightning, thunder, the face of Moses–radiant. A veil over his face.[248]

He awakened with a start. *Was it a dream? It seemed so real!* Just then, he looked up toward Mount Hermon again. This time he saw a bright cloud engulfing the entire peak of the summit. It was glorious! Even majestic! What was it? Should he awaken the old man again?

Once more he was reminded of the fire on the mountain that he had seen that night early in his watch. Fire on the mountain–a call to a feast?

He thought of Jesus and His words, calling the people–calling him–to feast on–Him. It all began to become clear to him. Jesus' words leapt into his mind:

"The words I speak to you, they are spirit and they are life[249] –I am the Bread of Life–Blessed are you who hunger and thirst after righteousness, for they shall be filled."[250]

". . . Be filled . . . this hungering in my soul can be filled?"

He remembered in conversations with His veteran disciples how John the Baptist had referred to Jesus as the Lamb of God.

Tears began to course down his cheeks. Was it too late? Hope, like a sputtering candle, was still alive. He was like a smoking flax, which the prophet Isaiah said that Messiah would not quench, and his heart was as a bruised reed, which He would not break.[251]

Dawn began to appear. The stars dimmed in the lavender and orange sky, as the great light took over the day watch. He stood up and quietly checked his flock. All was well.

Just then, he heard the sound of small pebbles tumbling down the slope just above him. Then the sound of several footsteps muffled by sand and dewy grass. He gripped his staff and cautiously peered up the jagged path and saw three–no, four men descending from the top of the mountain. Who were they? Had they been up there all night? What were they doing up there?

Wait a minute. They look familiar. No, it can't be. It looks like–yes! It is! Jesus! His face–it's so radiant! Like Moses, only–no–veil.

His head was swimming with flashbacks of what he had seen. The light up on that mountain. The bright cloud with glorious fire. Fire on the mountain. A call to a feast.

Jesus is the Fire on the mountain, calling the world to the feast.

He is the feast.

The Passover Lamb stopped and smiled a smile of all consuming love. The shepherd fell to his knees and glorified God for the gift of love that had been bestowed upon him, even in his faithless state. Jesus touched his face and whispered, "Welcome back."

Then He continued down the hill, His three climbing companions, Peter, James and John, in dreamlike movement, still dazed in speechless wonder at what they had seen, walked silently behind.

They had definitely seen Him
in another light.[252]

And the seventy returned again with joy, saying, Lord, even the devils are subject unto us through thy name.

Luke 10:17

"Lord!" one of them shouted, his eyes gleaming. "Even the demons submit to us in Your Name!"

Jesus grinned, "Yes! While you were out there, I was praying for you, and I saw Satan's power fall like flashes of lightning each time you overthrew a part of his domain!"

CHAPTER TWENTY-THREE

The War Zone

YOU COULD HEAR THEM coming a mile away. Their laughter rang through the air like bells. Jesus smiled as He watched them approaching. He was pleased with their progress. First He had taught the Twelve, and sent them out, and then appointed and dispatched seventy others. He had sent them out two-by-two into the villages to preach the kingdom of God and to heal the sick.

"Master!" They broke into a run when they saw Jesus standing at the top of the hill, His hands on his waist and His beautiful face framed in the twilight, smiling a warm greeting. They quickly gathered around Him, excited as children at a party.

"Lord!" one of them shouted, his eyes gleaming. "Even the demons submit to us in Your Name!" How excited they were to find that they had authority over the evil one who had for so long kept them bound under his control!

Jesus laughed, "Yes! While you were out there, I was praying for you, and I saw Satan's power fall like flashes of lightning each time you overthrew a part of his domain! Remember, I have given you power and authority to trample on the evil spirits that bite like snakes and sting like scorpions. And I have given you power and authority to overcome all the power of the enemy, and nothing, no evil entity will harm you!"

Peter puckered his lips in a defiant pout, drew up his huge fists and threw several punches at the air as if to say, *Take that, Devil!* "Those stinking demons have to obey us now!" The others laughed uproariously.

Jesus' expression grew more serious. "Don't put your focus on, nor rejoice only in the fact that the spirits are subject and must submit to you–" He raised His arms toward heaven, "But rejoice that your names are written in heaven!" Jesus wanted them to remain balanced in their view of who they were and where their authority came from. He turned the excitement of their newfound authority into praise to the One Who gave it to them.

An enormous company of angels, who always appeared whenever the Word was spoken,[253] had escorted the Seventy, fighting alongside them in the war zone, in the power of His Name. The angels had encircled them, their swords drawn and pointing outward, giving them a hedge of protection.[254] Captives were set free from Satan's hold, hundreds were delivered from oppression and many were healed. The glorious gospel was preached with great power and joy. After their mission was complete, the angels swept through the evil hordes sending the remaining ones screeching and tumbling wildly into the atmosphere. When the cloud of demons disappeared, the angels settled down around the disciples again to escort them back to the Presence of Jesus.

The good pleasure of His Father had been manifested through the disciples' childlike faith. Jesus looked up, "I praise You, Father, Lord of heaven and earth, because You have hidden these things from the wise and learned, and have revealed them to these little children. Yes, Father, this was Your good pleasure!"

God in His wisdom had given kingdom insight, not to those who were self-exalted and wise in their own esteem, but to those who with childlike faith, simplicity and humility leaned utterly in total dependence upon their Lord.

The circle of angels joined in worship with the Lamb. The Father and all of the angels in heaven had been rejoicing greatly for those who had been rescued and set free through His disciples and the Seventy, but when they saw Jesus so filled with joy and praise, they broke forth anew with singing and applause. All eighty-two disciples burst into worship as well. Their eyes filled with tears of joy as they joined in with the praise of their Lord.

Peter and Andrew praised God with all their hearts, and John breathed a sigh of love as he gazed upon the face of his Master Who was lost in praise and thanksgiving. Nathanael's tear-filled eyes were wide with wonder and awe.

Jesus, seeing the wonderment and joy in their eyes said, "All things have been given over into My power by My Father. Understand that no one knows Who I really am except the Father. And no one knows Who the Father really is except Me–" Their misty eyes widened. Jesus continued, "–And anyone to whom I choose to reveal and make Him known."

He turned to the Twelve. Their eyes were glued on Him. "Blessed are those whose eyes see what you see." He walked over to Simon Peter and put His hand on his broad shoulder and looked into the faces of His companions. "I'm telling you, that prophets and kings of old longed to see what you have the privilege to see and hear what you hear."

Peter and Andrew looked at one another. These simple fishermen had never been privy to anything of significance, and were dumbfounded by the magnitude of what they were a part of.

All but one of the disciples was caught up in the ecstasy of worship. Judas was glad to be back. He had felt uncomfortable the whole journey, since they were instructed not to carry money, or even an extra pair of shoes along. Jesus, once again, wanted them relying on His Father's provision, and to build the faith of the Seventy.

He instructed them that it was time to come away and rest. Some of the Seventy plus the Twelve headed for Bethany, a town on the eastern slope of the Mount of Olives, to the home of His dear friends Lazarus and his two sisters, Martha and Mary.

* * *

Jesus relaxed in the fine, spacious home while most of the men went outdoors and sat or stood around in the courtyard under the welcome and refreshing shade of the sycamore trees, chatting and laughing with excitement at the joy and thrill of having experienced firsthand the power of God. Never before had they been allowed to explore anything outside the letter of the Law. The spirit of the Law had been crushed under a load of outward ordinances and traditions. Jesus' teachings were alive and vibrant. The atmosphere was electric with enthusiasm.

Mary, the younger of the two sisters, was seated at the feet of the Master, listening intently to the glorious words that cascaded forth like a pure fountain of grace from the lips of her Lord. Jesus was thoroughly enjoying the rare moment of relaxation and refreshing with His friends.

Martha, on the other hand, was anything but relaxed. Flour from her early morning baking adorned her smock. She bustled around anxiously in the kitchen, making preparations for the meal, murmuring under her breath and slinging dishes and slamming cupboard doors. She felt put upon having all these extra mouths to feed. She was running out of flour and patience. And there's her young sister in the living room looking like a moonstruck puppy, sitting and doing nothing while she had all the work to do. Each time she passed the doorway, she could see Mary completely enraptured and totally oblivious to her sister's increasing wrath.

Finally she could take it no longer. Martha stood in the doorway, dishtowel in hand, hand on hip, hip thrown to one side, fuming. "Lord," she said in a whining tone, interrupting Jesus' teaching, "Does it not concern you that my sister is doing nothing but sitting and has left me to do the preparations and serving alone?"

Service ceases to be service when the server complains about having to serve.

There was a tone in her voice that insinuated Jesus was somehow being inconsiderate of her feelings and inattentive to her personally. Martha felt left out and resentment began to rise up in her, a mood that

Jesus would never react to favorably. Instead of taking Martha's side and shooing Mary off to help her, Jesus, as always, took the side of righteousness. Jesus loved Martha and knew she had more than the need of an attitude adjustment. She had another problem. Her priorities were wrong. In her attempt to honor her Guest, she was mentally distracted in her serving. Mary had honored Him by forgetting all else *but* Him.

"Martha, dear Martha, you are so upset over so many details."

Simon Peter sat across the room smiling and thinking about his own dear little wife who had busied herself in the kitchen to serve Jesus when He came to visit. He had invited her to join in their fellowship and conversation with the men. She slowly shook her head, big brown eyes wide with surprise. It was unheard of for a woman to join in the conversation with the men. Especially the Rabbi! Jesus had gently related to her that He welcomed women into fellowship and to hear His words.

How unlike the religious leaders He was in His treatment toward women. Their common morning prayers were "Blessed art Thou, O Lord our God that Thou hast not made me a Gentile, a servant nor a woman."

Jesus smiled tenderly and said, "Mary has chosen the better thing, and it will not be taken from her."[255]

Peter could see that Martha, in the midst of doing "women's work" was attempting to put Mary "in her place." As a woman she should be in the kitchen! He grinned at Martha and thought, *If you really knew how the Master operates, you would say to Him, 'Lord, I'm missing out on your teaching. I heard about how You fed the five thousand, so here's the bread and stew. How about multiplying it for this crowd so I can stay in here and listen!'* Peter smiled to himself, *And He would not have reproved her for it. He would commend her for her faith! As with the centurion, He would have said, "Wow!"*

"One thing is needed," Jesus told her. "And Mary has chosen it."

Martha was absorbed in the serving.

Mary was absorbed
in the Savior.

* * *

Trembling in fear at the sight of his master's rage, the demon captain continued his report, "He has recruited seventy more besides the original twelve, S-Sire. They're casting our demons out right and left and making well all those we've made sick! He has given these followers of His the same authority and power over us that He has! They merely act in His Name.[256] If it g-gets out to the rest of His adherents that they have dominion over us we're finished!"

"Stop!" Satan screeched, slapping his hands over his pointed ears. "I've heard enough!"

In extreme frustration the captain continued, "B-but Sire, that's not all, He's raising p-people from the dead as well! A young man in Nain, and a little girl in Capernaum!"

The news hit Satan broadside, sending him into an explosion of rage. The gauntlet was thrown down. The ultimate challenge was made. The Seed had trespassed into the very interior of Satan's domain. His voice trembled with anger. "I am the one who has power over death![257] He is challenging the very core of my kingdom!" His unleashed fury caused the captain to cringe in fear. A string of blasphemies vomited out of Satan's mouth. "I want Him dead, do you hear? I don't care how you do it, just get Him!"

"B-But how, S-Sire?"

"Use your imagination, you idiot! They traverse back and forth on the Sea. Stir up a storm and drown them!"

The demon captain sighed deeply. "Uh, Sire, there's a problem."

"Now what!" Satan bellowed, throwing his hands in the air in frustration.

"Twice we have accosted Him and those fool disciples of His with violent winds, and we thought surely we would drown the lot of them."

"Yes, yes," Satan urged him to get to the point.

"He slept right through one of them without the slightest tic of fear." A twisted grin crossed his face. "I must say, we did give His boys quite a fright."

"Go on, go on."

"Well, Sire, just as the boat was filling up and about to go under, they awakened Him, and He rebuked our splendid storm and it calmed immediately!"[258]

Satan groaned, "Don't tell me He has power over my air as well! I am the prince of power of the air![259] That's *my* territory–how *dare* He!"

"And the second time, we attacked His twelve dismal disciples when we caught them crossing the lake without the Seed. We stirred up a violent wind and nearly had them–and–uh,"

Satan's eyes blazed with rage. "And?"

"Well, Sire, He came walking on the water to them–"

"He what?"

"He, uh, walked on the water to them in the middle of the violent sea and rescued them from our assault."[260]

Satan erupted into another outburst. The captain cringed in fear. He wished he could escape, but knew he could only stand there trembling until his tirade subsided.

"There has to be a way! There has to be! And it must be once and for all! He'll not triumph over me! I shall conquer Him I shall–"

The demon captain blinked in surprise as his master abruptly stopped in mid-sentence.

"That's it! That's it! His tail jerked with excitement. Satan turned to the captain. "Call all my princes of darkness together. I have it! I have a plan!"

"What is it, my lord?"

A sly, monstrous smile slithered across his face like a snake.

"There can be only one way to get Him."

"What's that, Sire?"

Satan smiled mockingly.

"He must die
for His cause."

All these things spake Jesus unto the multitude in parables; and without a parable spake he not unto them: That it might be fulfilled which was spoken by the prophet, saying, I will open my mouth in parables; I will utter things which have been kept secret from the foundation of the world.

Matthew 13:34,35

He laid out for them in rapid sequence beautiful pearls of wisdom in simple story form and strung them like a heavenly necklace.

CHAPTER TWENTY-FOUR

A String Of Pearls

JESUS HAD A COMMUNICATIONS system that was connected directly to His Commander-in-Chief, and He carried out His orders in perfect obedience. "I only do what I see the Father doing." He saw His Father talking to a Samaritan woman at a well, healing nine ungrateful lepers,[261] sticking mud in a blind man's eyes to heal him, spitting on a man's tongue to loose it,[262] forgiving an adulteress, taking Peter fishing, and even doing a little catering on the side.

Whatever He saw His Father doing, He did the same thing. He heard His Father telling stories about His kingdom so that those who had ears to hear would have no trouble understanding. He told them of a way of life that was so wonderful that its value was that of a pearl of great price, a field that hid a treasure,[263] a place and a lifestyle that one must press into. A glorious rest and peace awaited them through faith, and that He would help them attain it.

He heard His Father telling them poignant parables that clearly defined His Father's kingdom. He laid out for them in rapid sequence beautiful pearls of wisdom in simple story form and strung these parable-pearls like a heavenly necklace,[264] teaching them about every area of this natural life, kingdom-life and after-life:

an invitation to a wedding feast and an unprepared guest,[265]
a barren fig tree,[266]
sheep and goats,[267]
the equality of laborers in His vineyard,[268]
the kingdom being like a seed growing in secret,[269]
ten talents[270] and ten virgins,[271]
two debtors[272] and two sons,[273]
an unjust judge[274] and an unjust steward,[275]
lost sheep, a lost coin and a lost prodigal boy,[276]
a wise steward[277] and wicked husbandmen.[278]

Every avenue of life was covered. Each pearl was beautifully laid out and arranged to perfection for their understanding and admonition. Each word of wisdom would aid in their freedom and peaceful living. His were words of life; words that would renew their minds,[279] clear out the darkness and free them from confusion and fear. His words were living things that held preeminence over all else and were forever settled in Heaven.[280] His words were sent to heal their diseases,[281] to tear down strongholds[282] and to eradicate the lies of the devil. His words would never return to Him void but would accomplish His purposes.[283] Each word was a pearl of wisdom and a gift from the Father's heart.

The pearls spoken, each one in place,
the necklace strung,
the ornament of wisdom,[284]
was theirs to wear
or to cast away to swine.[285]

And the scribes and Pharisees brought unto Him a woman taken in adultery–they set her in the midst–

John 8:3

He could see that the foundations of their lives were built on the shifting sands of deception, and their frames were uneven and bent. The Master Carpenter had a knack for straightening frames.

CHAPTER TWENTY-FIVE

The Great Architect

THE PHARISEES HAD MOVED in large numbers throughout Jerusalem and other cities in an all-out attempt to turn the people away from the popularity of Jesus and recruit them into their order. Upon gathering a crowd, they would cry loudly, "Take the yoke of the Law upon you and learn of it! It shall be life to you!" One morning, soon after their soliciting campaign was fresh in the minds of the townspeople, Jesus came from the Mount of Olives and sat with His disciples in the Temple courtyard. Immediately a crowd gathered. Their questions were lively and His answers were profound.

One of the young men who had been approached by the Pharisees to join their order said, "Master, the Pharisees call us to take the yoke of the Law upon us, to learn of it. They say it shall be life to us. What do You say?"

Jesus knew the true yoke of the Law was not what they were

offering, but their endless added laws. He stretched out His arms to them. "Come to Me, all you that labor and are heavily laden with the burden of man's laws, and I will give you rest. Take My yoke upon you. For My yoke is easy and My burden is light."

The Pharisees' commands had become veritable yokes of bondage to slavery, yet they would not lift a finger to help anyone.[286] They demanded that they *must* bear the yoke of the *Torah*, which when left in tact, was not a burdensome yoke, but was truly the Law of Love. But they had added hundreds of hairsplitting laws to it, making it a heavy load indeed. But Jesus invited them to voluntarily take up His yoke and He would shoulder it with them, making their burdens easy and light. Jesus' commands must also be submitted to, but His commands were easier kept through love. Man's unbearable yoke was to perform impossible works of self-righteousness. The Savior's yoke was one of quiet faith from which true righteousness springs.

The Blessed Carpenter had crafted many yokes in that little shop in Nazareth. He knew that an ill-fitting yoke would work against them, which meant pain and struggling for the yoke-bearers. He invited those who would co-labor with Him to cast the weight of their burdens upon Him, for He cared deeply for them.[287]

"Learn of Me," He said gently. He was offering to be their Teacher. He would impart truth, knowledge and wisdom to them that would change their lives forever. "For I am gentle and humble in heart, and you shall find rest for your souls."[288] He spoke of His own humility and invited His hearers to humble themselves and to become like Him.

Satan wanted to be like God and lost heaven. Jesus invited them to be like Him, and they would gain heaven.

He could see that the foundations of their lives were built on the shifting sands of deception, and their frames were uneven and bent.[289] The Master Carpenter had a knack for straightening frames. He took the ruler of discernment and measured their desire and capacity to receive His teachings. With the plane of His Word He smoothed out the misshapen concepts of their image of God. He took the compass of His love and drew a circle around their hearts and spoke truth in their inward parts.[290] He loosed the warped windows of their souls and poured in the Light of heaven.

Like any good Architect, He built structures with a distinct purpose in mind. They were created to glorify God in their bodies[291] by bearing much fruit[292]–the fruit of His Spirit.[293] That was why they were born–to bring glory to the Father. Their lives were a far cry from what God had in mind for His children. Jesus wasn't here to merely make adjustments in their lives; the Architect of Life was here to restore them to their original design.

The morning shadows crept silently across the courtyard as though being careful not to disturb the Savior's teachings. Suddenly, a commotion arose across the gallery. Screams of a woman and shouts of angry men echoed in their ears. They were heading this way!

The familiar scowls of the Pharisees and scribes burst upon the scene. Their fingers dug into the bare arms of a half-dressed woman, leaving bruises on her milky-white skin. As they approached Jesus, they threw her to the ground on her face, knocking the wind out of her and splitting her lip. Sand ground into her right cheek. Her long auburn hair covered her tear-stained face. She could picture her accusers gingerly fingering the stones they had scooped up along the way. She dared not lift up her throbbing head. It would only be met with a stone. Shame and fear engulfed her.

"Oh, God, oh, God, oh, God," was all she could whisper.

Little did she know–they had thrown her at His feet.

"Master, this woman was caught in the very act of adultery. Moses commands us in the law that she must be stoned. Don't You agree?"

Jesus remained silent.

They wouldn't leave it alone. They continued to badger Him, hoping to catch Him in a discrepancy so they could accuse Him.

He drew a line in the sand.

"Well, Jesus? Are You going to answer or not?"

He slowly stood up and looked them squarely in the eyes. "He that is without sin among you, let him cast the first stone at her." He stooped back down and continued writing on the ground.

Their mouths gaped open in speechless silence. What could they say? How could they answer? No one is without sin![294]

The only One Who was qualified to cast the first stone–didn't.

Instead, He doodled in the dirt.

The woman still didn't move a muscle. Her heart was pounding like a captured bird. She, who waited for stones to tear her flesh, now heard stones dropping on the ground.

Clop. Clop. Clop.

One by one they dropped their weapons and in the silence of their stinging consciences, dispersed and walked away with stooped shoulders and heads hung.

The woman dared not look up.

Jesus was still stooped down. God, stooping down to touch one of His creatures.

"Woman," Jesus said tenderly.

She didn't move.

Jesus could hear her heart pounding. He waited a few moments and then He spoke again. "Woman." This was not a condescending term. He called her the same name His Father had given before the fall.

Perfect creation of God. He already saw her . . . forgiven.

"Woman, where are your accusers?"

Slowly, she lifted up her head. Slowly brushing back her wild curls, she wiped the blood from her mouth with the back of her hand. Looking up, she met His gaze.

No man had ever looked at her that way before. Men always leered at her through eyes of lust. This Man looked at her through eyes of love, as though seeing her true self. She wasn't sure she had ever seen her true self until she looked into His eyes. Eyes of purity. Eyes of truth. She realized she had never seen truth before, and upon gazing into the eyes of Truth, they told her of a love that was unlike any she had been told of. A love that loved the real her. No one had ever reached that part of her. In fact, she never knew that part of her existed.

He reached over and gently brushed the sand from her cheek. Again He spoke. "Where are your accusers?"

She pushed herself up and drew her torn garment around her and looked around. "They–they're gone."

"Does anyone condemn you?"

"No. No one, Sir."

"Neither do I."

He came not into the world to condemn the world–

"You may go. Don't sin anymore."[295]

–But that the world through Him might be saved.[296]

Her eyes filled with tears. Tears of joy and gratitude. For the first time in her life she felt clean. Released. Accepted. She smiled and turned to go. But first, she glanced at the ground where He had been writing.

What was it? She wasn't certain, but it looked like–blueprints?

For–a mansion?[297]

And she wasn't sure,
but it looked like
her name
was written
on it.

But when the Pharisees heard it, they said, This fellow doth not cast out devils, but by . . . the prince of the devils.

Matthew 12:24

Deception eyed Fear carefully. “You have any ideas?” Fear grinned hatefully, “As a matter of fact, I do.” He spread his gleaming talons and admired them dramatically. “Why not make them believe He is aligned with us?”

CHAPTER TWENTY-SIX

Fear Tactics

THE MORE LEGALISTIC PHARISEES constantly dogged Jesus' steps in an attempt to snare Him in His words, only to set the stage for more of His radiant responses. Jesus took full advantage of their constant negative presence. Using contrast can often make a point more profoundly. Light shows up best in darkness. Just as a jeweler places a diamond against a black cloth to bring out its beauty and brilliance, Jesus was placing the jewel of the gospel against the "black cloth" of the Pharisees' antagonism. Their spirited rebuttals of His claims threw powerful rays of light on the deluded deductions they embraced, causing His truth to stand out even more.

God had chosen Israel as the covenant people through whom He would reveal His goodness.[298] They had been given the great privilege of being the unveilers of God's truth. Now truth was here in the flesh[299] and they were determined to silence it. Though they looked pure and religious, the populace had no problem seeing the inconsistencies of their lifestyles with their teachings; a strong indictment against them, and another "black cloth" against the diamond of Jesus' perfect profile.

The demon captain took note of the opposite effect the Pharisees' debates were causing. "Everything we do backfires on us!" he growled. He and his cohorts watched in despair as Jesus turned the Pharisees' inaccurate applications of the Word of God into an occasion for crystal clear clarification of His truths. "The people are not taking the side of the Pharisees! They're actually enjoying these confrontations! We must do something about this!" the captain declared to his subordinates, as though they had anything to say about it.

"Like what?" a briery little demon squawked.

"We must report to Deception. His scheme to snare Him in His words is not working. The more negative His antagonists are, the more clarification of the Seed's words it allows!"

"Deception's not going to like being told his plan is failing," another flunky demon cackled.

The demon captain's grotesque head settled down between his shoulders. "I know," he grunted, "But that's his problem. All I'm supposed to do is report what I see."

* * *

Deception's neck swelled like a cobra about to strike when the captain reported how the Seed was gaining more and more adherents.

"The more negative His opponents, the more support He receives from the masses!"

"Alright, alright, Captain, you've made your point. Now leave."

The grisly captain backed out of Deception's dark chamber and out of his presence, bowing and smirking to himself. He rather enjoyed seeing the pompous prince perplexed.

He nearly backed into Fear who was waiting to see Deception, and had overheard their conversation. Deception sat down with a thud and motioned for Fear to enter.

"Having a bit of a problem, are we?" the thorny, fiendish prince taunted. He sat down in a mountainous heap across from him.

"Nothing I can't handle."

Fear smirked. "Sounds like you need a new approach."

"I have some ideas I'm implementing. I must say your recent accomplishment was stunning. Stirring up Pilate to kill those Galilean worshipers right in the Temple in Jerusalem![300] Brilliant! That should cause a great deal of fear throughout the country. It was especially clever to have Murder butcher Galileans! The Seed's very own region! Nice touch, Fear!"

Fear snorted with pride. "Yes, I am counting on it to frighten the Seed's adherents that the same might happen to them if they continue to follow Him." He began filing his talons. "And what is your next move?"

"You'll see in a moment." Deception called an attendant who quickly sent for Doubt and Unbelief, twin entities that always did their dirty work together. The devilish duo arrived almost immediately and listened carefully as Deception gave them their orders

"Study the Seed's disciples. Find inroads into their minds. We must discover a way to turn them from Him. We have been counting too much on the Pharisees. They only drive the people to Him. There has to be another way." Deception dictated to them in the strongest of terms to attack unprohibited, using whatever strategy they wished to implement. "And work over the new followers. We cannot have truth spreading throughout all of Israel!"

Doubt, a murky, shadowy little demon, was noticeably disturbed. "We've never seen anything like this! There has never been One such as the Seed Who flagrantly attacks in open defiance our master and his powers of darkness!"

The Holy Warrior's attacks had been blatant against the one who had gone unchallenged for centuries.

"He has even multiplied Himself by twelve! And then seventy more! Who knows how many more He will recruit!"

Fear sat quietly listening, sharpening his talons into needles. He was getting irritated with Doubt's usual skepticism and apprehension. "What are you so worried about?" he grunted. "Afraid you can't do the job?"

Doubts beady eyes blazed. "I'm not afraid, I'm just uncertain how we should approach such a mammoth operation. After all, we've never encountered anything such as the Seed before!"

Fear smirked, "As usual, you're so wishy-washy and distracted by all your ridiculous questioning, that you've forgotten that our targets have already been prepared to receive anything we give them. All we have to do is reinforce what is already at work in them since the Great Fall. Our master has firmly lodged in them the seeds of suspicion and doubt. You, of all demons, should know that! You need only to manipulate what is already very much a part of them." Fear glared at him and continued filing his talons.

Deception eyed Fear carefully. "You have any ideas?"

"As a matter of fact, I do." He spread his gleaming talons and admired them dramatically. "Why not make them believe He is aligned with us?"

Unbelief cackled, "You really *are* wicked."

"Thank you." Fear sniffed. "I thought you would like that."

Deception leaned back and grinned horribly. "I must admit your plan is brilliant. That should frighten His followers away. Make them think His miracles are satanic!"

Doubt frowned. "How will you do it? Obviously people are being healed and set free from our hold. Why would they believe such a thing?"

Fear stood up, looming over the twins. "A simple task, really. Merely block in them the ability to believe, by making His claims seem absurd, unrealistic, even demonic. These stupid doubt-infested earthlings have a natural fear of the supernatural. Make them think He casts us out by the power of our master, Satan. They shall cringe with fear and leave His company speedily!"

Unbelief glared at his twin. "Do you have a better idea?" Doubt clammed up and glowered.

Deception leaned forward. "The religious leaders are meeting tonight. Hatred will be there and has done the preliminary work. All you have to do is drop these thoughts into their minds." The demon prince was exhilarated at the anticipation of a mass beguilement.

Fear glared at the twins. "I should like to be the one to plant this scheme into their minds myself. I don't want such a brilliant idea to be blundered. Perhaps I'll even bring along some of my spirits. It should be a great deal of fun."

"Perfect! I'll send these two ahead of you to tell Hatred the plan."

Deception stood up. "It should be a lovely evening with those insipid religionists. I'm sure you'll have no trouble out of them at all. They're wide open for suggestions."

The demons laughed wickedly. Even Doubt began to see the plan's potential.

* * *

Members of the Sanhedrin sat in their appointed places, talking among themselves. Some were murmuring caustically against the Nazarene. Others sat quietly watching the others.

Hatred had been working on several of the more prominent leaders. Fear's enormous form, along with several of his evil cohorts, floated down through the ceiling. Fear dispatched his spirits to move among the assembly and settled beside Hatred. "How are things going?"

"Wonderfully! I've been working over several candidates and Doubt and Unbelief have latched on to some of those who have shown some interest in the Seed."

"Excellent!"

The meeting was finally called to order. The high priest stood and a hush fell over the room. "Brethren, we have called this assembly to discuss the growing crisis concerning this–this fraud, Jesus of Nazareth. You have all seen how the crowds gather wherever He appears."

"Yes! And they gaze upon Him with adoration and wonder," a Pharisee responded loudly. "They believe He is the Messiah!"

"This is getting quite serious!" another said gravely.

The high priest looked at them through narrow eyes. "Brethren, we must put a stop to it!"

"But how? You see how they follow Him, how they cling to Him!"

The eldest of the robed leaders stood and spoke, his voice trembling with age. "You've seen the miracles. They are quite extraordinary, are they not? I have known that man who was healed in the synagogue all his life! His hand has always been withered and deformed. It's incredible to see him whole and able to work with his hands. It's truly remarkable!" He sat down and cupped his ear so he could hear the discussion.

Another Pharisee frowned, "Yes. Remarkable–and most upsetting!"

One of the younger members of the Academy who had been present at the miraculous healing stood and spoke up. "How can you say that? A miracle such as this could bring revival to our synagogue!"

The high priest retorted, "Revival? To whose credit? Those followers of His are not giving God glory for these displays–they are putting their focus on this unlearned Galilean!"

"Yes but . . ."

"Have you become one of His followers too?" he said sharply.

"No, I . . ."

"Then if I were you, I would speak no more of this deceiver!"

The young man looked around at the faces in the assembly. "There are others here who are amazed by these miracles as well!" He hoped that someone would come to his aid in defending the Nazarene, but no one dared to open his mouth. He couldn't see the spirits of fear that had them paralyzed.

"Others?" the high priest squinted angrily.

The elderly Pharisee looked down with his eyes closed and shook his head.

"Yes! No one has ever performed such miraculous deeds as these! Not even Elijah healed as many people as this Man Jesus has. He opens blind eyes and heals lepers, and the lame walk. He even raises the dead! Why is it so hard to see that He must be sent from God?"

"That's enough! Sit down!"

The young man's face reddened and he slowly sat down. He knew he was dangerously close to contempt against the high priest and that he was getting nowhere.

Hatred motioned to Fear. "Come! This one is ready. Make your move now!"

Fear moved like a mammoth cloud behind a middle-aged Pharisee who sat stroking his graying beard. His brows were in an intense knot and he seemed deep in thought. Fear grinned and sank his needle-sharp talons into his skull and the man stood up and spoke. "Brethren, it is true that this Man has done remarkable feats. And it is even understandable that some here are amazed at the miracles."

The young Pharisee looked at him hopefully and leaned forward in his seat, nodding in agreement.

The high priest looked at him cautiously. "Go on."

"But remember, Pharaoh's magicians could do miracles. Who knows where this Man gets His powers? Certainly not from God!"

The high priest walked over to him. "Do you mean . . . ?"

"Yes! I mean He drives out demons by the power of demons!"

The young Pharisee was flabbergasted. He jumped up, "That–that's unbelievable!"

"Is it? Think about it!"

"How else would a mere untrained Galilean perform such feats?"

The young man fell back in his seat, and looked at the floor, his mouth open. Doubt was on one side of him and Unbelief on the other.

"We've been looking for a way to deter His followers. We shall merely warn them that He is in league with the devil himself."

The high priest was ecstatic. "Well, gentlemen? What say you?"

Some of the others voiced their approval heartily and others simply stared and nodded numbly their agreement.

They were unable to see
the four gloating demons
and their cohorts
laughing hideously.

* * *

The next day, Jesus was teaching in the courtyard near the synagogue. He and His disciples sat on the ground with the eager crowd. He spoke with them freely in His usual relaxed manner. His hungry listeners hung onto every word.

The Pharisees waited nearby, waiting for the opportunity to hurl their demonically-inspired scheme into the minds of Jesus' listeners. They considered themselves engaging in a service to God to get rid of this young rabble-rouser in whatever maniacal means it may take, which delighted Hatred and Fear immensely. The Pharisees were beside themselves with contempt for Him, making them easily accessible to the wiles of the devil.[301]

Deception was thrilled at the report of the previous night's success at the Sanhedrin. He could not pass up the opportunity to personally attend and observe the implementation of the double-dealing treachery. It was one thing to poison the minds of the Seed's advocates, but more thrilling to his malicious, evil mind was the prospect of the religious leaders to commit blasphemy. It was the ultimate deception–his finest hour. The Pharisees could not wait to execute the evil plan. It was now just a matter of a favorable circumstance.

It didn't take long for the opportunity to arrive. A demonized man who was totally blind and unable to speak was brought to Jesus. He stood up and immediately cast out the demon. It shrieked loudly and took off, slamming hard against an enormous angel. The glorious being grabbed it by the throat and slung it into oblivion.

The man's eyes fluttered open and he looked around him. His blindness was gone! Suddenly his tongue was loosed and he began to glorify God. "Praise God! I can see! I can see!" All the people gasped in amazement and cried joyfully, "This is the Messiah! This has to be the Son of David!"

When the Pharisees heard this they seized the opportunity and ran into the crowd crying, "Can't you see this fraud is possessed Himself by Satan! That is how He casts out demons!"

Deception, watching nearby, was ecstatic. His enormous torso swelled with excitement. "They've done it! They have reached the supreme evil toward God! They have attributed His miracles to Satan!" A fiendish grin spread across his face. "Wait until the master hears about this!"

Jesus, hearing the assaults of the Pharisees, turned and looked at them. He was majestically calm. The crowd grew quiet. They knew another confrontation was coming.

A band of glorious angels appeared, knowing their Master's weapons, mighty through God,[302] were about to be implemented. As Jesus spoke words of war, gleaming, razor-sharp swords[303] made of Light appeared in the angels' hands.

"If Satan drives out Satan, he has divided his own kingdom and interests. How, then, will his kingdom stand?" The Pharisees were speechless. "But if I drive demons out by the Spirit of God, then obviously an opposing kingdom has come in your midst!" Jesus was clearly defining two kingdoms in conflict.

Deception and his cohorts began to scream in pain as the angels bearing the Swords of Truth pierced and wounded them with every word that proceeded out of the Seed's mouth. The shrieking demons became confused and disoriented.

The crowd watched wide-eyed as Jesus rebuked the religious leaders for speaking blasphemy.

The Pharisees were dumbfounded as Jesus continued to censure them. "You can say evil things about Me and you can say evil things about My Father, and it will be forgiven you, but if you speak blasphemies against the Holy Spirit, it will never be forgiven! Not in this age, nor the age to come!" He strongly warned them because they were accusing His own Spirit of being demonic.

The invisible battle raged about them. Jesus continued, "Trees are recognized by their fruit and yours is pretty obvious! You children of the devil! How can you speak anything good when you are full of evil! Out of the abundance that is in your heart is what will come out of your mouth!" They glared at Him, not daring to speak. "All that comes out of your mouths are evil, idle words, and in the day of judgment your very words will either acquit you or condemn you! Your words will be your own damnation."

The sputtering Pharisees were dazed and astonished at His strong words, and seeing their shameful scheme had failed, they could only return to their dogged demands that He show them a sign. For months He had been healing vast multitudes of people ravaged with every kind of disease, and raising the dead and they wanted to see a sign.

"An evil and faithless generation demands a sign for proof, but no sign will be shown you except the sign of Jonah. Three days and nights Jonah was in the belly of a whale, and the Son of Man will be three days and nights in the belly of the earth." They looked at each other, bewildered at His words. "The men of Ninevah will stand in judgment of you. They, unlike you, repented when they heard the truth. And the queen of the South will stand up on judgment day and condemn this generation as well. For, unlike you, she longed to hear truth and wisdom beyond what she already knew. She traveled far to hear the wisdom of Solomon, and I assure you, Someone far greater than Solomon is talking to you!"

Deception and the others had all they could take. They took off, flapping and floundering to get away from the piercing stabs of Truth.

Jesus looked at the Pharisees with great sadness, knowing the demons would be back to continue their assaults. He knew the devil had legal access to them because of their sinful rebellion and resistance to the truth. He sternly warned them of what they were dealing with.

"When a demon has gone out of a man, it roams around the dry places searching for another dwelling place in which it can legally enter. When it finds none, it returns to the one in whom it had dwelt, and finds it swept and adorned with self-righteousness, but empty of God. It then has the right to return to make the condition of that man much worse than before. It will bring with it seven more demons even more wicked than itself."

Instead of receiving the warning and thereby becoming converted, they answered Him with stony silence, their eyes wild with hatred. What a pitiful sight were the walking dead, adorned in their pompous robes. He was giving them fair warning concerning their fate. He was showing them His wisdom over which they could not gainsay.

Jesus turned to walk away and stopped. He turned around and said sadly. "And unless you repent, so shall it be with you!"[304]

From a distance, Deception, hiding behind his cloak and licking his wounds, could easily see that the Seed's words to the religious leaders were being cast aside. This opened the gate even wider for the evil prince, who, soon after Jesus left, returned limping with wounds from the Sword of Truth, but stronger than ever in his resolve.

And with him were
seven more demons,
led by the
spirit of Murder.

There was a woman that had a spirit of infirmity for eighteen years, and was bowed together, and could in no wise lift up herself.

Luke 13:11

Her body snapped, crackled and crunched at the rare experience of being able to stand up straight. The demon screeched, pulled its talons out of her back and fled, flapping furiously to get away from the holy one of God.

CHAPTER TWENTY-SEVEN

Let Them Come

HER DAYS WERE SPENT staring at her shoes. While others enjoyed watching the birds in the trees and little wispy clouds passing by, she never missed a weed or a spot of dirt on the floor. For eighteen long years she was bent over like a horseshoe. Pain wrenched her body like a torture rack. Children made fun of her as she painfully made her way along the narrow streets.

Her tears didn't roll down her cheeks; they trickled up her forehead. She longed to stand up straight; to be able to look her family and neighbors in the eyes; to carry her own water jug on her shoulder. But she could not lift herself up at all. A foul spirit of infirmity had taken up residence on her back and held her fast, leaving her chest staring at her knees.

The little woman walked sideways like an injured crab. It was easier for her to see sideways than straight-ahead. She held her arms close to her sides, reaching out to steady herself occasionally on the smooth marble steps that led up to the synagogue entrance.

Although the poor, crimped creature was suffering, she never lost her faith. She never blamed God. She was in Synagogue every Sabbath without fail.

One particular Sabbath it paid off. They had a guest Speaker. His Name was Jesus.

As always, when the townspeople heard that He would be speaking in their streets or their meeting places, an enormous crowd gathered. The synagogue had not seen such a turnout in years.

Jesus watched her climb the steps and enter through the wide doorway. She stopped to catch her breath before she tackled the stairs that led to the women's balcony. Compassion engulfed Jesus when He saw the crooked little woman. And anger welled up in Him at the sight of the nasty little demon that was happily riding on her back; its talons embedded deeply in her spine.

Typically, He let the needs of the people come before His reputation or the approval of man. He was a Man of no reputation.

He called the dear lady to Him. She turned sideways to look at the Man Who had just called her and wondered if she had heard right. "Is that young Man calling me?" No one had paid any attention to her for years. Most people avoided her, much less purposely engaging her in conversation.

The religious leaders looked at each other. "What is He doing?"

Slowly, she moved toward Him. She stopped and stared at His sandals. "You called me, Sir?"

Jesus smiled and spoke gently. "Woman, you are released from your infirmity."

Something went off inside her. Faith shot through her like a missile. He laid His hands on her back and immediately she straightened up. Her body snapped, crackled and crunched at the rare experience of being able to stand up straight. The demon screeched, pulled its talons out of her back and fled, flapping furiously to get away from the Holy One of God.

The woman's arms shot upward in praise, her heart pounding with joy. She grabbed Jesus' hands and kissed them over and over, tears streaming down her cheeks, not up her forehead. "Thank You! Thank You!" The crowd went wild with applause.

Jesus answered, heartily, "You're welcome!"

The religious leaders watched the astounding miracle from across the room. They were shocked and indignant because Jesus didn't stick to the rules. He had the audacity to heal on the Sabbath. A great miracle was done before their very eyes and they were angry because He had done it on the wrong day.

"There are six days on which to work," the synagogue leader said to the crowd in his starchiest tone. "Let them come on those days and be cured."

Obviously the little woman had come on those other days and no one had cured her.

Jesus shot back, "Let them come? Should they not be able to come to be healed on the Sabbath as well? It is apparent you would treat your animals better than this woman, a direct descendent of Abraham, whom Satan has kept bound for eighteen years! Should she not be set free on God's day?"[305]

His words once again shamed His enemies. They were so blinded by the letter of the law, they missed the majesty of the miracle. But the people rejoiced at the wonderful things He did.

The demon that Jesus had cast out shot straight up, spewing blasphemies all the way, and slammed hard into the demon captain whose patrol was flying overhead, nearly knocking the wind out of him.

"Oooofff! Watch where you're going, you little creep!" the captain blasted.

"Oh! S-sorry, sir. I haven't flown in eighteen years!"

The captain eyed him suspiciously, "Have you been cast out?"

"Y-yes, sir. Violently! I'm completely lost and disoriented. I-I don't know what to do, or where to go!"

"Stop your whining. You'll find another home," the captain growled, adjusting his wings as they settled down on a dead tree.

"B-but, sir! I've been rendered powerless! I have nothing with which to inflict pain!"

"The Seed again," the captain wheezed hatefully. He motioned to his patrol to follow him back into formation. The captain shook his ugly head and muttered,

"How long is this going to go on?"

* * *

Sometime later Jesus was ministering to the crowds, which were growing in number so much that the people were nearly trampling one another to get near Him.[306] The disciples were quickly learning about crowd control. Several prominent leaders came from Jerusalem and were listening to Him teach. They threw questions at Him as fast as He could answer them, not that they wanted the answers, they were merely attempting to snare Him in His words.

A young mother waited patiently for the Master to finish His discourse with the Pharisees. Why wouldn't they leave Him alone? All this wrangling about the Law. It was plain to see they wanted to catch Him in a trap of words. But they could not do it. His wisdom was so far beyond theirs; the expanse was that between the heavens and the earth.[307]

The young widow held her boy close, hoping for the Teacher's blessing upon her son. The young lad desperately needed a man to look up to. No model could be better than Jesus. Perhaps if He would but place His hands upon the boy and pronounce a blessing, he would not go in the way of some of the hate-filled Pharisees. She wanted her son to know the way of truth, peace and mercy, attributes that were not only in Jesus' teachings, but epitomized in His life as well.

Several parents were in the crowd hoping for an opportunity to bring their children, even infants, for a blessing.

There were Pharisees in the crowd listening. Many had come to believe in Jesus, although they did not let it be known for fear of being ostracized by their peers. They could not deny His words of wisdom or the mighty miracles He performed. Others challenged Him at every turn and continually attempted to trap Him in His words.

Jesus looked at the latter sorrowfully. Knowing that they were counting on their good works and were confident that they were right with God, but they were scornful and looked down on others. For they being ignorant of God's righteousness, and going about to establish their own righteousness, had not submitted themselves unto the righteousness of God.[308]

He began to teach. "Two men went up to the Temple to pray, one a Pharisee, the other a publican."

Already they didn't like His story. How dare He put them in the same story with a publican! As always He taught illustrations with dazzling contrast.

"The Pharisee stood proudly proclaiming his own righteousness, 'I thank God that I am not as other men, who are swindlers, adulterers, and especially that I am not like that publican over there! I'm a good person. I fast twice a week and I tithe all I posses.' And the publican, standing afar off, under great conviction of his sinful ways, would not dare even lift his eyes toward heaven, but beat his breast in mournful repentance and cried out to God for mercy, admitting he was a needy sinner."

Jesus' point was clear. The Pharisee in His story, in the pathetic pretense of praying, was merely boasting of his own righteousness and in doing so, was looking down upon others. Jesus told them clearly that the humble publican left there justified, counting on the goodness and mercy of God; not the Pharisee who counted on his good works, and considered his right–ness to be right–eousness, and saw pride as a virtue. God resisted pride, but Satan welcomed it with delight.

"Everyone who exalts himself eventually will be humbled, however, he who humbles himself, that one will be honored and exalted."[309] The proud Pharisees glared at Him while others received His words with joy.

The young lad standing with his mother was mesmerized. He gazed upon the Teacher and wondered if truly He was flesh and blood like himself, or if liquid love the color of the sun ran through His veins. He longed to run to Him and throw his arms around His neck.

His mother and he had watched Jesus' every move for days. The evidence was overwhelming that He truly cared about people. The sensitivity in His touch, the kindness in His eyes, the tenderness of His voice was beyond any human compassion they had ever witnessed. There were no pious platitudes awaiting them when He met them on the pebbled shores and on the grassy slopes; no hesitating or condescending to answer their fervent questions about their lives. He felt their emotions, His heart beat with their hearts, and His tears flowed with theirs. His enormous capacity for love was limitless.

His heart broke when He watched hundreds of men and women staggering, limping, hobbling, almost crawling to Him with hope in their eyes–hope mixed with fear that they might be overlooked, or worse, ignored. His profound sympathy to their plight intensified Him to His mission: to strip away the power of the one who had done this to them.

The young mother and her son had seen how He merely served expecting nothing in return. Smiling, touching, blessing, healing, wiping tears, cupping faces in His rugged yet tender hands, kneeling down to listen to a child's cry. Women and children wanted to touch those hands that had healed the lepers, opened blinded eyes, straightened limbs and spines; hands that had fed the hungry and raised the dead. They wanted to hear the voice of the One Who spoke truth to their longing hearts–that gave them words of hope–that spoke their language–that laughed when they laughed and wept when they wept.[310] Men wanted to gaze into His clear, lucid eyes that saw into their innermost being, that spoke understanding and love to their hearts, and that saw their problems and cared enough to give them genuine answers.

Jesus loved to be with them! He even spent hours playing with children and chasing butterflies whose jeweled wings He had designed. He ran in the meadow with them, laughing and playing hide-and-seek and tossing them in the air.

The people clung to Him and followed Him for days, hanging onto every word. They adored Him and begged Him to remain with them, sensing He was their very own. He enjoyed hearing their ideas and challenges. He loved meeting their families and friends. They brought their hearts to Him and He encouraged them in their endeavors and praised their accomplishments. He enjoyed their company, listening to them speak excitedly of their hopes and dreams.

Even in His strong answers to the religious leaders, love emanated from Him. The young lad couldn't understand why they always dogged His every step with taunts, insults, and jeers. Couldn't they see He was a good Man? At last the Pharisees left Him.

The young mother tenderly placed her hands on her son's shoulders and led him toward Jesus. Several parents lined up behind them to bring their infants and children to Him for a blessing. The lad's heart swelled with excitement. Timid as fawns, they approached Him, the boy's brown eyes wide with awe and wonder. He would get to meet the Teacher!

Suddenly, there were scowls in his face! Harsh words rang in his ears, forbidding him to come to Jesus! The boy cowered and clung to his mother.

Hearing the rebukes, Jesus turned and spoke forcefully an intense command, "Let them come!" He was sorely displeased.

Peter winced at the rebuke. The disciples sheepishly backed off and made room for them to pass.

"Always allow the little ones to come to Me!" He spoke firmly, yet His voice was gentle. He had just given a strong discourse of how the Pharisee had looked down upon one of God's "little ones". The illustration was not for the sake of the religious leaders only, but for all who heard, especially His own disciples. "Let the little children come" was not just a cry for infants and children, but for all who would come with childlike faith to Him.

"Do not forbid or hinder them–ever!"

The little mother led her son to Jesus and fought back tears of joy when He called the young lad by name.

"John Mark, come."

Jesus held out His arms and drew him close to Him. The boy could hear Jesus' heartbeat as He hugged him.

"Anyone who does not receive and welcome the kingdom of God like a little child, shall not enter into it."

The boy felt His strong hands upon his head and listened quietly as He pronounced a fervent blessing over him and wondered how He knew his name.

The blessing ended, Jesus looked deeply into the boy's eyes and spoke softly,

"For such as you–belongs the kingdom of heaven."[311]

* * *

Jesus had finished teaching for the day. The seeds of truth that the Sower freely broadcast to His hearers contained within themselves the germ of the promised flower, the kingdom of God, but there was no future kingdom growth for those whose hearts were filled with selfish and worldly cares.

Many religious leaders' hearts were pricked upon hearing Jesus' parable of the Pharisee and the publican. Others, who were truly seeking the kingdom of God and were open to kingdom truths, joyfully but fearfully welcomed the glorious seeds of wisdom, dreading persecution from their peers. Many, however, especially those of wealth and influence, found it hard to receive and sustain the truth. But the common people heard Him gladly.[312]

Some hearts were shallow and bereft of understanding; others were stony and hardened to truths for fear of persecution. Still other hearts were entangled with the cares of business and the lure of riches.

Deception and his minions worked feverishly attempting to steal the seeds of truth from all who heard Him. Like a flock of thieving crows, they descended upon the hearers, distracting them from the truth with their fiery darts of deception, and quickly snatched the seeds from many hearts. They had little difficulty stealing the seeds from some. For others they had to use multiple attacks to wrench the tiny truth seeds away before they could begin to take root.[313]

One such victim was a rich young ruler who had heard Jesus preach on several occasions and had been waiting for an opportunity to speak with Him. When he had found out that Jesus was once again in the area he ran quickly to see Him.

After Jesus blessed the children, the young man made his way toward Jesus. Upon recognizing him, the crowd moved aside and allowed him to the front. He was an upcoming young religious leader of much influence and possessed great riches.

Jesus looked at him lovingly, knowing that His parable had struck his conscience, but He also knew that his heart was entangled with his wealth, his good works and his stature as a religious leader.

The richly robed young man approached Jesus quickly and fell at His feet. "Good Teacher, what must I do to inherit the kingdom of God?"

In complete humility Jesus answered him, "Why are you calling Me good? No one is really good but God alone. You know the required commandments: Do not commit adultery, do not kill, nor steal, nor bear false witness, and, of course, honor your father and your mother."[314]

A look of relief came over his face. He replied proudly, "All these I have kept since I was a child!"

Jesus looked deeply into his eyes. "There is one thing you lack."

The young man was startled. His mind was racing, wondering what he had left undone.

"Go and sell everything that you have and distribute the money to the poor, and you will have great treasures in heaven; and then come back and follow Me."

His words hit him broadside. *Sell–all that I have? Surely He is jesting!* But seeing the look on Jesus' face, he knew He was dead serious. The young man stood there completely bewildered and speechless. All eyes were on him awaiting his answer. But he did not answer. He turned in deep sorrow and walked away.

His treasure was in his riches, not in heaven.[315] Jesus did not mind him having money. He minded the money having him. He did not understand that Jesus was not attempting to bring him to poverty, but that by selling all that he had and giving it to the needy, it would be multiplied back to him both in temporal riches and, more importantly, heavenly riches.[316] Had he obeyed Him, it would have been given back to him in a full, goodly measure, pressed down, shaken together and running over. For what measure is used shall be measured back again.[317] Jesus sadly watched him leave. "How difficult it is for the rich to enter the kingdom of God! It is easier for a camel to go through a needle's eye, than for a rich man to enter into the kingdom of God."

The disciples, thinking that wealth was a sign of God's blessing, were astounded. "Who, then can be saved?"

"The things which are impossible with men are possible with God."

Peter looked at the other disciples and back at Jesus. "We have left our homes, families and businesses to follow You!"

"Be assured that when I, the Son of Man, sit upon the throne in My glorious kingdom, you, My disciples, will sit on twelve thrones as well. You will be judging the twelve tribes of Israel." Their eyes widened with excitement. They looked at each other and grinned.

Jesus continued, "And those who have left their houses, brothers, parents, children, or property for My sake, will receive a hundred fold in return. And many who are thought to be important now will be unimportant then, and those who are considered to be the unimportant ones now will be seen as the greatest then."[318]

Peter smiled and folded his arms and nodded, feeling secure in the kingdom. Jesus noticed a hint of smugness in his heart and knew He would have to deal with it.

He said goodbye to John Mark and his mother and began to walk away. He pulled the apostles aside and said, "Listen closely. We are headed toward Jerusalem." He looked straight at Peter. "Prepare your hearts now, because it will be a time of great difficulty and danger."

Andrew and Matthew looked at each other. Danger? Peter's hands closed into fists at the thought of danger to his Master.

"All that has been written about the Son of Man through the prophets will soon be fulfilled."

The Twelve moved in closer. Here it comes! The prophecies of His glorious appearance! At last it will come to pass! They grinned and nodded at one another. But John saw a deep anguish in His eyes and unconsciously braced himself for His next words.

"He will be betrayed to the chief priests and teachers of the law, who will hand Him over to the Romans and will be insulted and spit upon. The Son of Man will be flogged and killed, and on the third day He will rise again."[319]

They were dumbfounded. It was as if their minds became mysteriously veiled.[320] All twelve faces fell. Peter's brows knit together. *There's that death-talk again. One minute He builds us up telling us about sitting on thrones and the next He says something like that. Why does He insist on talking like this?* He looked at the others and saw their reaction was the same, especially Judas, whose countenance immediately darkened. Peter became irritable and withdrawn. He kept to himself and said little as they left and headed for Jericho.

* * *

The word got out that the great Teacher from Nazareth was headed their way. People came running out of their homes and shops as He reached the outskirts of their city and began to swarm around Him. The disciples quickly surrounded Jesus to keep Him from getting trampled. As He walked toward the town the crowd grew so large that it seemed a parade was passing by in the streets.

A blind man by the name of Bartimaeus was sitting on the edge of the road. Hearing the noisy excitement, he reached out to the passersby and shouted, "What's happening?" They told him that Jesus of Nazareth was passing by. His heart began to pound. He immediately began yelling at the top of his voice, "Je-sus! Jeeeee-suuus! Son of Daaaa-vid! Have mercy on meeee!"

Peter, still bothered at Jesus' strange words, ran over to Bartimaeus and began to rebuke him. "Be quiet!"

The other disciples, equally upset and edgy about His warnings joined in. "Somebody shut this blind man up!"

They had seen Jesus do countless miracles–including opening many blind eyes–and they tried to shut him up!

But he screamed all the louder, "Son of Daaaaa-viiiid! Have mercy on meeee!" He was pressing in no matter what the cost.

A cry for mercy always stopped Jesus in His tracks. He looked at him and sternly commanded His disciples, "Bring him here to Me!"

Suddenly the same ones who tried to shut him up had a different tone. "Come, friend! The Master wants to see you!"

When they brought him to Jesus He asked him, "What do you want Me to do for you?"

Peter looked at Jesus sideways and thought, *What a question! The man is blind!*

But Jesus knew the power of one asking specifically for his petition and not merely presuming God knows, and that He will automatically comply with the need. He had taught on many occasions, "Ask and keep on asking–seek–and keep on seeking–knock–and keep on knocking–and the door will be opened unto you!"[321]

"Lord! I want to seeeee!"

Jesus spoke into his very being, "Receive your sight! Your faith and trust in God has healed you!"

Instantly his eyes were opened. "I can seeeee!" He began leaping and twirling and praising God. "I can seeeee!" The people burst out in applause and began to jump and shout praises to God. Jesus laughed and rejoiced with him. Bartimaeus was ecstatic. He ran to Jesus and grabbed Him and hugged Him and then took off dancing and running and crying, "I can really seeeee!!"[322]

Tears rushed into Peter's eyes, ashamed that he had been annoyed with his Master. He shook his head, and thought, *Three times I've shot off my mouth today. Once with that young boy–again bragging that I had left all to follow Him–and now with this precious blind man. I wonder if I'll ever be able to control my tongue.* He watched the happy sight and then looked at his Master Who was joyfully praising His Father. Peter wondered if he would ever get used to such extraordinary occurrences as this. He and the other disciples laughed at the jubilant sight and threw their hands in the air and shouted, "Hallelujah!"

Bartimaeus went skipping like a child down the street and the townspeople followed him, rejoicing and praising God for His goodness. The crowd dispersed and Jesus and the disciples began to move once again toward Jerusalem. Andrew looked at John and Peter and after a deep breath asked, "Well, are you ready for the difficulties that await us in Jerusalem?"

Peter looked at him confidently,
folded his arms across his chest,
jutted out his jaw and said,
"Let them come."

But when Herod heard thereof, he said, it is John, whom I beheaded: for he is risen from the dead.

Mark 6:16

Everyone in the palace could hear his haunted cries–those horrible sounds of anguish in the dark of night, echoing up and down the marble corridors and into the bedchambers throughout the palace, where others spent sleepless nights listening to the cries of his tormented soul.

CHAPTER TWENTY-EIGHT

Screams In The Night

CHUZA FOLDED HIS THICK arms and sighed heavily as he looked out the lofty palace window. A light rain was falling and tiny sparrows flitted about in the air. With his head cocked slightly to one side, he studied them. *How happy and carefree they are,* he mused. He even found himself envying them. They did not have the heavy responsibilities of man, but seemed to merely enjoy life, building their nests, singing their twittering little songs, and flying about. A rare smile formed on his lips. *Wouldn't it be wonderful to fly?* He breathed in the fresh spring air and watched the raindrops gently watering the earth. His mind was far from his work–work that he was quickly learning to despise. He was Herod's household manager.

His thoughts turned to his wife, Joanna. She had come to believe in the Nazarene Preacher Who was causing a significant stir throughout all of Israel. He had remarkably touched her somehow. Even Chuza could see the obvious peace and joy in her life where there had been only pain and anguish; not to mention the incredible healing of the chronic, debilitating pain in her back and legs that had nearly crippled her for years. But more than that, she told him, He had healed her soul. Chuza didn't understand such things. One thing he did understand was the danger she was in.

Chuza's bushy brows were fixed in a perpetual expression of worry. He had mixed emotions about the Nazarene Teacher. Because of Him, his lovely, petite wife was walking without pain and was able to get up and down out of bed without help. He smiled at the thought of her–her warmth, her playful wit. She loved to call him "her jug", for certainly he was shaped so. He loved her deeply and was glad to see the wonderful, newfound peace in her beautiful brown eyes, but at what cost?

He was afraid for her. Not because of the Nazarene Himself. He seemed harmless enough, but for several weeks he feared for her safety. This Jesus was drawing such enormous crowds and causing such turmoil that Chuza had feared her getting trampled in the throng.[323] He had begged her over and over to stay away from Him and the strange friends she had made within His company, but she would weep and beg and he had to let her go. How could he not? He had healed her! But now he feared for her life. Not because of the Nazarene. Not even because of the crowds. But because of his employer, Herod Antipas.

He walked away from the window and sat down at his desk, slumped forward and put his head in his hands. He was exhausted. For weeks sleep had been an impossibility. Tired in body and mind, he leaned back in his chair and closed his eyes.

Chuza no longer enjoyed the status of his position. The glamour and excitement of working for Herod had lost its luster. The Tetrarch had changed. He had always been harsh and often cruel, but ever since he had John the Baptizer beheaded he seemed to be getting worse. He seemed to be–possessed. This was especially evident in the night.

Everyone in the palace could hear his haunted cries–those horrible sounds of anguish in the dark of night, echoing up and down the marble corridors and into the bedchambers throughout the palace, where others spent sleepless nights listening to the cries of his tormented soul.

Just thinking about it sent a shudder surging through Chuza's broad frame. He was always amazed at how well his wife slept. She seemed to sleep in perfect peace.[324] But Chuza dreaded the nights in the palace. There seemed to be some sort of–evil in the atmosphere.

He was right. Fear was having a wonderful time tormenting the Tetrarch. He had dispatched several of his most effective spirits to harass him throughout the day, but he relished coming himself to the royal bedchamber in the black of night to torment his wretched mind.

The evil demons flew about his head like swarms of bats, whispering in his ears day and night, "This Man Jesus is John the Baptist raised from the dead.[325] He's come back to haunt you."

Herod bolted upright in his bed and screamed, "Stop it! Stop!"

Another spirit of fear hissed, "He was a prophet of God and you killed him!" Herod cried out in anguish, thrashing about in the bed and burying his head in his pillow. Throughout the night all he could see in his mind was the ghastly sight of John's head on that silver charger.

Tired of his noisy nightmares, Herodias had long since taken another bedchamber at the other end of the palace where she couldn't hear the loathsome cries. Why should she have to endure sleepless nights? After all, she had no trouble sleeping. Her conscience did not bother her in the least. Not even for the shameful way she used her young daughter to bring about the slaying of a prophet of God.[326]

Murder, too, loved to join Fear and his spirits in the evil nightly revelry at the palace. He had been in on beguiling Herod to have John the Baptizer beheaded, and now he mocked and tormented him for it. Now he hovered over him like a cold, evil shadow and whispered, "You'd better get rid of Him, or He'll get rid of you."

The spirits of fear continued their torture. "You've seen his miracles!" they hissed, "He has powers–powers–powers." Herod's screams were music to the demons' ears. They congratulated one another on a job well done.

The torment continued until a few hours before dawn, then Murder spoke to Fear, "Let me take over now. He's ready to do anything we tell him. But we must let him rest for a few hours so that he can think clearly enough to make his plans."

The spirits left Herod in a cold sweat, while Murder sat quietly at his side, silently stroking his head with his talons and whispering words that echoed throughout the corridors of his mind, "You must kill Him–kill Him–kill Him."[327]

The next day, Chuza sent Joanna and her handmaiden Susanna[328] to their summer home for a few days until he could get a better feel for what Herod was going to do. She left him reluctantly, but was glad to leave the palace. She hated the way Herod leered at her when Chuza wasn't looking.

After she was safely gone, Chuza quickly gathered up some papers and took them in for Herod to sign. When he approached the ornate doors of the royal chamber, he found them open. The guards ignored him as he entered.

The Roman influence in the décor of the spacious apartment was obvious. Gleaming white marble figures rested on shoulder-high columns. The gold patterns that had been artfully inlaid in the walls glistened in the sunrays that slanted through the large arched windows. Tapestries draped sumptuously over the exquisitely handcrafted furnishings. Herod was pacing up and down impatiently as though waiting for someone. He was dressed in his usual finery, yet looked disheveled. When he saw Chuza he frowned, "Oh, it's you. What do you want?"

Chuza quietly walked over and handed the papers to him and then backed away and waited for him to sign them. He studied Herod's face. It was drawn and unshaven. His eyes were wild and red. He looked as though he had aged ten years in just the last few days. He barely looked at the papers, signed them, thrust them back at him, and then ordered Chuza to leave.

Just then one of his highest ranked centurions entered. Herod yelled past him, "And make sure we're not disturbed!"

Chuza left quickly and pulled the massive doors closed, leaving one open just slightly. He sat at a nearby table and pretended to go over the papers. The guards paid no attention to him. He had done it countless times. He could overhear the voices inside. Herod began ranting about something. He could only get part of it, but he could tell that he was plotting all sorts of maniacal things. Then he overheard him say that he was going to kill the Nazarene! Even the guards looked at one another stunned.

Chuza stiffened, *This has gone far enough.*

I must warn Joanna
to stay away
from the Nazarene!

Lay not up for yourselves treasures upon earth . . . But lay up for yourselves treasures in heaven . . . For where your treasure is, there will your heart be also.

Matthew 6:19-21

"What if He's right? I have thought of little else since He spoke those words to me. And yet I find that my heart fails me at the thought of losing all that I have . . ." His voice trailed off.

CHAPTER TWENTY-NINE

"The Choice"

THE YOUNG RULER SAT silently in his usual place in the great chamber where the Sanhedrin met. The chief Pharisee noticed that he had been withdrawn lately and that his countenance was fallen. He approached him and asked him to remain after the meeting, that he would like to speak with him.

The council was adjourned and the older Pharisees stood around and talked for awhile, reviewing the business they had discussed in the meeting, and then the room slowly emptied. The religious leader in his long robes watched as the young man walked over to him. His glum appearance seemed even more pronounced. The older Pharisee motioned for him to sit beside him on a marble bench.

"What is troubling you? You seem distracted. And you certainly have not been engaging in your usual spirited discussions at our meetings."

"Nothing . . . I . . ."

"Come, come, now," he pressed, "I've known you since you were but a lad. You can talk to me."

The young man took a deep breath. "Sir, I went to see the Nazarene."

The old Pharisee gasped, "You what?"

"I went to see Him. In fact I have heard Him teach many times and secretly longed to speak with Him . . . to ask questions. His words . . . no Man speaks like this Man. I could listen to Him for hours! And His miracles!"

The robed leader's eyes narrowed. "I must say, I am surprised at you."

"Yes, I know you and the others think He is a rebel, but I . . . I don't."

"Oh you don't, do you?" He stood, folded his arms defensively and stared down at him. "And what did He say to you?"

"I asked Him what I must do to enter the kingdom of God."

The Pharisee was aghast. "Why on earth did you ask Him that? Do you not know the answer to that question already? Have you not been taught well?"

"I have been taught many things. But when I hear Him speak, I feel I know . . . so little."

"Really!" He was incensed. "So! Have you become one of His followers, too?"

The young man looked away. "Perhaps I would have," he gulped hard. "Except . . ."

His eyebrows went up. "Except?"

"He told me I must sell everything I have and give the money to the poor, and then come and follow Him."

The old Pharisee laughed so loud it echoed through the chamber. "Sell all that you have? For what possible reason?"

He slowly stood and shrugged, his head down. "I don't know. I suppose He thought I was entangled by my riches."

"Or perhaps He would like for you to sell all you have and give the money to *Him*!"

"That's not what He said . . ." He began walking toward the door.

"Surely that is what He meant! Why else?"

The young man jerked around angrily. "How should I know? I have given large sums of money to the Temple treasury, I've done all the Law requires, I'm not an adulterer, I've honored my parents, I . . ." He threw his hands in the air. "Why does He make it so hard to enter the kingdom of God?"

"That's what He told you?" he exploded. "That you must sell all that you have to enter the kingdom of God? Now I *know* He's a heretic!"

"I'm not so sure . . ."

"What?" he gasped, his veins protruding.

"Perhaps my riches *are* a hindrance."[329]

"How can you say that? You have lived an honorable life! You have kept all the commandments! You have . . ."

"He told a parable of a rich, unpitying, selfish man named Dives and a poor, wretched beggar named Lazarus, who received no help from him who had it to give. Once fixed in their places of eternity after death; the poor man was in a place of rest and bliss, the rich man in the tormenting fires of hell."

The Pharisee sputtered, "The beggar in heaven and the rich man in Hell . . . ?"

"Let me finish. A great gulf was fixed between the two, which no man could breach. Their relationships reversed, the rich man cried out to the poor man for help. But it was too late. The Teacher explained that this life is the time and place to make the choice for eternity.[330] Self-gratification or mercy. He made it crystal clear. The ultimate choice is ours."

"How can you believe such drivel?"

"What if He's right? I have thought of little else since He spoke those words to me. And yet I find that my heart fails me at the thought of losing . . . all that I have . . ." His voice trailed off.

"There! You see? He has brought only torment to your mind! How can that be from God?"

"Perhaps it is my conscience that torments me. Perhaps He's right."

"I've heard enough!" The old Pharisee began to pace. "Can't you see that He merely enjoys tormenting the religious leaders in any way He can? "He stopped and glared at him. "He was invited to dine at the home of one of our members of the Sanhedrin and He didn't even perform the ritual of ceremonial washing! It was a direct affront to us all! Especially the one in whose home He was a guest! And when we confronted Him with it, He railed against us and said that we were careful to clean the outside of the cup and dish but that inside we were filthy, full of greed and wickedness!"

The young man lifted is head, "Greed?"

His eyes were blazing. "Yes! He said to give to the poor what we so greedily possess and then we would be clean!"

"Almost the same words He spoke to me . . ."

"He accused us of taking the most honored seats and enjoying our status . . ."

"But his words are full of authority."

"Authority?" he exploded. "What authority? Does He have the authority to call us fools and accuse us of extortion and even keeping people out of the kingdom?[331] Do we not do good works and give to the poor?"

The young man lowered his eyes. "Perhaps we should not do it with such fanfare. We blow trumpets in the synagogues and streets to call attention to our works of charity. I heard Him say that in doing so, we should not expect to receive a reward from heaven. That we have our reward already–the accolades of men."

The religious leader's face reddened. He had done what he just described countless times. He squinted at him, "And what else did He tell you?"

"He said that we should not pray long prayers in the doors of the synagogues and on the street corners to be seen of men."[332]

"We pray long prayers because we have much to pray about! Our nation is under the bondage of Roman heathens! Did He ever think of *that*?"

The young ruler smiled slightly, "Some say we pray long prayers to keep from being bothered by those who are hurting and in need. Who would disturb a priest while he is praying?"

"That's completely absurd!"

"Is it?"

The religious leader was speechless. He knew he was guilty of that very thing. He cleared his throat nervously. "And just when does this fraud pray? I've *never* seen Him pray!"

A wistful look came across his face. He answered softly, "Jesus prays at night–sometimes all night–so that He is accessible to everyone in the day."[333]

The old priest fell silent. He stood glaring at him.

The young man sighed and turned to leave. "I suppose each of us must search his own heart about such things. All I know is I am deeply unsettled in my heart and I must get alone and sort things out."

The old Pharisee came after him and shook his finger in his face. "I'm warning you! You are dangerously close to falling under this imposter's spell. And if you do, you will be immediately cast out of the Sanhedrin!"

The young ruler looked at him squarely. "Perhaps. But I'd rather be cast out of the Sanhedrin than the kingdom of God. Goodnight, Sir!" He turned again and headed out the door.

The old man yelled after him, "Don't put too much effort in your devotion to the words of that fraud. He won't be around much longer!"

The young ruler stopped in his tracks and turned to face him. "What do you mean by that?"

The synagogue ruler's eyes blazed. "Word has it that Herod is seeking to kill Him."

The young man gasped, "What? I–I must warn Him!"

"Go ahead. But it will do little good. Herod has a very large army at his disposal."

"You want Him dead, don't you?"

"I wouldn't lose any sleep over it."

"You–you're a religious leader and you wish a man dead–simply because you don't agree with Him?"

The old man just stared at him.

"I suppose by your silence the answer is 'yes'!" He shook his head. "Don't look for me on the Sabbath. I'm sure I can find another place that will benefit from my riches. Perhaps I'll even do what the Teacher said and sell all I have and give the money away."

The priest gulped and sputtered, "Wait, now–now don't be a fool!"

"A fool, Sir?" He paused and smiled peacefully. "I think I'm beginning to see that the most foolish thing I could do would be to *not* do what He said."[334] With that, he walked away with a noticeable spring in his step.

The old Pharisee watched him walk away. He turned slowly and stepped back into the meeting hall and sat down on the cold marble bench. His heart was pounding with rage. *That rogue has caused us to lose one of our wealthiest benefactors. If Herod doesn't get Him, perhaps there's another way.*

He sat there alone in the massive room
and vowed he would do
whatever it took
to silence this One Who dared
to offend God's elect.

* * *

Many Pharisees had come to believe in Jesus, but they remained covert for fear of their peers and of losing their position. The chief priest, Caiaphas, had put out the word that if anyone of their order attempted to see Jesus, they were to be reported. The believing Pharisees kept their convictions to themselves. All but two. Nicodemus and Joseph of Arimathea.[335] They met together regularly and prayed for their Pharisee brothers. The wealthy young ruler heard about them. He longed to meet with them, but did not want to put them in danger. That night he silently followed Joseph to Nicodemus' spacious home. Just as he reached the gate to the courtyard, the young man whispered, "Brother Joseph!"

Joseph's hearing was not what it used to be, so he did not hear.

"Psssstt, Brother Joseph!"

The old Pharisee turned in the direction of the sound and saw the young ruler waving at him in the shadows.

"What . . . ?"

"Don't be afraid," he whispered loudly, "I must talk with you, Sir."

"How did you know I would be here tonight?"

"I–uh–followed you, Sir."

"You followed me?" Joseph's eyes widened, a hint of fear in them. He quickly looked around to see if he had led others to spy on him.

"I'm alone," the young man assured him.

"What can I do for you?" he said, still eyeing him with suspicion.

"Someone must go to Jesus and warn Him that Herod seeks to kill Him!"

"Herod!" He turned and motioned to him. "Come!" Joseph quickly led him through the gate. They found the door slightly ajar. Nicodemus had been watching and listening. He let them in quickly and closed the door.

"What is it? Is something wrong?"

Joseph nodded at the young man to tell Nicodemus what he knew.

"I just got word that Herod is plotting to kill Jesus!"

Nicodemus' eyes narrowed. "How do you know this? And why are you telling us?"

"Because I know that you are His followers."

Joseph and Nicodemus looked at one another. "Yes, it is true. How do you know about Herod?"

"I got it from a very good source. One who despises the Teacher and knows those who would like very much to see Him eliminated."

"Why did you not go to our Master yourself?"

The young man dropped his head. "I–He–He probably would not have listened to me."

"Are you one of His?" Nicodemus asked gently.

He avoided their eyes. "I must go. Won't you please give Him the message?"

"We will. But won't you come with us?"

"No–I–have some things that I must first take care of. Then I hope to see Him again."

They didn't question him. The two old gentlemen prayed for him and watched him go out into the night.

The next morning, at the break of dawn Joseph and Nicodemus met and headed toward the area where they last heard Jesus had been. They did not seek the cover of night but boldly in the light of day made their journey to their Master. The two could not walk as briskly as they would like, but at last they entered the village where Jesus was teaching. Just as they got to the outer edge of the crowd, they heard the sound of horses' hooves rapidly approaching. The two old Pharisees quickened their pace. "It's Herod's centurions coming for Jesus!" They elbowed their way through the crowd and ran up to Him, "Master, leave this place quickly! Herod seeks to kill you!"

The disciples moved closer to Jesus just as Chuza rode up on a spirited gray stallion and quickly dismounted. They were shocked to see that it was Herod's household steward approaching and unarmed.

He looked past the burly disciples, "Sir! May I speak with You?"

Jesus ordered His men to let him pass. They eyed him carefully and let him by. Jesus motioned for him to come. "Of course, what is it?"

"I've come to warn you that Herod is plotting your death!"

The Prince of Peace was completely serene. "You go and tell that sly fox that I will continue to drive out demons and heal people today, tomorrow and on the third day. And then My time will come. I will continue on to Jerusalem. It wouldn't do for a prophet to die outside of Jerusalem!"[336]

Nicodemus frowned in dismay. *Die? What does He mean by that?* He looked at Peter who winced at His death-words once again.

Jesus looked at Chuza with a warm gaze, "But you came to warn Me first even before your wife. I'm certain you have put yourself in jeopardy coming here to tell Me this."

John whispered to Andrew. "Sounds like he has the makings of a good disciple. He put the Master before himself and his own family."[337]

Andrew nodded enthusiastically.

Something stirred inside Chuza. An awakening began in his spirit that he was not yet fully aware of. At that moment, two enormous angels were dispatched and assigned to watch over him.[338] They settled down beside him and stood at attention in the presence of the Lamb.

Jesus put His hand on Chuza's shoulder and smiled, "Thank you for coming to Me. One day we shall sup together."[339]

Chuza blinked in bewilderment, not understanding what He meant.

The angels understood

and smiled.

And when He had thus spoken, he cried with a loud voice, Lazarus, come forth . . . And he that was dead came forth, bound hand and foot with grave clothes.

John 11:43,44

Death, who had been gloating over his victory screamed in pain as, once again, the Seed smashed him with a counter-blow, violently flinging him away from his victim.

CHAPTER THIRTY

The Awakening

THE WEARY MESSENGER RETURNED to Bethany. Mary and Martha ran up to meet him. "Did you see Jesus? Did you tell Him about our brother?"

"Yes, I gave Him the message."

"So? Is He coming?" Martha said as she looked past him toward the road, expecting to see Him and His disciples come around the bend any moment.

"He–He didn't move."

Martha's heart sank. "What do you mean?"

"He just told His men that Lazarus' sickness was not unto death. He said something else, but I didn't understand it. Something about receiving glory–or something."

Mary and Martha blinked in stunned bewilderment.

"What does He mean?" Martha asked. The messenger shrugged his shoulders and walked away.

"Oh, He'll be along," Mary said. "Go back home. I'll watch for Him and will let you know when He arrives."

Martha nodded in agreement and hurried off to the house to prepare food in case He and the disciples had not eaten. Lunchtime came and went. No Jesus.

Mary sat on a large rock and continued to watch the road. The day wore on. She rubbed her temples with her fingers. She was getting a headache from the bright afternoon sun. Where could He be?

Martha lovingly tended to her brother. She sat beside his bed and prayed silently, but Lazarus kept getting worse. Over and over in her mind, she thought of the words the messenger related to her that Jesus had said: "This sickness will not end in death." But it was obvious he was dying and hope was dwindling like oil in a lamp. Her heart could no longer feed on the second-hand words of the messenger. She needed the presence of her Friend Jesus. Here! Now!

Mary scanned the horizon the next day, certain that He would come. She watched and waited, waited and watched. The only ones she saw on the road were the townspeople who stared at her pitiably as they passed. Some made snide remarks behind cupped hands, while others shook their heads sympathetically and walked on. The shadows crept across the road. Still no Jesus.

The message that the sickness would not end in death was a hope deferred[340] and their hearts were sick. Lazarus' illness was indeed giving way to death. Was Jesus mistaken? They didn't want to believe that. Perhaps the messenger had heard Him wrong.

Martha, kneeling next to Lazarus and clutching his fevered hand, sent for Mary to come. She knew the end was near. When the message was quietly whispered to her, Mary sadly walked away from the place where she had waited and watched, shattered because their Friend had not come.

The sisters were completely devastated when Lazarus died. They spoke not a word as they washed his body, anointed it, and made funeral arrangements. None spoke it, but they felt that surely Jesus would make the funeral! They put Lazarus in the tomb and rolled the stone in place. Still no Jesus. Not even a message of sympathy.

Many prominent Jews had come the short distance from Jerusalem to attend the funeral. They were surprised to see that Jesus was not there. They whispered among themselves on the fringes of the weeping crowd. "I wonder why their good Friend didn't come to their aid."

The funeral over, the sisters quietly went home to grieve. No one was watching the road. No food was being prepared. They cried for four days. It was bad enough that their dear brother was gone. But their hearts carried the extra burden of feeling let down and forsaken. Had they done something to offend Him? Their minds went back to the last time they were together.

Mary thought, *Was I presumptuous to sit so near the Rabbi as He taught? After all, women aren't supposed to–*

Martha worried, *I'll bet He's upset with me because I interrupted His teaching to insist Mary help me in the kitchen.*[341]

Unconsciously, they felt that Jesus had forsaken them. That suspicion of God's goodness that is engrained in the fallen nature was at work. It screamed at them from the annals of the Garden of Eden– God's not good. You can't really trust Him to be there for you.

The disciples, too, had questions, knowing that His good friend Lazarus was dying. These people were some of His best friends.

Jesus had gotten the message about Lazarus, all right, but He received another message from Heaven.

"Stay where You are, Son."

Jesus only did what He saw the Father doing.[342]

He saw the Father trusting Mary and Martha with one of His silences. Those quiet, invisible stepping stones that would take them higher. Higher with Him.

Jesus finally arrived. When He came toward the area where Lazarus was buried, He could hear the woeful sounds of the mourners. Gloom hung in the air like a shroud. Martha had come to the tomb to weep. Some of the mourners hovered over her wailing and beating their breasts. One of them looked up and saw Jesus, and said sarcastically, "Well, look Who's here."

Another sneered, "It's a little late, isn't it?"

Martha ignored their remarks and ran to meet Him. "Lord!" He put His hands out and grasped hers. Her face was swollen from crying.

"Lord," she sobbed, "If You had been here, Lazarus would not have died." Jesus looked at her tenderly. Just seeing the love and peace in His face renewed her faith. "But even now I know that God will give You whatever You ask."

"Your brother will rise again."

"Yes, Lord, I know that he will rise again in the resurrection at the last day."

He spoke loudly enough so that all could hear. "I am the Resurrection and the Life. Those who believe in Me, even though they die, they will live again. They are given eternal Life because of their faith in Me and will never see permanent death." His voice softened. "Do you believe this, Martha?"

"Yes, Lord, I have always believed You are the Messiah, the Son of the Living God, Whom the Father has sent into the world."

Peter smiled, remembering when he first got that revelation.[343]

Jesus smiled down at her and nodded. She wiped away a tear and said, "I must tell Mary You are here."

She quickly went to where Mary was, called her aside from the mourners and said, "Mary, the Teacher is here."

Mary jumped up from her chair and ran out the door. The mourners were astonished at her quick departure and assumed she went to weep at her brother's tomb. They followed after her.

When she saw Jesus, she ran and fell at His feet. Her favorite place.[344] "Lord! If You had been here, my brother would not have died."

When Jesus saw her tear-stained face and the way the mourners kept wailing around her, He was moved with indignation and deeply troubled. Did they not yet understand that physical death does not extinguish spiritual Life?

"Where have you placed him?"

Mary stood up, wiped her tears and said, "Come, I'll show You."

As Jesus walked with Mary and Martha toward the gravesite, He wept. He mourned with those who mourned.[345]

Some of the people nearby said, "Look, He's weeping. How fond He was of Lazarus!"

Others frowned, "If this Man can heal a blind man, why could He not have kept His good friend from dying?"

Jesus heard them and was deeply troubled at the hardness of their hearts.

They came to the cave with a large stone over its entrance. Jesus looked at the stone; knowing that in just a few days, another stone would be rolled away, but it would be at the hands of angels. He hoped that what they were about to see would remove the stone from the hearts of those present.

"Roll the stone away."

"Lord, by now the smell will be awful. He's been dead four days," Martha said.

Time was *their* enemy. Not His. "Did I not tell you that you will see God's glory if you believe?"

By now a huge crowd had gathered. Jesus gestured to them to roll the stone away. Several men slowly walked toward the large stone. None dared speak. They gave each other side-glances of a mixture of skepticism and wonder. They slowly rolled the massive stone aside, then quickly moved away from the open cave. They gasped at the stench and threw their hands and shawls over their noses. They watched Jesus as He moved toward the grave opening. He stopped and looked up to heaven.

Mary and Martha grabbed each other's hands and held tightly. Their hearts were racing.

The wailing and chanting ceased. The silent mourners watched in amazement and whispered, "What is He doing?"

Jesus prayed aloud so that all could hear Him, "Father, I thank You that You always hear Me. I am saying these things out loud for the benefit of all those who are here so they may believe that You have sent Me."

As always, Jesus was providing for those present another glimpse of the goodness of His Father, further proof of His Messiahship and the oneness with His Father, that some might believe.

Everyone stood in awed silence. Jesus lifted His hand and shouted with a loud voice,

"Lazarus! Come!"

His command was so powerful that had He not called him by name, all that were buried in the surrounding tombs would have come forth.

The mourners stood with their eyes glued to the dark entrance of the cave. Mary and Martha, their lips pursed, and holding their breath, squeezed each other's hands so tightly they were cutting off their circulation.

His Word sent a powerful energy into that dark tomb. Suddenly, life sprang into Lazarus' body and new blood began to circulate and tingle through his veins. His organs began to function, and breath came into his lungs. His spirit returned to his body at the command of the Giver of Life! Consciousness awakened in him, and perfect health rushed through his body like a bubbling spring.

Two large, shining angels lifted him up into a sitting position, stepped back and applauded their Lord's marvelous work. They began shouting praises to their King. All of heaven rejoiced at the sight of it.

Lazarus, sitting up, swung his legs to the side of the wide ledge where he had been laying, and then stood. Through the thin, gauze-like cloth about his face, he could see a blurry but vivid light. He moved slowly in the direction of the bright portal and toward the gift of new and extended life! Joy beat heartily in his strong, healthy heart, and he longed to kick his heels and dance with all his might before the Lord. But he was only able to walk with small, confined steps in the grave clothes that bound him–back into the world from which he had departed, now very much alive.

Death, who had been gloating over his victory screamed in pain as, once again, the Seed smashed him with a counterblow, violently flinging him away from his victim. Just as David of old delivered the lamb out of the mouth of the lion,[346] Jesus, the Good Shepherd delivered Lazarus out of the jaws of Death and the mouth of the grave.

As Lazarus approached the entrance of the tomb–now an exit for him–the multitude gasped when they saw movement in the darkness of the cave. Were their eyes playing tricks on them? Their minds would not register what they were seeing–the eerie yet marvelous sight of a dead man walking. But he was not dead. He was alive!

Some of the mourners screamed, terrified at the ghostly sight. Mary and Martha stood there speechless, completely astounded. Their minds could not grasp what was happening. It was frighteningly wonderful!

Lazarus stepped out into the light of day, out of darkness, out of death, out of that place of the unknown, and into the blazing light of the sun.

The mouths of the people unhinged. They were thunderstruck. Someone finally was able to speak. "God be praised!" The rest of the crowd picked up the words and cried out praises to God. "The Lord be praised! Hallelujah!"

Jesus shouted, "Remove the grave clothes and let him go!"

No one moved. Not only could they not yet engage their minds enough to get their feet to obey, they were still awestruck at the sight and too frightened to touch him. When they were able to think, they were unsettled about touching a dead man, knowing they would be considered unclean. Yet, he was not dead! Finally, someone approached him carefully and began to remove the strips of cloth that wound around him. Others quickly joined in and began unwinding the shroud. Upon removing the cloth from his face, there emerged a pink-cheeked, stunned, grinning man who never looked better in his life!

Mary and Martha ran to him and threw their arms around him and clung to him, weeping for joy at the return of their dear brother. Many of the people who witnessed the incredible miracle believed in Jesus.

The angels in heaven laughed and praised God heartily and rejoiced with their dazzling angel-brothers who were standing on each side of Lazarus. "Glory to God!" they shouted. "Another battle won!"

Death screeched loudly as he was cast violently away, "Noooooooo!!! Not again!!" Trembling, he headed for his master's lair. Knowing he was bent on killing the Seed, he wondered how he was going to be able to hold *Him* in the grave.

The news of the great miracle spread like wildfire across Israel. It reached the ears of the Sanhedrin, which upon hearing it, instead of conceding to the repeated evidence that this Man must indeed be God-sent, it merely sealed His fate and made them even more determined to kill Him. Instead of realizing that only God can give back life, they were so blinded by hatred and jealousy that all they could think of

was how they could
put the Giver of Life
to death.[347]

And the multitudes that went before, and that followed, cried, saying, Hosanna to the son of David: Blessed is He that cometh in the name of the Lord; Hosanna in the highest.

Matthew 21:9

Satan stood high on the pinnacle of the Temple, watching the spectacle, spewing blasphemies, his wings fluttering in the wind like two enormous kites. "Enjoy Your little parade, Jesus," he muttered under his breath. "Your worshipers will soon be a murderous mob. I'll see to that!"

CHAPTER THIRTY-ONE

Palms And Purging

A STEADY STREAM OF pilgrims flowed into Jerusalem from all over Israel and beyond. The city was a humming beehive of activity. For weeks preparation had been made. Women scrubbed, cleaned and dusted and made room in their homes for old friends, while others opened their houses to welcome strangers. The Passover Feast was on everyone's mind. It was the talk of the street and the synagogues. The festive mood permeated the entire city.

Banners were displayed, and the sacrificial animals were herded through the gates of the Temple. Grand rituals took place through the week. But the Passover was not the only thing on the lips of the locals. The reports and rumors of the Prophet from Nazareth met every ear of the incoming flux of festive visitors as well.

"Will He be here?" they asked excitedly. "Will we get to see Him?"

"If He comes, perhaps He will do a miracle!"

The happy chatter added to the exhilarating atmosphere. Suddenly, a wave of excitement arose outside the city walls. Singing and cries of "Hosanna!" could be heard at a distance. The crowds poured through the gates to see what the commotion was all about. They strained their eyes to see.

"It's Him! It's Him!" someone cried. "It's the Prophet from Nazareth!"

He was still a long way off, yet the fervor of praise seemed to spread through the crowd like wildfire. Those who had been touched by His healing hand especially exalted Him with loud cries, sending a wave of worship through the throng. Soon the whole city was joining in.

"Hosanna! Hosanna in the highest!"

The disciples encircled Him. The little colt on which He rode seemed oblivious to the weight of his Blessed Burden. Palm branches waved and were cast before Him, creating a cool green carpet to welcome His entry.

"Hosanna! Hosanna!"

Satan stood high on the pinnacle of the Temple, watching the spectacle, spewing blasphemies, his wings fluttering in the wind like two enormous kites. "Enjoy Your little parade, Jesus," he muttered under his breath. "Your worshipers will soon be a murderous mob. I'll see to that!"

Some of the Pharisees came running toward the crowd, filled with rage. "See how the whole world has gone after Him!" They elbowed their way through the palm waving throng, determined to get His attention. "We'll put a stop to this," they muttered as they approached Him. Finally they got within earshot and screamed, "Master! Rebuke Your disciples!"

Jesus looked at them astounded. Didn't they know that prophecy was being fulfilled at this very moment–right before their eyes? Were they so blind that they could not remember the scriptures they had memorized since childhood?

"Rejoice greatly, my people! Shout aloud, O Daughter of Zion! Your King, the Righteous One comes to you. See? He is gentle and rides upon a donkey." [348]

He turned to them and shouted, "If these were to be silenced, the very stones on the ground would begin to cry out!" They stood there speechless as the crowd moved around them, continuing their joyful worship.

When the little donkey made the last turn in the rocky road, the whole panorama of the city came into view and spread out before Him like a great tapestry. He dismounted and stood gazing at Jerusalem. His disciples were astonished at the sudden change in His countenance. Peter and John looked at each other bewildered as Jesus cried out, His arms outstretched,

"Oh Jerusalem, Jerusalem! You who murder the prophets and stone those who are sent to you! How often would I have gathered your children together as a mother hen gathers her brood under her wings, but you refused!"

The band of Pharisees, who had been listening, came closer and glared at Him with disgust.

Jesus continued to cry out, "Behold! Your house is forsaken and desolate, abandoned and left destitute of God's help! For I declare to you, you will not see Me again until you say, Blessed is He Who comes in the name of the Lord!"

Upon hearing His lament over Jerusalem, one of the Pharisees who had caught up with Him frowned, "Why do You cry out in such a manner? We have not killed any prophets. And if we had lived in the days of our forefathers, we would not have joined in the shedding of their blood!"

Jesus turned quickly. "So you testify against yourselves that you are the descendants of those who murdered the prophets. Fill up, then, the measure of sin of your forefathers! Finish what they started! You snakes! You sons of vipers! You playactors! You've blocked the entrance of the kingdom of God for men and you think you'll be going in, but you won't! You travel all over the country to recruit one man into your order, and make him twice the deluded sons of hell that you are! You make great arguments about making vows, swearing by all sorts of things, and you can't even keep your vows to God! You're blind! You choke on a gnat and swallow a camel!"

His voice was hoarse with emotion. "Woe to you!" He roared.

"You're like white gravestones, but inside you're full of dead men's bones. You look so pious and scrubbed, but within you're full of hypocrisy and iniquity! How will you escape being condemned to hell?"[349]

The disciples closed in around them as Jesus continued to censure and warn the Pharisees. Peter's huge fists were drawn up tight just in case a fight broke out.

The Pharisees were incensed. They despised Him. Jesus, the Holy Warrior, the Seed of the woman, was in intense warfare with the seed of the devil.

He had come–for them–and they rejected Him.[350]

Jesus broke through the circle and headed down the rocky ledge toward Jerusalem. The Pharisees followed, pressing hard against Him and continuing to try to provoke Him. He headed for the Temple gates.

Upon entering the arched terrace courts, He could see it had been turned into a marketplace, a place of commerce and bargaining! His cheeks flushed in holy wrath upon seeing the greedy moneychangers profaning the hallowed halls of His Father's House.

The selling of the sacrificial animals to line the pockets of the sinful, gluttonous high priests, was the worst kind of affront to the Lamb of God. With incredible strength, He overthrew the tables of the moneychangers sending coins jangling and rolling across the marble floor. Doves flapped wildly and fled when their cage doors flew open. He cracked the whip He had quickly made, sending the Temple officials running for cover. His words echoed in the ears of the astounded onlookers and throughout the Temple court.

"–This is a House of prayer!–"

Craack!

"–But you have made it–"

Craack!

"–a den of thieves!"

The moneychangers fled out the door leaving their spilled moneyboxes on the floor. Goats and lambs ran bleating in every direction.

The angels gathered in glorious array around the Temple. They chased out Greed and all his demons as they shrieked and scattered, dipping and tumbling through the sky like inky clouds.

A band of angels settled down around Him with swords drawn. They could see Murder looming over the farthest end of the Temple with his evil spirits batting about excitedly. The angels' golden eyes scanned about, watching and waiting for the Lamb's command. But no command was given. He knew His time was near and that His Father would send more than twelve legions of angels if He asked for them and they would be dispatched immediately.[351] But the Seed would not shrink back from His Mission. Soon darkness would be unleashed like a great rolling wave upon Jerusalem–with the Temple at the center–a place for dark counsel and intrigue.

Never again would He enter there. Jesus' farewell to the Temple left it to its desolate future. He abandoned it to its ruin.[352]

The scribes and chief priests were beside themselves with savage hatred. Murder smiled as he watched them scramble to call their meeting to make their final plans. A grotesque grin crossed his bloody fangs. Drool seeped out of his monstrous mouth at the thought of the approaching atrocity he would administer at the hands of the deceived leaders of the nation of Israel. Deception had done his work well. Everything was falling into place. He and Murder were once again working together as they had done many times. For centuries they had carried out their evil plans, beginning with Adam and Eve's first offspring.[353] They had plenty of notches on their talons to prove it. They had instigated infanticide.[354] Conducted carnage and manipulated massacres.

A crucifixion should be a piece of cake.

* * *

The tormenting cries of the captive souls of men grew louder in Jesus' spirit. The time for His agony was nearing. Soon He would be leaving His dear disciples. Jesus longed for them to understand His heart. Although His words had the air of the extraordinary, His devoted apprentices could not help but be antagonistic against Christ's death message. If they were unable to reconcile His parting, how could they conceive His coming again?

He had answered their questions about Israel's political future with words that took their breath away. He spoke of wars and rumors of wars, about nations rising against nations. Their eyes blinked in bewildered horror as He spoke of earthquakes, famines, plagues of pestilence and a cosmic upheaval in the heavens. He had warned them about tremendous persecutions, family divisions, Jerusalem compassed about with armies, men's hearts failing for fear; even the Temple being overrun with Gentiles and then the Most Holy Place would be desecrated by an abominable anti-christ!

To mark in their minds that these events would take place over a period of time, and would not be fulfilled only in their lifetime, He gave many admonitions to His future corporate Church of internal corruptions through deception, heresies, failure of faith and persecutions from the secular influences and domination.

A dazed gleam of hope sprang into their eyes when He told them that He, the Son of Man, would be coming in a cloud with great power and glory, with a mighty trumpet blast and would be surrounded with angels.[355] His last warning to them had been one of constant watchfulness. He explained that He Himself would go and prepare a place for them,[356] a place so beautiful and wonderful it was beyond all they could ask or even imagine.[357] Exciting as all of that sounded, they knew they would soon have to release Him as a tree must release her leaves in the fall season.

Although His words were mixed with hope and told of a future reunion with Him, they found it difficult to comprehend what He was telling them about the One Who was to come, the Holy Spirit. Their sorrow and fear blurred the glorious message of His Father's grand design. They could not understand that Jesus had spoken of the completion of His mission and the next phase of the Great Plan, the ministry of the Holy Spirit.

In fact, there was much that they did not understand. All twelve disciples had experienced frustration with Jesus' constant suppression of success. They all had their hopes and expectations dashed when He refused to be made king by the throngs.[358] All twelve had expected a nationalist Messiah. Judas wasn't alone in anticipating a place of honor in the new kingdom.[359] He and the others had to constantly deal with the questions of "Why?"

Why didn't He aid John the Baptist, instead of withdrawing Himself?[360]

Why didn't he show a sign from heaven?[361]

And, above all, why did He harp on this thing about dying?

Their hopes, dreams, desires, even demands–not met.

They were disappointed. Their faith was frustrated. One by one all their props had been removed. Disappointment shook the very foundation of their faith.

The only difference between Judas and the rest of the disillusioned disciples was how he handled disappointment. Instead of trust, he chose treason. In place of faith, he chose falsehood. Instead of humility, he chose hatred. The seed of distrust in his fallen nature won out over the seed of faith. Disappointment had opened the door.

Judas became sullen and a strange darkness lurked in his eyes. His murky countenance was evident to all those around him. Hope for his kingdom dream had died like a feeble, sputtering fire that had once been unquenchable as phosphorus. Judas had not gotten his way. Jesus had not responded to his desires and did not meet with his idea of how God should behave; and in doing so, his faith was overthrown. A terrible price to pay for unfulfilled expectations.

Satan had planted an offense in his mind and made him feel betrayed. Such irony.

The Betrayer himself felt he was the betrayed.

Doubt and Unbelief, the twin tormentors, were on assignment to scrutinize the Seed's followers, especially those closest to Him, for a possible candidate to use against Him. They had not failed to notice Judas' hand dip into the moneybag.[362] His impatience with Jesus' obvious disinclination to set up a political rule was a dead give away.

The ever-increasing hardness of heart in Judas caused the dual demons to drool as they smelled the aroma of his sinful flesh. His penchant to greed, selfishness, discontent and ingratitude were all the invitations needed for Satan to come and dine; to "eat the dust" of the clay flesh that he was cursed to feed upon forever.[363]

They had found their foothold with which to infiltrate their foe's very foundation. One of His closest friends.

The twins acted swiftly and reported their findings to Deception, who wasted no time taking advantage of the open door. The demon prince waited for the right moment, and when Judas was alone, the evil predator buried his razor-sharp[364] talons deeply into his brain and whispered incessantly, echoing the words of the Waster:

"You can't trust Him.

He's holding out on you.

You'd better take it from here."

Then entered Satan into Judas surnamed Iscariot, being of the number of the twelve.

Luke 22:3

"Do what you have to do and do it quickly," He whispered to Judas. The betrayer slipped out into the night. The hoards of Hell hovered overhead and escorted the devil-possessed man into eternal darkness."

CHAPTER THIRTY-TWO

Communion

THE GOLDEN RAYS OF the afternoon sun slanted down upon the Holy City teeming with worshipers who had come for the Passover Feast. The festivities of the week were filled with music, worship and camaraderie. The sight of the grand and glorious Temple stirred national and religious fervor in their hearts. Pilgrims from all the nations had made their long journeys to see the ancient city, some for the first time. They chattered happily as they walked about, eyes gleaming with excitement to be in the Holy City, Jerusalem.

Every room in Jerusalem had been reserved for weeks for this occasion, and on the very day of the Feast, Peter and John were shown an upper-level room. Jesus had given them instructions to go into the city, and they would see a man carrying a pitcher of water. They were to follow him into the house he entered and say to the owner of the house, "Our Teacher asks you, 'Where is the guest chamber where I may eat the Passover with My disciples?'" He would show them a large upper room furnished with carpets and couches, and they would make the preparations there.

It all seemed so mysterious to learn of its location in such a peculiar way. They did not know that had Judas been privy to the plan, he would have told the high priest and Jesus would not have been able to have that final meal with them.

The Passover meal was instituted as a memorial to Israel's deliverance from the last plague visited upon Egypt: the death of the first born, and the setting free of God's children from the cruel bondage of Egypt.[365]

And now Jesus and His disciples were preparing to celebrate the Passover Feast. But this time it was different. He was instituting a new kind of Passover Supper, forever to be known as the Sacrament of the New Covenant. Holy Communion. The Holy Eucharist. God's children would once again commemorate the death of the first born. Only now it was the First Born Son, the final Sacrificial Lamb that would set them free from the bondage of Satan once and for all.

The upper chamber was ready. The owner saw to it that the couches were properly draped and Peter and John busied themselves making their final preparations and then lit the lamps.

Jesus and the remaining ten disciples once more descended the Mount of Olives into Jerusalem, now glowing with lamps in each window. Many people gathered on the porches and flat rooftops throughout the city to gaze at the spectacle of the receding sun casting a red and orange blaze against the gleaming Temple, causing it to appear as though it were on fire. Jesus looked at the sight longingly. He knew one day soon the true Temple–that of His beloved Bride–would be ablaze with the indwelling fire of His Holy Spirit.[366]

It was the last unfettered, unhindered view of the city Jesus would have until His resurrection. As they passed the magnificent Temple buildings, the disciples remembered what Jesus had recently told them; that these glorious structures would one day be cast down, not one stone being left upon another, left desolate.[367] A shudder moved through them at the prospect of it. In another's thoughts, a dark and sinister scheme rolled over and over in his mind, goaded by God's archenemy.

The withdrawing sun left behind a colorful, glowing horizon. Long shadows disappeared and the trees and hills became featureless silhouettes. The moon and the twilight stars appeared as though a part of the city's festive adornment.

The gathering together in fellowship with His disciples and the communion of hearts would have been an occasion of deep joy, but Jesus came with a heavy heart to the supper. He had looked forward to the intimacy of the hour and the Blessed Sacrament of Communion He was about to introduce to His embryo church, but a profound sadness was in His eyes.

The disciples sensed the eminent departure of their Lord. They wanted to be near Him, all longing to be at His side. John and the betrayer won out. What a contrast! John, his heart filled with deep oneness and love for the Savior, and Judas, his heart filled with ingratitude, greed and hatred. John, with his head on the Savior's breast, held fast to the moment and silently worshiped his Master with a deep love.

He could hear the heartbeat of God.

Jesus' breathing was interspersed with soundless sighs. There was a deep anguish in His soul. He had lost one of His disciples to the devil. The betrayer's foot was at the very edge of the abyss, sliding into the depths of it. Had he looked down between his feet he might have seen the mouth of hell.

The presence of Judas in the room and the very evil within him had brought an atmosphere of strife and contention. A quarrel broke out over who was the greatest in rank among them. Jesus had to deal with it swiftly. At His stirring, John quietly gave up his place of worship and removed his head from the warm sanctuary of His Lord's bosom.

Jesus stood, removed His outer garment and picked up the basin used for ceremonial handwashing. He poured water into it, tied a towel around His waist and knelt before His disciples and began washing their feet. They were incredulous.

When He approached Peter, he drew his feet tightly under himself on the couch and put his hands out as if to shove away the whole scenario. "You're not washing my feet Lord. Not ever!"

Jesus' straightened and looked at him. "If you don't let Me wash you, you can have no part of Me."

Peter pulled his feet out from under him and stuck them out and plopped them both in the basin and thrust his hands out and dropped his head. "Then wash my hands as well! And my head!"

Jesus began to wash his feet. "You don't understand what I'm doing now, but one day you will." Peter with an enormous lump in his throat, said nothing.

The lesson over, Jesus returned to His place, put His robe back on and sat down. "Do you understand what just happened?" They dared not speak, but sat in reverent awe. "You call Me Teacher and Master. And rightly so. These titles denote rank and respect, yet you must understand that as your Teacher and Lord, I have shown you an example of how to truly serve. Not by lording your rank over someone else, but by serving with humility and love. That is what I have called you to do and I have shown you an example of this tonight. An example I expect you to follow."

The emotional drama of the past few weeks had been heady indeed: the raising of Lazarus from the dead–the triumphant entry into the city–the violent purging of the Temple. The disciples had been flying high, fantasizing and even arguing about kingdom rank. He had to once again cut across the grain of all they expected or thought. He washed their feet. The humiliation of it clipped their wings and brought them down to where they belonged. Down to where the highest love is. His illustration was mind boggling. He had done the menial service of a slave. He had called them to serve, not to rule. Love serves. And He, once again, was the perfect example of the love-servant.

It should have been a moment of peace and oneness, but His heart was filled with anguish. "One of you will betray Me this very night."

The disciples, in innocence of conscience, were cut to the heart and each one asked, "Lord is it I?"

Judas' eyes darted about to see if any of them knew it was he. With a heart as cold as a gravestone, and not wanting to stand out by remaining silent, asked, "Master, is it I?"

Judas Iscariot always called Jesus Master or Rabbi, a mere title of honor, as one would call his teacher. Not once did Judas call Him Lord, for no man can say that Jesus is the Lord, but by the Holy Spirit.[368]

Jesus, full of agony of soul, yet in perfect control, leaned over and replied, "Yes, you know it is you. Now go do what you have to do and do it quickly."

The others did not hear the answer but looked at one another suspiciously and wondered who He was talking about.

Jesus, the pitying Savior had given three warnings from the deep compassion of His heart: First He washed the betrayer's feet, hoping the humility of the act would deter him; then He solemnly warned, "One of you will betray Me," and lastly He shared His bread with him. But no warning would dissuade him. The betrayer slipped out into the night. The hoards of hell hovered overhead and escorted the devil-possessed man into eternal darkness.

The traitor gone from the table, the air seemed to clear. Upon the completion of the Passover Supper, Jesus was ready to instate what would forever be known as the Lord's Supper. He took the bread, broke it apart and blessed it and gave it to His disciples.

"Take and eat this. It is My body."

The body they so desired to cling to and did not want to give up. The body that encased the heart of heaven, the true Passover Lamb that would be slain for the sins of the world. Jesus was limited in that human Body in which He moved about those brief thirty-three years. But soon, He would go to be with His Father Who would send His Spirit, and would cover the earth with His Presence. He would no longer be bound in the human predicament, having to walk from one town to the next to minister. He would no longer be confined to the tiny nation of Israel, but would be able to minister to millions around the world at the same time.

And Jesus would be taking a body home.

The very fact that He would be seated at the right hand of His Father[369] in a glorified body, bearing the nail scars of Calvary as covenant marks, would *be* intercession. The sacred wounds of the risen Christ would soon emanate such glory and invoke such praise that the heavens would tremble at the praises to the Lamb. Amid the glorious anthems to be raised by the myriad of angelic beings around the crowned King, the Father need only to look to His right, see that glorified body, and a word need not be spoken. Jesus' very presence there in a body would be intercession enough.[370] His blood will have been sprinkled upon the Mercy Seat.[371] That would say it all. Jesus' heart beat with excitement at just the thought of it.

"This is My body. Take and eat it."

Eat and be nourished in the provision the Father has made for your freedom. Let it become a part of you so that you will, in turn, be nourishment to someone else. Eat and come into fellowship in His suffering, His death and then the resurrection into true life in Him.

Then He took a cup of wine, gave thanks for it and gave it to them. They passed it around and each one drank from it.

"This is My blood."

His blood. The agent for cleansing and washing away all unrighteousness–the full, complete and final covering of sin–the agent that overcomes the world, the flesh and the devil.

"This is my blood, poured out for many."

Sealing the Covenant of the Ages, His blood–the very life-flow between the Father and His children.

"I declare to you that I will not drink of the vine again until that day when I drink a new and better wine in the kingdom of God."

Another wine and another feast awaited Him.[372]

The supper over, they sang a hymn and headed for the Mount of Olives. Time was short and there was still so much His disciples didn't understand. Their perception of the Great Plan was still misunderstood. He had spoken of His death, burial and resurrection on several occasions, but it only seemed to bewilder them. His teachings were often veiled in mystery. Frequently He had stunned His hearers with mysterious words and had often spoken in parables. They hoped that this, too, was merely another one of His spiritual sayings.

It was difficult for them to hear those words, 'I'm leaving.' The disciples' faces screamed in silent pain as Jesus unfolded in clear language His impending departure. Their limited grasp of the significance of it was evident in the forlorned questions they asked,

"What do You mean You're going to the Father?"

"What do You mean, 'In just a little while I will be gone, and you will see Me no more; but just a little while after that, and you will see Me again?'"[373]

They were having a hard time relating to His admonitions that their weeping would suddenly be turned to wonderful joy.[374]

Just days before, after stirring up the city with His violent purging of the Temple, they had asked Him many questions concerning the future of Israel and the signs to look for at the end of the age, their thoughts still being based on a political viewpoint. Again, He told them of His departure, which they regarded as some metaphorical mumbo-jumbo and sat with bewildered, glazed expressions, unable to consider such an irrational arrangement. A thick knot had formed in their stomachs when He spoke of such things. Their emotion-filled reactions blinded their ability to receive the Great Plan, the event of the ages, His death, burial and resurrection.

He knew their comprehension of the New Covenant He instated that evening at their last supper together was limited, and that the blessed sacrament of Communion would be passed down to generations through their hands. Hands which now trembled in confusion and fear.

The enjoyment of His personal presence was utmost in their minds. But the One Who was to come would bring to their remembrance the things He had told them and they would then understand and rejoice. They would grieve in the brief separations, but when His Spirit came, He would be closer to them than ever before.

He would not just be with them,
He would be in them.[375]
and millions more like them,
and it would
never end.

-BROW

And he that was called Judas, one of the twelve, went before them, and drew near unto Jesus to kiss him. But Jesus said unto him, Judas, betrayest thou the Son of Man with a kiss?

Luke 22:47,48

The moment was exhilarating for Satan and his minions. Just as he had led a mob of angels in rebellion in heaven, he would now lead a mob of God's own creatures in rebellion on earth.

CHAPTER THIRTY-THREE

Gethsemane

A HORRIBLE GRIN CROSSED Satan's hideous face as he made his move upon Judas Iscariot's heart. The prince of darkness silently moved into his heart,[376] a moment he had waited for longingly for months.

Judas' countenance changed completely. His appearance was dark, his eyes wild, his posture bent. He moved in the shadows like an animal. The devil-possessed man crept through the streets like a thief. As he approached the house of the high priest, he could see torches dotting the area of the courtyard. A Roman detachment, along with several servants from the high priest's palace and Jewish officers of the Sanhedrin awaited his arrival.

Satan had betrayed the Father. Now, embodied in one of the Seeds' closest friends, he would betray the Son. It brought the enemy great pleasure to win such a prize, to cause one so close to the Seed to double-cross Him.

As Judas neared, Annas, the director of the mob, was almost startled at the wild look in Judas' eyes. Satan's excitement heightened at the culmination of events, leading him to a near savage behavior.

The plans had been made the day before. There was nothing to discuss. They would only follow the betrayer into the night. The blood money had been paid. They were ready to collect their "possession."

Little did they know they had "paid" for the One Who was about to pay all for them.[377]

The procession began to weave its way through the streets. The moment was exhilarating for Satan and his minions. Just as he had led a mob of angels in rebellion in heaven, he would now lead a mob of God's own creatures in rebellion on earth.

A feverish swarm of demons flew overhead, following their master as he slinked in the shadows, hosted in the cowardly body of the betrayer, Judas.

* * *

The gales of hell blew fiercely over the Son of Man in the garden of Gethsemane. He had taken with Him His three closest friends to watch and pray with Him. Leaving them at the entrance of the garden, He went a little farther into the interior of the familiar oasis, a place where He and His disciples had come often, seeking peace and rest. This would be a night of neither peace nor rest for any of them.

Jesus knelt and cried out to His Father, "Oh My Father! If it be possible, let this cup pass from Me."

He lifted His bowed head and spoke tenderly. "But not My own will, Father–but Yours."

He stood, turned and walked toward His friends. He needed them. And He was concerned about them.

The sickly, pale light of the moon fell across the sleeping faces of Peter, James and John. Peter snored fitfully. Jesus dropped to His knees and shook them. "Can't you stay awake and watch and pray with Me just one hour?" He shook Peter's shoulder. "Simon! You must watch and pray so you won't enter into temptation. Your spirit is willing, but your flesh is weak. Pray!" At the time of His greatest agony, He was concerned about them.

The humanity of Jesus was at its peak. He needed the brace, even the embrace of His friends. Sleep held them fast. He stood and stumbled back to the place where He prayed and fell to the ground, His face buried in the earth. The earth He had formed.

The wet grass mingled with the sweat in His beard. Again He cried out to His Father.

"Oh My Father. If it is possible–let this cup–pass from Me."

He lifted Himself up to His hands and knees and raised His head. In the inner anguish of His soul, He remembered the covenant that He and His Father had discussed in Heaven.

"Yet not My will–not Mine, Father, but Yours alone."

He stood and walked back toward the disciples. He walked past the flowering shrubs and serene olive groves, a startling contrast to the anguish of His soul.

Seeing them deep in sleep, He sighed and left them, returning to His place of prayer.

Falling to His knees again, He stretched His arms toward heaven; His hands opened and closed, opened and closed as though He were grasping for His Father's hand.

"Oh–My–Father."

His throat was dry, His voice hoarse and raspy.

"If it is possible–"

He fell with His face to the ground. Drops of blood seeped through His skin and mingled with the sweat that ran down His face.

"If it is possible–let this cup–pass from–Me."

Silence. No answer.

"But," He whispered, "Not My will, but Yours alone."

The anguished cries of the Son of God pierced heaven. A massive archangel settled down to the ground next to Him[378] and covered Him with his wings, creating an arched tabernacle in which to give Him the message, the answer to the cry of the hour.

The answer to the question–is it possible?
An answer He already knew.
It was not possible.

* * *

The mob moved steadily closer, their torches burning. They passed by the festive lamps shining in windows and courtyards of the homes filled with travelers and guests who had come for the great Feast celebrations. People gawked out of their windows at the torch-lit company of soldiers and robed figures with staves and swords, and wondered at the strange spectacle.

"What's going on?" they asked each other excitedly as they watched them pass on their way up the steep hill of the valley of Kidron, Death working up momentum.

Jesus stood, brushed off His robe and victoriously left the blood, sweat and tears in the gouged ground of Gethsemane. He had passed through the valley of despair triumphant. He had prayed the most humble prayer ever prayed. In the face of torture, torment and death, and worse, separation from His Father, He prayed,

"Not My will–but Yours."

God gives grace to the humble.[379]

Grace.

God's assistance–God's ability–God's strength–God's favor.

Grace came.

He quietly bent over the sleeping disciples. Instead of chastising them, He told them to take their rest. He no longer needed their aid. God had given Him the grace to help in time of need.[380]

In the distance He could see the flickering lights of the throng approaching. "The hour has come," He said, waking the disciples. "Get up. We must be going. The prince of this world is coming and he has nothing in Me."[381]

The groggy disciples sat up and rubbed their eyes with their fingers. Peter jumped to his feet, embarrassed that he had fallen asleep again. James stood and held his hand out to John and helped him up. Their eyes bulged in fear at the sight of the oncoming mob.

They approached Jesus with swords drawn. He could see the contorted visage of the enemy peering from behind Judas' face.

"Whom do you seek?" Jesus said, as if He didn't know.

"Jesus of Nazareth," one of the soldiers demanded gruffly.

"I am He."

The power in the words, "I am"[382] knocked the entire throng backward onto the ground. They clambered awkwardly to their feet and scrambled frantically for their swords and torches.[383]

No man could take His life.

He laid it down.[384]

Their breath could be seen in the cold night air. Breath that He, the Giver of Life, had given them. He stood there majestically, His arms folded across His chest.

"Whom do you seek?"

"We–uh–told You, Jesus of Nazareth."

"I am He."

The demons swarming overhead screeched in pain at the power of those words and scattered like cockroaches caught in the light.

The chief priests, captains of the Temple guard and the elders pushed their way to the front. Jesus spoke directly to them. "You come with clubs and swords as though I were some dangerous criminal? I was with you daily teaching in the Temple. You could have easily arrested Me then. But this is your hour, and the time for the power of darkness."[385]

Judas strolled over to Jesus with freshly washed feet. Jesus could hear the muffled jingle of silver coins as the devil-possessed man leaned over to kiss His cheek.[386]

Thirty pieces of silver
taken out of the Temple treasury.
Money that was to be used
to purchase
a sacrifice.

And Peter followed Him afar off, even into the palace of the high priest: and he sat with the servants, and warmed himself at the fire.

Mark 14:54

Peter trailed behind the mob in the shadows with Fear, and the twin demons, Doubt and Unbelief working him over, Fear on one side and the dirty duo on the other, whispering in his ear.

CHAPTER THIRTY-FOUR

Sifting Seeds

PETER WAS DISCOURAGED AND disheartened. He followed Jesus from a distance. His thoughts were coming at him like arrows as he watched Jesus being led away by the angry mob. *All this talk about leaving. Is this what He meant?* His heavy feet stumbled over roots in the blackness of the night. *He said He was sending someone else. A Counselor?*[387] *I don't want anyone else! He actually said it would be better if He left.*[388] He gulped, *How could He say such a thing?*

He nearly stumbled over his own feet slowly making his way in the darkness. *Nothing has gone right tonight. Just before our last supper together, I get caught up in an argument about which one of us was the greatest. And all over the seating arrangements. The others started it!* He stopped to catch his breath. *I said the wrong thing when He approached me to wash my feet*–He swallowed hard at the painful thought of it, and mumbled out loud, "Then He tells me Satan wants to–sift me,[389] whatever that means! Why single me out? Why me?"

His eyes darted about to make sure no one was following him. His thoughts continued, *I told Him that even if all the others abandoned Him, I was ready to go to prison–even death with Him! And what does He do? He tells me I'll deny Him three times before the cock crows in the morning! Deny Him? I would never do that!*

He stopped and leaned against a tree for a moment to catch his breath. *So I couldn't stay awake when He asked me to watch and pray with Him–but it's been a rough week. And my heart has been so heavy–it just took its toll, that's all.*

He looked ahead at the flickering torches, their light blazing against their swords. *Then to top it all off, when that lynch mob, led by that traitor Judas–I never did trust that guy–came to arrest Him, I tried to defend Him with my sword. Alright, so this fellow–this member of the guard ducked and I only got his ear. But what does our Leader do? Is He grateful? No! He picks his ear up off the ground, blows the dirt off, puts it back on his head and heals him! And then He tells me to put my sword away!*[390] Tears coursed down his cheeks and into his beard. *I guess I can't do anything right!*

The sifting had begun.

Peter trailed behind the mob in the night shadows with Fear, and the twin demons, Doubt and Unbelief working him over, Fear on one side and the dirty duo on the other, whispering in his ear,

"See, Peter, you just can't please Him."

"Hard as you try, you'll never measure up. You're not worthy. Look at all your failures. He doesn't care about you." And then the ultimate weapon, "Why don't you just give up?"

The seeds of faith that had been planted in him[391] were being sifted like wheat. He was being shaken like a sieve. Satan would try his faith to the verge of near overthrow, counting on the seed of suspicion that was already in his fallen nature–the grain of doubt–the tares of distrust–to win out; to pulverize his faith–to grind it to powder. It was going to be a long night.

Up ahead he could see Jesus being led toward the high priest's house. He didn't look much like a Messiah now. Maybe it was all a mistake.

Upon entering the courtyard gate, the soldiers dispersed into little groups. They laughed and joked and flirted with the servant girls. The rest of the men found places to sit, some leaned on the courtyard wall, and others moved toward the door of the house and strained to hear what was being said inside.

When Peter reached the house, he could see a fire flickering in the corner of the courtyard. Several men stood around it warming themselves. He hesitated to go inside the gate, but quietly slipped over to the fire and warmed his hands.

A young servant girl brought an armload of kindling. As she threw it on the fire, the light of the flames blazed across Peter's weary face. She stared at him. "Say, aren't you one of the Nazarene's disciples?"

Peter turned his face from the fire. "Woman, I don't know what you're talking about!"

She glared at him, then left to fetch some more firewood, returning in a few minutes with a friend. They eyed him suspiciously and whispered behind cupped hands. Finally the friend said, "You are one of them!"

Peter denied it again, "I told you, I don't know Him!' He moved away from the fire and found an unoccupied corner of the courtyard.

Meanwhile, the high priest was questioning Jesus. Peter could see their silhouettes through the window. The chief priest and most of the Sanhedrin were there. Peter strained to hear. He couldn't quite make out their words, but their voices were angry. He could see one of the leaders tear his robe! The high priest's attendant slapped Jesus![392]

Little did he know he slapped the true High Priest.

Their voices grew louder and louder. Fear rose up in Peter and he headed for the gate. One of the high priest's servants came up behind him. "Hey, didn't I see you with Him in the olive grove?"

Peter began to curse. "I tell you, I don't know the Man!" In the distance, a rooster's crow cut through the predawn sky and pierced Peter's heart.

Just then, they led Jesus out the door to take Him to the palace of the Roman governor. Peter looked up. Jesus turned. His holy eyes looked straight at Peter.[393] Not eyes of disappointment. Not eyes of disapproval. Not eyes of denouncement.

But eyes of pity and deep discernment.

Peter went out
and wept bitterly.[394]

And he cast down the pieces of silver in the temple, and departed, and went and hanged himself.

Matthew 27:5

Judas, totally in the clutches of Death and his fiendish partner, Suicide, ran out the door and down the Temple steps, shoving anyone who got in his way.

CHAPTER THIRTY-FIVE

Death Money

As HE WANDERED THE streets of Jerusalem, the thirty pieces of silver jingled in Judas' money belt, which he had carefully wrapped and hid in his robe next to his greedy heart. But the blood money brought him no joy, no peace, no satisfaction.

He glanced wildly about him, his countenance darkened and distorted. Every face on the street seemed to stare at him as if to say, Betrayer! But it was only the accusing voices of his own conscience with the aid of the tormenting demons hovering about him and taunting him. The staring faces were only gazes of wonder at the haggard, disheveled man with the wild, tortured eyes stumbling toward them and clinging desperately to something under his robe.

He knew Jesus was condemned. All heaven and hope had receded from Judas. He no longer had companions; no one to counsel him, no one to help. He was alone. Alone with the price of innocent blood.

He reached into his bosom and pulled out the money belt containing the thirty pieces of silver, which now seemed like a bag of snakes. He must get rid of it. Perhaps then his torment would be relieved.

The priests and elders were huddled together in the Sanctuary of the Temple, speaking in hushed tones of their triumph of having finally arrested that pretender Jesus. Judas staggered in and interrupted their meeting. Their scornful eyes met his, giving him a look that sawed him in two. He could see there was to be no sympathy, no pity for him.

The accomplice in the joint arrangement was no longer needed, no longer welcome. Just hours before, he had been a most essential and significant figure to them. Now he was an intruder, useless and irrelevant. He was in the way. Completely alone, disjointed. An outsider, not only to the leaders to whom he had been a most necessary tool, but to all of life. He had known Life, now Death was calling. It would have been better had he never been born.[395]

"I–I have sinned!" he cried hoarsely. He stumbled toward them. They glared at him in disgust. "I have betrayed–" he broke into convulsive sobs, "–innocent blood!"

Judas repented to the wrong ones. Yet it was not true repentance but a realization of the tragedy he had been party to. He now saw the raw depravity of his evil enterprise and knew it could not be undone.

"What is that to us? That's your problem!" his accomplices spat with hateful contempt. "You deal with it!"

Judas' haunted eyes were dilated and bulging, completely encircled in bloodshot white. He opened the money belt he had feverishly clung to and with trembling hands threw the thirty pieces of silver violently to the floor. The coins rang loudly throughout the Temple, rolling and wobbling like tiny gleaming tops on the marble floor.

The seducer, Deception, laughed at the seduced.

They turned their backs on him and continued their conversation. Judas, totally in the clutches of Death and his fiendish partner, Suicide, ran out the door and down the Temple steps, shoving anyone who got in his way. He rushed up the side of the mountain where the Kidron and Hinnom valleys met. He found a dead, stunted old tree that leaned over the steep, rocky precipice, and unraveled the very money belt that had held the blood money, and coldly and solemnly, with trembling hands, made a noose. He placed one end of it around a branch of the tree, and the other around his neck, and threw himself off the edge. The old snag gave way under the weight of his body and he fell upon the jagged rocks below.[396]

Hell opened wide her mouth and swallowed him up.
Suicide and Death slapped each other on their backs
and took off to report
their vile victory.

Pilate therefore said unto Him, Art thou a king then? Jesus answered, Thou sayest that I am a king. To this end was I born, and for this cause came I into the world, that I should bear witness unto the truth.

John 18:37

The Heavenly Warrior Jesus was in the midst of settling issues of freedom or slavery, Heaven or Hell. If they knew Who He was, they would have fallen on their faces in reverent awe.

CHAPTER THIRTY-SIX

The Sentence

BY NOW THE WORD had spread through all of Jerusalem of the bizarre events. Jesus had been passed around like so much unwanted rubbish–from Annas to Caiaphas, to Pilate, to Herod, and back to Pilate again. The Captain of their souls was now their Captive.

The religious leaders' evasive answers had angered Pilate. Strangely reluctant to be His judge, he had picked up on the word "Nazarene" and thought he saw a way out. He had quickly turned Jesus back over to His captors and ordered them to take Him to Herod who was in Jerusalem for the feasts. Herod was glad to see the Nazarene's demise was imminent and hoped it would end his sleepless nights. And now Jesus was back in Pilate's presence again.

Pilate stared at Jesus. He found it difficult to look into His eyes. Something about Him made him feel uneasy. His heart longed to talk with Him privately; he had heard so many extraordinary things about

Him, but it was too late. He was now His judge. He stood looking at Jesus, feeling like a man with the weight of the world on his body. An unusual uneasiness scraped along his nerves. These feelings were foreign to Pilate. He had always been completely confident and had never felt the pangs of fear in his life. Now he wasn't so sure. He felt as though his feet were glued to the marble floor. He must not let on of the churning in his gut. He must remain in control.

His wife had heard many stories about this Man and had shown a great interest in Him. When he told her at dinner last evening that he had granted a Roman guard to aid the Jewish leaders in His arrest, she became terrified, which concerned Pilate greatly. She was not the type of woman to show undue emotion, nor was she superstitious in nature.

Pilate had gotten up before dawn and dressed that morning. His wife had not slept well all night and he had noticed she was still in a fitful, restless sleep as he slipped out of their bedchamber on his way to meet with the Jewish leaders concerning this Man Jesus.

And now He stood before him. He didn't seem to be the rabble-rouser they had made Him out to be. Jesus stood tall and quiet before him. Never had Pilate seen One so viciously accused, yet so calm, peaceful and poised. He didn't even try to defend Himself, much less the usual begging, pleading and bribing he had seen men do on so many occasions, attempting to lessen their fates. This Man stood here serene and quiet as though *He* was somehow in command of this strange event.

"Are You the King of the Jews?" Pilate asked flatly.

"Are those your words or theirs?"

"Do I look like a Jew? Your own countrymen and leaders turned You over to me." He backed up a half step, folded his arms and looked through narrow eyes at Him and said slowly, "What did You do?"

Jesus looked at him with tender majesty. "My kingdom is not of this world. If My kingdom were of this world, I assure you, My servants would have fought so that I would not have been handed over to the Jews. But My kingdom is nothing like you've ever seen or heard of."

The angels, held back by the Father's command, sighed and nodded.

Pilate looked at Him and frowned deeply, half in cynicism, half in awe as though looking at some sort of Alien Aristocracy. "You are a King then?"

Jesus stood there in the absolute rest of His Father. "As you say. Because I am a King, to this end was I born and for this cause came I into this world, to bear witness of the truth."

Pilate cocked his head to one side, tightened his tanned, muscular arms and raised one eyebrow. "And what is truth?"

The young God-Man knew it was a question that would be echoed down through the centuries through the corridors of governments, places of learning and in the hearts of men.

Pilate didn't know truth was not a what, but a Who.[397] The very embodiment of Truth was standing right in front of him and he could not see Him. It only made him nervous.

Pilate left Him and went out to the Jews, who had refused to enter the Palace for fear of becoming "defiled". The hypocrisy of that pathetic observance of the law was astounding.

"I find no fault at all with this Man! It is your custom that a prisoner be released at Passover. Shall I release the King of the Jews?" He knew that title would hit a nerve. He also knew they had Him sent there through sheer jealous resentment.

They shouted back, "Not this One, but Barabbas!" Jesus had talked about setting the captives free, but did nothing to get them free from Roman bondage. At least Barrabas had attempted an insurrection.

Just then a servant came with a pleading message to Pilate from his wife saying, "Have no dealings with this just and noble Man. I have suffered a long and difficult night because of a dream concerning Him." The message unsettled Pilate.

In the meantime, the religious leaders were busy goading and even bribing the gathering crowd to demand the release of Barabbas, a notorious thief, murderer and self-acclaimed freedom fighter. No one had fought more for their freedom than Jesus had. A boiling cloud of demons flew overhead, egging them on.

Pilate returned to them, "Who do you want me to release?"

They shouted back loudly, "Barabbas!"

Pilate glared at them in disgust and sent Jesus to be scourged, hoping that would satisfy them.

He was bound and beaten. Like flames across His back, each stinging lash brought hot, dizzying pain and a crimson ribbon of blood, each one a scourge against sickness and disease, fulfilling the Scripture,

"–and with His stripes we are healed."[398]

The soldiers then took Him and having braided a crown of needle-sharp thorns, shoved it down on that Sacred Head, threw a purple toga on His bloody back, put a stick in His hand for a scepter and began mocking Him cruelly and slapping His face.

They had no idea the life and death battle He was waging for their very souls; that the Heavenly Warrior Jesus was in the midst of settling issues of freedom or slavery, Heaven or Hell. If they knew Who He was, they would have fallen on their faces in reverent awe. Instead, they turned it into an unholy freak show. They spit on Him and slapped Him.

They slapped the face of God.

An ever-present army of angels stood ready at His command to come to His aid, but He did not summon them. The cloud of witnesses and the angels watched each step of the events with amazement. Even at the bewilderment of the prospect of His death, their faith in God's Great Plan brought an excitement to them. Jesus, too, looked beyond the shame and suffering He faced; His heart held a strange joy[399] at the anticipation of millions of souls being set free and the redemption of those who would cling to His cross and His wounds.

The cruel soldiers returned Him in that incongruous garment to Pilate. The old governor felt a pang of pity when he saw Jesus' mangled face from the sadistic fists of the soldiers. He couldn't bear to look at Him. He called one of the soldiers to lead Him out and Pilate presented Him to His accusers saying, "Behold the Man!"

Seeing Him even in mock apparel suggesting royalty incensed the crowd all the more, being scorned that they called Him their king.

Murder and Hatred were dancing in and out of the crowd stirring them to a frenzy. Many in the throng that had rolled like a living wave through the portals of Jerusalem crying Hosanna! were now shrieking their death cries.

"Crucify Him! Crucify Him!"

Pilate shouted, "You take Him and crucify Him. I find no fault with Him!"

The religious leaders cried out, "According to our law, He must die because He claims He is the Son of God!"

When Pilate heard this, terror struck his heart. He turned and faced Jesus. "Who are You? Where did You come from? Why don't You say something? Don't You understand that I have the authority to let You go or to let them crucify You?"

Jesus said in quiet majesty, "The only authority you have is what has been given you from heaven. Therefore the one who betrayed Me to you has committed a far greater sin."

Hearing this, Pilate went back and continued to try to reason with them to release Him, but they would have none of it. They threatened, "If you release this Man, you are no friend to Caesar, for this Man, calling Himself a King, defies Caesar's office!"

When Pilate heard this he led Jesus out and shouted, "Behold your King!"

A wild frenzy broke out, "Crucify Him! Crucify Him!" The cries shook the very foundations of the palace. Never had he seen so much hostility. Never had he witnessed such an uprising of violent hatred. Not even in the tumultuous uproars of the forum. He thought the very demons of hell must have been turned loose. He was right.

Pilate shouted, "You want me to crucify your King?"

The high priest shouted back, "We have no king but Caesar!"

Spiritual Blindness had placed a heavy shroud of darkness upon their minds.[400] Satan had so conquered their hearts that this incredible cry, a complete denial of Judaism was provoked, and worse, a denial of Jehovah God. It was, in the frenzied height of the hour, a blasphemy of unparalleled proportions, only to be echoed

with their self-cursing that,
"His Blood be upon us
and our children!"[401]

And the people stood beholding. And the rulers also with them derided him, saying, He saved others; let him save himself, if he be Christ, the chosen of God.

Matthew 27:41,42

Looking up at the inscription hanging over Jesus' head, Satan's cold hand reached out and touched the lips of one of the Sanhedrin, inciting him to cry out a mocking echo of the wilderness temptation, "If You are the Son of God–come down from the Cross!"

CHAPTER THIRTY-SEVEN

The Crucifixion

THE CENTURION THREW HIM down hard against the splintery cross that was lying in wait on the ground. He found the small hollow in His wrist and placed the square iron nail there, and with loud clanging blows, drove it into the Savior's flesh. He quickly moved to the other side and drove the other one in. Fire shot across His arms and slammed into His shoulders and chest as the spikes tore into His hands. Blood gushed out, spurting onto the harsh hands of the Roman soldier who drove them in. Jesus' eyes met his. The surly soldier expected to see a glare of hatred. Instead, through the excruciating pain–he saw pity and compassion.

Two criminals were crucified with Him, their crosses on either side of His.

Satan, surrounded by his most notorious princes of darkness, sat at a half-moon shaped banquet table directly in front of the center Cross, enjoying the ghastly spectacle.

Jesus' feet were positioned one upon the other so they could be secured together with one long spike–through the heel. With loud ringing clangs, the hammer drove it in.

Satan jumped up, thrust his fists into the air and shouted, "There! I've done it! I've crushed His heel! I'm the victor over that vile vow that has menaced me all these years! Let's see Him try to crush my head now!"[402]

"Here! Here!" his monstrous minions cheered, lifting their chalices in salute to their gloating master.

The soldier then nailed above His head an inscription that read, THIS IS JESUS, THE KING OF THE JEWS. With a heave, the soldiers silently lifted up the Cross. The base was inserted into a hole with a jolt, sending a new wave of pain through Jesus' body. The crowd gasped. His body slowly sagged and his wrists tore even more under the weight sending an explosion of pain up his neck and into His brain.

The demons laughed and applauded as their agonizing Enemy writhed in pain.

Debauchery stood and bowed to Satan, his eyes wild with excitement. "Now, Sire?"

"Yes! Let the celebration begin!"

Debauchery gave the signal. Hoards of his hellish demons flew to the crest of the Cross and began a descending dance about it, looping invisible chains around the tortured body of Jesus like a malevolent maypole.

Little did they know they were celebrating their own destruction, for had they known it, they would not have crucified the Lord of glory.[403]

Jesus tried to push Himself upward so He could breathe, but this movement began a series of spasms that caused even more torture.

One of the disciples watching from a distance ran to the others who were in hiding. He beat on the door and when they opened it, he fell in a heap in their arms and screamed with a loud voice,

"They'rrrrre killliiinngg Hiiimm!!!!! They wept so sorrowfully they barely had breath in them.

John, the only disciple who did not run, stayed from beginning to the end, holding onto his Lord's dear mother. While self-indulgent soldiers cast lots for Jesus' only worldly goods, Jesus, seeing His mourning mother faint with grief and leaning on John, unselfishly made provision for her.

"Woman! Behold your son!"

His lungs screamed for air. But He spoke once more.

"John! Behold your mother!"

So typical. Self-forgetfulness. The very emblem of the God-Man.

From then on, John took Mary into his home and took care of her.

Agonizing hours passed and the invisible revelry continued. Satan, drunk on the exhilaration of the long-awaited moment, threw his goblet to the ground. He haughtily strolled through the crowd and stood at the foot of the central Cross. Looking up at the inscription hanging over Jesus' head, he reached out his cold hand and touched the lips of one of the Sanhedrin, inciting him to cry out a mocking echo of the wilderness temptation,

"If You are the Son of God–"

The hollow voices seemed far away and echoed in Jesus' roaring ears.

"If You are the Son of God–come down from the Cross!"

Others joined it, "So! You're going to destroy the Temple and raise it again in three days, are You? Well then, if You are the Son of God, save Yourself and come down from your Cross!"

Simultaneously, the leading priests, the teachers of religious law, and elders picked up the spirit of the scornful sport from their father the devil,[404] and began to mock and ridicule the writhing Redeemer. "He saved others, but He can't save Himself! So! He's the King of Israel, eh? Let Him come down from the Cross and we will believe in Him!" The bloodthirsty crowd laughed. Even the criminals who were crucified with Him shouted insults at Him.

Another reviled Him saying, "He trusted God–now let God deliver Him! After all, didn't He say He was the Son of God?"

The Blessed Hope of Israel hung before their eyes, naked, bleeding and dying at their guilty hands. For them. The god of this world had them so blinded, they could only abase themselves to the very depths of hell, committing mortal suicide.

The soldiers joined in the mocking. One of them offered him strong vinegar wine mixed with myrrh, a drug to help numb the consciousness to the pain, but He refused it. He would not succumb to the aid of man to avoid the full suffering of the Cross as though He were a guilty victim.

He was an innocent Volunteer.

Jesus was able to push Himself up between the twisting cramps in His legs and joints for small gulps of air. He groaned as the pain became more unbearable.

Satan threw back his head and laughed horribly. He shook his bony fist at the sky and cried loudly, "There, God! I have finally won!" He looked back at Jesus and then bellowed toward the heavens once more, "Look at Him, God! How pained You must be just now. I have the Seed and Death shall soon swallow Him whole!"

The Heavenly Host gasped in horror.

Satan continued his harangue. "The world is still mine and You can't stop me! Not now or ever!" He screeched with laughter and his princes of darkness applauded and guffawed uproariously. Satan marched around the Cross and shouted, "I have accomplished even more than I had imagined, God. I have made You out the Liar!" He laughed insanely and jabbed his crooked finger at the sky. "Your word is no longer true! You said the woman's Seed would crush my head! Your ancient prophecy has failed. Your detestable oath of Eden lies beneath my heel in a pitiful heap! Your beloved Son in Whom You are so well pleased was not quite up to the task, God. He did not crush my head!" His blaring voice became more vicious with every word. "Now nobody will believe You, God. Not even your darling angels." Taunting laughter erupted once more from the demons.

Jesus rolled His head to the side and gasped for air. Savoring the moment, Satan cocked his head to one side and smiled caustically. "Well, Jesus! Where are all of Your followers now? You came to save the world and all You have left are a few blubbering women."

Bitterness, a briny, tentacled demon prince, stepped up alongside

Satan, joining him in his sadistic seduction. "Jesus! Look what they've done to their meek Messiah! Look where all Your kindness got You! How You must despise them!"

The languishing Lamb looked upon the bloodthirsty mob and whispered hoarsely with labored breath,

"Father–forgive them. They–don't know–what–they're–doing."

Had He not done that, all would have been lost. All thirty-three years of His sinless, unspotted Life would have been wasted.

But the Sacrificial Lamb remained unblemished.

Satan and his cruel cohort turned in disgust and rejoined their foul festivities. Masses of dark clouds tumbled overhead. Another hour of cruel mocking and pain passed. The crushing pain in the Savior's chest felt like a searing, iron vice closing in on His heart.

The Heavenly Host, held back by the command of God, was enduring their own agony as they helplessly watched the attacks of the adversary upon their dear Friend.

At the sixth hour, darkness gathered over all the land. A nauseating odor filled the air. Suddenly like a kick in the stomach, all of the sickness and sin of the world slammed into Jesus' already weakened Body.[405] He gasped at the magnitude and weight of it. The foreign feeling of sin slithered over His Body like a million snakes, then sank into His very Being.[406]

And He Who knew no sin became sin for us.[407]

Spasms of nausea racked His tortured torso. Then it happened. The moment that had caused Him to sweat great drops of blood at Gethsemane. The moment that had torn the anguished cry from His lips, "Oh My Father! If it be possible! Let this cup pass from Me!" The fevered horror of the God-forsakeness shattered His very soul. The last temptation, the final human experience that He had never before suffered–happened. Fear of abandonment by the Father,[408] the aftermath of Adams' folly, that dominates the fallen nature that God's not good, you can't trust Him, He really will leave you and forsake you–hit home.

In unparalleled pain, He wailed with a loud voice,

"Eli, Eli, lema sabachthani?"

"My God! My God! Why–have You forsaken–Me?"

Some of the crowd thought He was calling for the prophet Elijah. One of them once again ran and filled a sponge with sour wine and held it up to Him on a stick and offered it to Him to drink.

"Leave Him alone. Let's see if Elijah will come to His rescue!"

At that moment the fires of God's Holiness and His Righteous Judgment against sin, spread through the Savior's ravaged Body like roaring flames, consuming the Sacrificial Lamb. The supreme moment of the Cross had come.

He became the Curse,[409]
the Scapegoat,[410]
the Substitute,[411]
the Propitiation,[412]
the Victor.[413]

At the paramount point of His Passion, He, as Conqueror with a loud voice proclaimed,

"It is finished."[414]

Then, in the most sublime submission, with faith winning out to the end, He overcame the last, most tormenting fear of all. Abandonment of the Father. Trusting Him that He would not leave His soul in Hell, neither would He suffer His Holy One to see corruption,[415] and offering one last acknowledgement of His faith in His goodness, He bowed His Sacred Head, and almost like a lullaby whispered,

"Father, I entrust My spirit
into Your hands."
His last words
were a prayer
of faith.

* * *

Thick, dark clouds like a black crepe mourning veil covered the earth, blotting out the sun. The universe gasped as the Chosen Planet lost its earthlight. A moaning wind sang a mournful duet with the pining, sighing wails of the women. Loud rumbles interrupted the lamentation, changing their wails to shrieks of terror. The earth convulsed violently, sending a shudder through all of nature. Graves ripped open and many bodies of the saints, which slept, arose.[416]

Jesus' offering for the Passover. The firstfruits of the Resurrected.

Upon seeing the earth erupting, one of the centurions who watched Jesus die and several who had witnessed the crucifixion, cried out in horror, "Truly this was the Son of God!"

Rocks were rent and lightning flashed behind the three crosses, causing an eerie silhouette against the skull-shaped summit.

The face in the moon seemed to look upon the earth in an incredulous gasp. The crowd screamed and ran in every direction. The women stood helplessly, shuddering in the darkness, holding onto one another and sobbing convulsively. The earth swayed and swelled, knocking people off their feet as they ran screaming for shelter.

The heavy Temple veil was rent from top to bottom
by the Hand of God,
ripping open forever
the entrance to the Most Holy Place.[417]
The Final Lamb
had been slain.

I am he that liveth, and was dead; and, behold, I am alive for evermore, Amen; and have the keys of hell and of death.

Revelation 1:18

Satan and his demons shrieked and shivered as they beheld the Living Lamb of God. Satan screamed, "I killed You! You can't be alive! I buried You!"

CHAPTER THIRTY-EIGHT

The Victory

THE SIGHT OF THE Seed's Blood made Satan strangely weak. He had ordered the festivities to be moved to his domain. Debauchery, as usual, handled the festivities of feasting and licentiousness. The devil was intoxicated with his conquest. The queen of the she-spirits danced before him, her cobra-like movements mesmerized him.

The demon captain and his subordinates applauded as Deception and Murder toasted one another. The revelry and ovations echoed through the evil empire. Legions of imps and devils danced in undulating movements around their evil master.

Pride was seated at the right of Satan. Deception at his left. Smoke belched out of the cavern walls. They stood and signaled for the music and dancing to stop. Satan, in his longest, most ostentatious robe, with his medals of war gleaming on his chest, stood and moved to his place.

The time had come for the coronation, when Satan would claim himself the conqueror of God.

The evil minions scurried to take their places, lining the jagged walls of the enormous cavity. The demon princes in their order of authority moved to their positions behind Satan, their wings unfurled in tribute. Pride signaled for the procession to begin.

The course of the procession took Satan and his attendants around the cavernous hall, moving slowly to the rhythm of the drums. His subjects bowed deeply as he passed. Upon completing the circumference of the vast chamber, the subjects fell in behind the attendants to follow their master out the massive doors into the long Corridor of Captivity, the place where the hopeless souls were imprisoned in dark cells on either side.

At the entrance of the corridor, the procession stopped. Pride stepped out of his place and announced loudly that their king would be escorted by Deception and himself through the corridor of Satan's trophies, the lost souls of men, and would command the souls to fall down and worship him as he passed by.

The drums began the strange, pulsating rhythm. Deception joined Pride out in front of the procession. They began moving down the long passageway. Pride shouted loudly, "Bow down and worship the king of the universe! For he has conquered God and crushed His Seed!"

"All hail!" the attendants shouted as they entered the corridor.

Pride and Deception moved rhythmically to the beat of the drums. Satan followed, his long robe slithering behind him.

As they approached the first group of cells, Pride shouted his command that the interned souls begin to worship. Suddenly they stopped. Deception's eyes widened in horror. Pride's loud, commanding voice trailed off and Satan stood in a confused stupor.

The prison gates were standing open. The cells were empty.[418]

Pride signaled the drums to cease. Deception turned to Satan, still in a daze, and whispered in a guttural tone, "Where are they?"

Satan began to feel queasy. Barely able to speak, he wheezed, "It can't be!"

Just then at the end of the corridor, the gates of hell burst open and a blinding Light slammed into their eyes. "Oh! No!" Satan cried.

"It can't be!" Pride shrieked.

The demons screamed and flapped their wings trying to get away from the Light. Deception held his wing over his eyes and shouted, "We must close the gates!"

The attendants screamed, "We can't see!"

Satan, his eyes stinging, ran towards the gates screaming wildly, "No! It can't be! I crushed the Seed! I've conquered God!"

The princes, principalities and powers of darkness followed him, howling in pain. They reached the gates. Blinded by the Light, they fumbled around and grabbed hold of the massive gates. Heaving with everything they had, they pushed the gates with all their might, but were met with an incredible, invisible force.

The gates of hell could not prevail.[419]

Suddenly, a powerful blow knocked them backwards, flinging the gates open, sending them sprawling. Jesus stood there, dazzling Light flashing out of His eyes, His Body resplendent with Glory.

Satan and his demons shrieked and shivered as they beheld the Living Lamb of God.

Satan screamed, "I killed You! You can't be alive! I buried You!"

"No one takes My life from Me, but I lay it down of My own accord. I have the power to lay it down and I have the power to take it up again."[420]

The conquering King of kings and Lord of lords stood over His archenemy and fixed His foot squarely on Satan's chest over his evil heart, making His enemy His footstool. Satan screamed in agony. "Please! Please! I'll do anything! Just don't crush my head!"

Jesus looked at him and through gritted teeth demanded, "The keys of Hell and Death!"[421] The trembling devil slowly reached into his robe and agonizingly pulled the keys out, and handed over his kingdom to Jesus.

The Blood on His robe completely debilitated Satan and his demons, reducing them to powerless, impotent slugs. Jesus marched them through the streets of hell and past the fallen angels who were imprisoned there as they looked on in horror.

Heaven looked down and saw the defeat of Satan and the victory of Jesus and exploded into glorious praise. The first part of the Great Plan had been completed and the next Phase would be laid upon His Bride the Church to carry out, commanded by God the Holy Spirit.

The Heavenly Host suddenly appeared, millions of them, all glorifying God and singing praises to the Lamb.

Having spoiled the principalities and powers, He made a show of them openly, triumphing over them in it. He humbled Himself and became obedient, even unto death on the Cross. Therefore, God exalted Him to the highest place and gave Him the Name that is above every Name."[422] And at the Name of Jesus, every knee in heaven and earth

and *under* the earth should bow,
and every tongue confess that
Jesus Christ is Lord
to the glory of God."[423]

But Mary stood without at the sepulchre weeping: and as she wept, she stooped down, and looked into the sepulchre.

John 20:11

A familiar fragrance met her senses. She turned and saw a Man standing before her. She assumed He was the gardener. She was right. He had planted plenty of seeds.

CHAPTER THIRTY-NINE

The Resurrection

THE MORNING LIGHT WAS not yet above the horizon, yet the skies yielded the promise of a beautiful day. Soft lavender shadows lay across the winding stony path. A rabbit skittered away at the sound of footsteps crunching on pebbles and sand.

Two angels whispered, "Here they come."

The weary women had purchased sweet-smelling spices to anoint Jesus' body. They were concerned about who would help them roll the great stone away. Certainly the Roman soldiers would offer no help. If anything, they would offer only taunts and crude remarks.

Mary, the mother of Zebedee's sons sighed, "Perhaps we should have asked Joseph of Arimathea to accompany us."

Mary Magdalene agreed, "Yes, it was very courageous of him to go to Pilate and ask for our Lord's body and then to place it in his own tomb."

Joseph of Arimathea was one of the noble Pharisees, honorable in rank and a highly respected member of the Sanhedrin. He himself was waiting for the kingdom of God, and had been a secret disciple of Jesus–secret because he feared the reaction of his peers. Daring the consequences from the Roman government and his colleagues, he had gone to Pilate and asked to take the body of Jesus from the Cross. He and Nicodemus lovingly tended His body and placed it in Joseph's newly hewn tomb.[424]

As the women approached the burial site, their anxiety turned to shock when they saw the stone had already been moved and the Roman guards were gone. Would they remove it and then leave? Something was wrong.

Salome and the two Marys looked at each other in bewilderment. Had they stolen His body too? Mary Magdalene began to weep. "Oh, no! Not this too! Is there no end to this?" She wiped her tears and bent low and timidly looked inside the tomb. Two lightning-like beings in glistening, white robes sat where Jesus' body had laid, one at the head, the other at the foot of a burial cloth still intact like an empty cocoon. The face napkin was neatly folded beside it, a custom that meant He would be back.

Mary was startled to see the bright beings whose glory lit up the dark tomb, but something held her attention even more than they did. She gazed steadfastly at the empty place where her Lord's body had lain. It was gone!

To her amazement, one of them spoke to her. "Woman, why are you crying?"

Not being well versed in conversing with angels, she blurted out, "They've taken my Lord away and I don't know where they have laid Him!"

The angel announced the grandest words that would ever be spoken: "Why do you seek the Living among the dead? He is not here, but He is risen!"

She was so flabbergasted by their presence, the words didn't sink in. Trembling, she stepped out of the tomb. *Were those . . . angels?* Even from an angel she couldn't get comfort. Salome and the other Mary stood nearby, their faces in their hands, weeping quietly.

Mary's head was spinning. She had to think . . . to pray. Her hands holding her throbbing head, she began to walk further into the garden. *What is happening? What are we to do now?*

A familiar fragrance met her senses. She turned and saw a Man standing before her. She assumed He was the gardener. She was right. He had planted plenty of seeds. He spoke to her softly.

"Why are you so distressed?" He seemed truly concerned.

Mary replied with trembling lips, her voice hoarse from weeping all night. "Sir, if you have removed my Lord's body, please tell me where you have taken Him and I will make other arrangements for Him."

And then He said her name. "Mary–."

That voice–it was so familiar! That voice she had heard on so many occasions. That melodic voice that, when first heard, had released her from the clutches of seven afflicting demons and called her out of darkness and into Light. That voice that spoke with authority and power; that healed the sick and cleansed the lepers and raised the dead!

Her eyes flew open in full recognition, and she fell at His feet and cried, "*Rabboni*!" Hearing her excitement, the other women came running and, upon seeing Jesus, burst into glorious praise, their voices ringing with laughter and tears."

Mary reached to cling to His feet.

"Don't touch Me, for I am not yet ascended to My Father." He did not want her to worship a wounded body that had not yet been glorified. There was a completion that yet awaited Him in heaven.

His voice was filled with joy. This time He spoke to Mary from a different perspective. He had called her out of darkness and now He was calling her as a messenger, the first evangelist[425] to take the Good News to the despairing.

She was instructed to run quickly and tell His disciples, especially Peter,[426] that she had seen the Lord. "Go quickly! Tell them that I will see them in Galilee." Knowing the unique anguish of Peter's soul, having been the only disciple to openly deny Jesus, He especially wanted him to hear the good news.

The disciples were still in hiding but Mary knew where to find them. She ran like a gazelle over rocks and creeks, and up the hills, her feet were like hind's feet.[427] She couldn't wait to tell them! She pictured in her mind their excitement and joy.

Although their hopes and dreams had been shattered and their circle had been broken, and though they were plunged into the depths of despair, their love for their Master never waned; nor did their devotion to each other. But all seemed so hopeless. Yet a dim expectation of something–something yet to come was still alive. A flicker, a tiny spark of hope remained, though none were any longer sure for what they now awaited. He had said He would be raised from the dead. But they had not heard–they that had ears to hear had not heard with their spirits–yet His Word would not return unto Him void,[428] but would remain in their hearts as a tiny glimmer–like an illusive firefly that they could not seem to capture.

And what should they now call themselves? Surely no longer apostles–of a dead Messiah? How could they take up their former ministry as they had been taught–to heal the sick and to cast out demons? With what authority now? And to preach the gospel–the good news to the poor? What good news? There was no good news!

Their past seemed like a far away dream; their present was filled with crushing grief, and their future seemed bleak, to say the least. Where was their ministry? There was no ministry! There was only this feeling of despair that shook them to their very core. And what was their message now? That their Messiah had been murdered? That the Christ had been crucified? That was not good news–that was the worst news they had ever heard!

Had He only been a great prophet? Just another one to be numbered among all the others about whom He had so strongly censured the Pharisees? "Your fathers killed all the prophets–" Was He now just another dead prophet along with Zacharias and John?[429] Had the Good Shepherd been caught and devoured by raging lions?

They did not yet understand that the Great Shepherd had snatched them once and for all from the jaws of the lion, the devil.

Suddenly they heard footsteps. Their hearts pounded with fear once again. But the footsteps were light, like those of a deer–not the heavy tromping of soldier's boots that threatened them each time they passed by. A knock at the door. Not the heavy pounding of Roman fists that had beaten the dear face of their Lord, but a knock from small hands, yet urgent!

They reluctantly unbolted the door and stood there, defeated like dead men. They sighed in relief, "It's just Mary,"

Just Mary? She carried in her bosom news–the greatest tidings any human would ever proclaim. She burst in upon them, panting joyfully and exclaimed, "Peter! John! He's alive! I have seen Him!"

They met the greatest news of all time with stone silence of unbelief.[430] Even after having heard the precious sentences from the lips of their own dear Master, "I will rise again", they did not believe. The vivid fact of His death was so central in their natural thinking that they were not yet able to let the natural give way to the supernatural.

She thought perhaps that they did not hear. "He's alive! I tell you, I saw Him! He's not in the tomb! He is no longer dead! He is risen!"

They blinked at one another. Can it be true? At that, Peter followed by John bolted past Mary and ran as fast as they could, their souls longing–as a deer pants for water.[431]

They did what all must do–they went to seek the answer for themselves.

On that glorious spring morning, they ran past trees whose tender leaves and tiny buds shouted out the miracle of the Resurrection. For centuries, humanity had not noticed the message of the yearly bursting forth of life from death, always at the time of Passover. They had turned blinded eyes and deaf ears to the cries of creation.[432]

John got there first, and when he saw that the tomb was open, he ducked down and looked inside. His mouth unhinged and his eyes protruded. He was gone! There was not even the slightest hint of the odor of decay.[433] He quickly turned and shouted, "Where is He?"

They did not yet know that the world in future centuries would still cry–where is the Body of Christ? Is there any hope that He is alive?

John, who had seen Him die, had watched them bury Him, and now seeing the tomb empty, in shock said to Peter. "It's true! He is Risen!"

It all became clear to them now. The words of the past had become the gospel of the future. The Savior had bridged that dark chasm from death and brought Life as no one had known life.

Mary leapt for joy and clapped her hands. They finally believe! She touched Peter's arm. "He told me something more! He said, 'Go and tell My brethren to go into Galilee, and they will see Me there.'" The three of them held each other and wept for gladness.

That Easter morn with the sun beaming brightly was such a contrast from the horrible darkness just a few days back. The air seemed clearer as after a refreshing rain, and the birds were singing their joyful little praises–so unlike the wails and weeping of the women and the ghastly rumbling of the earthquake, the tearing of the rocks and the screams of the terrorized witnesses. Now the clouds were gone and all was at peace.

There even seemed to be an air of joy in the atmosphere. And, indeed, there was. Millions of angels were dancing and frolicking in the skies above. A celebration unparalleled was taking place in the heavens.

No longer was the serpent, that old dragon, in command. Something bigger than he, a Stronger Man than he,[434] a greater Warrior than he had come and had set the captives free.

He had purchased the very souls of mankind.
And the mouth of an empty grave
shouts the triumph of the Cross.[435]
HE IS NOT HERE!
HE IS RISEN![436]

Simon Peter saith unto them, I go a fishing. They say unto him, We also go with thee. They went forth, and entered into a ship immediately; and that night they caught nothing.

John 21:3

His thoughts tumbled about with questions. Jesus had appeared to Thomas the Doubter–and tonight He had come to James the Denouncer–would He deal with the Denyer?

CHAPTER FORTY

The Lord's Breakfast

SHE SAW HIM THROUGH the window. That unmistakable walk could be no one else. "Peter!" she cried, dropping her apron. Her mother jumped up from her needlework and clapped with joy as her daughter ran out the door to run to her husband. Gathering her skirt up in her hand, she ran as fast as she could. "Peter!" she cried through a rush of tears. "Oh, Peter! Thank God!" He lifted her up in his muscular arms and buried his face in her neck. She held him fast and wept joyfully, "You're home! At last! You're home!"

Peter was glad to leave the bloody city of Jerusalem; to return to the fresh air and friendliness of his beloved Capernaum; back to the vine-covered hills and green valleys that cradled his home by the sea; back to the smell of the nets and the fresh breeze that brushed across the shining blue water, the familiar cottages and the warmth of his wife's fawn-brown eyes.

Her hug was as warm as spring. "The rumors we've heard . . ."

He put her down gently. "I know. But I'm fine. And as you can see," he stepped back and spread his arms out wide and grinned, "I'm home!"

Her smile said it all. It was a smile of joy and relief. He squeezed her hand tenderly as they turned and walked toward their cottage.

Peter's mother-in-law, an older portrait of her daughter, only thinner and hair streaked with silver, stood in the doorway with her hands on her hips. The laugh lines around her eyes deepened as a broad grin stretched across even, yellowing teeth, welcoming him home.

"Tonight we celebrate!" she announced, jabbing her finger into the air and waving it about as though executing a command, and headed for the kitchen.

That night around the supper table, Andrew, James and John, Thomas, Nathanael and another disciple joined them.[437] They told Peter's wife and her mother the whole story. A mixture of laughter and tears punctuated the accounts of Jesus' countless miracles, the endless persecutions and the betrayal of Judas Iscariot. Peter's mother-in-law slapped the table with her open hand. "I always thought there was something shady about that young man!"

"He, uh, committed suicide soon after Jesus was arrested."

Peter's wife's mother looked down and shook her head.

As they recounted the events of Jesus' arrest, mock trial and crucifixion, the two women gasped in horror and burst into tears.

"Don't weep!" John said hurriedly as he stood and wiped away his own tears. "He is risen! The tomb is empty! We've seen Him!"

Peter's wife's enormous eyes blinked in wonder. "You've–seen Him?"

Thomas jumped up from the table. "Yes! We've seen Him with our own eyes!" His voice rose with excitement. "He's not an apparition! He has a body–still! It is a literal resurrection of His crucified, pierced Body! We–or that is–I did not expect to see Him in a glorified human Body. But He is indeed risen!"

They burst into joyful applause repeating those wondrous words, "He is risen! God be praised!"

"How awful it must have been for Mary!" Peter's mother-in-law said finally, her brows furrowing deeply.

"Yes, it was." John said quietly.

"The Lord placed her in John's care," James said reverently.

"Where is she now?"

John answered, "She's with James, the Lord's half-brother, and His other brothers and sisters. She hasn't seen them for quite awhile."

Thomas poured some more wine. "We are to meet Jesus again in Bethany."

Peter's wife gasped. "That's so close to Jerusalem. Won't that be dangerous?"

Nathanael smiled and placed his hand gently on her shoulder. "Not if He told us to go."

"Makes sense." Peter's mother-in-law said, clearing her throat and folding her napkin.

Just then, there was a loud knock at the door. "Who could that be?" Peter walked over and opened the heavy wooden door slowly. And there stood James. He was visibly shaken. James had been an antagonist of Jesus, his half-brother, claiming He was mad and should be locked up. He had even scoffed at Him and suggested He go to the Feast of Tabernacles and show off His miracles.[438]

Peter eyed him cautiously. "Hello, James."

John quickly stepped forward. "Where's your mother?" he asked, a note of concern in his voice. "Is she alright?"

"Yes . . . she's fine. I . . ."

"Come in," Peter opened the door wide and stepped back. "You look sort of . . . strange."

"I've . . . I've seen Him!"

"What?"

"Jesus. He . . . came to me." James began to sob. "Mother told me everything. I didn't believe her. I got angry and went outside to walk off some steam and . . . He came to me.[439] I saw His wounds. He . . . He forgave me for . . . everything." He sobbed like a child.

John put his arm around him. "It's alright, James."

"But I gave Him . . . and you–such a hard time. I'm so . . . sorry."

The disciples looked at one another and smiled knowingly. John held him and let him pour his heart out. Peter's wife quickly brought him a handkerchief and a cup of cold water.

"I've said so many unkind things about Him . . . and you!" he wept, looking at each disciple through a cascade of tears.

"Shhh, it's alright." John consoled.

James sniffed and blew his nose "I would go to synagogue on the Sabbath and–and bless God, then turn right around and curse Him . . . and you!" He blinked back the tears and frowned deeply. "You know, the tongue is an unruly thing, full of evil. No man can tame it!"[440]

His words pierced Peter's heart, reminding him of his own impulsive and unruly tongue with his three-fold denial of His Lord. He thought to himself, *Tell me about it.*

The men encircled James, forgave him joyously and comforted him. His countenance changed from deep remorse to peace and joy.

Peter looked at his glowing face, glad that his troubled heart had been restored and delighted that he had gained a brother. He then looked at the tranquil, contented look on Thomas' face, knowing the Lord had ministered to his problem with skepticism when He had once again appeared to them. Peter quietly stepped away from them and leaned against the wall, his arms folded across his broad chest. *What about me?* he wondered. *Why is my heart so unsettled?*

James had the peace of His Risen Lord in his heart, and left rejoicing in his forgiveness from the men he had so often reviled.

"Give our best to Mary!" Peter's wife waved goodbye to him then closed the door gently and began to clear the table.

Peter's mind was in turmoil. He grabbed his outer garment and announced abruptly, "I'm going fishing!"

The disciples looked at each other. "We're going with you!" and they headed out the door. Peter had wanted to be alone, but said nothing.

They shoved off and headed for deep waters. The familiar touch of the little ship was a welcome change for Peter. The emotional trauma he and the others had endured the last few weeks had been draining.

The purple twilight slid away into darkness. A pearl-tipped moon played hide-and-seek with the fading pink clouds. Lamps were lit in the little cottages that dotted the pebbled shores of the Sea of Galilee. The friendly lights in the windows dimmed into tiny, trembling sparkles like a lovely necklace lying gently upon the bosom of the Galilee.

Peter drew in a huge breath, filling his lungs with the fresh cool sea air. The breeze caressed his rugged face as his mind went back to the last time He saw Jesus. He had appeared to them, and then again to two others on the road to Emmaus.[441] All the disciples had seen Him by then except Thomas. Peter smiled and shook his head. Poor Thomas. He had such a hard time believing and had even declared, "Until I see Him face to face and thrust my finger into His wounds, I will not believe!" But Jesus in His goodness came into their midst–even walked through a wall! And he showed Himself to Thomas, who stood there with his jaws hanging open. He invited him to examine His wounds. Thomas fell on his knees and cried out, "My Lord and my God!" Thomas had swallowed hard at Jesus' answer. "Thomas, you believe because you've seen Me–but blessed are those who believe without seeing."[442]

The little ship rocked gently as it moved farther out into the deep. The darkness hid the tears that coursed down Peter's cheeks. His thoughts tumbled about with questions. Jesus had appeared to Thomas the Doubter–and tonight He had come to James the Denouncer–would He deal with the Denyer?

The night passed slowly. The fish were not schooling. Thomas and Nathanael were rocked to sleep by the gentle swaying of the boat. James and the others talked quietly in the stern. John instinctively watched the net and seemed to be lost in another world. He had discerned his friend Peter's turmoil and was silently praying for him.

The ship creaked softly as it slowly moved to the rhythm of the waves. Peter sighed dejectedly and wondered how he had gone from Peter the Rock[443] to Peter the Coward. He had gone over and over it in his mind for the past several days from the night he denied His Lord to the present. Nightmares constantly haunted him and every morning he would wake up in a cold sweat, gasping each time he heard a cock crow.

The joy of knowing that Jesus was alive had healed much of his hurting heart, but it didn't diminish from his mind the enormity of what he had done. He had been part of the most intimate circle of Jesus' friends. He, along with James and John, had been present at the raising of Jairus' daughter. And that incredible night on Mount Hermon when the same three had witnessed the transfiguration of His Lord and the appearance of Moses and Elijah! Peter winced at the remembrance of yet another time his impulsive tongue sounded off.

Jesus had taken Peter, James and John up Mount Hermon to pray. Suddenly, Jesus' face became as bright as the sun and his clothing was dazzling white. Then Moses and Elijah appeared and began talking with Jesus about the Great Plan and how Jesus would die in Jerusalem. The three disciples became drowsy and fell asleep. Upon awakening, they saw Jesus, Moses and Elijah all dazzling as if dressed in fire! As Moses and Elijah were about to depart, Peter in his excitement blurted out, "Lord! This is wonderful that we are here! Let us build three tabernacles–one for You and one for Moses and one for Elijah!" Just then a bright cloud came over them and a Voice said, "This is my beloved Son, with Whom I am well pleased. Listen to Him!" The terrified disciples fell face down on the ground. Jesus touched them and said, "Don't be afraid." And when they looked up they saw Jesus by Himself.[444]

Peter would never forget that dazzling cloud. All his life he had heard of the glorious cloud that had come down upon Sinai when God spoke to Moses.[445] *And then it came down and God spoke to me!* He closed his eyes and shook his head. *The one time God's cloud comes down to speak, He had to tell me to be quiet and listen!* Peter slapped his hand over his eyes and dragged it down to his mouth. He blinked hard as he thought, *At the most glorious occasion any human has ever witnessed–I wanted to start a building program!*

He looked at James and John. He thought of how Jesus had drawn him to Himself, and even seemed to be grooming him, James and John for leadership. *Leadership? Me?* he thought with a shake of his head. *Hah! Some leader I turned out to be. The only leading I seem to be able to do is having these men follow me back into my old life of fishing.* He looked at the empty net. *And I don't seem to be able to even do that!* He sighed dejectedly. *He said I would be a fisher of men. I can't even be a fisher of fish!*

The words of the Master whispered in his aching heart, "Apart from Me, you can do nothing."[446] Another tear formed in his eye. He prayed silently, *"Lord, I need you. I need you now!"*

The morning light began to paint a soft golden glow behind the gentle hills. The two sleeping disciples opened their eyes, yawned loudly and stretched. "What time is it?" Nathanael said groggily.

"It's time to head home," Peter said soulfully.

They saw the empty nets and decided not to say anything to their companions. It was obvious that they had fished all night and caught nothing. Thomas reached down, dipped his hands into the water and splashed it on his face in an attempt to wake up. John walked to the bow of the ship and stood next to Peter. The little sail billowed gently, drifting them toward the shore.

Approaching the water's edge, they saw a lone figure in the dimness of the morning light. A slight haze lifted off the surface of the water and through it they could see a red glow of hot coals at the feet of the stranger. They were about three hundred feet out and they strained their eyes, but didn't recognize Him in the veiled morning mist.

A melodious voice rang in the still clear air. "Good morning! Did you catch anything?"

John answered, "No. We fished all night and caught nothing!" His voice echoed against the shore.

"Cast your net on the right side of the boat!"

They looked at each other in wonderment. Somehow this all seemed familiar.[447] They looked at each other and shrugged and reluctantly threw their net expertly across the water. Within seconds, a strong, lively tug alerted them of a huge catch. They strained their muscles with all their might, but there were so many large fish caught in the net they couldn't bring it in.

John gulped hard and whispered hoarsely to Peter, "It's the Lord!"

When he heard that, he became aware of his nakedness and releasing his hand on the net, he grabbed his tunic and put it on. In his excitement he held his nose and jumped into the water and started swimming toward the shore. As he swam, his mind went back to the night he cried to Jesus to bid to him come to Him and how he had walked on the water, but had failed at that too.[448] *I've learned my lesson on that one,* he thought. *I'll just swim.* His impulsiveness had been tempered greatly.

The other six rowed to shore dragging the net full of fish behind them. They reached the shore just after Peter's feet touched the beach. Together they drew the net up and, out of habit, the four fishermen began to count their haul. One hundred and fifty-three! While they were counting, Jesus was preparing to feed them.

Fish and bread were already roasting on the fire. "Bring some of the fish you caught and we'll have breakfast." He wanted them to eat of the fruit of their labor.

None of the seven dared ask who He was. They knew it was the Master. It seemed too good to be true to once again be in the Presence of their Risen Lord. Their hearts danced with excitement and wonder as they timidly approached the little campfire and the heavenly chef. They stood with their mouths gaping open. "Please. Sit down," Jesus chuckled.

They settled themselves in a semi-circle around the campfire. Jesus took the bread and fish, blessed the food and served them.

The victorious, Risen Savior–still the humble servant.

As they ate, they just stared at Him and worshiped in awed silence.

Still deeply unsettled in his heart, Peter longed to speak to Jesus privately, but dared not ask. He fastened his eyes upon Jesus' face now framed in the light of dawn. The rising sun cast a luster on Jesus' hair, forming a luminous halo.

A lone sea gull flew overhead crying out his lonely call as if asking to be invited to their gathering. It seemed alone and out of place. Peter could relate.

The men finally relaxed and began talking joyfully. John thought of the contrast of their last supper together in Jerusalem–the sadness of their Lord's impending departure–and now the joy of His Presence with them once again. Their laughter was a much-needed medicine.[449]

After breakfast, Jesus looked intently at Peter and said quietly. "Let's take a walk."

Peter's heart began to pound. This was it. The moment he had waited for. A mixture of relief and dread plowed through his emotions. He stood up and brushed off the sand. His head was down like a schoolboy called out by his teacher. Jesus put His arm around Peter's shoulder as they walked slowly up the beach.

Peter started to speak, "Lord, I . . ."

"Simon . . ."

He was calling him by his original name. He always addressed him by his given name when he had been operating in the flesh.

"Y-yes, Lord."

"Simon, son of John, do you love Me more than these?" He swept His arm in a wide expanse, encompassing Peter's beloved lake, the great haul of fish, the hills and cottages, and his boat. He was bringing the natural-born leader to a choice between his old life and the new. The natural or the supernatural. Did he prize them more than Him?

Peter answered, "Yes, Master. You know I love you."

"Then feed My lambs."

His words startled Peter. *Feed His lambs? He still wants me in His service?*

They moved a little farther up the beach and Jesus moved a little farther into his heart. He again stopped and looked even deeper into his eyes. Peter felt Jesus could see into the depths of his troubled spirit.

"Simon, son of John, do you love Me?"

Peter refused to use the same word for love that Jesus used. Jesus' word denoted complete devotion; a higher, God-like love. Peter answered that he loved Him the best he could love as a sinful human being.[450]

Jesus looked at him keenly. "Be a shepherd to My sheep."

Shepherd? Caretaker? He would trust me to do that?

They turned and slowly headed back toward the others. Peter's mind was in a whirl. He still had not brought up the denial. *I wish He would get it over with,* he thought.

Jesus stopped and once again looked intently at Peter. "Simon, son of John, do you love Me?"

Peter was grieved that He should ask him a third time. He looked at Him sorrowfully and after a moment of silence answered, "Lord, You know everything and You know me. I love You as best I can."

Jesus smiled and placed His hand on Peter's wide shoulder and smiled, "Then feed My sheep."

Suddenly Peter felt the turmoil leave his heart. He realized the three questions were the answer to his heart's cry. The three-fold denial had been dealt with and treated with the Master's healing salve of grace and mercy. Jesus not only forgave him but also reinstated him to the place of leadership and authority for which he had been originally called, by giving him care of His flock. And with each question, the Savior had also tamed Peter's tongue. No longer careless with his answers, Peter had carefully examined his own heart and answered with humble truth.

A broad smile sprawled over his face. Looking once again at the huge haul of fish, suddenly he no longer saw fish, but instead he saw the souls of men.

He searched Jesus' face, amazed at His mercy and grace, but a familiar wondering arose within him if he would be strong enough and have courage enough to carry out His Lord's expectations. He did not yet understand the impending power of the Promise with which the Holy Spirit would soon endue him and the others not many days hence.

"Lord, I have failed so many times . . ."

Jesus smiled and assured him that he would endure to the end, even unto death, and in so doing, His Father would be greatly glorified.

They walked toward the other men. Peter's heart was at peace, even at the staggering revelation that he would one day be martyred. He looked at John, his shepherd's heart already stirring with love for Jesus' own. "Lord, what will happen to John?" he whispered.

"Don't be concerned about John. Even if he lives until I come again, it is nothing for you to be placing your attention upon. Just keep your focus on and follow Me."[451]

John started walking toward them grinning from ear to ear. He knew in his heart that his prayers had been answered and that his friend's troubled spirit was now free; that his beloved Master had once again healed the broken hearted.

The other men moved closer. Jesus then told them to gather the rest of His disciples and to go to the mountain near Bethany. "I will come to you there."

They quickly ran to tell the others that the Lord wanted to meet with all of them. Perhaps He would at last reveal His plan to them. A few days later, when they came together to the appointed place, He appeared to them. It was still mind boggling to their natural minds that He who had died was standing before them alive and well once again.

After a time of joyful rejoicing and worship, one of them spoke, "Lord, you know that we are but mere men. Some of us have doubted You, some of us have denied You, and nearly all of us left You when You needed us most. You tried to tell us that You would rise again but we did not understand. Please, Lord, tell us plainly, will You at *this* time set up Your kingdom and restore it to Israel?"[452]

They still didn't get it.

"It is not for you to know the times or the dates of future events. The Father has appointed certain things to take place by His own choice, power and authority. But go to Jerusalem and wait for the Promised One that I have spoken to You about. And when He, the Holy Spirit, comes upon you, you shall be clothed with power, ability and might and you shall be My witnesses in Jerusalem, and all of Judea and Samaria and to the very ends of the earth."

They were stunned at His words, and grateful that they were once again in His service. Their peace and their ministry were restored. They would tell everyone, who would listen, the Good News. Jesus the Savior of the world was risen–He had overcome death, hell and the grave! A mixture of great joy and sadness was evident in their eyes. They sensed once again His impending departure.

Seeing the perplexed look on their faces, He said gently, "Don't be afraid. Remember that I am with you always, even unto the end of the age."

The eleven disciples stood there speechless, hanging onto every word as though they were His last. Then He spoke words to them that would bring unimaginable horror to Satan and his minions.

In humble majesty He declared, "I have been given all power and authority in heaven and in earth. Therefore, I now commission you to go and make disciples of all nations. Baptize them in the name of the Father and the Son and the Holy Spirit, and teach them to obey all the commands I have given to you."[453]

Stunned that He was then giving His authority to them, they knelt before their victorious Messiah and Lord. He quietly spoke a blessing upon them, and then before their very eyes, He began to rise. They gasped and reached up for one last touch but He was soon taken up in the clouds. They stood there watching awestruck and dazed. He disappeared in the clouds and returned to heaven.

Two enormous, glittering angels dressed in the glory of God suddenly appeared before them. The disciples gasped and marveled at the sight of them.

One of the angels smiled and said, "Why do you stand here gazing into the clouds?" The men stood speechless. They continued, "This same Jesus, Who was caught away and rose up from among you into heaven, will return in just the same way."[454]

The disciples laughed joyfully and began shouting praises to their King. The angels joined in with them and then disappeared like flashes of lightning.

All of heaven exploded with praise and anthems of worship and joy. His mission was complete! It was finished! He had won and He was now seated at the right hand of His Father. The Heavenly Host burst forth with such glorious songs of victory that the whole universe joined in the celebration.

The disciples left arm in arm, the final words of Jesus echoing in their ears.

"I have been given all power and authority in heaven and in earth . . . go and make disciples of all nations."

So powerful were those final words that He spoke to His embryo church that they echoed throughout the kingdom of darkness and shook the very foundations of hell.

The Seed had won
and the defeated,
wounded dragon with his
crushed head of rulership
screamed in agony.

The Beginning

EPILOGUE

I tell you the truth,
unless a kernel of wheat falls to the ground
and dies,
it remains only a single Seed.
But if it dies, it produces
many seeds.
John 12:24

Satan did not consider that
if you bury a Seed,
it produces many others
like itself,
and brings forth
a great harvest.

PRAYER OF FAITH

Father in heaven, I come to You with faith as a little child. I come to You empty-handed. I have nothing to impress You with. I have nothing to bribe You with. I come just as I am, a sinner. And I come believing You are Who You say You are. I believe You died on the Cross, were buried and rose again on the third day and ascended to Heaven, paying the price for my sins. I ask You to forgive me of all my sins, especially for having lived independently of You and trying to find fulfillment in everything but You. I believe You have defeated Satan and I want no part of him or his lies or his work. Jesus, I step down off the throne of my heart and I ask You to come into my life. Save me, Lord. Change me and make me Your own. I offer You my life, which is the highest praise I can give. Please fill me with your Holy Spirit so that I may be a strong witness for you. And I will call You Lord from this day forward. In Jesus' Name, Amen.

Be of good cheer, for I have overcome the world.
John 16:33

For speaking engagements

please write:

TEMPE BROWN
P.O. BOX 5461
WASHINGTON, DC 20016
theseed4u@aol.com

BIBLIOGRAPHY

A Sermon by Rev. Tom Grazioso

Many sermons by Rev. Lyman B. Richardson

Gesenius' Hebrew-Chaldee Lexicon to the Old Testament by Dr. William Gesenius, Baker Book House Publishers

The Handbook for Spiritual Warfare by Ed Murphy, Thomas Nelson Publishers

Halley's Bible Handbook by Dr. Henry H. Halley, Zondervan Publishers

King James Version of the Bible

The Life and Times of Jesus the Messiah by Alfred Edersheim, Hendrickson Publishers

The Oxford Companion to the Bible by Bruce M.Metzger and Michael D. Coogan., Oxford University Press Publishers

Strong's Exhaustive Concordance by James Strong, Baker Book House Publishers

Thayer's Greek-English Lexicon of the New Testament by Joseph H. Thayer, Baker Book House Publishers

The New Ungers Bible Dictionary by Merrill F. Unger, Moody Press Publishers

Vines Complete Expository Dictionary of Old and New Testament Words by Vine, Unger and White, Thomas Nelson Publishers

ENDNOTES

[1] Isaiah 6:1-3 & Ezekiel 1:13

[2] I Corinthians 13:1

[3] Revelation 4:6

[4] Revelation 12:4

[5] Colossians 2:9, I John 5:7

[6] Ezekiel 28:2,15

[7] Exodus 26:31

[8] I Peter 1:19,20

[9] Job 38:7

[10] Ephesians 2:2

[11] I Peter 1:19,20

[12] John 1:14

[13] Genesis 3:15

[14] Psalm 2:7

[15] Isaiah 7:14, 8:8-10 & Matthew 1:23

[16] Galatians 4:4

[17] Psalm 72:19

[18] Isaiah 55:12

[19] Luke 2:13,14

[20] I John 3:8b

[21] Psalm 51:5

[22] Matthew 2:11

[23] Micah 4:8 & Matthew 2:8-17

[24] Genesis 35:21

[25] Adapted from a sermon by Rev. Tom Grazioso, Pastor of Full Gospel Church, Oceanside, NY. *Used with permission.*

[26] A quote by Christine Lamson White. *Used with permission.*

[27]Micah 5:2 & Matthew 2:6

[28] Genesis 3:15

[29] Genesis 4:8 & I John 3:12

[30] Exodus 1:16-22, 2:1-10

[31] I Samuel 18:6-11

[32] Genesis 37:12-20

[33] Daniel 6:16

[34] Isaiah 14:12

[35] Ezekiel 28:2,13,14

[36] Isaiah 14;13

[37] Ezekiel 28:15-17

[38] II Corinthians 11:14

[39] Genesis 2:7

[40] Genesis 3:8

[41] Matthew 7:18

[42] Genesis 1:28

[43] Genesis 1

[44] Luke 10:19

[45] Genesis 3:1-6

[46] Romans 5:12

[47] Matthew 2:13-15

[48] Matthew 2:1-18, Herod's brutal action fulfilled the prophecy of Jeremiah: *"A voice was heard in Ramah, lamentation, and bitter weeping; Rahel (Rachel) weeping for her children refused to be comforted for her children, because they were not."* Jeremiah 31:15

[49] Matthew 2:23

[50] Isaiah 11:1

[51] 1 Kings 22:17

[52] The writings of Josephus.

[53] Probably the great revivalists Hillel and Shammah, in their older years. They died a couple of years later. Rev. Ed Nelson.

[54] Luke 2:39-52

[55] Luke 12:27, Matthew 23:37 & John 4:35

[56] John 1:1-3

[57] Job 38:11

[58] Hebrews 4:15

[59] Matthew 13:55

[60] Luke 2:7

[61] Hebrews 2:9

[62] Luke 13:1
[63] John 1:4,5
[64] Luke 1:5-15
[65] Romans 11:3
[66] Matthew 14:1-10
[67] John 1:25-29
[68] Isaiah 40:3
[69] Luke 1:17
[70] John 3:30
[71] Matthew 3:1-17
[72] Luke 4:18
[73] Ephesians 6:12
[74] I Timothy 4:1
[75] II Timothy 1:7
[76] John 8:44
[77] Luke 13:11,12
[78] Romans 1:21-32
[79] Ephesians 2:2
[80] I Samuel 15:23
[81] Matthew 14:3
[82] James 3:14,15
[83] I Corinthians 15:55
[84] Proverbs 10:12
[85] Isaiah 14:11-15
[86] Revelation 12:9
[87] II Corinthians 4:4
[88] John 4:23,24
[89] Exodus 32:1-4
[90] Psalm 115:4-8
[91] Deuteronomy 17:3
[92] Ezekiel 8:16
[93] Deuteronomy 12:31
[94] Matthew 15:1-14
[95] James 4:6 & I Peter 5:5
[96] Matthew 15:6-12

[97] Matthew 23:15
[98] Matthew 23:4
[99] Ephesians 2:9
[100] Matthew 2:16
[101] John 3:34,35
[102] Genesis 3:8
[103] I Corinthians 15:45
[104] Mark 1:13
[105] Luke 11:24
[106] Daniel 6:16
[107] Ephesians 6:16
[108] II Corinthians 10:5
[109] I Peter 5:8
[110] Genesis 3:17
[111] John 10:10
[112] Titus 2:13
[113] Isaiah 61:3
[114] I Samuel 17
[115] I John 2:16
[116] Exodus 16:15
[117] John 6:48
[118] Hebrews 4:12
[119] Psalm 91:11,12
[120] Matthew 12:25
[121] I John 4:4
[122] John 1:3
[123] Hosea 5:14
[124] Matthew 4:1-11
[125] Proverbs 5:4
[126] Isaiah 53:3
[127] Revelation 21:9
[128] John 14:2
[129] John 4:1-42
[130] John 4:46-54
[131] John 15:1-5

[132] Galatians 5:22
[133] Psalm 53:6
[134] Edersheim.
[135] John 7:5
[136] Matthew 13:55 Some texts say Jude, some Judas, some Judah.
[137] I Kings 17:8-24
[138] II Kings 5:1-15
[139] John 1:11
[140] Luke 4:14-30
[141] Mark 1:14,15
[142] John 1:32-34
[143] Luke 4:31-41
[144] Luke 5:1-11
[145] Mark 1:32-34
[146] John 2:2
[147] John 2:1-11
[148] Isaiah 54:5, 62:5
[149] Revelation 19:7-9
[150] II Corinthians 11:2
[151] Ephesians 1:13
[152] Matthew 23:13
[153] Luke 5:3-7
[154] Mark 2:14 & Luke 5:27
[155] Matthew 9:9
[156] Genesis 2:22
[157] Ephesians 4:26,27 & Hebrews 12:15
[158] Matthew 9:13, 12:7
[159] Genesis 4:5-8
[160] II Corinthians 10:4
[161] Matthew 14:3,4
[162] John 3:29
[163] Matthew 9:14
[164] Luke 5:39
[165] II Corinthians 5:17
[166] Matthew 13:52

[167] Matthew 5:17,18

[168] Matthew 23:5

[169] Galatians 3:6

[170] Matthew 22:36-40

[171] *Only begotten Son*: Jesus knew that teachings would arise that would attempt to place Him on the same level as men from whom other religions would emerge. It has been said, that Jesus is the Son of God. But so are Buddha, Mohammed and others. They are created sons. Their bones are in the ground. Jesus is the only *begotten* Son of God; the only One Who was raised from the dead, and belief in Him alone results in everlasting life.

[172] John 3:1-17

[173] Hebrews 12:1

[174] Colossians 1:13

[175] Matthew 4:17

[176] Ephesians 2:2

[177] James 4:6 & I Peter 5:5

[178] Isaiah 60:1, John 1:4, 3:19

[179] Psalm 145:8,9

[180] Galatians 5:22,23

[181] Hebrews 4:12

[182] II Corinthians 10:4

[183] Matthew 5,6 & 7

[184] Matthew 11:12

[185] James 4:7

[186] Acts 26:18

[187] Psalm 44:5

[188] Psalm 118:11,12

[189] James 3:14-16

[190] Matthew 10

[191] Mark 6:17-20

[192] Malachi 4:6

[193] Matthew 11:1-6

[194] Mark 2:15

[195] Luke 8:2,3

[196] Matthew 5:14
[197] John 4:3-41
[198] II Corinthians 4:6
[199] Psalm 22:3
[200] Luke 8:3
[201] I Timothy 6:10
[202] Matthew 13:18-23
[203] I Chronicles 16:11
[204] Daniel 4:37, 6:11, & 10:13
[205] John 1:3
[206] Matthew 8:10-12
[207] Luke 9:1,2, 10:1,9 & 17
[208] Luke 8:24-40
[209] Luke 15:10
[210] Mark 5:1-21
[211] Numbers 15:38-40
[212] Leviticus 15:19
[213] John 5:19
[214] Hebrews 2:15
[215] Proverbs 13:12
[216] John 10:10
[217] John 8:44
[218] Luke 7:11-16
[219] Leviticus 21 A sermon by Rev. Edward Nelson.
[220] Hebrews 4:14,15
[221] John 1:1-4
[222] Mark 5:21-43
[223] I Corinthians 15:55
[224] I Kings 21:25 Jezebel is a real person. The "Jezebel spirit" is not mentioned in the Bible, but it seems to still be manifesting itself in manipulation and control in today's society and even in some churches.
[225] Malachi 4:5, Matthew 11:14-14, Matthew 17:10-13, & Luke 1:17
[226] I Kings 18:17-40
[227] I Kings 19:1-10

[228] Luke 7:24
[229] Mark 6:20
[230] I Samuel 30:1-6
[231] James 4:7
[232] Mark 6:14-29
[233] Matthew 25:21
[234] Matthew 11:12
[235] Revelation 7:17, & 21:4
[236] Matthew 13:31
[237] I Kings 17:8-16
[238] Proverbs 17:22
[239] Isaiah 61:3
[240] John 6:1-18
[241] Mark 3:30
[242] Matthew 14:22-33 & Mark 6:45-52
[243] Psalm 93:3-5 & Matthew 7:24-27
[244] Matthew 16:6-25
[245] Exodus 3:2-5
[246] Exodus 19:16
[247] Luke 7:11-17
[248] Exodus 34:28-35
[249] John 6:26-68
[250] Matthew 5:6
[251] Isaiah 42:3
[252] Mark 9:2-10
[253] I Peter 1:12
[254] Job 1:10 & Psalm 91:11
[255] Luke 10:38-42
[256] Luke 10:1-20
[257] Hebrews 2:14
[258] Matthew 8:23-27
[259] Ephesians 2:2
[260] Mark 6:45-51
[261] Luke 17:17
[262] John 9:1-37

[263] Matthew 13:45,46
[264] Proverbs 3:3
[265] Matthew 22:11-14
[266] Matthew 21:18,19
[267] Matthew 25:32,33
[268] Matthew 20:1-16
[269] Mark 4:26-29
[270] Matthew 25:14-30
[271] Matthew 25:1-13
[272] Luke 7:40-43
[273] Matthew 21:28-31
[274] Luke 18:1-8
[275] Luke 16:1-13
[276] Luke 15:3-32
[277] Luke 12:41-48
[278] Matthew 21:33-46
[279] Romans 12:2
[280] Psalm 119:89
[281] Psalm 107:20
[282] II Corinthians 10:4
[283] Isaiah 55:11
[284] Proverbs 4:5,9
[285] Matthew 7:6
[286] Matthew 23:4
[287] I Peter 5:7
[288] Matthew 11:28-30
[289] Psalm 103:14
[290] Psalm 51:6
[291] I Corinthians 6:19,20
[292] John 15:8
[293] Galatians 5:22
[294] I Kings 8:46
[295] John 8:1-11
[296] John 3:17
[297] John 14:2

[298] Deuteronomy 7:6-9
[299] John 1:14
[300] Luke 13:1
[301] Ephesians 6:11
[302] II Corinthians 10:4
[303] Hebrews 4:12
[304] Matthew 12:22-45
[305] Luke 13:10-17
[306] Luke 12:1
[307] Isaiah 55:8,9
[308] Romans 10:3
[309] Luke 18:9-14
[310] Romans 12:15
[311] Matthew 19:13-15, Mark 10:13-16 & Luke 18:15-17. It is not known that John Mark was that child that was rebuffed by the disciples. Literary license used here.
[312] Mark 12:37
[313] Matthew 13:1-9, 18-23
[314] Exodus 20:12-16
[315] Matthew 6:19-21
[316] Luke 6:38 & II Corinthians 9:6
[317] Matthew 7:2
[318] Matthew 19:30
[319] Matthew 20:17-19
[320] Luke 18:34
[321] Matthew 7:7,8
[322] Mark 10:46-52
[323] Luke 12:1
[324] Proverbs 3:24
[325] Mark 6:14-16
[326] Mark 6:14-29
[327] Luke 13:31
[328] Luke 8:3 The text does not say Susanna was Joanna's handmaiden, but it was a possibility.

[329] Luke 18:18-25 We do not know the outcome of the Rich Young Ruler. Literary license was used regarding his life.
[330] Luke 16:19-31
[331] Luke 11:37-53
[332] Matthew 6:2-7
[333] Luke 6:12
[334] Matthew 7:24-29
[335] John 19:38
[336] Luke 13:31,32
[337] Matthew 10:37
[338] Hebrews 1:14
[339] Revelation 3:20
[340] Proverbs 13:12
[341] Luke 10:38-42
[342] John 5:19
[343] Matthew 16:16
[344] Luke 10:39, John 11:32 & 12:3
[345] Romans 12:15
[346] I Samuel 17:35
[347] John 11
[348] Zechariah 9:9
[349] Matthew 23:13-39
[350] Isaiah 53:3
[351] Matthew 26:53
[352] Matthew 24:1,2 & Mark 11:15-18
[353] Genesis 4:8
[354] Exodus 1:16-22 & Matthew 2:16
[355] Matthew 24:3-31, Mark 13:3-37 & Luke 21:7-28
[356] John 14:1-3
[357] I Corinthians 2:9 & Ephesians 3:20
[358] John 6:14,15
[359] Matthew 18:1
[360] Matthew 12:14-16
[361] Matthew 12:38,39
[362] John 12:6

[363] Genesis 3:14b

[364] Psalm 52:2

[365] Exodus 12

[366] Acts 2:3 & I Corinthians 6:19,20

[367] Mark 13:1,2

[368] I Corinthians 12:3, a sermon by Rev. Kristian Davis.

[369] Hebrews 8:1

[370] Hebrews 7:25

[371] Leviticus 16:14,15

[372] Revelation 19:7,9

[373] John 13

[374] John 16:7-20

[375] John 14:7-31 & Luke 22:1-27

[376] Luke 22:3

[377] Matthew 20:28

[378] Luke 22:43

[379] James 4:6

[380] Hebrews 4:16

[381] John 14:30

[382] Exodus 3:14 & John 8:58

[383] John 18:1-8

[384] John 10:15,17

[385] Luke 22:53

[386] Matthew 26:36-49

[387] John 14:16

[388] John 16:7

[389] Luke 22:31

[390] John 18:10

[391] Matthew 13:18-23

[392] Matthew 26:65-67

[393] Luke 22:61

[394] Mark 14:54-72

[395] Matthew 26:24

[396] Matthew 27:1-5

[397] John 14:6

[398] Isaiah 53:5
[399] Hebrews 12:2
[400] II Corinthians 4:4
[401] Matthew 27:1-31
[402] Genesis 3:15
[403] I Corinthians 2:8
[404] John 8:44
[405] Isaiah 53:4-12
[406] John 3:14
[407] II Corinthians 5:21
[408] Hebrews 13:5 The original language here reveals God reiterating that He will not in any way fail us, nor give us up, or leave us floundering without His aid. He said "I will not, I will not, I will not" three times to make His point that in no way would He leave us helpless, forsake or let us down, or even relax His hold on us! And then He added, "Most assuredly not!" The Father, knowing this fear to be such an insidious enemy to His children, related in every way possible in this passage that He would never leave nor forsake us.
[409] Galatians 3:13
[410] Leviticus 16:10, 21,22
[411] I Peter 3:18
[412] I John 2:2
[413] I Corinthians 15:24
[414] John 19:26-30
[415] Psalm 16:10
[416] Matthew 27:52
[417] Matthew 27:51-54
[418] I Peter 3:19 & Psalm 68:18
[419] Matthew 16:18
[420] John 10:18
[421] Revelation 1:18
[422] Colossians 2:15
[423] Philippians 2:8-11
[424] Matthew 27:57-60 & Mark 15:43-46

425 The first woman was deceived by the serpent, and through the woman's seed redemption came, and here, once again, Jesus bestows honor upon the woman–she is the first to tell the news that He is Risen.

426 Mark 16:7

427 Psalm 18:33

428 Isaiah 55:11

429 II Chronicles 24:21

430 Mark 16:9-11

431 Psalm 42:1

432 Romans 1:20

433 Psalm 16:10 & John 11:39

434 Luke 11:22

435 A line from *"Triumph of the Cross,"* a song by Nancy G. Crowson. Used with permission.

436 Matthew 28:1-9, Mark 16:1-8, Luke 24:1-12 & John 20:1-10

437 John 21:1,2 The text does not name Andrew. It merely states there were two other disciples. The author placed Andrew's name in the story.

438 Mark 3:21

439 I Corinthians 15:7 Jesus appeared to His half-brother James, but it is not know on what occasion. Literary license used here.

440 James 3:8-10

441 Luke 24:13-35

442 John 20:24-29

443 Matthew 16:18, Mark 3:21 & John 7:2-8

444 Matthew 17:1-8

445 Exodus 19:16

446 John 15:5

447 Luke 5:4-7

448 Matthew 14:28-31

449 Proverbs 17:22

450 Jesus used the word *Agape,* which means God's kind of love. Peter used *Phileo,* which denotes a personal attachment, a matter of sentiment or feeling.

[451] John 21
[452] Acts 1:6
[453] Matthew 28:18-20
[454] Acts 1: 3-11

AUTHOR'S BIOGRAPHY

TEMPE BROWN HAS GAINED national recognition as an evangelist, Bible study teacher, and retreat and conference speaker. She formerly served as assistant pastor at Christ Church of Washington in Washington, DC where she currently resides. She is a portrait artist and a gifted songwriter. A native of Oklahoma, Brown is the mother of three and grandmother of nine. She serves as an elder in her church in Washington, DC.